DATE DUE

ALSO BY MAUREEN JENNINGS

Except the Dying
Under the Dragon's Tail
Poor Tom Is Cold
Let Loose the Dogs
Night's Child
Vices of My Blood

A Journeyman to Grief

MAUREEN JENNINGS

McCLELLAND & STEWART

Library and Archives Canada Cataloguing in Publication

Jennings, Maureen
A journeyman to grief / Maureen Jennings.

(A Detective Murdoch mystery)

ISBN 978-0-7710-4338-3

I. Title. II. Series: Jennings, Maureen. Detective Murdoch mystery.

PS8569.562J69 2007   C813'.54   C2006-904290-X

We acknowledge the financial support of the Government of Canada through the Book Publishing Industry Development Program and that of the Government of Ontario through the Ontario Media Development Corporation's Ontario Book Initiative. We further acknowledge the support of the Canada Council for the Arts and the Ontario Arts Council for our publishing program.

Typeset in Janson by M&S, Toronto
Printed and bound in Canada

This book is printed on acid-free paper that is 100% recycled, ancient-forest friendly (100% post-consumer recycled).

McClelland & Stewart Ltd.
75 Sherbourne Street
Toronto, Ontario
M5A 2P9
www.mcclelland.com

1 2 3 4 5   11 10 09 08 07

Henry Bolingbroke:
Nay, rather, every tedious stride I make
Will but remember me what a deal of world
I wander from the jewels that I love.
Must I not serve a long apprenticehood
To foreign passages, and in the end,
Having my freedom, boast of nothing else
But that I was a journeyman to grief?

– *Richard II*, Scene III

For Iden

And this time for Christina and Scott
and all the good folks at Shaftesbury Films

CHAPTER ONE

JULY 1858

She glanced over her shoulder to see if he was coming. What could he be doing? He'd been gone more than half an hour, and all he'd had to do was pick up the forgotten tobacco pouch from their hotel room and come right back. They had planned to take the steamer boat across the Falls, but they'd miss it if he didn't hurry. She shaded her eyes against the sun, but the road was deserted except for a carriage that was approaching slowly, the horse's head drooping wearily. She consulted the gold fob watch that had been her father's wedding present to her. It was a beautiful and extravagant gift, but the giving of it was marred by her father being in his cups and barely able to utter his congratulation, so that when she did consult the watch, her pride in its richness was tainted by her disappointment in him.

She shifted back on the bench. To her left, she could see a rainbow arching over the high-flung spray of the cascading water. She had been excited to come here for her honeymoon, but the week so far had been less than happy. Initially, she had been self-conscious, sure that the other guests were staring at them in disapproval. When she confessed this to her husband, he was dismissive rather than kind, but she clung to his words: "You are the most beautiful woman in the room. The men covet you and the women are envious. Nobody knows. They think you are a Spanish countess."

She longed for him to say more, but in the short time they had been married, she had learned not to press forward with any discussion he didn't want to have. When he was courting her, he had been tender and solicitous, but nothing, not even her Aunt Hattie's blunt warnings about "man's nature," had prepared her for the roughness of their conjugal relations. She couldn't hide her discomfort, and he was impatient with her. "I wouldn't have expected such coldness from you of all people." She had cried so hard the first night that he had finally relented and teased and tickled her into a precarious laughter. This morning, she'd woken to find him sitting on the edge of the bed, looking at her. He had kissed her fiercely. "Today, I want you to wear your best blue silk gown, your largest crinoline, and your big hat with the peacock feathers. You will be the belle of the promenade."

So she had, and laced herself with unnecessary tightness that she now regretted on this hot day. Another quick check of the watch. What could be keeping him?

She heard the soft jingle of a horse's bridle and looked over her shoulder again. The carriage had halted and a man was coming across the grass toward her. He was heavy-set with a full untrimmed beard and moustache. His clothes and skin looked grubby. She fancied she could smell his stale sweat, but that impression might have been born only later, when he was on top of her. Somehow, from the first, her flesh knew who he was even though her mind would not accept it. Ever afterwards, she scourged herself for not immediately running toward the protection of the few visitors who were hanging over the railings watching the water. But then he was talking to her and she made the terrible mistake of listening.

"Ma'am, I must ask you to accompany me. I have bad news. Your husband has been taken ill. He's in your hotel."

She gasped. "What has happened to him?"

The man shrugged. "I can't say. All I know is I was sent to find you and bring you to him at once. The doctor's been summoned. You're staying at the Grand, ain't you?"

She nodded, not taking her eyes from his face, from the mouth that was smiling at her so falsely. Suddenly he stepped forward, and in one swift movement he pulled her from the bench. In a ghastly parody of an embrace, he crushed her against his chest so that her hat was almost knocked off her head, her nose and mouth were smothered, and she couldn't breathe. She felt herself being carried to the carriage and thrust inside.

There was another man within whom she couldn't see because she was shoved to the floor face down and at the same time something was stuffed in her mouth. It was vile-tasting and leathery, like a glove. The man pinned her with his knee, and in a moment he'd tied her hands behind her back. The carriage lurched forward.

CHAPTER TWO

APRIL 1896

Professor Broske was late arriving, and his audience was becoming restive. In the past week, Murdoch had been suffering another bout of insomnia, and now he yawned, wishing he was at home, dozing in front of the fire, instead of here in a lecture theatre with Dr. Julia Ogden. Not that he'd had much choice in the matter, as she was not an easy woman to refuse. Her usual companion to such events was her father, Dr. Uzziel Ogden, but he was confined to bed with a fever, and yesterday she had telephoned Murdoch at the police station and asked if he would accompany her to the Toronto Medical School.

"If you don't, I shall be relegated to the seats at the rear of the room with the other women. Professor Broske is a highly respected authority in his field, and I couldn't bear to miss anything. Besides, his topic for tonight is the physiology of fear. As a police officer, you might find it useful."

So here Murdoch was, in a room jammed with privileged and well-connected young men, all of them, he assumed, the sons of rich fathers. He'd glimpsed only a handful of women, and they were indeed seated at the back.

The door to the stage opened, and the eminent man swept in, followed by two student assistants wearing holland aprons and wheeling small trolleys. Broske was bewhiskered, balding, and short, and he exuded confidence and assurance. He strode to the podium, held up his hand for silence, and addressed the audience. His voice, lightly accented, was as resonant as any actor's.

"Good evening, gentlemen, and I am glad also to welcome the members of the fairer sex who are gracing us with their presence." He took a monocle from his breast pocket. "The topic of tonight's lecture is fear. I shall be conducting a few experiments, but I will not ask for volunteers so none of you have anything to fear on that account." The audience laughed dutifully. "I 'ave no doubt there is no one in this room tonight who has not at some time in their life experienced the emotion of fear. We are all, I'm sure, familiar with its manifestations, such as heart palpitations, shortness of breath, pallor, trembling, flight, sometimes immobility. Even I experienced a tremor of the 'and as I prepared to meet you. Such an emotion is not termed 'stage fright' for nothing." He paused for his little joke to take effect. "I should add, 'owever, that although the experience of fear in all its many varieties is universal and connects us to the greater family of mankind, we should keep in mind that certain races are more naturally afraid than others and women are more fearful than their brothers."

Murdoch wondered how Dr. Ogden, who, in his opinion, possessed an unparalleled coolness of disposition, was reacting to her hero's statement. As far as he could tell without blatantly staring at her, she was unmoved.

His hands tucked beneath the tails of his frockcoat, the professor moved away from the podium and began to pace back and forth. He spoke now as if he were dictating a letter, his tone slightly abstracted. "In lesser degrees, these physical effects may be useful to us. If threatened, those men, or even women, who are normally of a timid or placid disposition may be roused to defend themselves. 'Owever, we who carry this fragile machine of our body about with us continually ought to remember that any shock that exceeds the usual measure may prove fatal. I can adumbrate several instances of men, women, and children who have literally been frightened to death." He stopped to scan the rows in front of him, and such was the power of his personality, Murdoch wondered for a moment if he were trying to illustrate his point.

"Let us remember that fear is a disease to be cured. The brave man may fail sometimes, but the coward always fails."

A bespectacled young man sitting close to the front raised his hand. "Excuse me, sir. I have a question."

The professor frowned. "Can it wait? I usually take questions at the end of the lecture."

"My query seems apropos to the moment, sir, if you don't mind."

"Very well."

"If, as you say, fear is a disease and yet you have also reminded us that we have all experienced fear, are you then saying that all of us in this room are, to a greater or lesser degree, in a state of ill health? And if that is the case, what may we do to effect a cure for ourselves?"

The smallest titter rippled through the audience, as nobody was going to risk an outright guffaw until they saw how Professor Broske reacted.

He smiled and some of the tension left the air. "First, we must understand that the physiological responses we experience when we are afraid are reflex movements." He wagged his finger in the direction of the young student. "If I were to publicly berate you for your impertinence, which I have no intention of doing, dear fellow, your heart would start to race, the pupils of your eyes would no doubt dilate, and the inspirations of your breath would be curtailed. Those reactions would be beyond your power to control. And let me hasten to add, no shame lies in that direction. Courage of character is another matter entirely. It can, and should be, taught. Let me say that courage springs from three sources: nature, education, and conviction."

Murdoch glimpsed several students scribbling earnestly in their notebooks.

Broske continued. "There is a culture which heredity transmits to the brains of our children. The future and the power of a nation do not lie solely in its commerce, its science, or its army but are also formed in the hearts of its citizens, the wombs of its mothers, and the courage or cowardice of its sons."

There was an outburst of applause in which Dr. Ogden joined heartily. Then Broske snapped his fingers at one of the assistants, who promptly wheeled his trolley forward. On it were a small electric battery and a glass jar that Murdoch could see contained frogs trying desperately to climb out. They were scrambling over one another in their haste but unable to get a grip on the smooth glass. The professor adjusted his monocle.

"Paradoxically, gentlemen, to understand the functions of the brain, you must first understand what it does and does not control. For instance, as I have said, our reflexes are controlled by our nervous systems and will continue to operate even if the brain is removed."

He picked up a large pair of scissors while the assistant reached in, removed one of the frogs, and handed it to him. With one snip, Broske decapitated the creature and laid the body on the tray. He dropped the head into a bin.

He took a brown bottle from the tray. "Watch what happens when I drop a small amount of this vinegar onto the leg." The frog's rear leg jumped.

"Even though the brain is obviously no longer functioning, the nervous system is intact," said Broske. "The frog will continue to react for two or more hours, even though death has supposedly occurred. Another, please."

Murdoch felt a nudge in his side from Dr. Julia Ogden.

She whispered, "Surely this isn't bothering you, William? It is only a frog, after all. You've seen far worse."

She was right, but Murdoch had never seen live creatures dispatched with such callousness in front of an audience before. None of the medical students in his vicinity seemed to be troubled, and he wasn't about to turn around and gawk at the female students at the back of the room to see how they were faring.

"I'm all right, ma'am," he whispered, trying to focus on what the professor was saying.

In the next half-hour, Broske decapitated four more frogs, and their headless bodies lay on the white, blood-stained cloth while he used various techniques to demonstrate how the nerves could be made to activate the muscles of their legs. Murdoch glanced at the big clock on the wall. How much longer? Finally, to his relief, Broske swept the dead frogs into the bin and rinsed his hands in a basin of water held by one of the assistants.

"These are simple experiments that can be repeated with various creatures, including warm-blooded ones. Professor Goltz, of whom, no doubt, you have heard, brought a dog, part of which had the brain removed, to the International Congress of Medicine in Milan. It was quite remarkable to see the animal react to stimuli. However, for our purposes, we must illustrate our point with human subjects." He nodded to one of his assistants. "Fetch the boys, if you please."

"I hope he doesn't intend to cut off their heads," Murdoch said to Dr. Ogden, who frowned at him.

The other assistant set up two chairs facing the audience, then wheeled forward the second cart on which sat an electric battery with wires attached and four cylinders covered with blank paper. The first helper, who had the thin, mangy look of a hungry fox, returned, bringing with him two boys about ten or eleven years old. They wore identical grey serge suits and cloth caps, but one was dark-skinned, the other fair and blond. They both looked apprehensive.

Broske smiled warmly and indicated the chairs. "Please take a seat, boys. I'd like you to put your caps and your jackets on the floor beside you." He addressed his audience. "These young gentlemen are residents of your St. Nicholas orphanage. I 'ave promised them, what you call, a bang-up feast after our little demonstration, so they were quite eager to come for a night out, weren't you, lads?"

They both grinned obediently, but Murdoch suspected that they were no longer so eager. The two assistants were busy getting the boys ready for Broske's demonstration. First, they tied a band around each boy's chest. A stiff wire led from the front of each band to a metal stylus attached to one of the cylinders on the cart, which had been wheeled between the chairs. Neither child uttered a word but each watched anxiously.

"Don't worry, my fine gentlemen," said the professor. "This apparatus is quite harmless and will not cause you a soupçon of pain. It is called a pneumograph, and it measures the degree of inspiration and expiration at any given time. That's a fancy way of saying, it measures how much air you breathe in and out." He nodded to his assistants. "Switch on the battery, if you please, Mr. MacKenzie, so these poor chaps can see, there is nothing to fear."

The assistant turned on the battery, and the cylinder began to rotate slowly.

"First of all," said Broske, "we take a reading when the subject is breathing normally. Ah, there you are, the young negro's inspirations are rather shallow. The other boy's are more normal."

Murdoch was close enough to see that the stylus attached to the cylinder was making zigzags on the paper.

"Continue, gentlemen," said Broske to his assistants, and quickly they attached bands to the wrists of each boy and hooked the dangling wires to the stylus on the second cylinder. The professor called out to the assistant who was strapping the coloured boy's wrists to the arms of the chair, "That looks a little too loose. It needs to be quite snug."

The problem was corrected.

"Take a reading, if you please."

The assistant flicked another switch on the battery, and the cylinder began to move, the stylus making a similar pattern to that of the pneumograph.

"Excellent. Let that run for a moment or two. Now fasten the clamps."

The assistants brought forward two stands and placed them directly behind the chairs. Each was equipped with leather clamps.

"These are simple stands that photographers were in the way of using with their subjects when the taking of a photograph required the subject to be absolutely still for a rather long time," said Broske. "They ensured that nobody moved and blurred the shot. For the purposes of our experiment, it is important that the boys do not move their heads."

The boys were fastened into the clamps so that they were looking straight ahead. The cylinders continued to rotate.

"Now, my fine lads, I am going to ask each of you in turn some simple questions. All I want you to do is answer clearly and, of course, with truth. As you speak, the instruments will record your heartbeat and your breathing. That is it, no more and no less. Now then, our good Sambo here. What is your name?"

"Archie King, sir."

"Why are you living in the St. Nicholas home?"

"I am an orphan, sir."

"No parents? No papa or mamma?"

"No, sir. They're both dead since I was five."

"And from what did they die, young sir?" Broske's tone was jocular.

"I dunno 'zactly. I think it was fluenza."

"How long have you been in the orphanage then, young Archie?"

The boy paused. "Three years."

Broske was walking up and down in front of the two chairs while he was talking. He wasn't looking at the boys.

"And our little blond friend. What is your name?"

"Jim Anderson, sir."

"And why are you in the orphanage, Jimmy?"

"My father was took with the consumption, and my mam couldn't look after us good enough so she placed us at St. Nick's. She's coming to get me and me sister as soon as she can."

"How commendable."

The professor turned around and briefly inspected the recordings on the cylinders. He addressed the coloured boy.

"Are you happy at the orphanage, young Archie?"

"Oh yes, sir. Quite happy."

Suddenly, Broske leaned over the boy. His expression changed to one of utter ferocity and he bellowed, "Liar! How dare you think you can deceive me!"

Archie was powerless to move away.

The professor's face was only a few inches away from the boy's. He yelled, "Your parents died from whisky poisoning, not influenza."

Archie tried to shake his head, but he couldn't.

"I don't –"

"Be quiet! You are going to tell me nothing but lies. How can a happy boy set fires?"

Archie's eyes were wide with terror and his bottom lip started to tremble.

"Your superintendent told me you set a fire to one of the rooms. Isn't that true?"

"No, sir. I never did."

"Liar again. Tell me the truth."

"It is the truth, sir." Archie tried to shrink away. "I never set no fire."

Broske swirled around and spoke to the other boy. However, this time his voice was at a normal pitch.

"Jimmy, tell me. Is your friend, Archie King, a liar?"

The boy looked terrified and stuttered out, "I, I . . . don't know, sir."

The professor stared at him for a few moments, then he beamed, stepped away from Archie, went over to Jimmy, and ruffled his hair.

"Enough. I shall not maintain this misery a moment longer. You and Archie have been most helpful in my little demonstration, and as I promised, you shall get the best supper of your lives. Mr. MacKenzie, Mr. Sutherland, you can disengage the apparatus now."

They removed the clamps and bands that were holding the boys, neither of whom moved from their chair. Broske picked up a wooden pointer. His audience remained silent.

"I will now show you the results of the pneumograph and the pulsometer." The assistants removed the roll of paper from each cylinder and stretched them out. "When I berated Archie, his inspiration was sharp and sudden, as you can see here on the graph." He tapped the spot with his pointer. "Interestingly, the expiration did not immediately follow. The lad was actually holding his breath for a few moments. This is a typical response to fear." Another tap. "Then there were four more quick inspirations, each quite shallow. Also typical. You can see here on the graph where the heartbeat jumped considerably. That was, of course, when I raised my voice and startled him. It continued to beat rapidly." He pointed to the second roll. "Now, here are the results from young Jim Anderson. You can compare the two. His pulse rate increased when he witnessed his pal getting what he believed to be a severe scolding. Then when I asked him a question, no doubt anticipating he would be likewise treated, his breathing became rapid. Not as much so as the other boy, but certainly considerably more than before."

Murdoch thought his own heart rate had increased when the professor had raised his voice so unexpectedly. He wondered if Dr. Ogden's had. He'd have to ask her.

Broske continued. "Archie King, the coloured child, is by virtue of his race disposed to be fearful and sensitive. If I had reversed the order of scolding, his pulse would probably have accelerated at a greater rate even than that of the other boy. But they are good lads. I have known grown men fare worse, involuntarily evacuating their bladder and even bowels. Now, are there any questions?"

A veritable forest of hands shot up, but Murdoch didn't have the opportunity to hear what the students wanted to know. A familiar figure, large and imposing in his cape and policeman's helmet, had appeared in the aisle beside him. It was Constable Crabtree. He leaned over and whispered in Murdoch's ear.

"I'm sorry to interrupt, Mr. Murdoch, but an urgent call has just come through to the station. A man's body has been discovered over on Mutual Street. It looks to be a homicide. Sergeant Seymour has sent Constable Fyfer over to investigate, but he thought you should go too. He seemed to think you wouldn't mind too much at being called away."

Murdoch grimaced. Seymour had heard him moaning about having to accompany Dr. Ogden to some bloody silly lecture. He tapped her on the arm.

"I'm afraid I have to leave, ma'am. A police matter."

"What a pity."

Some of the nearby students gazed curiously as he stood up, but the others were completely absorbed by an animated discussion with the professor. The two boys remained in their chairs, and Murdoch was close enough to the stage to see the tear stains marking the coloured boy's cheeks. His fellow orphan looked pale.

Murdoch followed Crabtree out of the hall.

"I just hope those lads stuff themselves."

"I beg your pardon, sir?"

"Never mind, George. I'll tell you about it later."

CHAPTER THREE

O nce outside the building, Murdoch took a deep breath of the cool night air, which had the merest hint of spring. The macadam was glistening in the lamplights from a recent rain.

"Where are we going?"

"The stables are at 73 Mutual Street."

They set off at a brisk pace along Gerrard Street, quiet at this time of the evening.

"Boring talk, was it, sir?"

"Far from it. It was quite riveting, really. Blood, drama, suspense. What more could you ask for? A damn theatre couldn't have provided more entertainment."

Crabtree gave him a curious glance. "Like that, was it, sir? That's medical students for you."

Murdoch shuddered. "All right, George, tell me what you know about the case."

"Not much more than I've said, sir. The victim is a man named Daniel Cooke, who owns a livery stable on Mutual Street.

It was one of his stable hands that found him. There's a telephone in the office, so he called us right away."

"Why does that name sound familiar?"

"About three months ago we received complaints that one of his cabbies was mistreating the horses."

"That's right, I remember now. You investigated, didn't you, George? What came of it?"

"Nothing really, sir. I met Cooke the once when I went to check things out, and he seemed a bit jumpy but that could have been nerves. You know how people can get when they see a police officer. He owns about a dozen horses, as I recall, and they all seemed in good health. Not that I am an equine connoisseur, you understand, but there wasn't enough evidence to lay a charge."

"And no identity of the complainant?"

"No. It was a man's voice, but he refused to say who he was. He called three times, I believe. I thought somebody was just making mischief."

"Did Cooke have a family?"

"I don't know if he had children, but there is a Mrs. Cooke. I met her too. Quite a tigress, I must say. She was furious about the accusations, might ruin their reputation, that sort of thing. She didn't seem that concerned whether they were true. She made all sorts of unpleasant threats to me as if I was the one responsible for stirring up trouble. It was no use trying to explain to her I was only doing my job."

"How old a man was Mr. Cooke?"

"He was getting on. He'd be close to sixty."

They continued in silence for a little while. The street gas lamps were lit and most of the houses, elegant in this part of town, glowed with light. In some of the houses, the blinds weren't drawn, and the rooms were as illuminated as brilliantly as a stage. In one drawing room, a white-haired man, dressed in evening clothes, was waltzing slowly with a woman, also elderly, who was smiling up into his face. The light from the chandelier glinted on a brilliant jewel in her hair. They must have recently returned from some fancy affair. Murdoch was tempted to stop and watch them complete the dance, they looked so good together. A maid and a butler, also older, were standing at the edge of the room.

Murdoch was touched by the apparent affection between the dancers. He'd become rather interested in observing married couples, he realized, ever since he had proposed marriage to Miss Amy Slade.

Crabtree and Murdoch turned down Jarvis Street, and here most of the houses were protected from curious eyes by firmly closed blinds or curtains.

"I'm surprised that we're being called to this area of town. On Mutual and Shuter Streets, there's a physician living in every second house."

"And as we all know, only the poorer classes of society commit crimes," added Crabtree. He'd made his tone heavily ironic, and Murdoch grinned at him.

"There's Fyfer."

The constable was standing at the corner of a laneway. There was a high wooden fence behind him, which Murdoch assumed hid the livery. As they approached, Fyfer saluted.

"Good evening, sir."

"Evening, Fyfer. How do we get in?"

"There's a side entry just down here."

Fyfer lit the way down the dark laneway with his lantern. They stepped through the door into a cobblestone yard. There were no lights.

"The body's in the barn. There are two entrances for the carriages, and I barred those gates right away. Nobody has come or gone since I've been here."

"Where's the fellow who found the body?"

"I've put him in the office. It's right there."

He flashed his light. The office was just inside the south gate, and the side that faced into the yard was glassed. Murdoch could barely make out the figure of a man sitting at the desk. He didn't move or make any attempt to come out to them.

"Have you talked to him yet?"

"Just a few questions. His name's Elijah Green and he cleans out the stables. We didn't go much further than that."

Murdoch had worked with Fyfer before, and he'd grown to respect the young man's efficiency. He was also well aware that the constable's good manners covered a ruthless ambition. Kid gloves over a tiger's paw.

"Good. All right, lead on."

Fyfer opened the door to the barn and they went in.

"He's in the tackle room, sir."

He turned to the left and led the way along the centre aisle, which was also cobbled and lightly covered with straw. There was a warm, not unpleasant smell of hay and manure in the air and the lantern's bull's-eye beam picked out the rear ends of horses in open stalls. One or two of them nickered as the men went past.

"In here." Fyfer pushed open a door at the far end of the aisle and stood back for Murdoch to enter the room.

A brass lamp sat on a low stool in the corner. By its light, Murdoch could see the body of a man hanging by the wrists from a strap hooked into the ceiling. He was twisting slightly, and his feet dangled in the straw. The sharp reek of vomit filled the air.

Murdoch went in closer, and Fyfer aimed his beam at the body.

The man's blue eyes were open and staring and he was naked from the waist up, his back criss-crossed with livid marks. Blood had clotted along the lines and pooled at his waist. Buzzing flies fed greedily on the wounds.

Murdoch drew in his breath. "Good Lord, he's been whipped."

"Yes, sir. Quite viciously, too, by the look of it."

Murdoch walked slowly around the body. "Are we certain this is Daniel Cooke?"

"I recognize him myself," said Crabtree, who was standing near the door.

In life, Cooke was slightly above average height. Not as tall as Murdoch, perhaps just under six feet. He had a full head of wavy grey hair and heavy sidewhiskers. He was overweight, his flabby pale flesh spilling over the band of his trousers. Vomit streaked his chest.

Murdoch placed the back of his hand against the dead man's cheek. The skin retained some warmth. Gently, he turned Cooke's jaw to the side. It moved easily.

"He hasn't been dead long at all. No rigor mortis and he's not completely cold." He turned to Fyfer. "Where are his clothes?"

"His jacket, shirt, and underwear are over there in that corner. They look as if they were cut away."

"Your light, please." Murdoch went over to the pile of clothes and examined them. There was a brown check wool jacket, a blue striped shirt, and a grey cotton undershirt. All were in shreds, but it was obvious they had been cut, not torn.

"I thought the assailant must have had a sharp knife and a strong hand to cut through the jacket so cleanly," said Fyfer.

Murdoch nodded and began to search through the jacket pockets. They were empty except for a handkerchief and two nickel pieces.

"Was that lamp here?"

"Yes, sir, and it was lit, just the wick turned down low."

"Shall we get him down now?" Crabtree asked.

"One minute."

Murdoch shone the beam around the area. The shelves around the walls were loaded with horse tackle, bulky collars mostly. Bridles and harnesses dangled from hooks in the ceiling out of the way of mice and rats. Nothing seemed out of place, that is if you discounted the half-naked body.

He waved the flies away and studied the stripes. They covered his entire back but seemed heavier near the middle. It was impossible without a magnifying glass to tell with any accuracy how many times Cooke had been whipped, but it was a considerable number.

"I'm surprised nobody heard him," said Crabtree. "He must have been screaming."

Murdoch turned up the wick in the brass lamp as high as it would go and set it on the floor. "There are bruises at the corners of his mouth. I'd say he was screaming, but he was gagged with something that was removed. I'll need your knife, George. You'll both have to take up some of the weight."

The two constables had the unpleasant task of clasping the dead man while they lifted him up and Murdoch cut through the strap tying Cooke to the hook. Finally, the body collapsed, and they lowered it gently to the ground. Murdoch knelt and cut the binding at the wrists and the arms flopped away helplessly.

He examined the strip of leather that had bound Cooke's wrists.

"It's a lead shank, by the look of it. The clip is still attached. It's been sliced cleanly at one end. There should be more of it. Do you see anything, gentlemen?"

The room was small, and all three of them searched quickly, but there was no sign of the remaining piece of leather. Murdoch put the strip on top of Cooke's clothes to be examined later. "What do you think happened, sir?" asked Fyfer.

"I wish I knew. The man was no youngster, but he was still strong by the look of him. There must surely have been more than one person to be able to overcome him . . . Wait a minute, I see he's got another wound on his head. It's not very deep so it probably wasn't that hard a blow. Maybe enough to stun him, certainly knock him down. If you take a man by surprise, it's not that difficult to pin him if he's on the ground. Perhaps I'm wrong and there was just one assailant."

"Do you think he was attacked in this room?" asked Fyfer.

"I can't say at the moment. We'll have to wait to find out when we have some daylight. All right, we'd better get the wheels of justice in motion. George, go back to the medical school and see if you can bring Dr. Ogden here. Fyfer, you might as well start rounding up a jury so they're at the ready. I'll stay here for now and have a word with the man who found the body before I inform Mrs. Cooke."

"I'm here, sir."

Murdoch hadn't heard him approach, as he was standing in the shadows just outside the door. He stepped more into the light, and Murdoch realized he was a negro.

"I was wondering when I could get on with my job." He avoided looking into the tack room. "The horses need their feed and I've got to muck out."

His tone was neutral, neither overly polite nor provocative, but Fyfer didn't like it and he said sharply, "You'll get on with your job when we tell you you can. Detective Murdoch here wants to ask you some questions first."

The man blinked at the retort, but there was no other expression on his face.

"All right," said Murdoch. "Speaking of jobs, why don't you two get on with yours. Green, will you bring me a blanket so I can cover Mr. Cooke's body?"

"Yes, sir."

He disappeared into the gloom.

"Mr. Murdoch, I wonder if I might have a word with you before I get going," said Fyfer.

"Does Crabtree need to be here?"

"No, I don't think so."

"Off with you then, George," said Murdoch, and the constable left.

Fyfer lowered his voice. "I have serious misgivings about the darkie, sir. There are two things that don't sit right as far as I am concerned. First, he seems unnaturally composed. You know darkies are usually very emotional, but he is as calm as anybody I've ever seen, given he just discovered the body of his employer in what I'd call a gruesome state. I myself even found it hard to look at him at first." He hesitated and gave a nervous little flick of his moustache. "Secondly, he told me this isn't his usual night to come to work. Somebody else mucks out the stables on Wednesdays, which is a day when they close early. I think it's too much of a coincidence that he comes this night of all nights. He'd know there was no risk of running into one of the cabbies, for instance. You know how easy it is for somebody to pretend to be the one who has discovered the body and, in fact, they're the one who made it a body, so to speak."

He was quite right about that, and Murdoch had also wondered about Green's lack of distress. At that moment, he saw the man in question had come up with a horse blanket over his arm. Damn, the fellow moved quietly.

"All right, Fyfer, I'll bear what you said in mind. You'd better get hopping. Keep the jurors in the yard until I tell you. Get them subpoenaed as fast as you can. Roust them out of bed if you have to."

The constable saluted and left.

"Give me the blanket," said Murdoch to Green. He went into the room and covered Cooke's body, then stood for a moment.

"May the Lord have mercy upon your soul."

He made the sign of the cross, aware that the stable hand was watching him from the doorway. He turned around.

"If it's that important that the horses are looked after, I don't doubt you can work and answer questions at the same time. Let's close this door and you get started with your chores. I'll follow you around and talk to you."

CHAPTER FOUR

Green stuck a pail underneath the spout and started to pump out water. Murdoch stopped him and took the handle.

"I'll do this. How many do you need?"

"Each horse gets one pail full, and we've got a dozen horses."

"Bring them then. I'll man the pump."

Green did as he was told, and for the next while they worked together, the stable hand carrying the pails to and from the stalls.

"How long have you been working for Mr. Cooke?"

"Twenty years."

"And how old are you now?"

"Thirty-six."

Murdoch had thought he was younger than that. He was wearing a snug-fitting woollen jersey, which revealed thick strong arms and wide shoulders, and his movements were easy and lithe. He was standing close to the hanging lantern and Murdoch noticed he had a small lump over his left eyebrow.

"How'd you get the goose egg?"

Green grimaced. "I bumped into a low-hanging beam. You'd think I'd know better by now, but it gets me all the time." He went into one of the stalls and, shoving the horse aside with his shoulder, poured the water into the trough.

"Was Mr. Cooke a good boss?" Murdoch asked.

"As good as any, I suppose."

"That sounds as if you didn't much care for him."

"Did it? It wasn't meant to. I was his hired hand. It was a business arrangement."

"Any idea who might have attacked him?"

Green concentrated on his task. "None at all."

Murdoch felt exasperated with the man's apparent indifference. "Aren't you worried about your job now that he's gone?"

"Stable hands are always in demand." He put down the pail and stroked the horse's neck as it drank.

"I get the impression you'd miss these horses if you had to move," said Murdoch.

"I'm not sure you're right about that, sir. It'd be foolish to get attached to cab horses. They don't last long after they come here." He bent down and ran his hand over the horse's hock, clicking his tongue softly. "Bendigo's got a bit of swelling there. I'll have to put a poultice on it. He probably should have a rest tomorrow, but he won't get it." He stopped.

Murdoch prompted, "Why won't he?"

"Mr. Musgrave usually has him and he's hard on his horses. Some cabbies won't make the horse canter, especially at the end of the day, but he'll always whip them up if it means an extra nickel."

He came out of the stall and picked up another pail of water.

"Was Mr. Cooke a man of regular habits?"

"Very regular. He was here without fail, rain or shine, summer and winter, by nine o'clock in the morning. He'd leave for his dinner at midday, come back no later than two, then stay until his supper at half past six. One hour and a half for his meal, then back here until the last cab checked in, which might be about half-past eleven. Except for the Sabbath, when nobody works, and Wednesday, when the last cab has to be back by eight. He liked to supervise the comings and goings."

"What about you? What sort of hours do you keep?"

"I come in round about six or half past six in the morning. I've got to feed and water the horses, then harness up those that are going out. I gets my supper at about the same time as Mr. Cooke, then I come back to clean out the carriages and tend to the horses." He brought the empty pail over to the pump and waited while Murdoch filled it. "I finish by eleven o'clock most nights."

"Those are policeman's hours."

"Are they? But like I said, I ain't usually in Wednesdays or Sundays."

Murdoch finished pumping. "That's the twelfth, by my count. I'll do it. Where do you want it?"

He picked up the heavy bucket.

"Amber's the only one left," said Green. "She's in the last stall."

The horse was a knock-kneed roan mare who pawed the ground and tossed her head as Murdoch stepped into the stall. Suddenly, she kicked out with her rear leg, just missing him but landing on the pail, sending it flying. The water splashed over his trousers and boots, soaking them.

"Whoa there." He backed out quickly.

Green came over at once. "I should've told you not to get too close, sir. She's a mean one, that. Don't like nobody coming up behind her."

Murdoch felt like a fool. He'd worn his best clothes and boots for the lecture and now look at them.

"Damn. You should have warned me."

"Beg pardon, sir. Sometimes she's like that, sometimes she

ain't." Green took a piece of grubby towelling from the rail and handed it to him. "Why don't you go into the office and dry off properly. Mr. Cooke has an oil heater in there."

Murdoch figured Crabtree would be returning with Dr. Ogden in about half an hour, but he expected they'd be in the barn for some time longer. He didn't fancy standing around with sopping-wet trousers.

"Have you got the key?"

"It's not locked."

"Never or just tonight?"

"Tonight. When I found him I ran to the telephone. I 'spected I'd have to break in, but the door was open. Mr. Cooke always kept it locked. He was nervous 'bout thieves."

Murdoch dabbed at his trousers with the towel. "So far the key hasn't shown up."

Green frowned. "That so?"

"Which way did you come in?"

"Through the west side entry door. I do have a key to that."

"Who else does?"

"Just me and Thomas Talbert. He helps out on Wednesdays and Sundays."

"Not the cabbies?"

"No, sir."

"What about the office?"

"Nobody but Mr. Cooke had that."

"I'll need the names and addresses of the rest of the cabbies and also your helper's."

"I'll give you Thomas's, but you'll have to look in Mr. Cooke's files for the others."

Murdoch scrutinized him for a moment, but his head was turned away and revealed nothing.

"I'd better go and dry off a bit."

Green pointed. "You can get to the office through the passageway down there. You don't mind if I get on, do you?"

"No. I'll come back to you later."

Murdoch picked up one of the lanterns and, making sure to keep to the middle of the centre aisle in case he drew the ire of other fractious mares, he went in the direction Green had indicated. His boots squelched as he walked.

The door to the office was ajar and he stepped in, holding the lantern up high. It was a small room, better furnished than his own cubicle at the station. An oil heater was in the opposite corner from a safe, and the room was warm and the air redolent with the smell of good tobacco.

Murdoch sat down on a well-padded chair, pulled off his boots and socks, and placed them on top of the heater. He wrung a little more water out of his trousers. Blasted horse.

A rough sisal carpet on the plank floor scratched his bare feet as he padded over to the long bank of windows facing into the stable yard. From his desk, Cooke would have had a perfect view of the comings and goings of his employees. The desk had once been a fine mahogany one, but the surface was scarred with marks from matches allowed to burn down, and there was a light film of dust over everything and clumps of cigar ash. In the left corner was a clean, dust-free circle where he assumed the lamp now in the tack room had stood. On the right were several papers on a spike, a new-looking telephone, and an open box of cigars, half empty. Murdoch flipped through the papers briefly. They all seemed to be invoices, but he'd examine them more carefully later. He turned and swung the lantern in an arc around the room. There were two doors: one that led to the passage into the stables and the other likely to the street. He walked over to check. It was not locked and opened directly onto Mutual Street. He assumed Cooke had entered the livery stable this way, as it was the most direct. Was this where he'd received the blow to his head? Murdoch brought the lantern close to the floor, but the sisal was too rough to show any sign of a man being dragged. How had his assailant got in, and how had he got Cooke into the tackle room?

A pungent smell wafted over from the oil heater and he went to check on his socks. Not dry yet.

The large, elaborately decorated safe was locked. Next to it was a wooden filing cabinet. Murdoch opened a couple of drawers and found them untidily stuffed with papers. A cursory examination showed they were also business invoices. Hanging on a hook next to the cabinet was a clipboard with a pencil tied to it.

Murdoch unhooked the clipboard and checked the piece of paper. Today's date was at the top, Wednesday, April 15, and underneath several scrawled signatures. In the column next to their names, the cabbies had written the time of taking out the carriages and the time of return. The third column was initialled D.C. Only four carriages had gone out on the afternoon shift. Two of the cabbies, R. Littlejohn and J. Wallace, had signed off at 5:00 and 5:10 respectively. The last two names were R. Robson and P. Musgrave. The former had signed off at 7:00 and the latter at 7:25. Cooke had not initialled these names.

A flash of light outside the window caught Murdoch's eye. The side door across the yard opened and Constable Crabtree stepped in, dark lantern in his hand, followed by Dr. Ogden. Behind her, muffled in a black double-tiered cape, was Professor Broske.

Damn. They'd come sooner than he expected. He grabbed his damp socks.

CHAPTER FIVE

Murdoch went outside to greet the newcomers.

"I do hope you don't mind me coming along," said the professor. "Dr. Ogden thought I would find it interesting."

"Did she, indeed? This is a murder investigation after all, not a laboratory experiment."

Broske halted and lowered the hand he had already extended toward Murdoch. Dr. Ogden looked disapproving.

"Dr. Broske is a world-renowned expert in fear, William. When your constable said that the victim had probably died of fright, he was naturally most interested."

"Died of fright? We don't know that." He turned to Crabtree. "Why did you say such a thing, George?"

The constable seemed discomfited. "It's his eyes, sir. They're almost out of his head. In fact, begging your pardon, Dr. Ogden, what I said was, 'He looked as if he had died of shock. I didn't use the word *fright*.'"

It was Julia Ogden's turn to look embarrassed. "I suppose I was so caught up in Dr. Broske's lecture that I heard it as 'fright.' I'm sorry, professor. I have brought you here under false pretences."

"Not at all, madam. Let's save our judgment until we have examined the case further. I am more than happy to accompany you. I'm sure the learning will be all mine."

Murdoch watched this exchange in astonishment. The prim doctor of formidable intellect was behaving like a coy young girl. As for Broske, he was speaking to her and looking at her as if she were an object of great attraction. Dr. Ogden!

She met Murdoch's gaze and suddenly became brisk and businesslike again.

"Where is the body, William?"

"In the tack room, ma'am. Light us, George."

Crabtree led the way across the cobbled yard, which was slick and dotted with puddles. Broske offered Dr. Ogden his arm and she accepted. She was a good six inches taller than he and had to bend toward him to hear what he was saying.

"I mustn't forget to tell you the story of my poor Bertino and his open skull through which I could study the workings of the human brain for several weeks and what invaluable experiments I was able to conduct."

Her response was lost to Murdoch, who was opening the barn door. Elijah Green was mucking out one of the stalls. He straightened up when they came in, but he didn't approach them.

They all followed Crabtree down the centre aisle, Dr. Ogden lifting her skirt fastidiously. Murdoch ushered them into the tack room, knelt down beside the body, and removed the blanket. Cooke's staring, protuberant eyes did make him look extremely fearful. His mouth had dropped open and his fingers had curled.

Murdoch beckoned to Crabtree and they rolled the body to its side so they could see the back.

"Goodness me!" exclaimed the doctor. "How extraordinary."

Broske fished in his pocket and, crouching down, fixed his monocle and looked at the wounds.

"Definitely a lash of some kind and it was wielded with great ferocity. It 'as broken through the flesh in several places."

Dr. Ogden also bent down beside the body, and Broske offered her his monocle, which she used as a magnifying glass.

"Do you have the whip that was used, Mr. Murdoch?" she asked.

"No, ma'am. We haven't had a chance to conduct a search yet."

"I see he has also suffered a blow to his head on the top left side, but it looks superficial. However, I won't know until I open up the skull. You can lower him now." She peered closely at Cooke's face. "There's a cut in the corner of his mouth."

"I believe he was gagged, ma'am."

"He vomited quite copiously. He has not lost a lot of blood so I doubt he died from exsanguination. However, I suspect our constable was right, the cause of death may very well be shock. Poor fellow, he wasn't a young man, was he? After a certain age, one would hope to die peacefully in one's bed, wouldn't you say, Dr. Broske?"

"Indeed I would, ma'am, but isn't that both the terror and the marvel of life that we mere mortals have really so little choice in the matter?"

Murdoch agreed with him on that point. He was intrigued. Suddenly the professor seemed less like an implacable, self-important man of science and more of a philosopher. A definite improvement.

Dr. Ogden started to get to her feet and Broske helped her up.

"How close are we to getting the jury, William?" she asked.

"I don't know, ma'am. George, can you find out? If Fyfer hasn't got twelve men yet, beat the bushes until he has. Then one of you had better fetch the ambulance."

"Yes, sir."

"One of the more cumbersome of our Canadian practices, professor," said Dr. Ogden, "is that when there is a questionable death, the law insists on the coroner's jury viewing the body *in situ*. I wish I could start the post-mortem examination right away before rigor truly has its grip on him, but we have to wait until the jury is assembled and I can instruct them."

"I am not at all fatigued, I assure you, madam. Perhaps if there is nothing else for you to do at the moment, we could sit apart and I could tell you my long-postponed story."

She smiled. "I would like that." She turned to Murdoch. "Has the victim's family been notified?"

"Not yet. I will go to his home as soon as I can."

"You'll leave somebody in charge here, won't you?"

Murdoch groaned to himself. One characteristic of Dr. Ogden with which he was now familiar was her propensity to tell him how to do his job.

"I will make sure the place is quite secure if I am not here myself, ma'am."

She got his point and looked discomfited as she always did when caught out in her transgression. That was the counter-balance to her bossiness and kept Murdoch liking her.

"May I suggest you wait in Cooke's office, ma'am. You will be more comfortable there."

Once again, Broske offered her his arm. "That sounds like sound advice. Shall we?"

They all left the tack room, and as Dr. Ogden and the professor disappeared down the passageway, Murdoch turned, intending to go in search of Green. He didn't have to because the negro suddenly stepped out of the nearest stall. He had a horsewhip in his hand.

"I found this in here laying atop of the wheelbarrow." He handed it to Murdoch.

The leather had split near the end, revealing the whalebone underneath. All around the tear was stained a brownish red.

"Does it belong to the livery?"

"It might. I'll have to check the carriages. The cabbies are supposed to leave them in the brackets."

"Show me."

Green led the way to the carriage shed. There were five single-horse carriages and one two-horse lined up in a tight row against the far wall. The light from his lantern winked on the gilt lettering painted on the carriage doors, a big letter C and underneath the words *Cooke's Livery*. Murdoch was struck with how clean and well kept everything was.

"The whip is missing from number six carriage," said Green.

"Who had that one out?"

"I don't know without checking the list. They are parked in the order of coming in so number six would have been the last one."

"According to the sheet I was just looking at, that would have been P. Musgrave. He came in at twenty-five past seven, just after Robson."

Green nodded. "They both like to work until the last minute. Like I said, they were supposed to be all done, and the horses unharnessed and in their stalls by eight o'clock."

"Did either of these men have any enmity toward Mr. Cooke?"

"Not that I know of."

"Do you get along with them yourself?"

Green looked surprised by the question and, once again, Murdoch saw the wariness in his face.

"They's cabbies. As long as I do my job and make sure they've got clean carriages and fit horses to go out, we all get along."

Murdoch opened his notebook.

"Give me your address, will you?"

"Number 262, Terauley Street."

"Really? Bit of a haul, isn't it, to come over here?"

Green shrugged. "I'm used to it."

"What is the address of the man who spells you off? Thomas Talbert, you said?"

"That's right. He lives close by, at 33 Shuter Street."

At that moment, they heard Crabtree's sonorous voice. "Wait here until I come and fetch you. Remember you are subpoenaed and sworn, so don't think you can weasel out of your duty."

Murdoch closed the notebook. "The jurymen have arrived."

"Do you want me to stay here when I'm finished, or can I go home?"

"You'd better wait at least until Dr. Ogden has done her instruction and announces the date of the inquest. You'll be called as a witness. Oh and by the way, Green, I'm also looking for a piece of leather. I'd guess part of a lead shank. If you find anything like that, bring it to me."

"Yes, sir."

As they returned to the main barn, Dr. Ogden and Professor Broske emerged from the passageway, smiling at each other as if they had just shared a joke.

"I see the jurors have been gathered," said Dr. Ogden. She addressed Crabtree, who had come into the barn. "I assume you have a sufficient number?"

"Yes, ma'am. More than enough. We've sworn in thirteen."

"Good, bring them in then."

Crabtree went back to the yard and they heard him shouting.

"This way, gentleman. Through this door, step lively. The sooner we get started, the sooner you can go home. I'll read you the oath when we're in the room."

The men began to trickle into the barn, Crabtree and Fyfer behind them, rounding them up like so many cattle.

On the whole, they were an affluent-looking lot, which wasn't surprising given the area. Two soot-blackened navvies were also a part of the group somehow having fallen into Crabtree's net. The other men flowed around them like a river around a tree stump.

"This way, mind the horses."

Dr. Ogden in the lead, they all walked down to the tackle room.

Murdoch called out. "Ma'am, I must go and notify Mrs. Cooke."

"Very well. Your constable can inform you of the date of the inquest and I will be doing the post-mortem examination tomorrow. You will, no doubt, want to attend."

"I shall, ma'am."

"Good night then, Mr. Murdoch," said the professor. "I will probably have left by the time you return. I have to give another lecture tomorrow at a most uncivilized hour in the morning." He smiled. "In case you wondered, detective, it is the twin lecture to the one you were attending. I'm entitling it 'Courage.'"

"That sounds fascinating. I'm sorry I can't attend."

Murdoch tipped his hat and left. Speaking of courage, one of the most difficult things he was ever called upon to do was to tell a family member that a loved one had been murdered.

CHAPTER SIX

t was close to midnight by now, and Cooke's house was in darkness except for a solitary lamp in the doorway, presumably left burning for the master. Murdoch had no choice but to wake up the household. He had rung the doorbell a few times when he saw the gleam of a candle moving toward the entrance. Finally, the door was opened a crack and a sleepy-looking man, who had obviously dressed hastily, peered at him.

"What'd you want?"

"I'm Detective Murdoch from number four station and I must speak to Mrs. Cooke."

"The mistress? She's a-bed."

"I must ask you to wake her."

"Oh dear me. Has something happened to the master?"

"Yes, I'm afraid so."

"What?"

All of this conversation was conducted through the crack in the door.

"I'd like to come in, if you don't mind."

Under normal circumstances, the servant was clearly a man with a keen eye for protocol and proper position. He hesitated.

"Well, I don't know about that. How do I know who you are?"

"I just told you. Here is my card. Now, please do as I say. Does Mrs. Cooke have a personal maid?"

"Why, yes –"

"Wake her up also."

He had to push a little, but the man reluctantly stepped back and allowed him into the hall. The butler studied the calling card carefully.

"You'd better wait here then."

Murdoch had no intention of delivering his news in the hall.

"I think we'll all be more comfortable in the drawing room."

"We can't do that. There's no fire lit. Why? What's 'appened?" He had a Cockney accent that was becoming more pronounced as he became more distressed.

"I can't give you any information until I've spoken to Mrs. Cooke."

He looked frightened.

"Of course, sir. I'm sorry. Please don't think me impertinent, I'm just trying to do me job. Come this way. I'll have Lucy wake the mistress at once."

Murdoch heard a door opening overhead and a light appeared on the landing. A stout, grey-haired woman in a red satin wrapper was standing at the top of the stairs. "What is it, Ferguson? What's going on?"

"A policeman wants to talk to you, madam. About the master."

She gave a little cry of alarm. "Something's happened, hasn't it? I knew it, I knew it. He'd never normally go rushing out like that without finishing his supper."

She hurried down the stairs, straight over to Murdoch, and caught him by the arm. "Something terrible's happened, hasn't it? I can see it in your face."

"Mrs. Cooke, er, I think you should sit down." There was a coat stand in the hall with a bench. Murdoch took the lamp from the woman's hand and gently guided her to the seat. The butler didn't move but stood clutching his candleholder, watching them.

"I'm Detective Murdoch, madam. I'm afraid I do have bad news . . . I am very sorry to have to tell you, but your husband, Daniel Cooke, is dead."

Her fingers flew to her mouth. "I knew it," she said again. "I knew there was trouble."

"What kind of trouble, Mrs. Cooke?" Murdoch asked.

"Somebody called at the house at suppertime with some kind of message. We hadn't even finished our meal, but Daniel, Mr. Cooke, got up at once. He said he had to go to the stable right away."

"Did he say why?"

A fleeting expression of anger passed across her face. "No, he did not. But ask Ferguson here. He was the one who brought in the letter."

Murdoch looked over at the butler, who became more jittery. "I don't know, I'm sure, sir. It was a sealed envelope that I handed him. I don't know what sort of message it was. I can say, though, sir, seeing as you are with the police, he did seem very upset by it."

He glanced at Mrs. Cooke furtively, as if he was being disloyal, but she nodded and said, "He turned quite white and I asks him, 'What's wrong, Daniel?' but he just jumped right up and says, 'I've got to go to the stable at once.'"

"Who brought the letter?"

"The porch was quite dark –"

"I told you to fix the lamp, Ferguson. How many times have I asked you to take care of it and now look what's happened."

Murdoch attributed the irrelevancy of this remark to shock on Mrs. Cooke's part. Certainly the reaction he'd anticipated in a woman suddenly widowed hadn't yet occurred.

"I did repair the lamp, madam, but it's situated in such a way that at night the porch is quite shadowy –"

"Can you describe the messenger at all?" Murdoch interrupted.

"It was a young coloured man –"

"So it must have been Green," said Mrs. Cooke.

"No, madam. I was about to say, it wasn't anybody I'd seen before. Elijah Green would have identified himself anyways."

Murdoch made a point of opening his notebook. "It would be helpful if you could give me any details at all about this person, Mr. Ferguson." He could see that the old man actually trembled at the question.

"I'm afraid I wasn't paying a great deal of attention, and as I said the porch was dark."

"But you saw he was negro?"

"Yes, sir. He did have a white scarf wrapped around his face and a black fedora pulled down low, but I could see part of his forehead and the skin was dark."

"It wasn't just the shadows of the porch?"

"No, sir. Besides he sounded like a negro when he spoke. He had a Yankee accent. He had a sort of raspy voice too, rather as if he had a sore throat."

"What did he say?"

"Not much. 'Give this letter to Mr. Cooke right away,' or some such words." Ferguson pursed his lips, his nervousness momentarily superseded by his indignation. "He was quite rude, I thought. Not so much as a 'By your leave' or 'If you please.'"

"Can you say anything else about him? How tall, for instance? What else was he wearing?"

"He was about my height, I'd say, which is five feet, three inches. He had on a long black overcoat and the hat I mentioned, but that's all I noticed."

He was so worried, Murdoch almost patted him. "That's good, Mr. Ferguson. Thank you."

Mrs. Cooke got back into the picture. "He must have been luring my husband to the stable so he could rob him." She stood up. "I'll go there with you, Mr. Murdoch." She paused. "I suppose there's no doubt it is my husband who is dead?"

"The stable hand, Elijah Green, identified him and so did my constable."

"And where is the body?"

"At the moment it is still in the barn, but he will be moved to the funeral parlour as soon as the coroner has instructed the jury."

"I shall get dressed as quickly as I can and we can go to the stable. You'll no doubt need me to see what has been stolen."

Murdoch was taken aback. "Er, well, that would be helpful, ma'am."

She hadn't shown any curiosity at all about the way Cooke had died, but, giving her the benefit of the doubt, Murdoch decided not to go into details until she asked.

She started up the stairs, calling out to her butler, "Fetch Lucy to help me."

"Yes, madam."

The butler looked as if he was consumed with curiosity even if his mistress wasn't, but he had no choice but to do as she commanded. He scurried off down the hall with his candle, and Murdoch was left in the semi-darkness of the foyer. He opened the front door. Ferguson was right, the lamp wasn't adequate, but there was enough light to make his description of the unknown messenger credible and Murdoch thought he was telling the truth.

He took out his pipe, stuffed it with tobacco, and lit it, drawing in deeply. He would have preferred to wait until there was daylight to go back to the stables, but Mrs. Cooke seemed quite determined. Down the street a cat yowled and was answered by the deep-throated bark of dog.

He wondered what sort of message the strange Yankee man had brought that would make Daniel Cooke abandon his dinner and run out. To his death.

As for Mrs. Cooke, he had never met a bereaved woman who seemed to grieve so little, but what that meant, he didn't yet know. For that matter, Ferguson hadn't been devastated either. Nor Elijah Green. What kind of man had Daniel Cooke been who left so little sorrow at his abrupt departure from this life?

For all her urgency, Mrs. Cooke took a long time to get dressed but eventually appeared properly pinned and corseted. When they got to the livery, the constable who was now on duty told them that Dr. Ogden, the professor, and the jury had left and Crabtree had removed the body and transported it to Humphrey's Funeral Parlour. Mrs. Cooke headed straight for the office.

She knew the combination to the safe and, at her command, Murdoch opened it at once. She gasped.

"The money's gone."

There was a five-dollar bill and a cardboard box tied with a shoelace and labelled *bills* lying in the bottom of the safe, but that was all.

"How much money was there, ma'am?"

"Yesterday he told me he had four hundred and five dollars in the strong box. I told him he should take it over to the bank, but he said he'd go later this week. Now see what's happened. We've been robbed."

She suddenly burst into tears. She was certainly showing more grief at the loss of the money than the loss of her husband, Murdoch thought, but again he excused her. People often behaved strangely when they were most upset. He waited for a moment for her to calm herself.

"Did anybody else know the combination to the safe other than you and your husband?"

"Nobody. You can't be too careful, we always said. But that darkie must have forced him to open it and then he took the money and killed Daniel." She looked vaguely around the office. "Where did you find him?"

"His body was in the stable." Murdoch wasn't sure she was ready yet to hear the facts. "Is there anything else missing, Mrs. Cooke?"

She came over to the desk and opened first one drawer and then the other. "His revolver's gone."

"He kept a revolver?"

"He stayed late at the stables almost every night. Cabbies can be a rough lot. We both felt it was safer for him to be armed. Only a few months ago, he surprised a burglar and he purchased the gun after that."

Murdoch took out his notebook. "Could you describe the revolver to me, Mrs. Cooke?"

"I certainly can. We discussed at length what was the best for his purpose. He finally decided on a bulldog, thirty-two calibre. It was nickel-plated and had a rubber stock."

"Thank you, ma'am. That is excellent. Did he always keep the gun in the desk?"

She averted her eyes. "Let's put it this way, Mr. Murdoch. My husband believed in keeping his work life and his home life quite separate. I can count on one hand the number of times I have been here. I did visit him one evening not so long ago and took him by surprise. He had the gun in his hand when I came into the office." She chuckled in an awkward sort of way. "We made quite the joke of it afterwards. He replaced the gun in that drawer, I do remember that."

"And did he lock the drawer?"

"I don't recall. But he did always made sure the office door was locked."

"There was no key on his person that we have discovered, ma'am. It's possible he dropped it somewhere in the barn. We will look in the morning."

"There were two on the ring. The office key and the master key to the side doors."

Murdoch made a note. "Did he report the previous incident to the police, ma'am?"

"No, he didn't. I told him he should have, but nothing was taken and he said he hadn't got a good look at the man anyway. He was too soft-hearted, is the truth. Didn't want to bring in trouble. He thought it might give other people ideas."

"Perhaps we could both take a look around the room, while you are here, just in case he did put the gun somewhere else and in case you notice anything else out of place."

"Very well."

There really wasn't anywhere else to look. There was nothing in the bookcase or the filing cabinet. However, in the lower drawer of the desk, Murdoch found a pile of racing forms. They went back several months and were heavily marked and notated.

"Mr. Cooke liked to gamble, did he, ma'am?"

She saw what he was referring to and she frowned. "He was a man who made his living by hiring out horses. Occasionally he could get a rundown racehorse for a reasonable price. They make good cab horses."

She'd come up with that answer pretty quickly, thought Murdoch, who didn't think comments such as "Closing fast in last race," "Likes slop," and "Now's the time" were about potential cab horses.

The search was soon completed, and Mrs. Cooke declared that as far as she knew nothing else had been taken. She returned to the safe and gave a cursory glance at the box of bills. She looked far worse now than she had when he first brought her the bad news. Even in her youth, Murdoch doubted she had ever been an attractive woman. Her chin and nose were too coarse for beauty, and a long-standing petulance had etched lines between her eyes.

She put the five-dollar bill in her reticule. "I'll take this."

"Do you have an objection if I take the box with me, ma'am?"

For a moment, she looked uneasy. "I cannot imagine it will be of any help. It just contains bills of sale."

"Everything we can learn about your husband's affairs might help," said Murdoch, and not giving her much chance to protest further he picked up the cardboard box, scooped the papers off the spike on the desk, and put them inside.

"It is obvious a thief lured him away on some pretext," she continued. "I assume he was shot?"

"As a matter of fact, ma'am, we are not sure at this moment what caused his death . . . he'd been tied up. I hate to have to tell you this, Mrs. Cooke, but he'd been whipped."

She gaped at him. "Whipped? What on Earth do you mean?"

"His jacket and shirt were cut off and his assailant horse-whipped him."

She sat down abruptly on the chair by the door. "Why would anybody do that?"

"I don't know, ma'am. Did your husband have any enemies that you were aware of?"

"None. He was very well liked. You can ask his employees. They were very loyal. What a dreadful, dreadful thing. To take all of our money is bad enough, but to hurt him in that way . . ."

Murdoch wished he had insisted on Mrs. Cooke's maid accompanying them, but she had refused, saying she didn't want Nosy Parkers involved in her business. As Lucy was well within earshot, Murdoch thought Mrs. Cooke was being unduly rude.

"Let me accompany you home, ma'am. We will continue the investigation tomorrow. Is there a friend or relative you would like me to send for to stay with you?"

"No. My servants will take care of me. That's what I pay them for, isn't it?"

Murdoch had no answer to that so he offered her his arm and, pulling on it rather heavily, she got to her feet.

"I realize you must do your job, but I hope you don't intend to close the stable for more than a morning. The cabbies need to go about their business. It is their livelihood, after all."

"Yes, ma'am. I quite understand. And speaking of that, I need a list of their names and addresses."

She pointed at the filing cabinet. "There's a ledger in the bottom drawer. They're in there."

"Thank you, ma'am. And I promise you, we will do our best to move quickly."

"I would expect as much," she said.

CHAPTER SEVEN

AUGUST 1858

I n the month since she had been abducted, she had learned to keep her eyes averted and her head slightly inclined, and she did that now as she and her captors approached the porch.

"Here she is, ma'am."

The woman was lying on a lounge chair, covered with a shawl even though it was a hot, muggy afternoon. Her untidily pinned hair was quite grey, and her skin seemed deadly white, her eyes deeply shadowed. A girl with dark skin was standing behind her, cooling her with a large palm fan.

"What's her name?" the woman asked.

She spoke in a quiet, enervated voice that had an unusual twang.

"She was last called Lena, ma'am. She's been a lady's maid before and can sew beautifully, dress hair in the best style, and is quiet and docile as a kitten."

"Kittens scratch." This remark came from another woman who was seated near the door. Lena managed a quick glance in her direction. She was younger with a thin, pinched face. Her brown hair was pulled down smooth and tight from a straight centre parting in the current fashion, and the severity of it did not enhance her looks.

"A figure of speech only, ma'am," Prescott gave Lena a poke in the ribs. "Come on, girl. Tell Mrs. Dickie that you're a good girl."

She curtsied. "I'm a good girl, ma'am. I won't be any trouble."

The younger woman snorted. "My, aren't we la-di-da. Where *did* she come from, Prescott?"

"She belonged to an English lady, ma'am. Over in Ohio. Must've picked up the way of talking from her. Her missus'd never have sold her 'cept she was going back to the homeland."

"I think you should reconsider, mother. You know what trouble these high-yaller girls are. They think they're better than anybody else and the others get fussed and come complaining all the time. It's so tiresome."

Prescott addressed Mrs. Dickie. "What's it to be then, ma'am? I can get a good price for her anywhere if you don't want her."

The older woman gave a weak wave. "Come over here, girl. Let me look at you." Lena walked over to the couch. "Kneel down, you're so tall you're making my neck crick by looking up at you . . . that's better. Now let me see your hands."

Lena held her hands out, palms up.

"Yes, they are soft. You're not lying about that Prescott. No, don't protest. You know perfectly well you'd pass off a mule as an Arabian if you could get away with it. Now, girl, let's see you smile. You're much too solemn. I can't have gloomy faces around me, only sunny ones. Isn't that right, Fidelia?"

The coloured girl beamed a dazzling white smile, marred only by a partly chipped front tooth.

"Yes, missus."

Lena forced herself to smile, and the woman looked at her critically.

"Much better. You're quite pretty with a happy expression. What do you think, Leigh? Caddie? Turn around, child, and show them how you can smile."

Lena did so. A man spoke.

"I think she'll do as well as any other, mamma. You are in need of a maid."

Lena hadn't noticed him at first, as he was standing at the far end of the porch. He was short, running to fat, with thinning hair, although he was probably still in his twenties.

The young woman who'd been addressed as Caddie frowned. "I tell you she'll cause trouble."

The man shrugged indifferently. "I don't give a fig either way. It is up to mamma."

Mrs. Dickie waved her hand in Prescott's direction. "I like her. It's settled then. Fidelia, you can take her to the cabin and show her where she'll sleep." She touched Lena's cheek with her dry finger. "Are you hungry, child?"

"Yes, ma'am."

"Beulah will fix you something. Come back in here in about an hour. Can you tell the time?"

"Yes, ma'am."

"Good. Now, Mr. Prescott, come around to the back and my son will settle up with you. Leigh, deduct at least twenty dollars from what he asks. He's a rogue through and through."

The slave trader tipped his hat. "Thank you, ma'am."

Lena felt a pang of fear. How bizarre that she should feel afraid seeing him go, but she did. He was the only link to her real life. He was the only one who knew who she was and where she came from. But even as she saw him bowing, grinning, ignoring her, she knew how foolish it was even to suppose for a moment he would tell the truth. She'd tried that on the steamer, she'd tried to talk to the captain, but Prescott had pulled her away. Later, he'd punched her so hard in the ribs that she couldn't breathe. He said if she did that again, he'd have her taken off to the loony bin and she could scream and carry on there until she went grey and they would never believe her because everybody in that place said they were somebody else. "You'll be chained up and starved and beaten, and if you think your husband will find you, he might as well look for a needle in a whole barn of straw because he never will."

That kept her silent even more than fear of the pain he could inflict. If she was at least visible to normal people, to civilized people, she might eventually be found.

CHAPTER EIGHT

Murdoch entered the house as quietly as he could. An oil lamp was burning low on the hall table, but there were no lights showing underneath the doors leading from the hallway. It was past one o'clock in the morning and everybody was sensibly asleep. He hung up his hat and coat, yawning enough to dislocate his own jaw. He stood still for a moment. He was so used to coming into the house and listening for Arthur Kitchen, his former landlord, it had become a habit. This time he was making sure no wail of a babe woken prematurely tore the air. Katie, one of his fellow boarders, had warned him that her twins were coming down with the sniffles.

He reached for the lamp and noticed there was a letter beside it. It was one he'd received from Beatrice Kitchen that morning and he must have left it in the kitchen. He put it in his pocket and started up the stairs, stepping carefully over the second step from the top, which always creaked badly. He should see to it. He was nominally the landlord now. When the Kitchens had moved to Muskoka in a desperate search for a cure for Arthur's consumption,

Murdoch had agreed to stay on in the house, rent-free, and look after the new tenants. Murdoch smiled to himself. Mrs. Kitchen, bless her heart, would probably be saying a dozen novenas if she knew what had developed in the household. In the front parlour were Katie and her twin boys. She had considered herself married and then, abruptly, a widow, but it transpired the marriage was a bigamous one, making her children bastards. Not that anybody in his house was going to bruit that abroad. Charlie Seymour, a fellow officer at number four station, was renting one of the upstairs rooms, and Murdoch was sure the once-confirmed bachelor was smitten by the young woman. She was a sweet-natured girl who also happened to be an excellent cook, so Murdoch wasn't surprised Charlie was feeling the way he did. What would distress dear Mrs. Kitchen more than anything else, however, was the presence of the third boarder, Miss Amy Slade, schoolteacher, ardent and unapologetic New Woman, atheist, and the object of Murdoch's affections.

At the top of the landing, he could see that the door to his little sitting room was open and the soft glow of a candle spilled out. He walked quietly down the landing and went in.

Amy was sitting in the armchair fast asleep. She was in her dressing gown, her hair in a night braid. He stood for a moment, still at the stage of love when it is a delight to study the sleeping face of your beloved and marvel at its mystery. Even in the shadowy candlelight, the softness of her well-shaped lips were visible and stirred him.

Suddenly she opened her eyes with a gasp. "Will, you startled me. What are you doing standing there?"

"Looking at you."

"For how long?"

"Only a moment."

"Thank goodness for that, I was probably sleeping with my mouth open."

"No, you weren't. And even if you had been I would still consider you a sight for sore eyes."

She made a sort of harrumph sound and picked up the book
that was lying in her lap. "I was intending just to wait for you and
read a book, but I fell asleep. What time is it?"

"Almost half past one."

"Why are you so late? Surely the lecture didn't go this long?
Don't tell me you were called to a case." She scrutinized his face for
a moment. "You were. You're wearing your detective look."

"I'm not even going to ask what you mean by that, but yes,
you're right. Crabtree came to the lecture hall and fetched me."

"A murder?"

"We don't know yet, but it was very nasty."

"If it's all right with you then, you can tell me that part in the
morning. I don't want nightmares."

He bent over and touched his finger to her chin tenderly.
"Nightmares? I can't imagine my brave Amy having nightmares."

"But I do. You haven't known me long enough yet."

"I shall be glad to ensure that at any time, as you know."

She smiled. "Speaking of beds, which you were about to, I had
better get to my own. I believe the school inspector might pay me
a visit tomorrow and I should have all my wits about me."

"Was there a particular reason you were sitting up for me?"

"There was, but it can wait." She gave him a quick kiss.
"Good night. I'll see you in the morning."

In spite of his jangling alarm clock, Murdoch found it hard to
wake up, and Amy had left by the time he went down to the
kitchen. When he arrived at the station it was well after eight and
later than he'd wanted. Gardiner was the sergeant on duty,
Seymour having the luxury after a twenty-four-hour shift of a
long sleep-in.

"Morning, Will. Crabtree has given me the report on last night's incident and I took the liberty of sending him and Fyfer to start the search of the stable."

"Thanks, John. Is there any tea brewed? I need a large cuppa before I join them."

"I just mashed a pot half an hour ago. It'll be good and fresh."

The front door opened and a man entered. He was middle-aged, with a neatly trimmed beard and soberly dressed in a grey fedora and long tweed coat. Murdoch couldn't quite place his occupation. Not a doctor, nor a minister, but with an air of calm authority about him that men in those professions often have. The man lifted his hat to Murdoch.

"Good morning, do I have the privilege of addressing Detective William Murdoch?"

"I'm Murdoch."

The man extended his hand. "My name is Cherry, Earl Cherry, and I am actually conveying a message from Inspector Brackenreid." He held out an envelope.

Murdoch opened it, bewildered. Brackenreid had been away from the station for the past few days, supposedly suffering from a bad cold, which had become code for a severe hangover.

Dear Murdoch. I know we have had our differences, but when it comes to the wall, you are a man whose discretion I trust. I am sending a friend of mine with this letter. I am temporarily incapacitated with the aftermath of what was probably an attack of gastritis and I am staying at a lodge to recuperate. With some time on my hands, I have need of something to read and what better opportunity than to make a thorough study of the minutes of the city council. I'll settle for the ones for 1894. They are bound in a volume on the second shelf from the top in the bookcase by the window. As it includes the report of the chief constable, it would be better if it were kept private. I would like you to wrap it securely and give it to Mr. Cherry, who will bring it to me. Your help in this matter is much appreciated and will not be forgotten.

Your servant, Thomas Brackenreid.

Murdoch couldn't hide his astonishment. It was impossible to imagine the inspector recovering on his sickbed with a rousing volume of the council's report. Besides which, the request to keep it private was absurd. The minutes were available to the public, who were encouraged to look at them. Cherry was watching him.

"Mr. Brackenreid speaks highly of you, Mr. Murdoch."

"Does he, indeed? He has certainly kept that a secret from me."

"Ah," replied Cherry with an understanding nod that to Murdoch looked far too professional. Now he knew what the man reminded him of. An undertaker.

"The inspector says he's at a lodge, recuperating from gastritis. Where is he?"

Cherry glanced over at Gardiner with a little shake of his head. The sergeant was rather obviously trying to pretend he wasn't listening.

"John," said Murdoch, "would you be so good as to fetch me the tea you mentioned? And perhaps one for Mr. Cherry, here."

"No, no, not for me, thank you, I just breakfasted."

With some ill grace, Gardiner headed for the duty room where the officers took their tea breaks.

"Well, Mr. Cherry. What is this all about?"

Cherry lowered his voice. "This must be kept in strictest confidence, Mr. Murdoch." He paused and Murdoch almost expected him to bring out a Bible for him to swear on.

"Yes?"

"Inspector Brackenreid is at the moment a resident at the Ollapod Club."

It was all Murdoch could do not to burst out laughing. So the old sot had finally admitted his problem. The Ollapod Club was a nobby establishment over on Wellesley Street that claimed to cure chronic addictions to liquor. It had the reputation for being a conscience sop to wealthy clientele who stayed there for months at a time in well-tended sobriety. Rumour had it, however, that when released, a high proportion of the graduates fell back into their old ways with alarming speed.

"I see you know of us, Mr. Murdoch. You can understand therefore why the inspector wants discretion. Not everybody would see his decision to enter the club in the correct light."

"Which is?"

"An act of courage. To acknowledge one's weaknesses is not always easy, especially for a man with such pride and integrity as Thomas Brackenreid."

Murdoch had never previously ascribed these qualities to his inspector. It was a novel view.

Gardiner returned with a mug of tea that Murdoch accepted gratefully, gulping down a big swallow of the hot strong brew.

"Mr. Cherry, why don't you have a seat on the bench over there. The inspector has asked me to find a certain book for him. I'll just be a moment."

Brackenreid's office was on the second floor of the station. In spite of his complaints that the division didn't receive enough money to function as he wanted it to, the inspector had furnished his office in a luxurious fashion. There was a thick Axminster carpet on the floor and the large desk by the window was polished oak, a far cry from Murdoch's scarred and stained pine desk, which had been dragged in from God knows where.

The room was chilly because the fire hadn't been lit for some days, but there was a lingering smell of the rich cigars that Brackenreid favoured. Murdoch went over to the glass-fronted bookcase. There were several fat volumes of the council's minutes, all pristine-looking. He took down the one for 1894. What was Brackenreid after? He was about to riffle through the pages but found he couldn't because they were glued together and there tucked snugly into a little nest cut into the pages was a silver flask. He pried it out and opened the top. One whiff confirmed what he suspected. The minutes of the city council for 1894 had become the inspector's private cellar. No wonder he'd made a weak excuse for wrapping the book. If he was at a facility devoted to curing ine-briates, it wasn't too likely they would want him to have a flask of good whisky in his possession. What to do? Tell on him? Murdoch went over to the desk and took out a piece of paper.

Dear Inspector Brackenreid. I have great sympathy for your current struggle. Some days will be more difficult than others I'm sure, but I know you will come through it. All the best, William Murdoch.

He folded the paper and put it into the empty space. He poured the whisky into the aspidistra on the window ledge. It needed watering anyway. Then he took a sheet of one of the newspapers stacked ready to light the fire and wrapped the book. He found a ball of twine in the desk drawer and tied up the parcel, cutting the string with Brackenreid's cigar clippers.

Cherry was waiting quietly in the hall. He did not seem to have engaged Gardiner in any conversation, and the sergeant was busy writing his night report in the duty roster.

Murdoch handed Cherry the package. "Here you are, sir. And please give the inspector my condolences and wish him a speedy recovery."

"I will." He paused. "I understand Mr. Brackenreid was requesting a particular volume. Was it in good condition, would you say? What I mean is, was it suitable for reading?"

There was a look of friendly skepticism in his eyes, and suddenly Murdoch liked him much better.

"Let's say, I removed any unnecessary items so that the inspector wouldn't be distracted."

Cherry smiled. "Ah, I see. The old flask-in-the-middle trick, was it?"

Murdoch nodded.

"You'd never believe the tricks some of our pat – I mean, some of our guests can get up to when they are in still in the grip of the demon," said Cherry. "I thank you, sir. Your good inspector might not have the same gratitude now, but he will, I promise you he will."

"I hope so. How much longer will he be with you, do you think?"

"It depends on his progress. So far, he has been somewhat resistant. He did not enter the club solely of his own choice. I believe his wife was adamant."

"A week then? Two? More?"

"I'm afraid it is impossible to tell, but what I will do is to see if he can give some direction as to what he wants done at the station here. We are trying to avoid his condition becoming widely known. He seemed to think you would be able to manage without him, but you might need a more formal acknowledgement. Perhaps he could appoint you deputy inspector or something like that."

"Me? Oh I don't think so. I doubt he'd want that."

"No, I meant what I said, Mr. Murdoch. He does speak of you with admiration."

Suddenly he glanced up at the clock on the wall. "My goodness, I am late. It will be time for the morning medicine and I should be there. Good morning to you, sir. And thank you for your help."

He left and Murdoch picked up his mug. "I'm going to my office, sergeant. Tell Crabtree to come and see me when he gets back."

Hmm . . . if he was deputy inspector for a few weeks maybe he could sit upstairs and enjoy a nice coal fire and a couple of cigars. Perhaps he'd been too hasty in emptying the whisky flask.

CHAPTER NINE

M urdoch untied the shoelace that secured the cardboard box, removed the lid, and took out the papers, spreading them across the top of his desk. They were indeed bills, many of them months old and, by the looks of it, none yet paid. He skimmed through them, but they seemed the normal transactions for a small livery. Bills for hay, oats, bran; one from a veterinarian who'd disposed of a horse afflicted with glanders. A small sum owing to a carpenter for repair of one of the carriages. The sheets he'd taken from the spike were more recent but more demanding. The veterinarian was now threatening legal action if his bill wasn't paid within five days of receipt. On top was a handwritten piece of paper requesting the payment of three weeks' back wages in the amount of eighteen dollars. The note was signed by Elijah Green. Murdoch removed that paper and put it in his inside pocket. The other tradesmen's names he wrote down to check later.

According to Mrs. Cooke, her husband had kept four hundred dollars in his safe. That was a lot of money and would easily cover his debts. Murdoch wondered if the racing forms he'd found were a tipoff as to what that money might be earmarked for. He was about to gather up the papers and return them to the box when he saw he'd almost overlooked a side pocket. He fished inside and took out a cloth wallet tied with ribbon. Inside was a creased piece of paper. He smoothed it out.

> Purchased from Thomas Talbert, Esquire, for the sum of 200 dollars. The Livery, 27 Mutual Street. Including the six horses and three carriages and all the tack presently in use. Also the present feed as noted.
> Signed. Daniel Cooke
> Eleventh day of October 1863. at Toronto. Acknowledged as stated, Thomas Talbert.

Elijah Green had referred to a man named Talbert who spelled him a couple of days of the week taking care of the stables. Were these two men related? If it was the same man, he'd be quite elderly by now.

He restored everything to the box and put it in his drawer.

There was a tap on the wall outside his cubicle, and Constable Crabtree's large shape appeared behind the reed curtain that made do as a door.

"Come in, George."

The constable shoved through the curtain that clacked noisily in his wake.

"Good morning, sir. I've come to report on the search me and Constable Fyfer did of the livery barn this morning."

"Did you find anything?"

"I'd say so."

He was carrying a lumpy-looking bundle wrapped in sacking and looked around for somewhere to put it.

"The desk is fine, George, what've you got? Not money, is it? There's quite a large sum missing, according to Mrs. Cooke."

"No, sir. No money, I'm afraid, but treasure, if I may put it that way."

Crabtree unwrapped his prize as carefully, as if it contained a glass piece. Inside was another scrap of bleached-out sacking, a length of rope, two Indian clubs, and a sheet of grubby, crumpled notepaper.

"There's a little space in the loft, not much bigger than a wardrobe, but the darkie has a cot there. There's a packing box next to it and I found these articles in there." He shook out the piece of sackcloth. "There's a stain on this one that looks like fresh blood to me."

Murdoch examined it. "It does, indeed. We'll have to get Dr. Ogden to take a look at it. Where was it exactly?"

"At the bottom of the crate. Green claims he had to bleed one of the horses, but if that's true, why take it up to the loft? Why not leave it in the barn?" Crabtree picked up one of the Indian clubs, held it in one hand, then slammed it into his open palm. "Mr. Cooke had been hit on the head. I'll wager this was the weapon used."

Murdoch focused a magnifying glass on the club. "I don't see any evidence of blood, George. Let's have a look at the other one. No, nothing on this either."

"He would have made sure to wipe them clean though, wouldn't he, sir?"

"I suppose so. What did he say about them?"

"That he used them for exercise."

"That could be true. I have a pair myself."

"It doesn't mean he didn't use one of them to bash Mr. Cooke on the head."

"True. What else have you got?"

"This rope. He would have used it to tie up Cooke before he strung him up to the rafters. It was coiled in the bottom of the crate under a piece of newspaper. Green said he used it as a lead for the horses, but if that's the case, why not keep it in the tack room with the other equipment?"

"Good point, George."

Murdoch examined the rope, which was about an inch in diameter and knotted at each end. He thought that was odd, but he couldn't find any sign of blood along its entire length, or traces of horsehair for that matter, which he thought was also odd. He decided for the moment to keep these doubts to himself. George didn't need any further convincing that they had their culprit.

"What's the paper all about?"

"Ah, yes, sir. That's the clincher, as far as I'm concerned. Have a look at what's written on it. Green was just in front of me and he actually snatched this out of my hand. Said it was private property and nothing to do with the murder. He was about to tear it up, but I got to it first. He was quite surly, so of course that got my dander up immediately. I told him what for and snaffled it, but for a minute I truly thought he'd be willing to fight me for it."

Murdoch picked up the piece of notepaper. Somebody, he presumed Green, had printed in a bold clear hand: _The Master_. *Advance Retreat Bar Bottom Chop Hit Mark Fall.*

The words were in a column on the left side of the page. The rest of the sheet was blank.

"It doesn't make much sense to me, George, does it you?"

"I think it's a plan of attack. See, it starts with the Master, which I assume is his employer, Mr. Cooke. Then it's *hit, mark, fall*. Mr. Cooke was marked all right."

"What about the other words?"

"He was probably planning how to do it."

"Did he have an explanation?"

"No, he did not. He admitted it was his and his hand, but he kept saying it had nothing to do with Cooke's death and it was private. Like I said, he was highly disturbed. Most I've seen from him yet."

Murdoch folded the paper again.

"Why would Green commit such a vicious act? What's his motivation?"

"I can't say, sir. Maybe he got it into his head that Mr. Cooke had slighted him somehow and he wanted his revenge."

"That's possible. I don't know about slighting him, but Cooke did owe him for three weeks' wages."

"There you go then." Crabtree had an expectant look on his face, and Murdoch had the impression the constable was disappointed with his lack of enthusiasm for his findings. "Are you going to arrest him?"

"Not immediately, George. We don't have quite enough to go on. But that was good work. I'll follow it up."

Crabtree fished in his pocket and took out some sheets of paper. "Constable Fyfer wanted me to pass this along to you, sir. He's relieving Burley at the livery. When we arrived the cabbies were waiting because they hadn't heard what had happened. Fyfer decided to question them and save you the trouble. He wrote out everything for you."

"Did he indeed? He's a diligent fellow, I must say. In the meantime, George, I'd like you to start doing the usual rounds. Check out all the houses up and down the street. Find out if anybody saw the coloured man who came to the Cooke house and apparently so upset Daniel Cooke. Here, I've written out the names and addresses of all the tradesmen that Cooke owed money to. Talk to them as well."

"Yes, sir."

"I'll look over what Fyfer has written, then I'm going to have a chat with Green's helper, Mr. Talbert."

Crabtree left. Murdoch pushed the little treasure trove to one side, took out his pipe and tobacco, lit up, and unfolded Fyfer's report.

CHAPTER TEN

THURSDAY, APRIL 16, 1896

*R*eport *of Constable Second Class Frank Fyfer.*
Mr. Daniel Cooke, deceased, employed six cab drivers. Four of them were present when constable first class George Crabtree and I arrived at the livery stable, 76 Mutual Street, city of Toronto. They were Robert Littlejohn, Joseph Wallace, Albert Carney, and Robert Robson; Thomas Muckle is down with pneumonia and has not been working for a month; Paul Musgrave was expected in later this morning. I interviewed each man separately, but as I was asking the same question of each I thought it would be simpler and add clarification if I listed first the question then the answer each man made. The comparisons might prove fruitful. I have written down in their own words what they said.

"Get on with it, Frank," Murdoch muttered out loud and drew in another puff of tobacco.

1. When did you last see Mr. Cooke?

Robert Littlejohn: When I returned the carriage at three o'clock yesterday.

Joseph Wallace: Twice. First when I took out the carriage at eleven o'clock and second when I brought it back at one o'clock. The bloody horse had cast a shoe, so I didn't get much business. I considered going out on another shift, but it's hardly worth it when we have to be all done by eight o'clock on Wednesdays.

Albert Carney: I saw him when I took out Mercer at nine o'clock and again when I brought her back at two o'clock.

Robert Robson: I checked out at ten minutes past three and he signed the sheet. When I returned at seven o'clock he was not present to initial my sign-off but that was not so unusual so I left not thinking anything of it. Wednesday is an early closing day.

2. How did he seem?

Littlejohn: I didn't notice. Businesslike, I suppose. He said I owed him money, which I didn't, but we cleared it up.

Wallace: He seemed like usual. We didn't say much. I'm not one for chatting with the boss like some are. I signed in and he initialled. He might have asked me if I'd had a good run, but I don't really remember. He was only fishing anyways. Always worried in case we're cheating him and not reporting the fares.

(Note from F.F.: Joseph Wallace showed himself to be a chronic complainer with a sour attitude toward life.)

Carney: I can't say as I noticed anything different. He's not the cheeriest of fellows, God forgive me for speaking ill of the dead, but it is the truth.

<u>Robson:</u> He wasn't no different from usual.

3. Do you know if Mr. Cooke had any disagreements with anybody that might have led to his death?

<u>Littlejohn:</u> I don't know. I just do my job. I've only worked here three months.

<u>Wallace:</u> If anybody had disagreements with Mr. Cooke, I'd say it was his tradesmen. He never paid his bills on time. He couldn't do that to us because we pay him our commission on fares and we pay for rental, but he was on top of every nickel. Get a tear in the upholstery and he'd expect you to pay for the repair. On the other hand, you never know what's going on in people's minds, do you? It might be a good idea to have a chin with Paul Musgrave. I'm not accusing him, mind, but I doubt he's grieving too much at the boss's demise, given the wife is now available.

(Note from F.F.: Here Wallace actually gave me a sly wink. I did, of course, ask him what he was referring to, but he clammed up completely. Said he meant nothing by it. Musgrave is a bachelor, that's all, and aren't all bachelors in need of wives? He refused to say any more and said to ask the man in question who as I said wasn't present.)

<u>Carney:</u> Well, he had tradesmen coming to the door two or three times a week for the past month. They was all pretty hot under the collars cos they said as they hadn't been paid. God forgive me for speaking ill of the dead.

(Note from F.F.: I thought it necessary to ask him at this point if he knew the names of the tradesmen and he said there were two he knew: Walter Hammill, the feed merchant, and Timothy Mishaw, a carpenter.)

<u>Robson.</u> He had a barney with his wife a few days ago, if that's what you mean. I saw them in the office. Real

fierce it was, but she's not a woman I'd like to cross. I felt more sorry for him than her.

(Note from F.F.: I pressed Robson on this matter as to what the quarrel was all about, but he couldn't enlighten me. Said he didn't hear anything because they were in the office, but he could see them. He does also admit to being a little deaf. When I pinned him down as to the exact time of this supposed row, he said it occurred Friday last, April 10, when he returned in the evening at nine o'clock. No one else was in the barn except the stable hand, Green.)

4. Would you say that you yourself got along with Mr. Cooke?

Littlejohn: He was my boss, I didn't need to like him. I can work anywhere. His cut isn't no different from the others. One dollar per shift for the carriage and 5 per cent commission on fares.

Wallace: Why are you asking me? Don't think you can throw suspicion on me, young man. I had no quarrel with Daniel Cooke, and you can't twist my words to make it seem that way.

(Note from F.F.: It took a while to calm Mr. Wallace's fears.)

Carney: I get along with everybody, ask my wife.

Robson: We got along all right. He's not a man I'd invite over for dinner, mind you.

5. We know that Mr. Cooke died somewhere between eight o'clock and nine o'clock. Can you give me an account of your whereabouts at that time and the names of a person or persons who will verify that.

Littlejohn: I don't know where I was. I went for a walk on Queen Street, nowhere near the stables. I got home about ten o'clock.

(Note from F.F.: This was a most unsatisfactory answer, and the man was obviously uncomfortable. I threatened to charge him with obstructing justice if he didn't tell the truth, and after much beating about the bush, he admitted he had been visiting a house of ill repute on Queen Street. I did get the address from him and the name of the woman he was visiting. This can easily be verified if she is willing to testify, which may not be the case. Mr. Littlejohn lives at home with his elderly mother and was distraught at the thought of her knowing what he was up to.)

Wallace: I can't believe you're asking me all these questions. Much more and I will hire a solicitor. I was at home all evening sitting in front of my own hearth, minding my own business. My wife can vouch for that and so can my brother and sister-in-law, who live with us.

Carney: I was at the Mechanics Institute with my wife. We were listening to a visiting preacher from America. Very good he was too. Most uplifting.

Robson: I know what you're getting at. I was one of the last to leave the stables along with Musgrave, but I went straight home. My wife was waiting for me and so were my two sons and three daughters. They are all old enough to know and tell the truth, and we are all good Christians.

(Note from F.F.: As Mr. Robson was indeed the last one to sign out except for Mr. Musgrave, I asked him if he had noticed any strangers in the area who might be considered suspicious.)

Robson: No. Didn't see anybody. It was raining when I turned in, and I just tucked my head in and went straight home. I've just got shut of a cold and I didn't want to get pneumonia like Muckle.

(Note from F.F.: Given the peculiar character of the assault on Mr. Cooke and what Constable Crabtree discovered in his box, I thought it might be prudent to ask the men specifically about the stable hand, Elijah Green.)

6. How did Mr. Cooke get along with Elijah Green?

<u>Littlejohn:</u> How should I know? Elijah did a good job, but you don't really see him much.

<u>Wallace:</u> Another ridiculous question. I never saw them together. All I know is that I've been here for going on ten years and Green was here when I came so he must be doing all right.

<u>Carney:</u> I don't know the answer to that. Why? Are you saying the darkie killed him?

<u>Robson:</u> Elijah is a fine fellow, as far as I'm concerned. He takes good care of the horses. Cooke was lucky to have him.

7. Do any of you have a key to the stables or the office?

All answered no.

(Note from F.F.: My assessment after interviewing these men is that Daniel Cooke was not particularly liked but neither was he hated. I think it is well worth our while to follow up on the reported quarrel between Mr. Cooke and his wife and also the tradesmen who wanted their money. Deprivation can make men desperate, as we know. In terms of alibis for the time of death, I can pursue that, but my feeling was that these men were telling the truth. I will also interview Paul Musgrave if you want me to.)

End of report.

Signed, Francis Fyfer.

Murdoch put down the paper. The first line of suspects in a murder case was always the victim's immediate circle, which in this case meant his employees. The cabbies would have been familiar with Cooke's schedule and with the stable itself, which he thought was an important factor in the case unless the killer was blessed with extraordinary good luck not to be interrupted. Fyfer had saved him time by questioning the men, but Murdoch would have liked to be present. He'd learned to trust his own instincts about the unspoken revelations that people made during questioning. When he'd shared this with Amy one night, she said he was probably "air scenting" like a hound does. "As long as my nose doesn't twitch," was his retort, but he thought there was truth in what she said. He couldn't pick up the trail from a written report, however thorough it was. He supposed he should trust Fyfer's instincts too, but he almost wished the fellow wasn't quite so eager. He was right, though. Adelaide Cooke had said she hadn't stepped into the livery since Christmas, which obviously wasn't the case if Mr. Robson was to be believed. He wondered what Wallace's "sly wink" meant. Did it imply something between the ungrieving widow and the cabbie Musgrave? Given the amount of debt Cooke had incurred, Murdoch could understand irate tradesman being driven to some act of desperation. He put Fyfer's report in the drawer and extinguished his pipe.

He frowned. He seemed to have a veritable shoal of suspects.

CHAPTER ELEVEN

Murdoch had been sitting in Humphrey's embalming room for at least half an hour. Daniel Cooke was lying on his back on the gurney in the centre of the room. His skin was fishbelly grey and he was already beginning to smell. The only sound that disturbed the thick silence of death was the buzzing of two or three elusive flies. They were hovering around the corpse and had so far managed to evade Murdoch's attempts to get rid of them. The door swung open and Professor Broske and Dr. Ogden bustled in.

"I do apologize for keeping you waiting, Mr. Murdoch," said Dr. Ogden. "Professor Broske was showing me some utterly fascinating photographs he took recently of a young patient who had broken his elbow. It fixed in place, alas, and had to be straightened. The doctor used his camera to record the young boy's expressions throughout the entire procedure. Quite amazing."

"That must have been painful for the boy," said Murdoch.

"Dreadfully so," answered Broske. "He was a brave young lad, but his face revealed everything. It was extremely distressing to witness."

Not to mention experience, thought Murdoch.

Broske slipped on one of the holland aprons hanging on hooks by the door. Dr. Ogden did likewise.

"Miss Julia has invited me to do the examination," he said. "I am so happy to be given this opportunity."

Why the man had taken to calling her that, Murdoch didn't know, but she seemed to like it and smiled prettily.

"I will be writing down the notes," she said.

"Before we start, Dr. Ogden, I have a request. One of my constables found some objects in the stable that I'd like to have examined more closely. They're over on the shelf wrapped in newspaper. I also found what is very likely the horsewhip that was used on Cooke. I've put that there also."

"I'll look at them afterwards. Professor Broske can corroborate my findings for me."

"Delighted to."

That little preamble taken care of, the professor got to work. The first part of the post-mortem he conducted in the conventional way, leaving the corpse clothed and simply dictating notes as to what he observed as he walked around the gurney.

"Daniel Cooke was well nourished, almost too much so. His height is five feet, ten and one-quarter inches. At time of death, he was dressed in a pair of plaid trousers, brown socks, and boots, no shirt or undergarment. All garments are of good quality. Mr. Murdoch, I will leave it to you to write out the report concerning his other apparel."

While he was waiting for them to arrive, Murdoch had done just that. Nothing new had been revealed.

Broske called over to him, "Mr. Murdoch? Help me turn him over, will you?"

Together they rolled over the body. "We have already remarked on the nature of the wounds to his back, but perhaps you could note down our observations now, Miss Julia? He has been struck many times. I will endeavour to make a more precise count, but as they overlap we might not be able to be completely exact. The marks appear to be slightly deeper on his left side and more concentrated on the lower end of the torso." Broske smiled at Murdoch. "What would you say that indicates?"

"His assailant was short. Or certainly shorter than Mr. Cooke. Even allowing for the fact that he had been hoisted up, the strikes of the whip didn't reach up any farther than his shoulder blades. And the assailant was right-handed."

"Very good, very good. I agree with that, don't you, Miss Julia?"

"I do."

Together they examined Cooke's back, disputing in a friendly way whether that stripe or this was an overlay or not. Finally, Broske straightened up.

"I would say he was struck between thirty-seven and thirty-nine times, but some of the blows were done after death."

"And I agree with that assessment," added Dr. Ogden. "The lashes as they cross here and here have broken the skin, which to me indicates that the perpetrator was becoming more ferocious as he continued."

The professor nodded. "That happens. When I was serving in the army, I saw men completely lose their tempers over the most trivial incident, but once they had embarked, the rage seemed to overtake them and they would have killed if not separated. Dogs are the same."

He began to undo Cooke's trouser buttons. "If you'll remove the boots, Murdoch, it will be easier to take off his trolleywags, if I may use such an expression."

They worked together while Dr. Ogden watched. Underneath his trousers, Cooke was wearing flannel underwear, which Broske pulled off.

"Ah look at that." He poked at the flaccid penis. "I'd say the man had at least one bout with venereal disease, wouldn't you, Miss Julia?"

She leaned forward to take a look, and Broske cradled Cooke's member in his hand.

"Yes, indeed. That's quite a scar. A large chancre."

"He must have contracted it some time ago, it's not recent. So far, I don't see any other signs of syphilis, but we'll see more when we open up his brain. Mr. Murdoch, will you be so good as to wheel over the instrument trolley. I'll need the scalpel first."

He proceeded to make an incision across the top of Cooke's head from ear to ear. He pulled back the scalp.

"Pass me the saw, if you please, Mr. Murdoch."

Murdoch thought he would rather prefer to take notes than be the assistant, but it was too late now. Broske sawed through the skull, removed the dome, put it in a dish, severed the nerves, then lifted out the brain, which was the size of his fist.

"Ah good, the brain looks normal, fortunately for his wife. There is no current disease that I can see."

He held it in his hand for a moment, then lifted it to the light. "Often in contemplating the brain of one of my patients, when it was visible to me, I have pondered over its structure and functions and seeing the blood coursing through it, I have imagined that I might penetrate into the inner life of the brain cells. I have thought I might learn the laws of organic change, the order, the harmony, the most perfect concatenations, but I must admit, I never yet saw anything, not the faintest gleam that gave me hope of penetrating to the source of thought."

He spoke with such yearning and reverence that Murdoch was astonished. As for Dr. Ogden, she was staring at Broske transfixed.

She spoke softly. "I myself have had such similar feelings. We know so little, do we not? I often think it is as if we are at the very base of the mountain that towers above us in all its grandeur and in our lifetime we can expect to climb only a few feet, hoping that the next generation will go on toward the top."

There was silence while Broske laid Cooke's brain in the dish. Murdoch didn't utter his own thoughts, but he didn't have to. There was an unspoken sympathy among the three of them.

Broske returned to his job. He was meticulous and thorough and moved quickly. He opened up the front of Cooke's chest and removed his heart.

"My, my, look at that. There is an equal amount of blood in each cavity. I would say that Mr. Cooke died from shock brought about by an intense emotion." He glanced over at Murdoch and Dr. Ogden. "I have it on the best authority that the human heart is capable of breaking in twain if confronted by grief. A certain captain came home to port expecting to be greeted by 'is beloved wife and children only to be informed that all of them had perished in a fire. He dropped to the ground dead, and when the post-mortem examination was conducted it was discovered his heart had literally burst."

"Do you think sorrow killed Mr. Cooke?" asked Dr. Ogden.

"Not necessarily. Any of the most powerful emotions can cause such a shock, even joy. But given the lividity in his face when we found him, I would say it more likely that he died from sheer terror. He struggled against his fate. In another man, what-ever emotion he went through might not have killed him, but you can observe here that the pulmonary artery is thickened."

Dr. Ogden leaned forward. "And see the roughness of his liver. I'd say that was early stages of cirrhosis."

"Quite so. Well, let us continue. I'll take that knife, please, Mr. Murdoch."

Murdoch handed him a long knife from the tray. Broske plunged it underneath Cooke's jaw and thrust upward, then he drew two lines away from the incision on either side. The whole of the lower jaw dropped, revealing the knife sticking up in the mouth.

"Would you be so good as to grasp hold of the tongue, Mr. Murdoch, and pull it forward so I can get to the pharynx."

Murdoch thought it was possibly the most unpleasant thing he had ever been asked to do, but his pride was involved now and he wasn't about to back away. He grasped the muscular cold piece of meat that had once served Daniel Cooke to utter words of many hues and tugged it out of the way until the professor had removed the pharynx, larynx, and the upper esophagus and examined them.

"No blockage anywhere. No bruising on the carotid arteries. He wasn't strangled or suffocated. He did vomit, but it did not get swallowed so his air passages are clear. Oh dear, Mr. Murdoch, you've stained your cuff."

"I'll replace it later."

"We're nearing the end. Let's take out the bladder and the urethra. They have emptied, which is quite normal with sudden death. I'll do the stomach next, Miss Julia. A ligature, if you please."

She handed him a long piece of twine, and he tied off the upper end of the stomach, then knotted two other pieces at the other end. He cut the stomach away and laid it on the tray.

"We'll put the contents in one of those glass jars, please, Mr. Murdoch. They'll have to be examined more closely later on."

Murdoch gave him the jar, and he emptied the contents of the stomach into it, squeezing the organ as if it were a bagpipe.

"He certainly didn't have time to digest his supper before he died."

That fit in with what Mrs. Cooke had told Murdoch about Cooke being called from the dinner table before he'd finished eating.

"Now we'll do the same with the intestines, and, Miss Julia, I'd be grateful if you would take care of labelling the jars."

"I will indeed."

Broske stepped away from the gurney and surveyed his hand-iwork. "I don't know if I speak for you, Miss Julia, but no matter how many dissections I have performed, I never fail to be in awe of the wondrous workings and mechanics of the human body."

She beamed. "You do indeed speak for me, doctor."

Murdoch surveyed the bloody carcass. Broske had a point, but all Murdoch could see was a body that has been cut into pieces and whose various organs were distributed like meat in a market. Then to his surprise, the doctor said, "Poor fellow. I don't know what his life was like or his character, but it is hard not to feel a twinge of pity for him." He crossed himself. "May God have mercy on his soul."

"Amen," said Murdoch, and he crossed himself likewise.

Dr. Ogden nodded.

CHAPTER TWELVE

Murdoch was glad of the opportunity to clear his nostrils of the stink of death, and he bicycled slower than usual over to Shuter Street, where Thomas Talbert lived. The warm spring sun seemed to have drawn out half the city's population, and Yonge Street was crowded with passersby. Women with enormous hats decorated with enough flowers to fill his front yard strolled arm in arm down the street, studiously ignoring the loud pleas from the shopkeepers standing outside their stores to "come in and look around, no obligation." A flock of four or five boys, playing truant from school, raced alongside him in the gutter, pretending they were horses and agilely avoiding the droppings of the real creatures.

"Why aren't you in school?" he called out, and they scattered into the crowd. He turned onto Wilton Street, less busy, but still humming. Two elderly priests in their saucer hats, countrymen for certain, dark crows amid colourful birds of paradise, threaded their way nervously in and out of the throngs of women. As he went by, Murdoch called out, "Bless me, fathers." And they both hastily made the sign of the cross in his direction. He grinned. This life may be transitory, but it was preferable to the irrevocable stillness of death that he had just been so close to.

Mutual and Shuter Streets were a physician's enclave with brass plates on almost every second gate. The houses were large and elegant with generous private grounds, all impeccably maintained by fleets of gardeners. Number thirty-three Shuter was a tall, narrow house that looked squeezed in as an afterthought between the two wider houses on either side. However, it, too, looked well cared for. There were bushes in the front yard, already in bud, and the flowerbed that edged the path was thick with yellow and purple crocus and scattered with snowdrops. The grass, albeit still anemic, was freshly raked, cleared of all the sodden leaves of autumn. Murdoch wondered how Mr. Talbert, a stable hand, could afford to live in such a nobby neighbourhood. He knocked on the door. The shiny brass knocker was in the shape of a horse's hoof.

He didn't have to wait long. The door was opened by a plump, pink-cheeked woman wearing the dark formal gown and white starched apron of a housekeeper. Murdoch tipped his hat.

"Good morning, ma'am. I wonder if I might have a word with Mr. Talbert?"

"He doesn't usually see visitors in the morning. He does his correspondence." Her voice was pleasant.

He took out his calling card and handed it to her. "I'm Detective William Murdoch from number four station. I'm afraid it's a matter of some urgency."

"Oh dearie me, is it about Mr. Cooke? We heard there was a terrible incident in the livery."

Murdoch wondered how much had already been distorted by rumour. "Yes, ma'am. I am here concerning Mr. Cooke."

"You'd better come in. I'll see if Mr. Talbot is available."

Murdoch stepped into the narrow foyer while she scurried away, disappearing through a curtained archway at the end of the hall. Sunlight was streaming through a beautiful stained-glass window above the door lintel, but there were no dust motes to catch the light in this foyer. There was a pleasant smell of beeswax, and the wooden floor gleamed with polish as did the simple coat stand and small table beside it. Murdoch was about to have a look at the framed pictures hanging on the wall when the housekeeper emerged.

"He said he'll see you but for no more than an hour." She smiled apologetically. "I'm afraid he can be rather determined about his timetable no matter who it is. Let me take your hat. Come this way, if you please."

For a stout, middle-aged woman, she moved quickly and lightly. She pulled back the green flowered portière at the end of the hall and opened the door to usher him in.

"Detective Murdoch, Mr. Talbert."

She bustled off immediately, leaving Murdoch on the threshold.

An elderly man with long white hair was seated by the fire, which had been built up to a roaring blaze, making the room stiflingly hot. He turned around at Murdoch's entrance.

"You wanted to see me?" His voice was flat and unwelcoming, his expression suspicious and unfriendly.

Murdoch could barely hide his surprise. Talbert was a negro.

"You are Thomas Talbert, are you not? You work at the livery owned by Mr. Daniel Cooke?"

"Yes, I do."

"I understand from your housekeeper, sir, that you already know about the death of your employer."

Talbert stared at him for a moment, then he got out of his chair and walked over to the tea trolley that was nearby. He was a tall, wide-shouldered man, thin and straight-backed, who even at his advanced age emanated strength and authority. However, Murdoch wondered if he had even heard what he'd said or comprehended it.

"Mr. Talbert?"

"I do know. Elijah Green came and told me last night. He said Cooke had been whipped." Talbert started to pour himself a cup of tea, his back toward Murdoch.

"The assault brought on a heart seizure, so it has become a case of manslaughter. Which is why I am here."

"What do you want from me?" Talbert returned to his chair with his teacup in his hand. "Don't tell me you've got me in your sights? Why is that, mister? Is it because I'm a nigger man? I'm a bit too old to be going around *assaulting* men, wouldn't you think?"

His tone of voice was conversational, but a sharp edge was close beneath the surface and he'd got under Murdoch's skin.

"I haven't got you in my sights, as you put it. And, frankly, I had no idea you were a negro until I came into this room."

For some reason that amused Talbert and he laughed out loud. "I could see that. It was written all over your face. For a frog, begging your pardon for the expression, you reveal too much. Just because I live on the same street as a dozen rich sawbones and my house is well kept and I have a nice plump pink housekeeper, you thought I was white. Must have been a shock when you found yourself staring at an old darkie."

"A surprise, more like."

Talbert waved in the direction of one of the chairs. "Why don't you pull over that chair and sit down. And I suppose you'll be wanting some tea?"

"Thank you, I'd like that."

Talbert put his cup on the floor beside him. With a little grunt, he pushed himself to his feet and went over to an ornately embroidered bell pull beside the mantelpiece and gave it a hard tug.

Murdoch had never been in the house of a negro before, and he glanced around as discretely as he could. The room was well furnished and it looked like many others he'd been in. Not quite as jammed with furniture as some, but the pieces were of good quality, and like the foyer, any wood that was visible gleamed from beeswax. Over the mantel, there was a large oil painting of Jesus ascending to heaven, next to it, a large gold cross – without the crucified Christ that Murdoch was used to.

The housekeeper appeared immediately. "Yes, Mr. Talbert?"

"Bring another cup for the detective, will you, Mrs. Stokely? And if there's any of your caraway-seed cake left, bring that too."

She gave a little bob and hurried off. Talbert resumed his seat in the Windsor chair. He picked Murdoch's calling card off the lap desk where he'd tucked it.

"So, Mr., er, Murdoch, just why have you come to talk to me?"

For some reason Murdoch couldn't quite fathom, Talbert's mood had altered and his tone was more friendly. He hadn't yet expressed a single word of regret at Cooke's death.

"Because I spoke to Elijah Green, who said you spell him off at the stables a couple of days a week. I understand you usually go in on Wednesdays."

"I do, but I had a bout with my lumbago yesterday and begged off. Good thing I did, in the circumstances. I'm sure it wasn't pleasant for Elijah to find the man strung up like that, but better him than me. He's young."

"Are you feeling better?" Murdoch asked politely. Talbert had been moving stiffly, but no worse than a man of his age.

"Yes, it's almost gone. Thank you."

"As I understand it, you used to own the stables. Or do I have that wrong?"

"Who told you that?"

"Nobody told me. I found a bill of sale in Mr. Cooke's safe. I'm just making sure you're the same Talbert who was named as the original proprietor."

"Yes, that's me. That was a long time ago." He paused, then sipped some more tea. "Robbed, was he?"

"Why do you say that?"

Talbert chuckled. "Easy to work that out. You said you'd been looking in his safe. Probably Adelaide Cooke made you check, didn't she?"

Murdoch shrugged. He'd never felt so much on the defensive during an interrogation.

"The first thing on that woman's mind would be money," Talbert continued. "She'd say he was robbed even if he weren't. Dan was a fool about his money. He liked to see it mount up so he could gloat over it, but I doubt he let his missus know everything he had."

There was a quick tap on the door and Mr. Stokely entered carrying a dainty china cup and saucer. She went to the trolley.

"Shall I pour, sir?"

"Yes, please. I hope you like your tea robust, Mr. Murdoch, because that's what it is."

"I do."

Mr. Stokely smiled. "Sugar?"

"Two lumps and some milk will do fine, thank you, ma'am."

"There was no more cake, Mr. Talbert."

"Mr. Murdoch's loss."

The housekeeper was addressing her employer formally, but there was an easiness between them that seemed to Murdoch to come from more than long service. Or was he misreading the comfortable sense of warmth between then?

Another quick bob and she left. Talbert waited until Murdoch had sipped his tea.

"Strong enough for you?"

"Indeed."

Talbert helped himself to more tea. "Daniel kept a revolver in the drawer. Did you find it?"

"No we haven't as yet."

Talbert leaned back against his chair, his long, wavy hair showed startlingly white against the red brocade.

"You're probably expecting me to express some sorrow for the poor deceased, some indignation about what has befallen him."

"People react differently. Maybe you're a man who doesn't show his feelings."

Talbert guffawed. "But I'm a darkie. Don't you know all us coloured folks are emotional to the point of excess? We can't help ourselves, so I've heard."

"I have no comment about that, Mr. Talbert."

"Good. The truth is that Cooke and I didn't move in the same circles. I hardly saw the man."

It wasn't quite what he'd conveyed earlier, but Murdoch let that ride.

"We know that Mr. Cooke died sometime between eight o'clock and half past nine last night. Do you mind telling me where you were you at that time, Mr. Talbert?"

"I was right here. Same chair, same room. I never go out at night."

"Is there anybody who can vouch for you?"

"Mrs. Stokely will. She has a room upstairs, but she always keeps me company in the evening. But you can't ask her now, I heard her go out. It's market day."

"I'll have to come back and talk to her."

"Suit yourself, but she won't say anything different."

"Why? Because you'll tell her not to?"

"No, because it's the truth."

Talbert was probably old enough to be Murdoch's grandfather, but there was nothing frail about him. From the beginning he had taken charge of the situation and kept Murdoch off balance.

"Did Mr. Cooke have any enemies that you know of, Mr. Talbert?"

"He was a boss and he was well off. That'll get you enemies every time. There's always men who like to grub around in their own jealousy and malice." Talbert dabbed at his mouth with a napkin. "He was also a man who enjoyed a little flutter now and again so he knew a few touts. He wasn't always quick to pay his debts, perhaps one of them lost patience."

Murdoch put his cup and saucer on the trolley and took out his notebook. "Do you know the names of these men?"

"No, not a one. I'm not a gambler myself. I don't like to squander my hard-earned money."

"Would anybody else know who these men were?"

"That's for you to find out, isn't it? I only go to the livery twice a week. I didn't hob and nob with the others, nor they with me."

"Did Elijah Green and Cooke get along?"

"'Course they did. Why shouldn't they? Elijah took damn good care of those horses, and Dan got away with paying him a pittance because he's a coloured man."

"What about the other cabbies? What's your opinion of them?"

"I don't have any one way or the other. We don't mix."

"Mr. Wallace implied there might be something a little un-toward going on between Mrs. Cooke and Mr. Musgrave."

Talbert laughed. "That's hard to believe. She's not the most attractive specimen of the fair sex I've ever known. But there's no accounting for taste, is there? And now I suppose she will inherit a nice sum of money. That can surely turn a pig's ear into a silk purse, can't it? You should investigate those two, Mr. Murdoch. Dan's death sounds suspiciously convenient to me and Musgrave's a man I wouldn't trust as far as I could throw him, which isn't far these days. He has a keen nose for which side his bread is buttered."

Murdoch put away his notebook.

"That's it, then? You're done?"

"For the moment. But there is one thing I could ask you . . . you sold your livery to Mr. Cooke for a paltry two hundred dollars. Why was that?"

This clearly wasn't a question Talbert was expecting and he paused for a moment.

"I'd had a run of bad luck, horses getting ill, a fire in the tack room. He bailed me out. At the time I was grateful for whatever I could get."

"It must have been difficult to go from being the boss to being an employee."

The old man's face revealed nothing. "I didn't work for him right away. I did other things. I've only been going into the stable the last couple of years. Elijah asked me and I accepted to help him out." He raised his head and glanced over at the clock on the mantelpiece. "That's all the time I can spare you, detective. I have more letters to write. Your hour is up." He picked up his lap desk and began to shuffle through sheets of paper.

Murdoch stood up. "Thank you for your co-operation, sir."

Talbert waved his hand at the door. "Let yourself out, will you?"

CHAPTER THIRTEEN

JUNE 1859

S he didn't know how long she'd been strung up, the rope hoisted tight over the beam hook until her toes barely brushed the ground. The muscles in her arms were screaming with the pain, and her wrists burned as if they were dipped in lye where the rope bit into her skin. She moaned. She had vowed she wouldn't cry out or beg for mercy, but that was at the beginning. Now she would have blubbered and wept without control even to the woman she hated with a bitterness that paradoxically kept her alive. Her father had always said, "My daughter's a good hater. Don't seem that way, she's so sweet and buttery to strangers, but I know her. She takes after me, she don't ever forgive when she thinks there's a wrong." Her mother, ever the soother, had protested, but Lena had experienced an odd sort of pride. To hate made her strong, made her not give in, made her endure the cruelty that was more and more frequently visited upon her now that Mrs. Dickie was so ill and not at home any more.

The row this time had been because Caddie's tartan gown wasn't ready for her to wear to church. The night had been too wet for any washing to dry properly, and there was nothing Lena could do about it.

"You're a lazy slut. I don't know why I keep you. You are one ugly nigger." This was accompanied by hard slaps to the head. It was only because Leigh had come into the room at that moment that Caddie had stopped, but he couldn't, or wouldn't, protect her completely. All three of them knew the never-acknowledged cause of his wife's jealousy. Just before they left for church, Caddie had ordered Sam, their lone field hand, to string Lena up to teach her a lesson and to think about what a wicked, sly girl she was. She may or may not have her whipped when she returned.

The door to the shed opened, but she couldn't see who came in and her body tensed with fear.

"It's me. I've brought you some milk."

"Fidelia, bless you, bless you."

"First off, I'm gonna get you on this stool."

The girl caught hold of Lena's legs and heaved her up, holding her with one arm while she thrust a milking stool underneath her feet. Some of the weight was taken off Lena's arms and she cried out with the relief of it.

Fidelia dipped a ladle into her pail of milk and lifted it to Lena's lips. She drank thirstily.

"More?"

"No, I'm afraid I'll be sick."

"D'you want me cut you down?"

"You'll get into worse trouble."

"I don't care. T'aint right what she's doing to you."

Lena was weeping now, she couldn't help it. "My arms are in agony, Fiddie. I think I'd prefer a whipping to this."

"Tell you what, I'm gonna climb on the stool and you can sit on my shoulders. That'll take you up higher even."

"Don't be silly. I'm far too heavy."

"No you ain't. 'Sides I worked in the fields since I was seven, before Mrs. Dickie bought me. I'm strong as a mule."

"Fiddie . . ."

"We can do it for bits at a time till they come back. You'll see." Fidelia suited her action to the words and was able to stand on the stool, crouch down, and get her shoulders under Lena's legs. With much initial wobbling, she straightened up, and Lena was lifted almost as high as the rafter so that she could bend her arms. Lena breathed her thanks, trying hard not to cry out with the sweetness of the relief.

"You know my father used to lift me on his shoulders when I was a child. I thought I was queen of the world then, up so high, I could touch the tree branches and pick off some of the best of the apples."

Fidelia grunted. "I don't have a rememory of my pappy. Nor my mammy, if you was to ask. There's always been just me."

"But now you have me. That's better, isn't it, Fiddie?"

"'Course it is. Like it's better to have roast chicken off the spit than acorn soup. Like it's better to have fresh blackberries off the bush than dried raisins with weevils in them. Like it's better to have –"

Lena managed to dredge up a chuckle. "Don't go on, please."

They stayed silently in that strange position, the young, skinny girl holding the bigger, heavier one on her shoulders, her hands around Lena's legs.

"I heard Missus Caddie say that Missus Dickie won't be coming home no more. She's got the white sickness and she ain't never gonna get better."

"I know."

"Does that mean we'll belong to Mr. Leigh and Missus Caddie?"

Lena whispered, "God help us, Fiddie, but it will mean that."

"We should run away."

"You know I can't now. But you should. Fiddie, you should get out of here as fast and as far as you can."

Fidelia eased her burden as best she could. "I ain't going nowhere without you. You know that."

Leigh Dickie and his wife didn't return from church for another hour and a half. The two in the barn heard them coming and Fidelia had to get Lena off her aching shoulders. Then, after waiting as long as she dared, she removed the stool and Lena was once again hanging by her wrists. She felt the child in her belly shift in protest.

CHAPTER FOURTEEN

Somebody had put two large clay pots of early daffodils beside the station door. Murdoch leaned his wheel against the wall and went inside.

"You're looking a bit knackered, Will," said Charlie Seymour, who was sitting at the duty desk. To Murdoch's ears, the sergeant's voice was tinged with reproach. Murdoch suspected he disapproved of the relationship between he and Amy Slade. It's not me who won't make it legal, he thought.

"I am. I didn't get home until the early hours of the morning," answered Murdoch, trying not to sound defensive. "You know about the case, don't you?"

"I do. Crabtree and Fyfer filled me in. It's a strange one. Any suspects?"

Murdoch shrugged. "You know how it is at this stage. Could be anybody. There are several unpaid tradesmen who might have lost their patience. Talbert, one of the stable hands, said Cooke ran with a fast crowd and liked to gamble. Talbert's an old man, but he could be carrying a grudge from years ago when, I believe,

Cooke cheated him over the purchase of his livery. Mrs. Cooke says her husband was robbed. One of the cabbies says another cabbie, Musgrave, was interested in Mrs. Cooke and implied he might have disposed of Mrs. Cooke for that reason. Another man claims to have witnessed a right barney between Mrs. Cooke and her husband a few days ago. Then Crabtree found a piece of blood-stained sacking in the closet of the other stable hand, Elijah Green, plus two Indian clubs and a strange-sounding note, so he's putting his money on the darkie as the assailant."

Seymour grinned. "You're right, you've got more possibilities than the prince at a garden party. And speaking of George, he just got in. He's in the duty room having his tea. He looks knackered too. You'd better watch it, might be something going around."

Murdoch stared at Seymour, not sure whether he was making a joke, but Charlie's face was impassive and Murdoch wondered, not for the first time, if it wasn't his own guilty conscience that was making him project judgments onto his friend. Only last Sunday, Father Fair had chosen as his homily text the sacrament of marriage, denouncing in ringing tones those sinners who had carnal knowledge of each other outside of holy wedlock. Murdoch hadn't been to confession for some weeks or he would have assumed the priest was particularly referring to him, but he'd shifted uneasily in the pew. When he was engaged to be married to Liza, both of them Roman Catholics, they had accepted, albeit impatiently, the church's injunctions to remain chaste until their marriage. That chastity had become a cruel jest when she had died so suddenly of typhoid fever and he still regretted it. But when he had declared his love to Amy and he had actually proposed marriage, she had laughed. "It's not for me, Will. We don't need any public declaration and contract to bind us together. I believe we are quite capable of determining our own destiny. If you want me in your bed, unwed but faithful, I will come happily." And so she had, and he had never known such pleasure in his life before.

Seymour snapped his fingers. "Will! Where are you? I said Crabtree claims he's got some important news."

"Oh, right! Sorry. I just went off in a little daydream."

"You certainly did." He reached underneath the desk. "I almost forgot myself. This was delivered this morning for you." He handed Murdoch a plain white envelope. There was no stamp, just his name neatly printed on the front.

<u>Detective William Murdoch. Strictest Confidence.</u>

"Some little street arab brought it in, but he was off before I could find out who it was from."

Murdoch tore open the envelope and took out a single sheet of paper.

<u>For no eyes other than yours.</u>
I would much appreciate it if you would pay me a visit. I am still in the place where I was before. We are allowed to walk in the gardens from 5 till 6. Meet me there today. It will be private. No matter what, Murdoch, please don't let me down. I am counting on you.

Thomas Brackenreid.

P.S. As I will probably be away from the station for a while longer, you have my permission to use my personal office on such occasions as you need to.

"What is it?" Seymour asked.

Murdoch hesitated. Charlie was his friend and he respected him, but there was something about the situation with the inspector that silenced him. He'd poked fun at the man many a time and shared in the general disrespect Brackenreid had engendered in the station, but he didn't feel like betraying a confidence placed in him even if he hadn't exactly agreed to it.

"I'll tell you later." He put the envelope in his pocket. "By the way, who put the daffies out front?"

"I did." Seymour gave him a shy smile. "It was Katie's idea. She thinks the station should look a little more friendly. Improve our relationship with the general public."

"Quite right too. The trouble with us, Charlie, is that we think too much like men and not women."

Seymour laughed. "I don't know if we can do much about that, but I know what you mean. On the other hand, God save me from women who want to wear the trousers." He stopped short. "Oh, I'm not referring to Amy. I just meant, er, metaphorically."

"Of course."

The door opened and a man came in. He was short and wiry with the tanned face of an outdoorsman. In spite of the mild weather, he was wearing a long caped houndstooth coat and astrakhan hat.

"Afternoon, gentlemen, I'm here to see Detective Murdoch."

"I'm Murdoch. What can I do for you?"

The man held out his hand. "My name's Musgrave, Paul Musgrave. I'm a cabbie at the Cooke stables. Cooke that was, may he rest in peace. Dreadful doings that, dreadful." Musgrave's tone and expression were cheerful. His eyes were crinkled at the sides, but whether that was from perpetual squinting into the sun or from being forever affable with his customers, Murdoch couldn't tell.

"One of your constables came over to my house. I was having a bit of a sleep-in and I didn't know anything that had happened. Shocking, it was. Completely shocking. Anyway, the constable and me had quite a chin wag and he told me to come here this afternoon and talk to you. So here I am." He was chewing vigorously on a wad of tobacco, and he looked around for somewhere to spit.

Simultaneously, both Murdoch and Seymour pointed at the closest spittoon and Musgrave skilfully deposited a stream of juice. He wiped his mouth with the back of his sleeve. "Don't worry about keeping me from my work. Today, I couldn't get a customer to get inside my cab if I paid him. Sunshine's bad for business, it is, especially in the spring. Hot summer's better, but then, most of the time, the ladies don't want to go out at all, do they?"

"Come with me then, Mr. Musgrave. Sergeant, would you tell Constable Crabtree to join us as soon as he can."

Murdoch began to lead the way to his cubicle at the rear of the station, then he halted. Why not? He went back to Seymour and whispered, "Charlie, believe it or not, Inspector Brackenreid has offered me the use of his office while he is away. Tell George to come up there."

Seymour gaped at him. "You're joking with me."

"Not at all. His exact words were 'You have my permission to use my office on such occasions as you need to.' I'm counting this as an occasion."

Charlie grinned. "Be careful, Will, you might get to like being an inspector."

CHAPTER FIFTEEN

"Got a new chair, did you, sir?" Musgrave asked.

Murdoch stopped abruptly. He'd taken a seat behind the inspector's desk and was enjoying testing the chair that tilted and revolved. He stopped quickly.

"Something like that," he muttered.

The top of the desk was pristine except for a tray filled with papers, the first one marked urgent. He'd better have a look at that later. Couldn't let down the reputation of station number four, after all. To the side of the desk was a squat walnut boxy container that he hadn't seen before. On the top was an ivory button, which he pressed. Immediately the sides of the box sprung open, revealing rows of cigars held in by a wire frame. Murdoch hesitated. Borrowing the office was one thing, taking cigars that didn't belong to him was another. Nobly, he closed it again.

There was a tap at the door.

"Come in," Murdoch called, and George Crabtree entered. If he was surprised to see Murdoch sitting behind the desk, he didn't show it.

"George, Mr. Musgrave is about to give me his formal statement. Write it down for me, will you?" Crabtree would spot any discrepancies or embellishments to what he'd already heard. "Mr. Musgrave, will you proceed? Start with your name and address please."

The cabbie removed his tobacco plug from his mouth and wrapped it in his handkerchief, which from the look of it had been used in this way many times before.

"My name is Paul Musgrave and I live at 210 Wilton Street."

"How long have you worked for Daniel Cooke?"

"Oh, 'bout three years now."

"What sort of employer was Mr. Cooke?"

Musgrave slapped his hand on his knee. "As good as they come. Conscientious to a fault. He was there when we booked out and sitting waiting when we booked back in. Mind you, he kept his distance, which is only proper, in my opinion. People will take advantage if you don't, it's only human nature. But you always knew where you stood with him. Pay your dues and he was pleasant as could be. We rents out the cabs, you see, and we pay that no matter what. One dollar a shift, which you've got to make up in your fares. We keeps what we take in, but we pass over 5 per cent of that to Cooke for wear and tear, as he calls it." He rubbed his hand over his face. "Or should I say, *called it*, may he rest in peace. That's why he was always on us to look at our dockets, which, as you know, the city council has strict rules about. In the first division, which is city limits, it's fifty cents. If you go to the second division, that is to Dufferin Street West or Pape in the east, it goes up to seventy-five cents."

Murdoch had been scribbling the figures in his notebook, and he made some quick calculations.

"If all you cabbies were getting steady business, I'd say Mr. Cooke could make a decent income even after paying for upkeep of the horses and carriages."

"He could. And we are in a prime location. A lot of professional men in the vicinity. Not all of them keep their own carriages, or if they do, the gentleman uses it. This means the ladies like to hire us to take them shopping or on their calls and so forth. We have a lot of regulars for that reason."

Crabtree gave a little discrete cough. "Mr. Musgrave had something else to say about the money, Mr. Murdoch."

"Yes?"

The cabbie settled back in his chair. "In spite of what I just told you, being a cab driver is a thankless job when you get right down to it. You never can say from one day to the next what money you're going to bring in. The best days are those when it starts off sunny but rains in the afternoon, so all the ladies get out to do their shopping, then get caught. Rainy all day long is not as good as you think because they don't want to go out. Same with cold. But I always tries to be pleasant and cheerful and I get a lot of steady customers. Especially because the stables is right near Shuter Street, I'll have a call a lot of times from the doctors' nurses that Mrs. So-and-So would like me to pick her up. They often gives me a nice gratuity. Them's the best jobs."

Murdoch waited. He could see by Crabtree's expression, Musgrave hadn't got to the point yet. The constable leaned forward.

"Tell the detective about Mr. Cooke's attitude to money."

"Right. Well as I was saying, the cabbie's life is an unpredictable one. Mr. Cooke was doing all right in my opinion, but lately he's been, that is, was, quite testy. Not like him at all. He was on us about working harder and kept saying as how we had to go after fares, not just wait for them to fall into our laps. He was starting to ride us to the point of aggravation. I don't know what had got into him. He didn't used to be like that. Not that I'm speaking ill of the dead, you understand, he was one of the best."

Another long pause. The cabbie was apparently studying the plant in the window.

"Go on, Musgrave. We don't have all day," said Crabtree, finally losing patience.

"Sorry, officer. Your aspidistra looks a bit wilted. It needs watering, I'd say."

"Mr. Musgrave, please continue," said Murdoch.

The cabbie nodded. "Here it is then. It's my belief there's been something going on with Mr. Cooke and the darkie."

"Elijah Green?"

"Him. Mind you, I'd never utter a bad word about the man except under these circumstances. He's been a good worker, I'd say. Makes sure the carriages are all spic and span and the horses fit, which you've got to have if you're in the business . . . but two times this month I came in a bit later than expected and I saw him in the office with Mr. Cooke and they were having a barney. A big up-and-a-downer, by the look of it."

"What about?" Murdoch asked.

"Wish I could help you there, but I can't. I come in the other end of the barn so I couldn't quite hear them, but I saw Mr. Cooke grab Green by his shirt. He was mad as the devil about something."

"What did Green do?"

"Nothing. He sort of shrugged him off, but I thought he was furious too."

"This happened twice, you say?"

"That's right. Once about two weeks ago and the other time was just this past Tuesday."

"The day before Mr. Cooke died?"

"Yes. It was just after eleven at night. Like I said, I was a bit later than expected."

"Was the earlier quarrel the same? Did Cooke grab Green?"

"Not that time. But he was yelling, I could see that. He banged his fist on the desk."

"Did you say anything to Green?"

"Not the first time, but when he came in I sort of made a joke of it. 'The boss found you cheating on the hay bills, did he?'"

"And?"

"Nothing. He just sort of shrugged and said something about the boss getting out of bed the wrong way. But if looks could kill, I wouldn't be sitting here talking to you today."

"That's it, then? That's what you have to tell us?"

Musgrave looked distinctly aggrieved at the question. "That's more than enough, ain't it? The darkie is a deep one. I'm a good judge of character, you have to be if you're a cabbie. You see all sides of human nature, and I tell you he keeps a lot hidden."

"Did any of the other cabbies ever quarrel with Mr. Cooke? Did you yourself, for instance?"

Musgrave shrugged. "Me and him got along good. The others I couldn't really say. Wallace is as sour as a pickle, so he and Mr. Cooke weren't exactly chummy, but I don't know as you'd call that a quarrel exactly. Besides, there's always going to be the odd squabble where a man's livelihood is concerned. Sometimes, Mr. Cooke would take a bigger cut if he thought you'd run the horse too hard or if there was any damage to the carriages. But like I said, he was a shrewd businessman. You can't be too soft or people won't give you any respect."

"That happened to you, did it?"

"Once or twice."

"You know, don't you, that we received a complaint that the horses in the livery were being mistreated."

For the first time, Musgrave lost some of his affability. Without the crinkly eyed smile, his face was hard. "Some interfering old so-and-so, I gather. No doubt a silly old dame who don't understand what a cabbie's life is like. I love my horses like they was my own children. But the truth is the more fares we get in an hour, the more money we makes. And if customers want you to scorch them down to the station so's they'll catch their train, I ain't going to say no, am I? They give big bonuses, some of them doctors."

"Mr. Cooke objected, did he? Wearing out his horses like that?"

"Not him. He knew that's the life of a cab horse, isn't it?"

He pulled a big steel watch out of his waistcoat pocket and stared at it. "I should get back to work. This is costing me money, you know."

"Is the livery operational, then?"

"According to Mrs. Cooke it is."

"You've talked to her, have you?"

Musgrave went still. His cold blue eyes were wary. "Yes, she was good enough to come over to my lodgings this morning. Even in the depths of her grief she is a considerate woman. She wanted to tell me what had happened."

"I've heard that there is a special relationship between you and she. Is that true?"

Musgrave's slapped his hands on his knees in anger. "Who's been gossiping behind my back, and the poor woman a new-made widow. Who said that?"

"It doesn't matter who said it, Mr. Musgrave. Is it true?"

"So help me God, it is not. At least not in the sense you're implying. She's got a good heart, has Adelaide Cooke, and to tell you the truth, her husband neglected her pitifully. You can't do that to a woman and expect her not to get real lonesome. She liked to go to concerts and so do I, and what's the harm in a man accompanying a lady to a concert once in a while, for God's sake?"

"I see no harm, Mr. Musgrave, no harm at all. Unfortunately others seemed to have, er, misconstrued the situation."

Musgrave was still fuming, but Murdoch thought it had the hue of a man who'd been found out rather than one innocent of wrongdoing.

The cabbie got to his feet. "I'm going to miss the afternoon calls if I don't go soon. Is that all you want to ask me?"

"Not quite. We found a whip that belongs to the carriage you use. Did you know it was missing?"

"It wasn't when I checked in last night. Cabbies are always borrowing from one another, a whip, a lantern, whatever it is they need at the time and are too lazy to replace. Why does it matter?"

"Let's say it's part of our investigation. But before you go, there is one more question. Can you give an account of your whereabouts between eight o'clock and half past nine on Wednesday night?"

Musgrave showed his teeth in what might pass for a smile. "That's easy. After I signed out at about half past seven, I decided to wet my whistle at the John O'Neil on Queen Street. I was there till closing time at ten. You can ask them."

"I will. That's it for now, but I will probably have to talk to you again."

"Beggin' your pardon, sir, but I don't see why. I've given you the best information you're likely to get. It's Elijah Green you should be talking to, not honest, decent men like me."

"I'll keep that in mind, Mr. Musgrave. Constable Crabtree will escort you downstairs."

CHAPTER SIXTEEN

Murdoch swivelled in the chair. "George, did you ever play blind man's bluff when you were a titch?"

"Yes, I did, sir."

"Well, I feel as Mr. Musgrave was having just such a game with us, trying to turn us round and round so that we don't know where we are. Going on about what a good man Mr. Cooke was, while making sure he painted a picture of an avaricious, cold-hearted tyrant. And the same with Green. 'A good fellow all round,' but capable of killing somebody if he's crossed. He quite made me dizzy, did Mr. Musgrave."

"He was a slippery one all right, but there's no reason to believe he wasn't telling the truth about the negro having a quarrel with Cooke. I thought he was giving me a lot of gammon about how that blood got on the sacking. I'll wager the boss gave him a stotter over something or other and that's where he got his goose egg from."

Murdoch frowned. "Maybe, but I'm putting my money on Musgrave. He's got the soul of a rat if ever I saw one."

"He did give us an alibi."

"Come off it, George. You know what the O'Neil's like. I'd as soon try to hold water in a sieve than catch the truth from the lot who frequent that place."

"I suppose you could be right about that, sir," said Crabtree reluctantly.

Murdoch whipped the chair around again. "There's something that bothers me about this whole business. Cooke wasn't blindfolded, so I have to assume his attacker didn't mean for him to live, otherwise he would have been identified. Was the intention to whip him to death?"

"Perhaps his attacker meant to shoot him. The revolver has disappeared, after all."

"Yes, I thought of that. Perhaps Cooke died too soon for his attacker to use it. Or he already knew Cooke had a weak heart. The disturbing thing, George, is that according to Dr. Ogden and her friend Professor Broske, some of the lashes were administered after Cooke was dead. That changes the picture quite a bit, I'd say. Did somebody hate Cooke that much? Or are we dealing with a lunatic?"

Crabtree shifted his feet. "I think that bears out what I'm saying about the darkie. You said yourself Cooke owed him back wages. Maybe he *was* intending to beat him to death."

Murdoch shook his head. "I find that hard to believe, George. For one thing, surely it would take a long time to actually bring about death? You would have to be extraordinarily determined, not to mention callous, to do that."

"Musgrave saw them have a barney."

"If he's to be believed, but even he didn't describe it as a blazing row, just raised voices and a shove on Cooke's part. That doesn't sound too lethal to me."

"You don't know what will send a man over the edge though, do you, sir? Besides, we can't forget about the mysterious messenger. Whatever it was he had to say, he got Cooke up from his supper pretty fast. And this cove was a coloured man, sir. He could have been an accomplice of Green's."

"Let's go and ask the man in person, shall we, George?" Murdoch swung around in the chair once more. "I've quite enjoyed our little stay in the inspector's crib. Rather more comfortable than my cubicle, wouldn't you say?"

"I would indeed, sir. No offence. When is Mr. Brackenreid due to return? Is he recovered from his influenza?"

"I don't know, George, but in the meantime, I see no reason why we shouldn't avail ourselves of his generous offer and conduct all further interviews here." He stood up. "Perhaps it will all be very simple and Green will confess on the spot."

Murdoch and Crabtree retrieved their wheels from the shed and set off for Terauley Street. The afternoon sun was gilding the spires of both St. Michael's Cathedral and the Metropolitan Church just below it, making no distinction between Catholic and Protestant, both equally blessed for once. They'd bicycled in silence for a while. Murdoch thought Crabtree was looking peaked.

"Are you feeling unwell, George?"

"Oh no, sir. I'm in the pink, just a little tired. Billy is getting the last of his teeth in so he's mardy as all get out."

"Katie rubbed her twins' gums with oil of cloves and gave them stale crusts to chew. That seemed to give them relief."

"Ellen's thinking of having his gums lanced. We did it with George junior and he was all smiles within the hour."

They biked on, both lost in the burdens of domesticity. Murdoch had come to dote on Katie Tibbett's twins, and he found himself more and more thinking about what it would be like to have his own family, even mardy children. Without realizing it, he sighed deeply and Crabtree glanced over at him.

"How's the house working out, sir? Is Miss Slade as ever, er, that is, is Miss Slade . . . ?"

Murdoch rescued him. "She is still a fierce advocate and representative of the New Woman, if that's what you mean, George."

"Ah, yes. You must have some lively chins about that."

"We certainly do."

Murdoch wasn't going to unburden himself to his constable about the nature of those talks.

"Speaking of Ellen, how is your better half, George?"

An expression of unhappiness crossed the constable's face. "As well as can be expected, sir, considering." He looked embarrassed and his voice tailed off.

"Good heavens, don't tell me she's in the family way again?"

"As a matter of fact, she is."

"Are you planning to start a colony or something, George? What's this, number five?"

"Yes, sir. I mean, er, it's our fifth, not that we're starting a colony."

For no reason that he could think of, Murdoch felt irritated. It was none of his business and he liked the constable, but there were many days lately when Crabtree seemed tired and out of sorts. Then he usually mumbled something about the baby keeping him awake. And now there'd be another one before this one was out of nappies.

He realized Crabtree had been saying something to him.

". . . it's hard to know what to do. We thought that because Ellen was still nursing we wouldn't, er, I mean, er, there was less likelihood of getting a baby, but that proved not to be the case."

Good heavens, George was confiding in him.

"To tell you the truth, sir, she had a very difficult time with the last one and she's fair worn out. She's at her wit's end about what to do."

Murdoch didn't have the vaguest idea what to reply, so he just nodded sympathetically.

"Beg your pardon, sir. I shouldn't be talking like this."

"Not at all, George. I wish I could be of more help. Have you spoken to your physician?"

"Yes, sir. He just prescribed her a tonic."

"That should help then." Murdoch knew how lame that sounded.

Crabtree sighed, tucking the brief intimacy back inside his heart. "Yes, sir. I'm sure it will."

Terauley Street was on the western side of Yonge Street, an area of the city that Murdoch didn't often visit, as most of his working life was concentrated on the area covered by number four division. Yonge Street on the western perimeter to River Street in the east, Carlton in the north, and Front Street in the south. A diverse population lived within its boundaries from very rich to very poor, expansive private grounds standing next to dirty foundries belching black smoke all day.

They crossed Yonge Street as quickly as they could, dodging the carriages that were clogging the city's main thoroughfare. Elijah Green's house was the end one of a row of narrow two-storey houses. There was no front yard, and they leaned their wheels against the wall of the house. Murdoch knocked hard on the door, which had once been blue but now needed a new coat of paint. The curtains of the windows at 262 were whisked aside. Murdoch had a glimpse of a dark face, then the curtain was dropped immediately. Before he could knock a second time, the door opened and a woman with a child close at her side stood in the threshold. She was a negress perhaps thirty years of age. The child, a curly haired boy, was six or seven. He shrank into his mother's skirt when he saw Crabtree in his tall helmet towering in front of them.

"Mrs. Green?" Murdoch tipped his hat.

She nodded nervously.

"Good afternoon, ma'am. My name is Murdoch. I'm a detective at number four station. This is Constable Crabtree. I wonder if I might have a word with your husband?"

Her eyes flickered away. "He's resting right now."

"Would you mind fetching him? I'm sorry to have to disturb him, but it is important."

She tapped the boy on the shoulder. "Donnie, go get your pa." The boy scuttled away.

The woman didn't move or make any attempt to bring them into the house, and there was an awkward silence while they all waited.

"It's been a lovely day, hasn't it?" said Murdoch. "I do believe spring has finally arrived."

Her brown eyes met his. She revealed nothing, but suddenly Murdoch felt foolish. She was a frightened woman and him uttering such banalities was absurd.

"Do you mind if we come in?" he asked, his voice gentle. "We want to ask some questions and I don't think we can do that standing in the street."

Suddenly Green appeared, his son right behind him. He had heard these words.

"Of course you can come in, Mr. Murdoch." He nodded at Crabtree. "I don't know about you, constable. You might be bumping your head on the ceiling."

He stepped back so he could usher them in. "This is my wife, Mary Ann. Donnie here, who is going to take his thumb out of his mouth, 'cause he's a big boy now, is my middle sprout."

The door opened directly into the living room, and Crabtree did have to bend his head to go through the low threshold. Opposite the door was a staircase partly curtained off at the bottom, but the family essentially occupied one room shaped like a L, in the foot of which Murdoch glimpsed a cooking range and a sink. Two girls were seated at a table near the fire, both of them had sewing on their laps. They, too, regarded Murdoch and Crabtree with considerable alarm.

Green spoke to them sharply. "Sophie and Alexandra, take your work upstairs. You too, Donnie."

They didn't utter a word but bundled the cloths they were working on and hurried up the staircase. Green pulled the curtain closed after them. "We can sit at the table," he said. "My wife will brew us some tea."

Murdoch was about to refuse, but she was already heading for the little kitchen alcove and he didn't want to give offence. He sat down, Crabtree squeezing himself into the chair opposite. Green's home was very different from Talbert's. Not only was it much smaller, it was furnished with mismatched furniture. The plank floor was covered with multi-coloured rag rugs and the armchairs had cheery crocheted covers flung over them. It was like many another workmen's cottage he'd been in. Green took the chair across from him and Crabtree. He sat quietly, waiting for them to start, but Murdoch could feel his tension. Was he capable of inflicting such violence on an older man? Physically yes, easily, but mentally Murdoch couldn't believe it.

Green put his hands on the table. The knuckles were swollen and criss-crossed with small scars. He saw Murdoch looking at his hands and immediately removed them and placed them on this knees. Then his eyes met Murdoch's.

"I suppose you're going to arrest me," he said, his voice dead.

CHAPTER SEVENTEEN

S uddenly the curtains across the bottom of the stairs were whisked aside and a man came through into the room.

"I heard that, you foolish brother, you. Of course they ain't gonna charge you." He was younger than Green, not as tall, and heavier and much darker-skinned. Whereas Green had given the impression of well-contained strength, Murdoch thought this man looked on the verge of explosive rage. On the other hand, that impression could have been created by the fact he was wearing only summer trousers and a white undervest that seemed too small for him and accentuated his muscular shoulders and arms. His feet were bare.

"You are?" asked Murdoch.

"Lincoln Green, his brother. And you are?" His tone was one of barely reined-in insolence.

"I'm Detective William Murdoch from number four station. This is Constable Crabtree. We are investigating the death of Daniel Cooke. Your brother worked for him."

"I know that. So did several other men, are you questioning them as well?"

"Linc, watch your manners," Elijah intervened in a sharp voice. "The detective has a job to do."

"In answer to your question," said Murdoch, "yes, we are. Why wouldn't we?"

Lincoln gave him an odd look, then lowered his head and muttered. "Where there's trouble, it always lands first on us coloured folk."

"Trouble ends up with them that deserves it," said Crabtree.

Lincoln looked as if he was about to give an angry retort, but his brother touched him on the arm. "Why don't you join us, Linc, and hear what the officers have to say for themselves?" He waited until Lincoln took the remaining seat at the table, then he turned to Murdoch. "My brother sometimes comes over to the stables if I need an extra hand. He's familiar with the routine and the other cabbies."

"You didn't mention that before."

"It didn't seem important. It only happens occasionally."

"Where does he work normally?"

"I haul freight down at the harbour," interjected Lincoln, but Murdoch didn't respond to him. He thought he'd put a bit of pressure on the situation by being deliberately rude.

"Does he know what happened?" he asked Elijah.

"I do." Lincoln answered for himself, clearly nettled. "Cooke got a thorough whipping."

"That sounds like you thought he deserved it," said Murdoch.

"No, it don't. I was just stating a fact. It ain't for me to say if he deserved it or not, although –"

Elijah gave him another warning glance and he subsided a little. "Don't mind my brother, Mr. Murdoch. We're both worried about the situation." He gave a rueful grin. "I'm probably looking like a good bet to pin the whole thing on. At least your constable seems to think so."

"I'm interested in the truth and the facts, Mr. Green, not speculation." Murdoch hadn't intended it as a reprimand to Crabtree, but the expression that crossed the constable's face told him it had been taken as such. He turned back to Elijah. "There are one or two things I need to clarify with you. I was speaking to Paul Musgrave, and he said there was bad blood between you and Mr. Cooke, that you'd had a couple of rows recently."

Elijah looked down at the table and began to fidget with a knife that had been left there. "I thought he'd get around to dropping that sooner or later. The so-called row weren't no more than happens between any boss and his stable hand from time to time. I wouldn't call it bad blood. That implies something ongoing and it weren't."

"What did you quarrel about?"

"Nothing serious. He'd got behind with my wages and I was asking him for what was my due. He liked to hold on to his money till the last minute so he was trying to fob me off."

His explanation didn't quite fit the picture that Musgrave had drawn, which suggested Cooke was the aggrieved man, but Murdoch let it go for now.

Lincoln leaned forward. "There's a lot more to this than my brother is letting on. Musgrave has it in for him and has for a long time. He's hard on his horses and Elijah challenged him more than once. He didn't like that. Thought the nigger man was stepping out of place, so he held it against him. He'd snatch at any chance he could to make trouble."

"Is that true?" Murdoch asked Elijah.

"It's true what Linc says about Musgrave misusing his horses, and it's true that I did challenge him about it. He's a man that holds grudges for all he looks like a friendly gnome. But he wasn't lying about me having a barney with Mr. Cooke. I saw him stand-ing outside in the yard, trying to listen, but he wouldn't have known what we was quarrelling about so I guess he's free to spec-ulate all he wants."

Elijah Green was a convincing witness, and Murdoch thought a clever one or an honest one or both.

"Why did you ask earlier if we were going to charge you?"

"You had a certain look about you."

Crabtree snorted in disgust, and it was Murdoch's turn to cast a warning glance. "Mr. Cooke says that money is missing from the safe. A lot of money. Do you know about that?"

"No."

"Did you know the combination?"

"No. The boss was very careful on that matter. He wouldn't open it if anybody was there. He sent me out of the room more than once in case I saw what he was doing."

There was the merest inflection of contempt in his voice.

"Mr. Cooke also said her husband kept a revolver in the drawer. It's not there. Did you know about that?"

"Yes, that weren't no secret. He was mortal afraid of robbers. He made sure everybody who worked for him knew he had a weapon."

"Had he ever been robbed?"

"Not in the twenty-odd years I've worked there." Elijah gave a sly grin. "I guess the threat worked."

"His wife says he surprised an intruder just three months ago. Did you know about that?"

"No, I didn't. He never mentioned it."

There was silence for a moment and Crabtree shifted in his chair. It was too small for him, but then most chairs were. Murdoch knew his constable was getting impatient. He wanted to return to the station with the suspect in cuffs. He heard the floorboards creaking overhead and he wondered if Mrs. Green was sitting at the top of the stairs, listening the way Lincoln had been. She had seemed so nervous when they came in, and Elijah and Lincoln were both tense and wary. Was it as simple as they said, a negro family on the fringes of a crime that they feared they might be easily blamed for?

"Mr. Green, I understand you sometimes sleep on a cot in the barn, and during his search, my constable here found some articles that might be viewed with suspicion."

"What's that supposed to mean?" Lincoln burst out.

"Exactly what I said, no more and no less. We are investigating a suspicious death and among things, we find a blood-stained piece of sacking apparently hidden –"

"It wasn't hidden," interrupted Elijah.

"Yes, it was. You never said you had a hideaway up there." It was Crabtree's turn to raise his voice.

"I never said anything because it isn't. It's just a place I kip down in if I have to. I explained about the sacking."

Elijah looked away. Lincoln was staring at the scrubbed table, not moving.

"Did you sleep there on Tuesday?" Murdoch asked.

"I did. Like I said, I was concerned about one of the horses."

Murdoch took out the envelope he had brought with him and handed Elijah the piece of paper Crabtree had found.

"You have admitted that this is your handwriting, but you have refused to say what is the significance of the words."

"There isn't no particular significance."

Lincoln glanced over and made an overly hearty gesture.

"I know what that is, Elijah. Them's the words you made up for little Donnie so he could practise his handwriting. Show them."

Elijah nodded. "Right. Of course they are."

"Does the child have a notebook I can see?" Murdoch asked. Catch them in the small details and they'll trip up on the bigger lies. But he saw immediately he hadn't trapped them. Lincoln got up and went over to the kitchen where the children had been earlier. He made rather a point of shifting away some newspaper. "Ah here it is." He returned to the table with a dog-eared scribbler, opened it, and handed it to Murdoch.

The last page was filled with a large, childish scrawl and sure enough there were the words from the piece of paper: *The Master. Advance, Retreat,* and so on.

"You look surprised, detective. Did you think coloured folk don't know how to read and write?"

"'Course he don't think that, Linc. But does that answer your question, Mr. Murdoch?"

"Why didn't you tell the constable that at the time? Constable Crabtree said you wouldn't offer any explanation and you were quite belligerent with him."

Elijah looked down at the table. "Begging your pardon, sir. But the constable was trampling all over my own place as it were. I got riled up a bit, that's all. I didn't feel like answering what is nobody's business but my own. And Linc here can attest to the fact that I have a stubborn streak a mile wide."

"That's right, he does."

Elijah tapped on the sheet of paper. "I can see looking at this list of words, they might seem odd but they don't really seem relevant to what happened to Mr. Cooke, do they? I mean there is 'hit' and 'mark' and 'fall,' but that's about it."

You are a cunning fox, aren't you? Murdoch thought. There's just enough plausibility in what you're saying. Enough but not sufficient. He decided to try another tack.

"Mrs. Cooke told us that her husband received a message while he was finishing his supper that seemed to alarm him. He rushed out immediately but didn't tell her why." The two brothers were both looking at him now with real curiosity.

"The butler said the message was delivered by a man he hadn't seen before. He described him as stocky build, about five-foot-four or -five inches tall. He was wearing a fedora pulled down tight over his eyes, a long dark overcoat, and he had a white muffler wrapped around the lower part of his face. It was a fairly mild night, so I am assuming the scarf was to disguise him rather than for warmth. There wasn't a good light in the porch so the butler can't give a really good description. However, he is sure the man was a negro."

Lincoln pounded on the table. "What do you mean, 'sure he was a negro'?"

"His skin was dark."

"Anybody can black their faces and pretend to be one of us. Only last month our pastor had to go to city council and protest about the minstrel show that was coming to town. They're all white men and they daub on burnt cork and paint their lips red and never heed for a minute that they are insulting us coloured folk. It would be easy for a white man to darken himself and make out he was a negro."

Crabtree was making it obvious what he thought, but Murdoch didn't answer. It was something he hadn't considered. Lincoln was quite right, and if it was true what he said, the messenger had certainly succeeded in throwing suspicion onto the stable hand.

"Has anybody been around the livery recently who might fit the description I just gave you?" Murdoch asked.

Elijah shook his head. "Nobody."

Lincoln poked him. "What about that coloured woman you told us about? She was a stranger. You should tell the detective what happened. We want to help him solve his case, don't we?"

Elijah shrugged. "There's nothing to tell, really. This woman was just a casual visitor. She only came by once. About a week ago, it was."

"What did she want?"

"She said she was the personal maid for an American visitor, a widow lady who wanted to inquire about hiring a cab privately while she was in town. That's all there was to it. She said she would come back the next day and make final arrangements, but she never did."

"Can you describe this woman?" Murdoch asked.

"I suppose so. She was dark-skinned, medium height, a bit on the stout side."

He paused, clearly reluctant to say much.

"What else?" Murdoch asked impatiently. "What was she wearing? How old would you say?"

Elijah shrugged. "Quite well dressed but very sober, as I recall. Her walking suit was navy or black. She had on a felt hat with a bit of ribbon, but, as I say, all very plain. Age? Not young, probably close to fifty."

"And you'd never seen her before?"

"Never."

"She could have been scouting out the place," said Lincoln. "Whoever attacked Mr. Cooke knew there wouldn't be anybody around on Wednesdays after half past seven."

"How did you know what time Mr. Cooke died?" Murdoch jumped in.

Lincoln grinned. "Elijah told me he found him at half past nine. He locked the stable sharp at half past seven, then came home for his supper. What happened must have been between those two times. And in case you was wondering, we were all of us here and can vouch for him."

Murdoch looked at Elijah. "Why did you bother to come home? You had to get right back again to feed the horses. Why didn't you stay at the stables?"

"My children like to see their pa before they go to bed. My wife and me say their prayers with them. So I come home whenever I can."

"I could call them down here and ask them if that's true," said Murdoch.

That got a reaction out of Lincoln especially, but Elijah also tensed. "It's your right to do that, mister. They've been brought up to be truthful, but if it isn't absolutely necessary, I'd prefer they were left out of it. It'll only upset them. Look, we have a Bible over there on the dresser. If you want me to, I'll swear on it that I didn't have nothing to do with Mr. Cooke's death."

His brother shoved back his chair and went to the dresser. "Here's the Good Book, mister. I'll swear on it too if that'll keep you away from those children. We're telling the truth."

He brought a large black Bible to the table and stood with it at the ready. Murdoch waved him away. "This isn't a law court. Was anybody else in the barn when this strange woman appeared?"

"There may have been, I don't really remember. If the cabbies aren't working they sit out in the room next to the tack room, but she didn't come in really, just stood in the doorway."

"And that was all she said to you, that she wanted to hire a carriage?"

Elijah bit his lip. "I suppose we remarked about the rain. It was coming down cats and dogs at that point . . . oh, she did ask me about church. She said she'd heard about a preacher named Archer and she wondered if he was still with us because she wanted to go to church. I said as how he was elderly now and wasn't preaching any more but Pastor Laing was and he could drum up as powerful a sermon as I ever heard. She asked where the church was, I told her, and that's it."

"Did the woman mention where she was staying?"

"No, she didn't. As I said, the encounter only lasted five minutes or so."

"I'm surprised you did remember such a casual meeting when you have such a busy job."

Elijah gave him the same rueful smile. "Mr. Murdoch, if you're a coloured man, you remember another coloured folk coming into your barn even if there was a hundred white folk passing through."

CHAPTER EIGHTEEN

t wasn't hard to tell that Constable Crabtree was angry, and when they got outside to where they'd left their wheels, he couldn't contain it any longer.

"I know you've got your reasons, Mr. Murdoch, but for the life of me I don't see why you didn't clap the cuffs on that man. On both of them, for that matter. As guilty a pair as I've ever seen."

"They were willing to swear on the Bible, George."

"Ha. That might mean something to men like me and you but not to them. You might as well hand the city directory to a savage and get him to swear his oath on it. Don't mean nothing. You notice how quick they were to offer when you said you'd question the children. They might have had a different tale to tell before their pa got to them. I was sorry you didn't go and get them like you said you would."

Murdoch was surprised at his constable's vehemence. George was normally mild-mannered and kind in his dealings with people of lesser status.

The constable continued, "That story about another darkie coming to the stables. That was intended to throw us off the scent. You did give away a description of the so-called messenger."

Murdoch winced. "That was probably a mistake."

"Not if they were innocent it wasn't, but Green conveniently remembered the woman after you said that."

"Why say it was a woman, though? If he was lying, why not just say a man who fitted the description the butler gave us came to the stables?"

"He's cunning, that's why. Didn't want to make it too obvious. I'd wager both him and his brother are in on the attack. You said yourself you thought it would have taken two people. I'd bet Lincoln was the one who went to Cooke's house, wrote something that would bring him running, and there they were waiting for him. They intended to kill him after the whipping. It had to be somebody who knew the stable would be empty of cabbies and also somebody who could get in. If you want my opinion, sir, we should get a warrant and search that house top to toe, if it isn't too late, that is."

They biked on for a while longer, not talking. Murdoch chewed over what Crabtree had said, some of which he'd thought himself. However, in spite of the nagging dissatisfaction, he'd been inclined to believe both brothers. It wasn't just the resort to the Bible that had convinced him, he thought Green's concern for his children was genuine.

"I'm going to proceed initially as if what Green said is true about this visitor. It may be important, it may not, but at least if we find her, we'll know if he was telling the truth. A middle-aged woman isn't going to walk too far in the pouring rain. The weather was terrible all last week. I know I didn't even get out my wheel. If she is indeed a visitor with her mistress, they must have been staying not too far away."

They were approaching Church Street as the bell of St. James Cathedral tolled out the half-hour. Murdoch braked hard. Crabtree sailed on until he realized what was happening. Murdoch called after him.

"There's somebody I have to see, George. I'll join you at the station in an hour."

Crabtree turned back. "Is there anything I should do in the meantime, sir?"

"Get me a list of all the hotels and guest houses that are within walking distance of the livery. Most hotels these days have telephones and so does the livery. I'm wondering why if this unknown woman wanted a cab, she didn't ring for one."

Crabtree couldn't hide his skepticism, but he saluted, remounted, and biked off while Murdoch retraced his path, heading for the Ollapod Club.

He was there in less than five minutes. The house was a grand pile surrounded by well-tended grounds and a high wrought-iron fence. A discrete brass plaque on the gate read, *Please ring the bell for admittance.* Murdoch was about to obey when suddenly a man virtually leaped out from behind one of the trees that lined the path and hissed, "Don't touch it." For a brief second, Murdoch thought a lunatic was addressing him, then he recognized Inspector Brackenreid. He was dressed in indoor clothes, bedroom garb to be exact. A blue velvet dressing gown underneath which his white stockinged, rather bandy legs protruded. He had on leather slippers and a night cap with a tassel. His hair was wild and dishevelled.

"Come through quickly, Murdoch. They mustn't see you."

He opened the gate and hustled Murdoch by the arm to the shelter of the big tree.

"Sir –"

"Shh. Don't talk just yet." Brackenreid peered around the tree trunk. "All clear. Follow me."

He scuttled across the lawn to a big maple and Murdoch had no choice but to follow him. Once there, Brackenreid did the same careful scanning of the territory, then beckoning, he took off again, this time to a small shed tucked beneath some evergreens farther away from the house. He flung open the door and dragged Murdoch inside. It was a tool shed and smelled of earth, overlaid with the pungent aroma of cigars. There was a chair in there and an upturned box. Brackenreid plumped himself down on the box. He was panting.

"Sit down, Murdoch. We don't have a lot of time. They'll be looking for me soon."

Cautiously Murdoch took the seat, afraid the inspector had taken leave of his senses.

Brackenreid saw his expression and he flapped his hands irritably. "I'm quite sane, don't worry. But this place is beset with rules and if you break them you lose privileges. That's why I'm still in these damn nightclothes. You know me, punctuality is not one of my virtues. I was late for meals two times in a row. They take your clothes away when you're first admitted and you only get them back if you do what you're told and follow the rules."

The late-afternoon sun was fading rapidly and the shed was gloomy. However, Murdoch could see well enough the changes in the inspector's face and body. He was several pounds lighter than when Murdoch had seen him last and most of the puffiness around his eyes had gone. Except that his hair was standing on end, he looked much healthier.

"The program does seem to be agreeing with you, if I may say so, sir."

Brackenreid snarled at him. "I might as well be in one of our own jails. Every minute of the day is accounted for. There are morning meetings with prayers, hot baths in the afternoon with a massage every second day. They claim that music heals you, so in the evening there is singing together or a musical entertainment that consists of caterwauling violins most of the time. I suppose you could call that healing, if you mean it makes you want to get out of here as fast as you can. If it's not that it's a talk by Cavanaugh, the Irish rogue who runs the place, or one of the former residents who rubs it in your face how well he's doing after the cure. And all of that sandwiched between three meals a day and a morning and nighttime purge. Not to mention having to line up four times a day for our medicine."

He stood up and, moving aside a clay pot, felt along the top shelf by the door.

"Ahh, here we are." He took down the stub of a cigar and a box of matches. "They won't let us smoke either, but I was able to smuggle some of my havanas into this shed. I'd offer you one, Murdoch, but this is my last." He leaned into Murdoch and sniffed. "You've been smoking recently, unless my nose deceives me."

"Er, yes. In fact, to be honest, I took the liberty of having one of yours . . . when I used your office as you so generously offered me."

Murdoch watched the inspector, readying himself for a reprimand, but Brackenreid actually smiled. "You did, did you? Good, aren't they?"

"Yes, sir. Very tasty."

Brackenreid blew out some thick smoke. "We're allowed one hour private time a day," he continued. "I'm supposed to stay in the lounge, but it was mild enough to come out and walk in the grounds. I never thought I'd appreciate solitude as much. One of the worst things about this place is that fellow I sent to the station, Earl Cherry. He's my personal attendant, and he never lets me out of his sight. He's always talking to me, never stops. He's so damned encouraging, it makes me sick. Two days ago I was on the point of walking out and he stopped me. Made me stay in my room while he and Cavanaugh went through all the virtues of temperance and the vices of drink. They kept saying I was changing my life, and it was worth all the pain and torment I was going through . . ."

He stopped and Murdoch could see drops of spittle in the corners of his mouth.

"They do have a point, sir. You do look very well, indeed. Better than I've seen you in a few years."

"You don't understand how difficult it is. You're probably a teetotaller."

"I'm not. I enjoy a jar as much as any man. But I do know what havoc a drunk can cause in a family."

Brackenreid stared at him. "You do? How?"

"My father, actually."

Murdoch could feel the bitterness on his tongue. After all these years, it was still a painful subject. Fortunately, Brackenreid didn't press him.

Murdoch continued quickly. "I must say, sir, that I admire your resolve. It takes courage to change your ways so drastically."

Brackenreid scrutinized his face for sincerity, then he sighed. "I don't know if I can accept that compliment, Murdoch. The truth is my wife and father-in-law approached Mr. Cavanaugh, and the three of them essentially held me prisoner in my own bedroom while they brought home to me in no uncertain terms the error of my ways. Both my marriage and my job were at stake and the good opinion of everybody we knew. Cavanaugh, of course, had a lot to say about his program and how successful it was. How could I refuse?"

"That is certainly a potent argument, sir."

"It is. I was not unaware of the pain and anger I was causing to those who cared about me. Unfortunately, as Cavanaugh says,

the demon drink had me firmly by the foot. He was running the
show, not me. That's what we're aiming to reverse. To cast off
the shackles of the slavish addiction, as he puts it, and emerge a
free man. He's partial to metaphors, is Cavanaugh." He blew out
more smoke.

"Why did you want to talk to me, sir? You said it was a matter
of some urgency."

"Yes. I know we've had our little set-to's, Murdoch, but
you're one of the few people I feel I can trust. My wife means
well, but she is completely under Cavanaugh's spell. Whatever
he says is gospel for her. They want me to stay here another
month until I'm completely cured, as they put it, as if I've been
suffering from measles or some such thing. I don't need a cure.
I'm not ill. I'm weak willed and I can't let the drink alone, no
matter what I tell myself. My own father was the same and most
of the people I knew, men that is, were the same as him. I despise
them and I despise myself."

His voice was so harsh, Murdoch felt a pang of sympathy.

"Whatever reason we give for inebriety, surely that doesn't
matter so much as the solution to the problem. Cavanaugh's has
a good reputation and they claim a lot of success. If you can stand
it, sir, a month should put you on the right path. After that it's just
a matter of sticking to it."

"You sound like Earl. It's so easy for somebody on the
outside."

He'd slipped back into self-pity, and Murdoch's momentary
sympathy vanished. This was the same old Brackenreid he knew
and had run foul of so many times.

Murdoch took out his pocket watch from his vest and consulted it. "I am on an investigation, sir. I can't stay much longer.
What can I do to help you?"

Brackenreid stubbed out his cigar in the plant pot and fished in the pocket of his dressing gown. He pulled out a small vial of gold-coloured liquid.

"I want you to get a doctor to analyze this. The residents here are supposed to have four special concoctions a day that are Cavanaugh's secret recipes. He refuses to say what's in them. The one we get in the morning is purgative and makes you nauseous. One later on is a tonic, and the evening one probably has some laudanum to put us to sleep. But it's this I'm interested in. At two o'clock we get this, the so-called gold cure. We don't drink this one, it's injected. Most of the residents can't wait to get their shot and they say it makes them happier and more energetic. I'd like to know what's in it." He smiled at Murdoch, another most unusual behaviour. "I'm still a copper, Will, even though I got booted upstairs and lost a grip on things. I'm curious about this. Every time I bring it up I'm told I'm just avoiding the real issues. Earl says in his solemn voice, 'These are safe medicines developed by Mr. Cavanaugh, but he doesn't want the ingredients stolen by unscrupulous competitors, so he prefers to keep them secret.' 'Come off it,' says I, 'I'm hardly likely to start a clinic for drunks. I couldn't think of anything worse.' But I can't budge him. Here, see what the doctor has to say."

"Have you received the injections yourself, sir?"

"I had to. My buttocks feel like my wife's pin cushion. It does seem to have a beneficial effect, I feel quite buoyed up afterwards, but now I'm curious about what's in it. Are they slipping in a brandy base? I've heard some places do that just to keep the residents on the hook even though they claim it's weaning them. This place is very costly, and I want to make sure it's worth it."

"I'll get on to it right –" Before Murdoch could say any more, they heard a man's voice shouting from the direction of the house.

"Tom. Thomas Brackenreid? Where are you? It's suppertime."

Brackenreid peered through the shed window. "Oh Lord, just what I thought. It's Earl. I'd better go. If he finds you here, I swear he'll have you searched. They do. It's in the best interests of the patients, they claim. Friends and family members have been caught smuggling in liquor."

"Not all of them in the city council minutes, I hope."

Brackenreid grinned at him and looked years younger. "You were a bit sly there, Murdoch. But you were right to do that. I'm not in the grip of the craving quite as much. I'm actually starting to enjoy being sober . . . and it's been a long time."

He peered through the window again. "Lord, he's coming here. I have to leave. Wait till we go into the house, then get out as fast as you can."

"How shall I get in touch with you when I have the analysis of the medicine?"

"I'm allowed letters, but they read them so you'll have to disguise what you write. When you are ready to meet, I'll do the same thing as I did today. I'll give Earl the slip and come over to the gate. Keep it the same time. But we'll need a code word."

"What if I write, 'Today is fire station inspection day,' and that means I'll be here."

"Excellent, Murdoch. Add bits and dabs of other things to disguise it."

"Yes, I was thinking of doing that, sir. It would sound a little odd on its own."

Brackenreid gave him a hard slap on the arm, which Murdoch interpreted as an awkward way of saying thank you.

"I'm grateful, William. I knew I could trust you."

"Tom! Mr. Brackenreid! Time to come in before you catch cold."

With a groan the inspector opened the door a crack and slipped out. Murdoch watched him hurrying across the grass toward his attendant, who greeted him warmly. Then, his arm through Brackenreid's, Earl escorted him to the house where lamps were being lit and Murdoch could see the residents lining up for their final tonic of the day. The inspector joined the end of the queue, Earl beside him.

CHAPTER NINETEEN

DECEMBER 1859

Lena daubed the goose grease ointment as gently as she could over Fidelia's lacerated back. The girl flinched but was silent. She was lying face down on a straw pallet in the lean-to, to which she and Lena had been relegated.

"You can holler if you like, Fiddie, there's nobody here. They've all gone to the meeting at the town hall."

"I ain't going to holler ever again. Not for them."

Lena continued what she was doing. She was almost blinded by her own tears but was trying to hide them from Fidelia.

"I should never have asked you to take him. You might have got away on your own. Carrying him slowed you down too much."

"Only a bit. He was good, didn't fuss hardly at all." Fidelia allowed a little smile at the corners of her mouth. "He sure done like that dried chicken I give him. I done chew it up real soft till it was like mush and stuck it in his mouth. He acted like he was a little bird in a nest and I was the mother. I thought he was gonna open up his little beak and chirp at me when I picked him up."

Lena had to stop for a moment to wipe her eyes. "If only he could have grown wings and flown to freedom."

Fidelia rolled over and sat up, wincing with the pain from her whipping. She clutched Lena's hand. "Don't fret, dear one. He's in heaven now and he surely has wings there. You know what Preacher told us just last month. Jesus done love all his children and he done pick the best to go and live in his mansion where they play all sun long and eat as much as they want and have pretty clothes and get to kiss Jesus whenever they feels like it."

"Oh, Fiddie, do you believe that?"

"Of course I does. Don't nothing else make sense otherwise. It was a comfort to remember those words when I knew your babe had died."

Lena rocked back on her heels. "And you're certain of that? Absolutely certain. There's no chance that the preacher got out before the fire?"

"I tells you, there weren't no chance at all. I done ask everybodys I could. I done see the flames myself. That slave catcher made me look. 'See what happens to niggers who get uppity. You shouldn't have gone in there. Too bad for that preacher man. He must've knocked over a lamp or something.' But we all knew it was them white folks done thrown their torches through the windows. It weren't no accident. I'd have been in that church myself, but that good old man took Ise from me and told me to get out and run like the devil himself was after me." Fidelia shuddered. "I knows them slave catchers done see me. They would have taken Ise and me both, but after the preacher says what he says, I took off from that church like a spooked horse. I was hoping I could draw them away and they would follow and they does for a bit till I fell over a foot that some fat pig of a white-folk passerby done stuck out to trip me up."

"How much later did you see the fire start?"

"Not long. There were two of them slave catchers, and one done hold me down and the other ran back to the church. He was one of them that set it on fire. Oh my dear one, I wish I could tell you something else but I can't. Ise's with Jesus." She grabbed Lena's hand. "You ain't after blaming me, is you?"

Lena embraced her. "How could I ever do that? Better he be there at peace than grow up a slave. That you got as far as you did is a miracle. You are my good and faithful friend, Fiddie. What would I do without you? And I am sorry with all my heart that the missus had you whipped so hard. And I'm sorry I had to lie and say you stole him from me. Will you forgive me for that?"

Fidelia grinned. "No sense in both of us getting whipped. Missus don't like me, never did. She wants to break my spirit. I heard her saying so to the master. But she hates you worse and would likely have killed you if you told the truth and mister hadn't been there." Fidelia stroked Lena's arm. "I've heard stories from Missus Craddock's man. Moses says as there's going to be a war coming soon and when that happens we'll all be freed. So don't fret, my dear one. We'll get away from here."

Lena touched the girl's face tenderly. "I hope with all my heart and soul it's true what they're saying. But we must be ready. As soon as we can, as soon as the war is declared, we, my dearest, are going to run away as fast as our feet will carry us. I'm almost well again and even if I'm not, we're going."

"To the Promised Land?"

"Yes, to the Promised Land."

"And we'll be free?"

For a moment, Lena allowed her face to reveal the emotions she had within her all the time, subdued only by tremendous self-discipline. "I almost forget what's that like, Fiddie. Oh I pray to the Lord that I haven't forgotten how to live like a free woman again."

"I ain't never been free, not since I was borned, but don't you fret yourself I'll find out quick as a rat what it means. And so will you remember."

Although they'd had this argument several times before, they still pursued it to the end, a sort of ritual, comforting in itself.

"When we're there, in the Promised Land, we can do whatever we like. You'll go to school, I'll be a fine lady again with servants of my own."

"I don't want to go to school. I'll be your servant."

"No, you won't. Dearest friends are never servants. You will be my companion, my sister. I shall ask my father to adopt you."

"What if they don't come? Them folks you're counting on. What if them chickens ain't going to hatch no how?"

"Don't be silly, Fiddie. Why wouldn't they? They've been searching all this time and just haven't found me. I know it."

"I ain't heard no stories about no man searching for his love down this way."

"He doesn't know where I am. He's searching, all right."

"But what if he does get you back, how's he going to feel knowing you had a bastard son with Leigh Dickie?"

Her words were so cruel, Lena flinched.

"I don't think he needs to know. Ise's dead, so it doesn't matter. But it will be our secret, yours and mine. To the grave, promise?"

"Promise."

"Now lie back down and I'll finish tending to you."

Fiddie did as she said, and Lena layered on more goose grease, then carefully covered the girl's back with a piece of muslin.

"He cut through the skin in a few places, so we should keep this cover on for now." She stroked the girl's hair. "See if you can sleep a bit, Fiddie. You're exhausted still. I'll do your chores for you."

Fidelia yawned. "Preacher says we must pray every day and he says as how we must forgive our enemies, but I don't think he means forgive Missus Caddie or Mister Leigh. I don't imagine even Jesus himself would forgive them."

"You're right about that. The preacher is a frightened old man. I'm not going to forgive my enemies, ever. I will never forgive the men who caused the death of my child, I will never forgive those who keep us here as slaves. And my revenge shall be terrible and exacted even on to their descendants and their descendants after that. So help me God."

Lena went out to the vegetable garden at the back of the house, leaving Fidelia to rest. "War is coming." The words were being whispered through the slave quarters like wind through the rushes. "War's coming, war's coming. Them Yankees are going to free us." "If we don't get killed first." "Pray the Lord we don't get killed first out of spite." "They won't do that, they needs us." "Don't you bet on it, missie, they's as spiteful as adders. They'd kill us for spite." "Not if the Yankees get here first." "War's coming." "When? When?" "Soon, war's coming soon and we'll be free." "Or dead, but that's freedom too." "I'd rather be a slave and alive than free and dead." "Not me, not me. I'd rather be dead than live like this for the rest of my life." "War's coming."

She looked over at the house. Leigh Dickie claimed he was a poor man and had no money for maintenance, but everybody knew he was a gambler and spent everything he could on dice and cards. His marriage was miserable, and Caddie never stopped nagging and complaining. There were times that Lena almost felt pity for him, but she shrugged it off. Nobody had pitied her when calamity befell her. *War's coming, war's coming.*

On impulse she walked toward the house. Everybody was gone to the meeting about the secession and the war and she doubted they would be back for a while. The other slaves were in the cabin. Quickly, she opened the door, slipped inside, and headed for Mrs. Dickie's bedroom. Everything was tidy, but she could see the dust everywhere. Caddie didn't let her clean because she said bluntly it was a waste of time. Mrs. Dickie wasn't ever coming back.

Lena went over to the dainty painted lady's desk under the window. All clear so far and she could see if anybody was returning. She lifted the lid. Inside were piles of papers, neatly tied with ribbon. A quick look confirmed they were old letters that Mrs. Dickie had kept from the friends of her youth. She pulled open the little drawer at the back of the desk. There were more papers there, a last will and testament, a deed to the house, and a creased document, handwritten, which she recognized as the bill of sale that Prescott had drawn up and given to Mrs. Dickie in exchange for four hundred dollars. She took it out.

Know all by these presents that I, James Prescott, of the County of Guildwood and the State of Maryland have this day delivered to Mrs. Catherine Dickie of the city of Baltimore, a negro slave woman aged seventeen years old, named Lena, for the sum of four hundred dollars and the right and title to said woman I warrant and defend now and forever. I also warrant her to be sound and healthy of meek character although inclined to be fanciful. She can read and write. Signed and dated this twenty-eighth day of August, 1858.

She knew there had been two papers: this bill of sale and the forged right and title that Prescott had also handed over. Frantic now, driven by need but not even acknowledging to herself what she wanted to know, she upended the drawer, spilling the contents onto the floor.

There it was. A piece of paper on the outside of which was written *Original title to slave called Lena*. She grabbed it up and unfolded it.

Know all men by these presents, that I . . .

The name of the seller was written in the space provided, a neat, legible hand that she recognized at once.

> In consideration of the sum of three hundred dollars, in
> hand paid by James Prescott to have and to hold, I deliver
> the said described negro girl unto the said James Prescott

A second signature, the witness's, was scrawled at the bottom of the page. She was familiar with that hand as well.

She had to sit down, otherwise she might have fainted. Her temples were throbbing so violently she thought her head would burst open. *War's coming, war's coming.*

CHAPTER TWENTY

Murdoch lit his bicycle lamp and set off back along Wellesley Street. His encounter with the inspector was bemusing. When Murdoch had been accepted into Inspector Stark's newly created department of detectives three years earlier, Brackenreid had made no bones about the fact that he didn't trust Roman Catholics and insisted Murdoch have the lesser position of acting detective. It was only after Murdoch had solved a major case earlier this year that Brackenreid had promoted him to full detective. That's why all his words about trust and respect had rung a false note. Murdoch wondered whether he was being set up as a scapegoat if this so-called cure collapsed. He wouldn't put it past him.

Murdoch thought back to Elijah Green's remark that if you were a negro man living in Toronto, you'd notice another coloured person, however brief the encounter. He'd felt a pang of empathy on hearing that. He'd had similar experiences as a Roman Catholic in this city, which was governed by Protestants who tended to fear and despise other faiths, even those under the banner of Christ. Forget about Jews or the few Chinese residents. They were even more ostracized. None of them could have public office, and there were none at all on the police force. Not that Catholics were immune from prejudice and self-righteousness. He'd seen vicious diatribes in both the *Orange Banner* and the *Catholic Register*, one against the other.

He wondered if Jesus wept.

He had been picking up speed as he rode along Wilton Street and now he smiled, knowing he was like a lost dog heading for home as fast as it could. He scorched down Ontario Street to his boarding house, which beckoned a welcome with bright lamplight.

He wheeled his bicycle into the hall and Amy immediately came out of the kitchen to greet him with a kiss.

"You taste like wine," said Murdoch.

"We're celebrating."

"Don't tell me the school board has offered you a permanent position?"

She grimaced. "I'll expect that when it snows in July. Come on, we're all in the kitchen. We've been waiting for you." She took him by the hand.

"Just a minute, let me take my things off."

"Only your hat and coat for now." She said it with a mischievous grin, and the implication made Murdoch blush like a shy schoolboy. This relationship was so new, he couldn't help himself. He was always chagrined when he reacted like this, he was almost thirty-five years old, for God's sake. But what his mind wanted and what his body did weren't always compatible.

Amy thrust open the door to the kitchen.

"Here he is at last."

"Hurrah!"

Charlie Seymour was sitting beside Katie Tibbett, the fourth resident of the boarding house. Her twin boys were in high chairs across from them. Somebody had given them each a wooden spoon and a pot to bang on and excited by the liveliness around them they slammed away enthusiastically. Both of them had cream smeared around their mouths. There was a bottle of wine on the table and the delicious aroma of a meal filled the kitchen. Katie got up to bring Murdoch his dinner, but Amy forestalled her.

"Stay where you are, I'll get it. Tell him your news."

Katie glanced at Charlie shyly. "You do it."

"With pleasure. Will, Katie and me are going to put up the banns. We've set a wedding date for May 16."

"Amy is going to be my maid of honour, and Charlie wants you to be the best man. Will you?" interjected Katie.

"I wouldn't miss it," said Murdoch. He thrust out his hand. "Congratulations, Charlie. I can't say I'm surprised, but I couldn't be happier for you."

Both boys yelled and waved their spoons like conductor's batons. Amy laced her fingers together and blew through her thumbs, making a shrill whistle.

"I don't know why she's said yes to an old codger like me," said Charlie, "but I'm not going to talk her out of it."

Katie gave him a kiss on the cheek. "Don't you dare say you're an old codger. You're the dearest, kindest man I've ever known."

Charlie groaned. "You'd say that to your granddad."

"Tell him he's a grumpy beast and all you want is his money," said Murdoch. "That'll make him happy."

"I couldn't do that, it's not true."

Katie was still an innocent and didn't always understand teasing.

Amy started to whistle a lively rendition of "For He's a Jolly Good Fellow," and Katie and Murdoch sang lustily to Seymour, who hung his head bashfully. When they'd finished, Charlie solicited another kiss from his betrothed, which was gladly bestowed.

Then Katie looked at Murdoch in dismay. "What are we thinking? You haven't had your supper yet." She bustled over to the oven, took out a plate of food, and put it on the table.

"It's your favourite, baked ham and cabbage with roasted potatoes."

"Let me pour you some wine," said Charlie.

Murdoch tucked into the dinner. "What are you going to do after you're married? Please tell me you're not going to leave."

"Seeing you stuff your face like that, Will, I would suspect you have designs on my fiancée," said Seymour. "But we have talked it over and we intend to stay here for at least a year so we can save money for our own house. Amy has kindly agreed to switch rooms with me so we'll put the twins in the middle room and Katie and I will have the parlour."

Murdoch liked that idea. It meant Amy and he would have more privacy. He glanced over at her and saw she had read his mind. She smiled at him.

"More wine, everybody?" Charlie reached for the bottle.

"Not for me," said Amy. "One is enough. I can't go to Councillor Blong's house smelling of drink."

"Are you going out tonight?" asked Murdoch in dismay.

"I have to. Mary Blong hasn't been in school for almost three weeks. I received a note today asking if I would visit her and bring her up to date with her lessons."

"What's wrong with her?" asked Katie.

"I don't know. He didn't say, but one of her friends whispered in my ear that Mary is having fits and the doctor is lost. I think she meant at a loss. My belief is that Mary would recover quickly if her new little brother disappeared."

"Oh, Amy, don't say that."

"Sorry, Katie, but it's true. Mary, poor thing, is consumed by jealousy over the newcomer, a longed-for boy, and I think this is her way of getting attention. But we'll see."

"There's a fresh junket in the pantry," said Katie. "Why don't you take some of it? That's sure to put you into the councillor's good graces."

"Thank you, Katie, but I refuse to curry favour just because he's a member of the school board." She smiled ruefully. "Besides, Mary doesn't like me much at all, and I wouldn't trust her not to spit it out in disgust just to make a point."

"Nobody would turn down Katie's junket once tasted," said Murdoch. "I'll have Mary's portion, though, if you think taking it is a waste of time. I can see the boys have already enjoyed their share."

Seymour raised his glass. "A toast to James and Jacob, also jolly good fellows."

He was a little tipsy because he was not a drinking man, but the wine and his obvious happiness had softened his usually austere features and took years off his age. Katie's first husband had been a scoundrel, and Murdoch was glad she had now found a man who so obviously would treat her well.

Murdoch clinked glasses. "To the lads. And lucky fellows they are."

Amy stood up. "I'll be off then."

"It's getting rather late," said Murdoch. "Why don't I come with you?"

"That's really not necessary, Will. They live over on Sackville Street not far from the school. It won't take me long to get there. I'm sure you've had an arduous day."

Murdoch felt a brief flash of frustration. This was not the first time they'd had a minor clash like this. "Amy! You're the one who looks tired. A little fresh air will do me good."

She hesitated. "Very well. At least we can give the lovebirds a little time to themselves."

Murdoch picked up his plate.

"Leave it, Will. I'll clean up," said Katie. "You should get going."

James bonged his spoon on the upturned pot in agreement.

Once outside, Murdoch and Amy walked in silence. He was damned if he was going to relent, but they hadn't gone far when he felt her slip her arm through his.

"I'm sorry to be so pig-headed, Will. It's just that I can't bear to be treated as if I were fragile or incapable."

"You think I'm not aware of that by now? Didn't it occur to you that I wanted your company?"

"I'm sorry, sir. I'll never do it again," she said meekly.

"Ha. I'll believe that when it snows in July."

They crossed over the street and he suddenly grabbed her round the waist and swung her over his hip to lift her up and over some horse dung that she had been about to tread in. He set her down on the sidewalk.

"See, you do need me. What would Councillor Blong think if you showed up smelling of wine and your skirt and boots covered in manure?"

She lifted her head. "I don't still smell of wine, do I?"

"To properly determine that I will have to come very close to your mouth and if I do that I will have to kiss you, and seeing that we are being approached by a respectable middle-aged couple, I had better not."

Amy stepped away from him. "No, you certainly had better not. They might recognize me and report me to the board for conduct unbecoming to a schoolteacher."

The couple passed them and the man raised his hat.

"Good evening, Miss Slade."

"Good evening, Mr. Hall."

Murdoch waited until they were out of earshot. "It's bad luck that he was somebody you knew. Not that we were doing anything."

She slipped her arm through his again. "Let's put it this way, that was Mr. Hall all right, but that wasn't Mrs. Hall. The woman clinging to his arm was a rather attractive woman, don't you think?"

"Very. And most stylishly dressed."

"She could be his sister, of course."

"Of course. And it meant nothing that he was in a hurry to go past us and seemed most disconcerted to see you."

Amy laughed. "Your policeman's eye, Will. But my heart did skip a beat when I realized we knew each other."

"Good heavens, I thought you were a New Woman."

"That's got nothing to do with it. I don't want to lose my position."

He almost burst out that she wouldn't get the shoot if she were a respectable married woman kissing her husband, even on the street, but he didn't want to spoil the mood again. Besides, she would have to leave teaching if she were married, and he knew that was one of the reasons she wouldn't agree to do it. In his blue moments, he wondered if the real reason was that she didn't love him enough but when she lay in his arms in bed, he believed her when she said she had never cared for anybody the way she cared for him. He sighed. Patience, patience.

"What's the matter?" Amy asked.

"Nothing."

The rest of the way to the Blong house he filled her in on what had been happening in the course of his investigation. She listened intently, as she always did.

"How cruel to whip a man in that way. No matter what he's done, nothing can excuse it. This feels like a bad case, Will. Be careful."

CHAPTER TWENTY-ONE

SEPTEMBER 1862

The late-afternoon sun had turned the river red and there was a sharp nip in the air. Summer was almost done. They had been on the move for two weeks, travelling mostly at night and both of them were exhausted. A few apples they'd picked had been the only thing to sustain them for three days, wormy and sour as they were. Lena stopped on the crest of the hill.

"Look, Fiddie, there's a farmhouse down there. Maybe we can find something to eat."

"And maybe we'll get taken. I'd rather stay hungry. We'd better scout it out first."

"But we must be in Union territory by now. They won't turn us in."

"They sure enough will if they think there's a reward. Come on, crouch down here, it's out of the wind a bit and we can watch."

Lena huddled close to Fidelia and they sat until the sun disappeared behind the horizon. They saw a wink of light from the farmhouse as somebody lit a lamp.

"Let's get closer. See who's at home," said Lena.

Cautiously, they slithered down the hill, keeping to the shrubs that dotted the slope until they were within a hundred feet of the house. The windows were uncurtained and they could see clearly into the front room, which from the look of it was the only room in the house. They could see a kitchen range, a table, and steep stairs leading to the upper floor. A grey-haired woman sat sewing by a fire that burned low. She was dressed in black.

"I think she's alone," said Fidelia.

"Let's wait a bit longer to make sure."

A cow started to bellow from the shed that adjoined the house, and the woman got up stiffly, put down her sewing, and walked over to the door. Shortly afterwards she came out with a shawl around her head and shuffled across the muddy yard to the shed. The cow was louder than ever.

"That critter's gonna bust if that old woman don't get there soon," said Fidelia.

They waited, but nobody else came out of the house, no new lights appeared in the upper window. The cow had quieted down.

Suddenly, the piercing bray of a mule came from the shed. Fidelia nudged Lena.

"The Lord done sent us a gift. Come on."

They stood up and walked across the yard toward the out-house just as the woman emerged carrying a pail of milk. She stopped when she saw the two of them.

"Vot you want?"

She had a thick, guttural accent and she looked afraid.

"We're in need of food and shelter, ma'am," said Lena politely. "I wonder if you'd be so good as to let us have some of your fresh milk and a place to bed down for the night? We can work for it."

The woman shook her head. "Nein. I sell this milk. You go away. No niggers here."

Close up she wasn't as old as she had first appeared, but her face was careworn and weathered.

She continued to walk past them to the house, but before she had gone more than a few steps, Fidelia grabbed a spade that was leaning against the wall and brought it down as hard as she could on the back of the woman's head. She dropped to the ground, blood leaking through her grey hair. The pail fell and tipped on its side, but Lena was there in an instant and righted it, saving most of the milk. The woman was convulsing and twitching, but Fidelia hit her again and she was still.

"It was her or us," she said.

Lena stared down at the body for a few moments. "Let's go into the house, I'm freezing."

"Shall we bury her first?"

"Later. We should make absolutely sure she is alone. Bring the spade just in case. I'll carry the milk pail."

They went inside. The room was plainly furnished, the plank floor well scuffed and worn, but the woman had been able to maintain herself somehow, and to their starved eyes the place was cozy and inviting, especially the sight of a half a loaf of bread on the table and the smell of something cooking on the well-blacked stove.

"Jesus, hallelujah," whispered Fidelia.

Lena nodded. "Amen to that." She went to the tall cabinet that was by the stove and quickly opened some of the drawers. She removed a long bread knife and handed it to Fidelia.

"Run upstairs and have a look in the bedroom. Leave the spade with me."

Fidelia did so, climbing the stairs, the knife behind her back. A few minutes later, she called down.

"Not a soul. That old ugly white biddy lives alone, all right."

At that, Lena tore a chunk of bread from the loaf and stuffed it in her mouth. She lifted the lid from the steaming pot and flinched at the heat of the handle. She grabbed two bowls from the shelf and started to ladle the soup into each one.

"Fiddie, come on down now, we can eat." She heard a thump from up above. "What are you doing?"

"Just goin' exploring. Hey!" Fidelia yelled out with excitement and the next thing she was hurtling down the stairs, almost falling.

"Lena, look what I done found under her mattress." She was holding a fistful of paper money. "Is it Confederate money?"

"No, Yankee."

"Quick, count it."

Lena took the notes. "It's mostly ones and twos, probably her milk money. Oh, Fiddie, there's almost a hundred dollars here."

"She most likely got more hidden somewhere about, we should search."

"Not right now. We've got to eat or I shall faint. Put the money on the table where we can look at it."

Lena went to the window and pulled the heavy woollen curtains closed.

"We don't want anybody looking in."

"We didn't pass no farmhouse since yesterday. We're all right."

They didn't speak until the soup was devoured and Fidelia filled their bowls again. She was shovelling up the thick stew into her mouth when Lena rapped her hard on the hand with her spoon.

"Don't gulp your food. Where are your manners?"

"I lost them long time 'go," said Fiddie with a scowl.

"Well you've got to acquire some. You're not an ignorant nigger gal now."

"I knows that."

"And you've got to start talking properly. You must say, I *know* that. And it's incorrect to say, 'The Lord done sent us,' it should be 'The Lord has sent –'"

"What you doing, missus?"

"I'm trying to teach you. These things are important, Fiddie. When we're in New York, you might as well wave a Cessie flag saying 'ex-slave, ex-slave' when you talk like that."

"Why you raging on me, missus high and mighty?"

"I'm not raging on you, I'm –"

"Yes, you are. I know you. You're roaring at me, ain't you, for hitting that old woman?"

"I might have been able to talk her into helping us."

"Not her. You heard her. She don't have no time for niggers."

Lena shuddered.

"What's the matter?" asked Fidelia.

"Nothing, I'm just cold that's all. Let's light all the lamps and stoke up the fire."

"Not before you 'pologize to me. I saved us."

There was a long silence. Lena stared down at the table, then her body sagged and she reached out her hand. "You're right, Fiddie. Please forgive me. It's just that . . ."

"I know what you're thinking. You're saying to yourself that this old white woman is all soft and helpless, but she weren't. She'd have shot us soon as blink if she had a chance."

"You're right again, Fiddie." Another pause while Fidelia wiped her bowl clean with the last crust of bread.

"While we're talking bout 'pologies and 'you're rights' are flying round the table, I'll give you one back. From now on you can correct me all you want. I'm not gonna be a nigger gal any more."

Lena leaned forward and kissed her. "My angel, my dove. Your price is above rubies."

Fiddie gave her a slap on the arm. "That so? I hope you ain't thinking of selling me."

Lena touched the girl's cheek. "Not God Himself, nor the Archangel Gabriel, not all the company of heaven could tempt me."

"You and your poetry," repeated Fidelia. "Now come on, I'se full of beans now. Let's you and me give this place the spring cleaning of its life and see what we can find."

They searched for two more hours and discovered another forty dollars in coins hidden in an old cigar box in the kitchen cabinet. Fidelia made up a bundle of things they could use or perhaps sell later when they got to New York. There were a few good pieces of silver cutlery, a man's steel watch; several picture frames. One of them contained the photograph of a young man in a Confederate uniform.

"See, what I tell you?" said Fiddie. "She wouldn't have helped no nigger women."

She removed the photograph from the frame, tore it up, and threw it on the fire.

"It's almost midnight, Fiddie," said Lena. "We've got to stop. We can't take the entire household with us."

"We'll take much as we can carry. You'll see. It'll be worth it."

She had been going through the wardrobe in the corner of the room and she took out a navy blue worsted suit. She sniffed at it.

"Smells like tobacco. Must have belonged to her old massa man." She slipped on the jacket. "Looka this, Lena honey chile. It fits me snug as a bug in massa's ass. See, there's boots as well." She thrust her bare feet into the boots that were at the back of the wardrobe. "They's perfect." She beamed at Lena. "You know what I think, missus? I think Miss Fidelia and Miss Lena, slaves in the possession of Mr. Leigh Dickie and his wife, may she rot in hell, Missus Caddie, have now died and here we have two new folks. One a respectable widow lady and the other her faithful boy, Solomon."

"Solomon? Why Solomon?"

"He was very wise, wasn't he? And ain't I very wise too?"

Lena chuckled. "You most certainly are. You're going to have to bind your little rosebuds down though, if you want to be convincing."

"Missus Caddie told me just last month I was as flat as an ironing table and as ugly as spoiled porridge."

"She was wrong on both counts. You're sprouting every day and you're as pretty as any coloured gal I ever saw."

Fidelia touched her own breasts tentatively. "Good thing we got out of there then."

Lena turned away. "I've changed my mind, Fiddie. I don't care if it is late, I'm going to have a bath."

"What for? You're only gonna get dirty again."

"Never mind about that. Look, she's got a tin tub. I'm going to boil up some water and sit in that old tin tub till I wrinkle up. You can go to bed if you like."

"No. I'll stay. You'll probably need somebody to wash your back for you."

After Lena's bath, they decided it would be warmer and safer to sleep downstairs, so they hauled the mattress off the bed and brought it down in front of the fire. The old lady had more than one nightgown, and Fiddie insisted Lena take the cleaner of the two.

"We can burn our clothes," said Lena. "I never want to see them again. I'll take hers, they're decent enough."

"What name you gonna take as your new self?" Fidelia asked.

"I don't know yet, I'll have to think about it." She pulled the girl closer. "It's cold, snuggle up. I don't think I've stopped shivering yet."

Fidelia rolled over so she was facing Lena. "I've been a thinking, the best thing to do is to set the house on fire. We can bring the old woman's body in here. When the neighbours find her, they'll think she just gone and knocked over a lamp or something like that. They might not even know 'bout her money and if they did they'll think it burned in the fire. We can get ourselves a good start that way."

"Surely, they'll notice if the mule is missing?"

"He could just have escaped."

"But what about the cow? It would be suspicious with the cow gone as well. Cows don't ever wander far."

"If we leave her, she'll holler if she ain't milked and that could bring the neighbours over too soon. We'll have to kill her."

"We could take her with us. We won't be travelling that fast and it means we could have fresh milk."

"No, she'll slow us down."

Lena sighed. "If we leave her in the shed, it most likely catch fire and she'll be burned alive."

"If it bothers you that much, I'll cut her throat first."

"If you say so, Solomon."

At daybreak they were up. Silently, they carried the corpse of the old woman, now stiffened in death, into the house. Lena made a pile of their old clothes, then splashed lamp oil on the furniture and the floor while Fiddie packed the mule's panniers. She milked the cow and added the pannikin of fresh milk to the mule's burden. Then as Lena started to throw lit matches onto the oil-soaked carpet, Fidelia released the cow to a merciful death.

CHAPTER TWENTY-TWO

Amy had found her visit with Mary Blong unsettling. The girl had had some sort of fit in her presence, but Amy thought she was acting.

"Her mother is forced to wait on her hand and foot, to the detriment apparently of the little brother, who is also clearly the apple of his father's eye," she told Murdoch. There was a sharp note in her voice. Amy was, Murdoch knew, the only girl in a family of boys.

"I tell you what, I'll have a word with Professor Broske. He might be able to give some advice, even see the girl if need be. I'm sure he'd be more than happy to do so, and it will enhance your value in the councillor's eyes . . . No, I'm only joking."

"I'm not offended. What sort of tight-laced spinster do you take me for? I'd polish Mr. Blong's shoes and anything else, if that would get me a permanent position."

Murdoch had made a sound of disbelief.

Later, he invited her to share his bed, but she declined,

pleading fatigue. She left with a deep kiss and a whispered promise and he went to bed alone but content.

The following morning, he slept late again and had to get moving in a hurry. He washed and shaved as fast as he could, swallowed a cup of cold tea left over from the night before, and jumped on his bicycle. He decided to drop off the vial of medicine that Brackenreid had given him at Dr. Ogden's house before going to the station and to ask her how he could get in touch with Professor Broske. It was a glorious spring morning, with clouds like dandelion fluff, scattered across a robin's egg blue sky, and he happily took a shortcut through the Horticultural Gardens. Buds had burst out on the trees and shrubs overnight, and flocks of starlings were twittering shrilly in the branches. He would have broken out into song himself if he hadn't feared to upset passersby, so he hummed loudly instead, until he realized he had unconsciously been singing "Ave Maria," which seemed incongruously ecclesiastical for his decidedly carnal feeling of well-being.

When he arrived at Dr. Ogden's house near the corner of Gerrard and Parliament Streets, a prim, elderly maid told him he was too late and that Dr. Ogden had already left.

"Friday is her surgery morning," she said in a disapproving tone, as if he should know that.

"Ah, yes. Did Professor Broske call for her, by any chance?"

"He did." More disapproval, but Murdoch thought it was for a different reason.

He'd packed the vial in a box with an explanatory note and he handed it to the maid. "Will you ask Dr. Ogden to telephone me at the station as soon as she can?"

The maid dropped a perfunctory curtsy. "Very well, sir. But I don't know when she will return home."

He tipped his hat and left. He hoped the good doctor and professor weren't going to go sightseeing after she'd dealt with her patients. He was curious to know what Broske would say about Mary Blong.

He bicycled back to the station, stopping briefly at a baker's shop to buy half a dozen macaroons, two of which he crammed into his mouth almost before he left the shop.

Gardiner was on duty again.

"Good afternoon, er I mean, morning, Murdoch. Your clock still isn't working properly, I see."

Murdoch grinned back at him. "Yes, it is. I had to bike up to see Dr. Ogden, which is why I am ten minutes past the hour."

"Constable Fyfer is waiting for you in the duty room. He says he's got some news regarding that case you're working on."

"Good."

"I warned him to make sure the tea was fresh," Gardiner called after him.

Murdoch tossed his hat on the hook by the door and went into the duty room, where Fyfer was filling a tea pot with boiling water.

"Good morning, sir. Lovely day, isn't it?"

"It is indeed, Fyfer, it is indeed."

He dropped the bag of macaroons on the table. "Pour me a mug of tea, there's a good lad, and you can have one of these."

The young constable did as he asked and handed a steaming mug to Murdoch.

"The sergeant says you have some news for me."

"Yes, sir." Fyfer took his notebook out of his chest pocket and flipped the pages. He glanced at Murdoch, his eyes shining with excitement. "I have found a witness, a reliable one, I swear. His name is James Whatling and he is a coachman to a Dr. Maguire who lives on Mutual Street right at the corner of Shuter Street.

You know where those private grounds are on the west side?"

"Yes. A nobby place. What's he have to say for himself?"

"When Constable Crabtree and I were going door to door on Thursday, both the doctor and Whatling were out of town. He'd taken him to Markham early that morning and got back late last night, which is why I only just got his statement. I made a point of going around before I came to work this morning."

"Please read it, Fyfer, I can hardly contain myself."

"Yes, sir, sorry, I didn't want you to wonder why I didn't give this to your earlier. Anyway, here's what the man had to say for himself. I took it down verbatim." He took up a somewhat formal pose, the notebook held in front of him like a hymn book.

"He said the following. 'I had driven Dr. Maguire, my employer for the past twelve years, to a concert at the new Massey Music Hall, which was to start at eight o'clock. The weather was inclement so rather than wait for him as I might ordinarily do, he gave permission for me to return home and he would take a public cab at the conclusion of the concert or stay at his club, which is within easy walking distance. The doctor is a bachelor so would not disappoint anyone who might be waiting up for him –' "

"My God, Fyfer, the man is long-winded. Can you get to the point?"

"Yes, sir, I'm almost there. 'I came home via my usual route at quite a fast pace because it was raining heavily and neither the horse nor I wanted to be out longer than need be' – it's coming, Mr. Murdoch, I promise. 'As I traversed in a southerly direction down Mutual Street, I crossed over the intersection at Wilton Avenue which meant I was passing the Cooke Livery stable where I now know Mr. Daniel Cooke was the victim of a savage attack –' "

"Is that how we referred to it, 'a savage attack'?"

"That didn't come from me, sir. I merely said that Mr. Cooke had been found dead under suspicious circumstances. I believe it was one or two of the newspapers that called it 'a savage attack.'"

"All right, go on."

"'As I went past the stables, I saw a woman standing under-neath a tree close to the fence that surrounds the livery. She turned on her heel on seeing me coming and walked away in the direction of Wilton Street . . .' That's not the exciting bit, sir. It's coming. 'Shortly afterwards, I saw a man walking very quickly, almost running, in fact, also going in a northerly direction, that is to say in the direction of the stables. I continued on my way, not paying too much attention –'"

"Sounds like he was paying a lot of attention, but never mind, continue."

"'I was about to turn into the gates of Dr. Maguire's estate, with some relief I must admit, when I saw yet another person also hurrying toward the stables. This man I recognized. It was Daniel Cooke himself.'" Fyfer stopped reading.

"Is that all?"

"No, sir. Sorry, Mr. Murdoch, I couldn't help but save the best to last. I asked Mr. Whatling if he could give me a description of the two people he had seen on the street before he saw Mr. Cooke. Here's what he said. 'I had the merest glimpse of the woman, who I am certain was trying to avoid detection but she was dressed in dark clothing, perhaps a mackintosh. She was of an average height. She had a black large umbrella –'"

"Oh very useful, Fyfer. No sense as to age or anything that would distinguish the poor woman from a half the female popu-lation of the city?"

"No, sir. But this is what he had to say about the second fellow, the one he thought was hurrying toward the stables."

"It was pouring with rain, who wouldn't hurry?"

"I know, sir, but I pressed him on this question. Obviously Cooke was rushing to his unknown rendezvous from his own house. The times fit perfectly if we give Whatling five minutes or so to get from Massey Hall. Did you get a good look at the man ahead of Cooke? I asks him and he says, 'Yes, I did. He wasn't carrying an umbrella. He was of medium height and of a stocky build. There is a lamp on that side of the street and as he went past his face was clearly visible in the light. There is no doubt in my mind, he was a coloured man, not young but with a hard cruel look to him as if he had lived a life of depravity.'"

"That does sound like our messenger fellow, although the life of depravity didn't impress itself on Ferguson. So we have confirmed that Mr. Cooke was running to a rendezvous set up by this mysterious darkie. It's impossible to say if the woman in the mackintosh was involved, but for the moment let's assume she was and she was waiting for them to arrive. As I've said, I think the attack required two people."

"But a woman to do something so cruel, sir? It's hard to believe."

"It is, indeed, constable, but we can't let our bias cloud our mind. The fair sex is just as capable of crime as we are. I'd like you to continue making your inquiries. Go farther afield. I want everybody in the vicinity questioned."

"Could we be dealing with a mad man, sir? I could telephone the lunatic asylum and see if they've had any elopements."

Murdoch clicked his tongue. "I can't see our fellow being insane. There's evidence of careful planning here. Besides if there were two of them, it's hard to imagine *two* mad men working well together. But there's no harm in following up on that. Give the matron my regards."

"Yes, sir. And Constable Crabtree and I have been making progress with the tradesmen. They are to a man angry with Mr. Cooke about his failure to pay and were wondering if, now he's dead, they will be properly reimbursed."

"I wouldn't count on it, not from what I've seen of his widow. I presume all their alibis check out?"

"So far they do, sir, but we still have three more to talk to. Cardington, the roofer, Kirkpatrick, the harness man, and McArthur, who delivers the wood."

"Go and do that right away then. I'll speak to Whatling. You've done a good job, Fyfer, but a second interview is often even more productive."

"Yes sir, of course." But Murdoch knew the young constable considered he had done all that could be done. He'd learn. Police work wasn't like that.

CHAPTER TWENTY-THREE

Given how garrulous he was, Murdoch had expected Whatling to be an older man, but he wasn't, probably barely thirty. He was in his shirt sleeves out in the yard of the coach house, polishing the carriage. He didn't look pleased at being interrupted. Murdoch introduced himself.

"I don't know what more I can add to what I already told your constable," said Whatling.

"That was most helpful, but there were a couple of things I'd like to clarify."

"Such as?"

"First off, I'd like to confirm the time when you saw the woman by the stable and the coloured man and Mr. Cooke. You had taken your employer to Massey Hall, I understand, and that would have been for an eight-o'clock concert, I presume."

Whatling continued his work, shaking out the cushions from inside the carriage.

"That's right. He's a very punctual man, is Dr. Maguire. Can't stand to be late, so whenever I take him anywhere I make sure to leave in plenty of time, to allow for unexpected delays. You can't be too careful in this job, the horse might throw a shoe, for instance, then what do you do if you've only allowed yourself a few minutes to get there before the curtain rises?"

He slapped at the cushions with a carpet beater, and Murdoch took advantage of the short break in his speech.

"So what time would you say you were crossing Wilton on your way back?"

"Well now, I let off the doctor at ten minutes before eight, a little later than I would have wanted but there were a lot of carriages arriving at the same time and we had to wait in line to get to the entrance. I couldn't let him off sooner because of the rain . . . so I'd say it took me only five or six minutes from the concert hall to home, which means I would have been there shortly before eight o'clock."

Murdoch was beginning to dread asking another question, but he pressed on.

"You said that you saw a woman standing underneath the tree across from the livery and she was trying to avoid being identified."

"That's right. That's what I told the constable. She –"

"It was an inhospitable night. Could she have just been in a hurry to get out of the rain?"

Whatling looked triumphant. "When I first noticed her, she was standing, distinctly standing, and waiting under that tree on the corner. She didn't move until she heard the sound of my carriage, then she scooted away up Mutual Street, and in my humble opinion, she deliberately bent her umbrella in my direction so I couldn't see her."

"Was she a white woman?"

"To be honest, I didn't see her face clearly. She was as well dressed as any white woman in a long, dark mackintosh, but, no, the gospel truth is I didn't really see her face."

"How close behind her was the man?"

"He was at the bottom of the road as if he'd just turned onto Mutual Street from Shuter."

"You described him as a coloured man, not young, and with a look of depravity. Can you tell me what constitutes that sort of look, in your opinion?"

Whatling frowned. "Not just my opinion. I've seen pictures of criminals and they had the same sort of expression. His face was all squeezed together like this." He demonstrated, but Murdoch thought he looked as if he had tasted something unpleasant, got some dirt in his eyes, or was straining on a commode. Depravity was not the first thing that came to mind.

"One thing that did intrigue me, Mr. Whatling, was that you got such a good look at the man. Was he not wearing a hat?"

"Yes, he was, a black fedora, as I recall, but as I drove past he looked up at me, fearful like, and as we were right by the street-lamp I saw him very clearly. Remember, I'm up in my seat so I'm looking down at him. I thought to myself, I thought, You are a thoroughly bad character as ever I saw one and I'm going to make good and sure all the doors are properly locked tonight."

"I see. You said he was of medium height and rather stocky."

"That's right. He was taller than me, who is medium height, you might say, and probably not as tall as you, who would be considered a tallish man."

He replaced the cushions in the carriage, then breathed on the side lamp of the carriage and polished it with a clean cloth.

"And Mr. Cooke, who you said was quite close behind this coloured man, did he catch up with him at any point?"

"Not that I saw, but I was turning into the driveway by then so they were out of my view. But I thought it odd that Mr. Cooke didn't call out a good night to me. He's familiar with the carriage. He just looked like he was a man in fear for his life and he wouldn't have noticed if the Prince himself in his royal coach was going down Mutual Street."

Murdoch sighed. "Can you tell me why you assumed Mr. Cooke was a man in fear of his life?"

Whatling hunched his shoulders, tucked his chin into his collar, and trotted a few paces around the yard. "He was walking like this."

This demonstration was slightly more convincing than the previous one but could as easily have been depicting a man who was facing into a heavy rain and getting soaked.

"Was he also wearing a hat?"

"No, which I thought was odd as it was pouring, but he wasn't in his right state of mind, if you ask me. Besides, we know Mr. Cooke was going to meet his death, don't we?" added Whatling.

We do now, thought Murdoch, but you didn't know it then. It was unfortunate that Fyfer hadn't got to the coachman before he'd heard any details about what had happened in the livery. He wondered how much Whatling had embroidered, not maliciously, but like so many witnesses, convinced after the fact about details they didn't think of at the time. There wasn't much else to be got from him, although the man looked as if he could go on talking ad infinitum. Perhaps being a coachman to a bachelor was a lonely job.

"Are you married, Mr. Whatling?"

"No, still hopeful. Why do you ask?"

"No reason, just getting all our facts straight. Are you acquainted with the Cooke household by any chance?"

"On occasion I drop in on my day off and have a chin with the butler, Ferguson. He's from over the pond and my father was from there too, so we like to share stories, as it were."

"And you have seen him since Mr. Cooke's death, I presume?"

"Yes, I saw him when I went over to the house to give my condolences to madam." Whatling was starting to look restive under all the questions. He wrung out his cloth in the pail of water and pointedly started to wipe down the wheels. Murdoch wasn't finished with him yet.

"How did you hear about Mr. Cooke's death?"

"Mr. Ferguson came by to tell me the news on Thursday night. He was dreadfully upset, poor fellow. He felt quite responsible because he was the one who had taken Mr. Cooke the message from the negro who came to the door. But I told him it was hardly his fault, was it? How was he to know the man was a murderer?"

"Quite so. We don't even know if that was the case ourselves."

Whatling gaped at him in genuine astonishment. "Who else would it be? When I realized I had seen the very man myself heading for the stables, we knew he was the one. The woman was probably in cahoots with him or was set to keep a lookout."

"Did Mr. Ferguson have any theories as to why somebody would attack Mr. Cooke or what the message was that drew him away so urgently?"

Whatling rubbed hard at a muddy splotch. "You probably should talk to him yourself." He paused and looked at Murdoch slyly. "I must say, he did tell me, in confidence of course, that Mr. Cooke had dealings with a fast crowd. This wasn't the first time Ferguson had taken messages."

"Really? Did he say what the others were?"

"No, he didn't, but he suspects they were from local touts. Mr. Cooke had a taste for gambling."

"Horses?"

"Horses and other things. Whatever sport was up, apparently. Lacrosse, boxing, skulling." Whatling gave Murdoch another look. "He even made some bets on the police games last summer, which of course he shouldn't have." He shook his head. "Poor man wasn't very successful, according to Mr. Ferguson. It caused, er" – he coughed delicately – "it caused, shall we say, some disagreements with Mrs. Cooke, who was dead against it. As are most of the ladies."

He pulled a handsome silver watch from his waistcoat pocket and consulted it. "I'm sorry, sir, but I must get on with my business. Dr. Maguire is going out to dine this evening. Is that all you need to ask me?"

Murdoch hadn't noticed the coachman being appreciably slowed down in his work, but he thought he'd got as much as he could at the moment.

"Thank you, Mr. Whatling, you have been very helpful. I may have other questions at a later date, and one of the constables will subpoena you to testify at the inquest. That should take place in a few days. We will let you know."

"Testify? Oh dear, I'm not sure the doctor will like that. He has his reputation to consider."

Murdoch was irritated. "First of all, it's the law. You have no choice. And, secondly, I don't see that you presenting your evidence honestly to the coroner will in any way reflect on your employer. Quite the opposite. You will be respected and admired for your acute observations."

Whatling looked doubtful. "You say that, sir, but you're not a coachman. People don't want their servants to be the centre of attention, do they? Especially not when murder is involved."

CHAPTER TWENTY-FOUR

F rom Whatling, Murdoch went directly to Cooke's house. Ferguson opened the door to him and flinched back when he saw who it was.

"Mrs. Cooke is not at home. She has gone to the stables to conduct affairs."

"It's actually you I'd like to talk to, Mr. Ferguson."

"Oh dear. Perhaps you could step inside then."

Murdoch did so and the butler closed the door quickly behind him.

"People do like to gossip, don't they?" said Ferguson. They stood awkwardly in the hall. "How may I help with your inquiries, sir?"

Murdoch could see the man trying to pull the formality of his position around him like a tattered cloak.

"I just wanted to go over your statement again. If you don't mind, I'll sit here on the bench." Murdoch sat down and took out his notebook. "You said that the person who brought the message to Mr. Cooke on the night he died was a coloured man?"

"Yes, sir. That's right."

"You described him as young?"

Ferguson pursed his lips. "It was dark and it's a little hard to say with coloureds. Perhaps it would be more accurate to say of middle age or more."

"What sort of build? Skinny? Fat?"

"Definitely not fat. I'd say, rather on the stocky side."

"And this was no one you recognized?"

"No."

"You have met Elijah Green and Thomas Talbert, the men who work at the stables, I presume?"

"Yes, on one or two occasions I believe both of them have come here to see Mr. Cooke about some matter of other."

"And you're sure it was neither man who brought the message that night?"

Ferguson pondered. "As sure as one can be about these matters. As I have said, it was quite dark in the porch and our interaction was very brief."

"The message was in an envelope, was it not?"

"Yes, sir."

"We have been unable as yet to find either the contents or this envelope. Did Mr. Cooke leave it here by chance?"

"I believe not. Lucy would have found it and handed it to me. Besides, I waited in the dining-room pantry to see if there would be a reply and I saw Mr. Cooke placing the letter back in the envelope and putting it in his inner pocket."

"Was there anything else that you noticed that might have come back to you on further reflection?"

"As a matter of fact, there was something. Mrs. Cooke spoke to Mr. Cooke quite sharply that he was going out so abruptly without finishing his supper, but he just said something like, 'I've got to go to the stables, I won't be long.'"

This was new information, and again Murdoch wondered how much Ferguson's recollections were being influenced by Whatling's and vice versa.

"It was raining heavily at that time. Did Mr. Cooke take a mackintosh with him or his hat, or even an umbrella?"

"He didn't take anything. I was about to hand him the umbrella, but he had gone out of the door before I had the opportunity."

Murdoch decided to get to the point. "I've heard that he liked to gamble. Did you know that?"

"My employers affairs are none of my business, sir."

"Of course, but that's not what I asked you, I merely wondered if you knew about his habits. Your friend, Mr. Whatling, seems quite aware of them."

Ferguson flushed. "As I said earlier, people do like to gossip."

"Was that a yes or a no answer?"

"In my position, one cannot fail to pay attention to visitors, and I must admit that I have seen some unsavoury men coming to the door."

"A yes, then?"

Ferguson nodded. Murdoch wanted to shake it out of him, but he also knew that he was afraid for his job. If it got back to Mrs. Cooke that he had been telling tales, she might dismiss him at once and with no references. He was at an age where finding other work would be difficult.

"Thank you Mr. Ferguson. You have been most helpful."

"Shall I tell Mrs. Cooke that you called?"

"I'm actually going to the stables now to see if I can find her."

Ferguson let him out with the same furtive movements as before, and Murdoch got on his bicycle and headed for the livery.

Mrs. Cooke was in the office, seated at the desk. She was dressed in mourning black but had tossed back her crepe veil. One of the cabbies, a lanky, rough-haired fellow, was standing in front of her, looking like a defiant schoolboy. Murdoch knocked on the window and when she saw who it was, she waved to him to come in.

"It wasn't me, missus, I swear," the man was saying angrily. "I've got a wife and five children, I'm not going to be cavorting all over the country in the middle of the night."

Mrs. Cooke greeted Murdoch. "You've come at a good time, Mr. Murdoch. One of my employees is a cheat and a liar, and I am just trying to determine which one it is." She wagged her finger at the cabbie. "This man is a detective. He'll be able to tell if you're lying or not."

The cabbie justifiably glared at Murdoch.

"I might be of more use if you tell me what this is all about, Mrs. Cooke," said Murdoch.

"I have discovered that one of my cab drivers is returning to the stables in the middle of the night and stealing one of the horse-and-carriages. I am trying to determine who is the culprit."

"Begging your pardon, ma'am," said the cabbie, "but how do you know it was one of us as did that? For that matter, how do you know the horse has been taken out?"

"Because, Mr. Wallace, when I came in early this morning, I discovered the carriage you had hired was quite filthy. Simply covered in mud. As for the horse you usually take out, it seemed quite worn out as well."

"That horse is ready for the knackers. I can't get any work out of him. In fact, if you check the sheet you'll see I signed off early, which is what I had to do as he wouldn't go no faster than a turtle no matter how I whipped him. As for the carriage being dirty, speak to Elijah Green. Perhaps he didn't do his job last night."

"I did. He says all of the carriages were cleaned before he went home. I am of the mind to believe him."

Wallace shrugged. "Well, I tell you it weren't me. You can ask my missus if you don't believe me."

Mrs. Cooke's expression showed clearly what she thought of that, but she made no comment.

"Have you spoken to all the cabbies?" Murdoch asked.

"Yes, I have, and they all deny any knowledge."

"Did you ask Musgrave?" snapped Wallace.

Mrs. Cooke stiffened. "Certainly I did. Why do you single him out?"

"No reason except I'd like to make sure nobody's playing favourites in this here inquiry."

Murdoch saw an angry flush sweep across Mrs. Cooke's face. She was obviously aware of the gossip surrounding her and Musgrave.

"You might not consider it so serious, detective, but it is theft. How dare somebody take my carriages without permission. I would like you to pursue the matter."

Murdoch shrugged. "I wish I could be of more help, Mrs. Cooke, but I can see no obvious explanation. At the moment, my other investigation is my priority. I was actually wanting to have a few words with you in private."

"What about?"

Murdoch gazed at her in astonishment. "Your husband's death, ma'am."

"Quite so." Her jet ear bobs jingled as she swung her head. "You can go, Mr. Wallace. But I am warning you, in my opinion, my husband tended to be too lax and I have no intention of continuing in that manner."

And you're going to lose a lot of your employees, thought Murdoch.

The cabbie left, anger in every movement.

Mrs. Cooke flashed Murdoch a self-satisfied smile. "You have to be firm with these people. They are like children and think they can get away with anything unless you show them from the beginning that they cannot. I'm sure some unscrupulous man thought he would take advantage of my misfortune to cheat me, but whoever it is has another think coming."

She took out a black-bordered handkerchief from her reticule and dabbed at her eyes, which seemed quite dry. Murdoch almost expected her to throw her veil over her face as she transformed from hard-headed businesswoman to bereft widow.

"Have you made any progress with the case?" she asked.

"We are still gathering information, ma'am, which is why I wanted to speak to you."

"What now?"

"I asked you before if your husband was a gambler and you denied it."

"Of course I denied it. He was no such thing."

"I have heard from different sources that, indeed, he was. That he was deeply involved with a gambling crowd."

Mrs. Cooke drew in her breath sharply, rather like a fierce horse. "Who told you such dreadful lies? He was a church-going man and as honest as the day is long." She leaned her head in her hands. "I can't believe such slander is being spoken about him. Who told you?" she demanded again.

Murdoch wasn't about to lose Ferguson his job. "My intent is not to malign your husband but to find out if he had enemies who wanted to do him harm."

"Well, I have no such knowledge. He was a most respected and loved individual. It is as obvious as the nose on your face that he surprised a thief, a cruel and, if I may use the word, perverted man."

"Mrs. Cooke, I have no desire to add to your unhappiness at this time, but your husband received a message that so alarmed him, he rushed from your house. Perhaps his assailant was a thief, but whoever it was knew enough about your husband to lure him to the stables. We have not found that message, so we are in the dark as to its contents."

"I assume he was told that something was amiss, one of the horses taken ill, for instance."

"Wouldn't he have mentioned that to you? It would seem natural to do so."

"My husband kept business matters to himself. He didn't want to bother me with such things."

"And yet you knew exactly how much money was in his safe."

Mrs. Cooke turned quite red again. Tough as she was, she couldn't control that telltale flush. "That is different. That was our livelihood, sick horses are not my concern, they are Elijah Green's."

"Mr. Musgrave told me that he overheard a quarrel between your husband and Green. Do you know what they were arguing about?"

"His wages probably. Green has worked for us for many years, and in my view he is quite adequately paid but you know how these people are, they're never content. Mr. Cooke did mention to me on more than one occasion that Green was pressing him for a raise."

Murdoch felt like catching her in her contradictions but refrained. Speaking of being a betting man, he would wager a week's wages himself that Adelaide Cooke was the kind of woman who would winkle every detail of business out of her husband. She wasn't sitting behind that desk with absolute authority for no reason. Whether this sharing included Cooke's little sideline, Murdoch wasn't sure.

"I also heard that you yourself recently had quite a barney with your husband."

For a moment she looked as if she would explode into a flurry of protestations, but instead she nodded. "I regret to say that is true. It was nothing, just a squabble that married people have from time to time. I wished he would spend more time at home and he said he had the business to take care of. It was nothing more than that."

Although she was presenting it as only a trifle, Murdoch had the feeling she was basically telling the truth. However, as the post-mortem had revealed, Cooke had contracted a venereal disease at some point. His adventures hadn't been limited to placing wagers.

Mrs. Cooke tapped her fingers on the desk. "Are you thinking of arresting Elijah?"

"I do not have a suspect in mind at the moment, ma'am."

"Good," she said. "I can't afford to be without a stable hand right now, and he is quite a reliable worker."

CHAPTER TWENTY-FIVE

Crabtree had written out a list of hotels and guest houses that were within comfortable walking distance of Cooke's Livery, and Murdoch decided that the nearest of them would be his next call. Even though he knew Ferguson and Whatling had talked over the events of Wednesday night, and had probably influenced each other, he saw no reason to doubt Whatling's statement. The negro messenger was likely the same man the coachman had seen heading up Mutual Street in the direction of the stables. As for the woman by the tree, whether she was connected with the case or just an innocent passerby, at this point, Murdoch couldn't tell.

Also gnawing at the back of his mind was an incident that had shaken the city two years earlier. A young man from an affluent and respectable family had been shot on the threshold of his own home. The victim had not died immediately and was able to give a description of his assailant, but for a while the police went off on the wrong track, searching for a slim, dark-skinned male. Shortly afterwards, a mulatto woman confessed to the crime. She had been seen on several occasions dressed in men's clothes, and it was difficult to know what had shocked the city more, the shooting or the masquerade.

That particular woman had passed easily as a man, and Murdoch wondered if Cooke's messenger was in disguise. Both the messenger and the coloured woman who had inquired at the livery had been described as stocky, middle-aged, medium height. The raspy voice that Ferguson had mentioned was suspicious. But then, heaven forbid, it could be the other way around. The maid who had come to the stables might be a man, for all he knew.

He braked, stopped, and looked over his list. The closest hotel to the livery was the Elliott House, on the corner of Church and Shuter. It had the reputation for excellent service at a high price and for catering to American visitors, the proprietor being a Yankee himself. The widow that Green had mentioned seeking a cab could afford to keep her servant well dressed, and the maid had told Green they were American. He turned along Shuter and soon reached Church Street. To walk from there to Cooke's Livery, he guessed, would take ten minutes at the most.

Elliott House was a large, gracious building, which sat in private grounds dotted with shrubs and well-placed benches, and he could see some of the guests walking on the sun-dappled lawn, enjoying the air. He parked his bike against the low iron fence that ringed the property and walked up the path to the door. A doorman, his back as straight as a sentry's, was standing on the steps and he swept the door open for Murdoch to enter.

"Reception straight ahead, sir," he said. Murdoch wondered if this little courtesy merited a tip but decided against it. Another young man with a ruler-straight parting in his black hair was standing behind the desk engaged in a telephone conversation.

"Yes, ma'am, certainly. I'll make a note of that immediately. Have a good journey, it will be most delightful to see you again."

He hung up, saw Murdoch, and greeted him effusively in a high-pitched voice.

"How may I help you, sir?"

Murdoch took his calling card out of his pocket and handed it to the young man, whose name plate identified him as Mr. Oatley.

"I'm trying to find two people who I have reason to believe are guests here, or were until recently."

Oatley examined the calling card and looked at Murdoch apprehensively. "Not counterfeiters, are they? We had trouble last year, but I thought the gang had been broken up."

"No, not counterfeiters. More like witnesses that I'd like to question. One is a widow from America, the other is her servant, a negress, middle-aged, medium height, dark skin. Are they staying here, perchance?"

Oatley frowned. "Oh dear, you're talking about Mrs. Dittman. She arrived last week from New York. She does have a coloured servant with her. She's the only one of our guests who answers to that description. Mrs. Dittman herself is not well and regrettably she has seldom been out since she got here. Is she in, er, is she in difficulties?"

"I don't believe so, but I would like to speak to her."

Oatley looked nervous and his voice squeaked even more. "Is it absolutely necessary, detective? We rely on our unblemished reputation for catering to a good class of people."

"I shall be most discreet, I assure you. But, yes, it is quite necessary." Murdoch was tempted to ruffle the clerk's smooth feathers by telling him he was working on a case of assault and suspicious death, but he was afraid the clerk might have hysterics.

Oatley stood on his tiptoes, leaned over the counter, and pointed with the tip of his gold-nibbed pen. "She is in the dining room for her luncheon. The waiter will take you to her."

"And her maid?"

"She is eating in the servants' hall downstairs."

For a moment, the young man's eyes showed a spark of avid curiosity. "Am I to know the nature of the case, detective?"

"Not at this moment, sir. I cannot disclose details."

With a nod, Murdoch headed for the dining room. Another liveried servant opened the door for him.

There was only a smattering of guests present, which gave the pristine white tablecloths and silver cutlery the opportunity to shine in the sunlight pouring in from the deep windows. The wall covering was flowered burgundy, the thick carpet was also lush with flowers. The room spoke of money. Lots of it.

"May I show you to your table, sir?" A waiter, as formally dressed as a clergyman, stepped toward him. He was holding a velvet-covered menu in his hand.

"I'm not eating, thank you. I'm looking for a Mrs. Dittman. Mr. Oatley said I would find her here."

With the merest of sighs, the waiter returned the menu to the podium by the door. "Mrs. Dittman is the lady seated by the window. Come this way."

"No, don't bother. You have another guest to deal with."

A portly man had entered the dining room. The waiter greeted him warmly and led him away. Murdoch stood for a moment, wanting to get a look at the woman in question, but either by choice or because she had been assigned that particular spot, she was partly obscured by a large potted fern. All Murdoch could see was the back of a thin woman, soberly dressed in grey. She was wearing a widow's bonnet, but she had lifted the short veil while she ate. Her clothes signified she was no longer in deepest mourning, but it was anybody's guess, with Her Majesty Queen Victoria as a model, how long she had been widowed.

Murdoch walked over to the table, his footsteps completely muffled by the carpet.

"Excuse me, ma'am."

He hadn't intended to startle her, but she jumped and twisted around to look at him. Murdoch removed his hat. "Mrs. Dittman?"

"Yes. Who are you?"

"Detective William Murdoch, ma'am. I wonder if I might have a few words with you?"

"What about?"

She had the abrupt, straightforward manner of speaking that he tended to associate with American ladies. Murdoch hesitated.

"It's a rather private matter, ma'am. Do you mind if I sit down?"

"Not as long as you don't mind if I finish my meal. I have paid enough for it and I don't like cold bacon, even if you Canadians do."

"Of course, ma'am. Please continue. I wouldn't interrupt you in this way if it weren't a matter of some urgency."

"Pull up that chair, then."

Mrs. Dittman must have been well into middle age, but she was still a strikingly handsome woman with strong, chiselled features and well-shaped hazel eyes. She would have been more so except for the gauntness of her cheeks and eyes that were too deeply shadowed. Her dark hair, drawn back into a knot at the nape of her neck, was liberally streaked with grey but was still thick and abundant.

He sat down, and she went back to her meal.

"I understand you have a maid, a negress?"

"That's right, Faith. The best there is. Why? Surely there's no problem with her staying with me. I'm not well. I need her. She's not eating in here. She's in the servants' kitchen, but Mr. Hirsh said he had no objection to her sleeping in my suite. It costs enough."

Murdoch was a little taken aback by the rush of words. "I'm not here to question your personal arrangements, ma'am. The reason I asked about your maid is because I am investigating a suspicious death and I have to track down anybody who might be considered a witness to the case."

Mrs. Dittman dabbed at her mouth with the napkin. "You are being most mysterious, sir. What suspicious death are you referring to and how could Faith possibly be a witness? We are visitors here."

"Did your maid go to Cooke's Livery last week, to try to hire you a cab for the evening?"

"What day are you referring to?"

"A week ago, Tuesday last."

"Ah yes. I did not know that was the name of the place but, yes, I sent her to find a cab. I wanted to attend a special lecture by a visiting professor of physiology, but as it turned out I was not well enough to go out. Why is it of import?"

"The stable hand said a woman of her description was inquiring at the livery on that particular night, and I need to confirm his statement."

"I see." Again she wiped the corners of her mouth with the napkin. "I do hope you're not going to tell me he is the one who has suffered an unnatural death?"

"No, ma'am. It is the owner who has died. His name was Daniel Cooke. You don't know him by any chance, do you?"

She frowned. "How could I know of him? As I just said, I am a stranger here."

She pushed her plate forward and a waiter who had not been in Murdoch's view suddenly appeared and whisked it away.

"May I bring over the sweet trolley, ma'am?"

"No, thank you. I have had more than enough."

In spite of her insistence on continuing to eat and the price of the meal, Murdoch saw she had left most of the food on her plate.

"I do beg your pardon if I spoiled your luncheon, ma'am."

"You didn't. I lose my appetite very quickly these days, but that's neither here nor there. Is there anything else you want to ask me?"

"I don't think so, but I would like to have a word with your maid."

"Faith? She won't add anything to what I've just said."

"I'd just like to hear from her personally, if you don't mind, ma'am. It won't take long."

"Very well. They probably won't let her in here and you probably don't want to go to the servants' hall. We'll have to go to my room. I'll have Oatley ring for her."

She stood up, pulled the veil down across her face, and walked to the door. Her stride was steady enough, but Murdoch had the impression that it cost her something to move like that.

CHAPTER TWENTY-SIX

Mrs. Dittman's room was on the ground floor at the rear of the hotel. She didn't wait for Murdoch but led the way down the hall, unlocked her door and went in, leaving him to follow. It was an airy room, elegantly furnished, and by the look of it one of the more expensive apartments in the hotel.

"Please take a seat, Mr., er, what was your name again?"

"Murdoch, ma'am. Detective William Murdoch."

She went over to the windows and began to draw the curtains.

"I find the sunlight hard on my eyes. I hope you don't mind," she said.

He made a noncommittal nod, noting as the curtains closed that the French doors opened onto a small patio and a wide lawn. Easy to come and go unseen.

"Do you have other servants, ma'am?"

"Not travelling with me, if that's what you mean. I have a housekeeper and a groom back in New York. Don't tell me you want to question them as well?"

Murdoch smiled benignly. "Not at all, ma'am. I was only inquiring because Mrs. Cooke reported a strange visitor the night her husband died. Her butler hadn't seen him before but thought the man was a negro."

"Really? Surely Toronto isn't so devoid of coloured people that every negro is related to every other? Just because I employ a negress doesn't mean I am responsible for all the darkies in the city. Both my housekeeper and groom are of Irish stock, by the way. I took in Faith when she was a young woman, and she has been as reliable as her name. Ah, here she is."

The door opened and a coloured woman entered. She was neatly dressed, middle-aged, medium height, and rather stout. She was carrying a tray with a silver coffee pot and china on it.

"I thought you'd like your coffee. Mr. Oatley mentioned that you didn't take any in the dining room."

She had a rather harsh accent that Murdoch had heard before from New Yorkers. She glanced over at Murdoch. "I didn't know you had a visitor, madam. Shall I fetch an extra cup?"

"No, thank you, please don't bother," Murdoch said quickly.

"This is Mr. Murdoch, Faith. He's a local detective and he wants to ask you some questions."

"Really, madam? Concerning what?"

"Last week you tried to hire a carriage for me from one of the local stables."

"Ah, yes, I remember, madam. Tuesday it was. We wanted one for the next day, but they weren't available. Is there something wrong?"

Murdoch answered. "The proprietor of that particular livery has died under suspicious circumstances and I am investigating the case, Miss . . . ?" He waited for one of them to fill in the maid's surname but neither did. "I understand that you had a conversation with the stable hand who was in the barn at the time? His name is Green."

Faith studied him with her dark eyes, but she didn't answer immediately. She poured out some coffee for her mistress first and handed it to her.

"Bring my medicine, will you, Faith? I hope you don't mind, Mr. Murdoch. I am supposed to take it at a regular time. Go on talking, though, you have our attention."

He might have their attention, thought Murdoch, but he didn't have control of the situation. Mrs. Dittman was very much in command. He waited while the maid went to the table at the side of the bed and returned with a brown bottle. She poured some of the contents into her mistress's coffee. Murdoch thought the drink looked like brandy, but that could be considered medicine, he supposed.

"Do you recall the man I am referring to?"

Faith addressed him without looking at him.

"It is rather vague in my mind, but I believe I do. I never knew his name, but if you're talking about a coloured man, big build, soft spoke, it must be this Green cove."

"It was a wet night on Tuesday. I wonder why you didn't make use of the hotel telephone for your inquiry."

Mrs. Dittman answered, "Faith is frequently confined indoors because of my state of health. She needed some fresh air."

"It wasn't raining hard when I went," added the maid. "I ain't, pardon me, I isn't made of sugar."

"According to Mr. Green, you also asked after one of the local ministers. A Reverend Archer. Is he an acquaintance of yours?"

"I have never met the man. But somebody at my own church told me about him. I hear he's a powerful good preacher. I likes a lively sermon so I thought I'd introduce myself."

"Faith is quite a devout Baptist, aren't you, dear?"

"I am."

"Just one more question then, ma'am. Did you notice anybody else on the street near the livery? Anybody at all?"

Faith pursed her lips, thinking. "No, can't say I did. There might have been somebody, but I didn't pay no mind."

Murdoch closed his notebook. "Thank you so much for your help."

He stood up.

"Show the gentleman out, will you, Faith? Thank you, Mr. Murdoch. You have livened up a rather dreary day."

"I'm glad to hear it. It must be disappointing to visit a strange city and not be able to get around as you must have hoped."

He was being deliberately disingenuous, but she wasn't in the least put out.

"Yes, it is. But we are planning to hire a Bath chair and Faith will wheel me. I am eager to see the cathedrals, in particular. After all, Toronto is the city of spires, is it not? Unfortunately, the weather has been against us, until now."

The maid was standing at the door, holding it open for Murdoch.

"Good afternoon to you then, ma'am."

Mrs. Dittman bowed her head graciously while Faith stared straight ahead.

She'd answered readily enough, but he thought it odd that she'd shown no curiosity about his questions. Usually people were agog to hear lurid details of deaths. It might be because she was a servant and didn't feel she had the right to ask. On the other hand, her mistress hadn't inquired either.

Inside the room, Mrs. Dittman added some more brandy from the brown bottle into her coffee cup.

"Do you want some, Fiddie?"

"I won't say no to that. My nerves are fair frayed. I didn't expect no detéctive to be sitting here jawing with you."

"I had no way to warn you but you were quite superb. Bernhardt herself couldn't have done better."

She poured them each a full glass of brandy.

"*Oh be joyful*," said Mrs. Dittman.

Faith laughed. "You got me out of an awkward spot there when he asked why we hadn't used the telephone. But butter wouldn't melt in your mouth." She imitated Mrs. Dittman's softer voice. "Toronto *is* the city of spires, is it not? Where'd you hear that?"

"I read it in the guidebook. Do you know there are one hundred and seventy-two churches in Toronto now."

"And most of them dull as dishwater, I'll wager."

Mrs. Dittman smiled. "Seriously, Fiddie, the detective struck me as a shrewd man."

"Not if he's a policeman, he ain't."

"He did have nice manners."

"Phony. Besides he didn't have nice manners to me."

"I thought he treated us the same."

Faith hooted. "You might think so, but I can tell the difference. 'Yes, ma'am, no ma'am, to you, yes, miss, no miss to me.'"

"I don't think so . . . Oh never mind, it's not worth arguing about."

"If he's as clever as you say, shall we fly the coop then?"

"No, of course not. We haven't finished our task yet. When that's done, we'll go."

"Are you up to it?"

For an answer, Mrs. Dittman beckoned her maid to sit beside her on the couch. "By myself, no. But with you beside me, my rod and my staff, I am invincible and have always been so."

Faith laughed out loud. "You and your fancy talk. You never stop, do you? Here, lie back and put your feet up on my lap and I'll rub them for you. I can tell you've been in pain today."

"Pour some more brandy and it will all be forgotten. Besides, I have eaten the sweet meat of revenge and that has soothed my pain."

"There you go again."

CHAPTER TWENTY-SEVEN

Amy lifted up Jacob from the sink where she had been bathing him and handed him over to Murdoch, who was standing at the ready with a warm towel. James was already bathed and dried and lay contentedly in his cradle watching them. Charlie and Katie had gone out for the evening to celebrate their engagement, and Amy and Murdoch were taking care of the twins. It had taken a bit of persuading to get Katie out of the door, but with repeated assurances from Amy (*It won't be too much trouble*) that the boys would be well taken care of (*Oh, I know that*), the two of them had left.

Murdoch was enjoying himself. "I remember my mother giving Bertie a bath. He was always afraid of water and she'd get me to distract him by blowing bubbles." He sighed. "I took a lot of pride in getting him to laugh, and momma often let me do the whole business myself."

"Poor Bertie," Amy said softly.

"Yes, he didn't have much of a life, sad little titch."

After they became lovers, Murdoch and Amy had spent many hours talking far into the night about their own lives. She had been born into a well-educated family, the only girl and the youngest of five, both mother and father teachers themselves. "I knew from childhood that I wanted to be a teacher and the best I could be. My father, bless him, was considered slightly mad by the folks in the town because of his unorthodox habits and teaching methods, but he was well loved. He died far too early, and my mother grieved herself to death. As I was only twelve at the time, I considered that very selfish of her and I still do. My brothers all went into professional life, two doctors, a lawyer, a clergyman, very High Church. Except for my brother, the lawyer, who is distinctly eccentric, I cannot understand why they are so conventional, considering how we were brought up, but they are and they do not approve of my bohemian ways."

Even though she had said it lightly, Murdoch thought he detected a hint of wistfulness in her voice and he had pulled her close to him.

"Well, I thoroughly approve."

She tweaked his nose. "That's because I come to your bed without benefit of clergy."

"No, it's not. I'd make us legitimate any time you say the word."

"Never. Sorry, Will. I can't."

He'd been hurt by that answer, but as she had taken away the sting by sitting astride him and kissing him, he recovered quickly.

On another occasion, he had told her some of his own tales; of the cruel treatment his father, Harry, meted out to all the family, including his wife; of his sister, Susannah, who had fled to a cloistered convent as a young girl and died there; of Bertie, a simpleton, and the youngest, who shortly after their mother's premature death had suffered a heart attack when he was only twelve years old.

"Only Harry is left and who knows where he is?"

It was Amy's turn to comfort him. "Perhaps someday that look will be gone from your eyes, Will."

Jacob was wriggling in his arms so Murdoch placed him in his cradle and rocked it gently.

"How do you like your new beds, boys?" he asked them.

The single cradle Katie had arrived with was far too small, and Charlie had immediately set to work to make two new ones. Murdoch had done his part by painting them light blue. He'd even sketched galloping black horses across the headboards. Amy had provided material for Katie to quilt, and now the twins lay, plump and well cared for by their new family.

Amy cleaned up the bathing area while Murdoch rocked both cradles.

"I hope Charlie and Katie do stay here. I'd miss these little fellows." He addressed the twins. "Even though you do wake me up at all hours, don't you? Not to mention periodically plucking the hair out of my moustache." James dribbled happily at him. "Ha, you think that's funny, do you? Wait till you've got more hair, I might have a go at pulling that."

He suddenly became aware that Amy was watching him. She had an expression on her face that he couldn't quite read, but before he could ask her what was wrong, they heard knocking at the front door.

"Oh no, I hope that's nobody from the station come to fetch you," said Amy.

"I'll answer it."

The knocking was repeated.

"Hold on, I'm coming."

He opened the door expecting it to be indeed an urgent

message from the station, but to his surprise, there on the doorstep were Dr. Julia Ogden and Professor Broske. It was the professor who had been doing the impatient knocking as his hand was already raised to knock again. "Good evening, Mr. Murdoch," said Dr. Ogden. "I hope you don't mind us disturbing you, but we were out for an evening stroll. I've been showing Marc, er, Professor Broske, some of the delights our city has to offer."

It flashed through Murdoch's mind that perhaps that meant they'd gone walking in the Mount Pleasant Cemetery on the off chance of stumbling over some old bones.

"I've examined the objects you asked me to and analyzed both the piece of sacking and that potion you brought me and I thought you'd be interested in the results," continued Dr. Ogden.

"And I understand you wanted to ask my opinion about something," said Broske. "So here we are, at your service."

Murdoch stepped back from the threshold.

"Please come in."

Broske gestured to Julia to go in front of him and they entered the hall. They were both wearing summer boaters and the professor had on a pale yellow linen suit that was undeniably foreign.

"One of my fellow boarders and I are taking care of Mrs. Tibbett's twins for the evening," said Murdoch as he led the way down the hall. "We are in the kitchen."

Broske's eyes brightened. "Twins! How marvellous. I am always happy to encounter them. I have conducted several experiments with twins that have yielded remarkable results."

Murdoch could feel himself stiffen. Given what he'd already seen of the professor's experiments, he wouldn't let him get within ten feet of the boys.

He pushed open the kitchen door. Amy turned around to greet them and put her finger to her lips. "They are almost asleep."

Murdoch made gestures to indicate they would go upstairs and Amy nodded.

"I'll come up shortly," she whispered.

Broske was casting acquisitive glances at the twins, but he kept quiet and the three of them trooped out again.

Murdoch ushered his guests into his sitting room.

"I'd offer you some tea, but I'd better not go down to the kitchen just yet."

"Do not fret, Mr. Murdoch. I am so experienced a traveller I always come prepared," said Broske, and he took a small silver flask from his inside pocket. "This is what in my country we call pomace brandy or, more popularly, grappa. It is not as smooth as the brandy I have sampled in Canada, but consequently, one drinks less. May I pour you a little, Miss Julia?"

"No, no, thank you." Dr. Ogden's hasty refusal did not bode well for the brandy, but Murdoch was curious.

Broske poured some of the liquid into the flask cap and handed it to him. "Good health."

Murdoch took a sip and almost choked. His lips and tongue caught fire and the brandy blazed a trail down his throat, taking layers of skin with it. His eyes watered and he coughed.

The professor grinned at him. "Grappa is something of what you would call a taste of acquirement."

Murdoch handed him back the cap. "I think that's enough for me, thank you."

Casually, Broske tossed back the remaining brandy in one gulp, wiping his thin moustache delicately. "Ah, that warms the heart, does it not?"

Murdoch thought that for a physiologist, the professor's sense of anatomy was decidedly inaccurate. The grappa had gone nowhere near his heart but had headed directly for his stomach, where it was now burning a hole.

"To quote one of England's eminent men, Mr. Samuel Johnson, 'Claret is the liquor for boys; port, for men; but he who aspires to be a hero must drink brandy.' And perhaps we must admit that is especially true of those who drink our Italian brandy."

Broske tossed back another capful of grappa and waved the flask at Murdoch questioningly. Dr. Ogden rescued him.

"Shall I tell you my findings now?"

Murdoch didn't trust his voice, so he nodded.

"First I should say that the piece of sacking was not very useful. The blood was mammalian and of fairly recent origin, but that was all I could determine. There were some hairs that were likely equine, but as it was in a stable, that proves nothing. The same was true of the whip. I saw nothing at all on either of the Indian clubs or the rope."

"And the vial?"

"That, on the other hand, proved to be quite interesting. Considering it is called the gold cure, I found no gold at all. Professor Broske confirmed my analysis of the contents."

"No gold. Much cocaine." The professor's English was rather suddenly truncated.

"Quite so," added Julia. "There was a small per cent of chloral, which as you know has a sedating effect, water, and a 10 per cent solution of cocaine. I've heard of this before. Unscrupulous or ignorant practitioners claim to cure addictions to alcohol and so they do, but they replace one addiction with another. Men stop drinking but then they begin craving the 'cure' or the cordial or whatever they want to call it, not knowing they are now dependent on another drug."

"Friend should be got out," Broske slurred. "And soon."

There was a tap at the door and Amy came in. She was still wearing her comfortable at-home clothes with silk pantaloons fastened at the ankle and full over-tunic. Broske jumped to his feet, his brown eyes glowing with admiration.

"Allow me to present Miss Amy Slade," said Murdoch. "You know Dr. Ogden, of course, and this is Professor Marc Broske. He is visiting here from Italy."

Amy held out her hand to Broske and, predictably, he held it in both of his for an instant, then planted a kiss on her fingers.

"Enchanting, mademoiselle."

Dr. Ogden pursed her lips. "We can't stay much longer, but I understand you have a question you wish to ask the professor, Miss Slade."

Amy described her visit to the Blongs' house and the condition of Mary Blong.

"I suspected she was faking the seizure, but I'm not sure. William thought you might be able to help. Perhaps you might even come to see the girl yourself."

Broske beamed. "I have a most simple method to detect fakery, which is infallible. But I am due to return to my homeland in five days so we must do something soon. Can you make an appointment for me to come to see the girl?"

"I'll arrange it as soon as possible," said Amy. "I do thank you, professor."

"Not at all, I am only to happy to demonstrate my skill." He turned to Dr. Ogden. "Perhaps you will come also, Miss Julia? I am sure you will be most fascinating to see the test."

"I would love to be there." She smiled at him, her annoyance gone.

CHAPTER TWENTY-EIGHT

The following morning, Murdoch decided to pay another visit to Thomas Talbert. He had supposedly known Cooke for a long time, and he might be able to confirm what Whatling and Ferguson had said about Cooke's predilection for gambling.

It was another lovely fresh morning and Murdoch found himself whistling as he rode down Mutual Street. Last night, just as Dr. Ogden and Professor Broske were about to leave, Charlie and Katie had returned and somehow in the introductions the news of their engagement came out. Broske insisted on celebrating but, fortunately, Charlie had a bottle of good whisky in his room and they were able to avoid the grappa in the several toasts that had followed. It was almost midnight when the doctor and her companion had finally left, Broske kissing Amy and Katie's hands with much gusto. Murdoch noticed he even slipped in a quick kiss to his Miss Julia's cheek. He smiled at the memory and at how pink Dr. Ogden had turned.

He leaned his wheel against the fence and opened the gate to Talbert's front garden. He paused. All of the front-room blinds were pulled down. It was almost nine o'clock, surely it was not too early to call on the man? He checked the upper windows and there the blinds were up. A sharp pinch of alarm gripped him. Of course, it was quite possible that Talbert had fallen asleep downstairs, but where was his housekeeper? There was a quiet to the house, a feeling of something not normal that was troubling. He went up to the door and knocked. Nothing stirred. He knocked again harder and this time he turned the door handle, pushed open the door, and stepped into the hall.

"Mr. Talbert? Mr. Talbert? Detective Murdoch here."

The unmistakable odour of death hit his nostrils.

The portières to the parlour had been drawn back and that door was wide open. He could see Talbert lying on the floor, near the fireplace. He was on his right side with his knees tucked tight to his chest.

Murdoch ran to the body and crouched down. He could see a single bullet hole in the neck just below the jaw. The bullet must have pierced the artery and there was a wide spatter of blood around the area where Talbert was lying. He was fully dressed and wearing the same light-blue smoking jacket that Murdoch had seen him in before. It was covered with blood down the left side. His wrists were tied in front of him and his arms had been drawn down over his bent legs. A poker was thrust behind his knees and over his elbows, pulling him almost into a ball. Incongruously, on top of the body was a scattering of bills, mostly five- and two-dollar notes, some of them stuck to his jacket by the blood.

Murdoch tried to lift the arms so he could get a better look at the other side, but rigor was at its height and the body was completely stiff.

Suddenly, Murdoch heard the front door open.

"Hello, Thom, I'm back," called a female voice.

"Damn." He jumped to his feet and ran over to the door, but he wasn't in time to prevent Mrs. Stokely from entering the room. Seeing him, she stood stock-still at the threshold.

"Who are you?"

Murdoch managed to get himself between her and the body. "I'm Detective Murdoch, ma'am. I was here the other day. Please don't come in here, ma'am. Let's go out into the hall."

She stared at him for a moment, then peered over his shoulder. The colour bleached out of her face and she suddenly looked like an old woman.

"Thom, oh my God."

She would have run over to the body, but Murdoch anticipated her and caught her by the arms. She wasn't screaming, but she was saying desperately over and over, "Oh my God. Oh my God."

"Mrs. Stokely, you cannot come any farther. A crime has been committed. Please do as I ask."

As gently but as firmly as he could, Murdoch eased her back through the door, pulling it closed behind him. Once in the hall, he got her into the chair by the hat stand. She was shaking from head to toe and there were flecks of saliva at the corners of her mouth. Murdoch crouched in front of her so he could meet her eyes.

She stared at him, uncomprehending. "What happened to him?"

"He has been shot."

That elicited more agonized exclamations.

"Shot? Who did it? Who? Who in God's name would kill a good man like Thom?"

"I don't know yet, ma'am. I came here to talk to him and this is how I found him."

He took a handkerchief from his pocket and handed it to her, but she gazed at it as if she hadn't seen one before and the tears slid unchecked down her face.

"I should have been here. I should have. Oh why did I leave him last night, of all nights?" He could hardly make out what she was saying.

"Were you away from home, ma'am?"

"Yes, I, I . . . visit my granddaughter on Friday nights. I just got back."

"When did you leave?"

"Leave? I don't know. It must have been at my usual time."

"When would that be, ma'am?"

"When? At eight o'clock, I suppose."

"Did Mr. Talbert have any visitors?"

"No. He never did on Fridays. He . . . he liked to have his weekly pipe . . . I don't like tobacco, you see . . ." Her voice trailed off.

"Did he mention anything about expecting anyone?"

"Not at all. He told me to enjoy myself, gave me a k –" She halted. "He told me to have a nice time and . . . and give his regards to my granddaughter. She has been recently confined, you see. Oh, how will I ever tell her?"

Murdoch straightened up. "Mrs. Stokely, do you have any brandy in the house?"

"Brandy?" She fluttered her hand. "Yes, Thom, Mr. Talbert, always kept a bottle in the kitchen. He didn't drink himself, but sometimes offered it . . . offered it to his . . . to his visitors."

Murdoch held out his hand. "Let's go into the kitchen, shall we?"

Unsteadily, she got to her feet and allowed him to lead her down the hall. She was leaning heavily on his arm and he could feel the violent trembling of her body. He sat her at the kitchen table, elicited the location of the brandy, and poured her a stiff cupful.

"Take a good swallow," he instructed her and was pleased to see a little colour return to her cheeks as she did so. She wiped her eyes and nose.

Murdoch took the chair across from her. "I know this has been a terrible shock, ma'am, but I must ask you to do something for me. I need to send for a constable. Do you think you can get to your neighbour's house and have them go to the station?"

"Yes. I can go to Dr. Pollard's. They have a telephone."

"Excellent. Tell them to have the operator connect them with number four station. Say that I need three or four constables here right away. They should also send for the coroner, Dr. Ogden, and we will need the ambulance. Do you remember my name, Mrs. Stokely?"

"No, I'm sorry, the shock has driven everything quite out of my head."

"I'm Detective Murdoch from number four station. Will you repeat that for me?"

"Murdoch from number four station. I'll remember." Her voice was a little stronger now.

"Very good. You are being most brave. Now, let me escort you to the door. Would you prefer to go out of the back door or the front?"

She shook her head violently. "There is a high fence between our property and theirs. What if somebody is still there?"

"I think that is most unlikely, ma'am, but let's use the front entrance so I can watch out for you. Then I want you to remain at the doctor's house until I come over myself. Will you promise me you will do that?"

"Yes, Mr., er, Mr. Murdoch. Oh dear, oh dear, what is to become of me?"

"Try not to think of that right now, Mrs. Stokely. The most important thing at the moment is that we get on the trail of Mr. Talbert's killer as soon as possible. Give me your hand. That's good. Now let me help you with your jacket."

As obediently as a child, she slipped her arms through the sleeves. She was normally a stout, buxom woman, but it was as if she had suddenly shrivelled.

"We'll leave your hat, shall we?"

She shook her head. "I'm not going to Mrs. Pollard's house bare-headed."

Murdoch handed her the hat, probably her Sunday best, of beige felt, wide-brimmed, and profusely decorated with brown taffeta ribbons and yellow feathers. She put it on and straightened up.

He offered her his arm again. "Here we go, then. Hold on tight."

Making sure he was walking on the side nearest to the parlour, he escorted her to the front door and stood on the porch while she made her way to the large house next to them. He waited until she had knocked and been admitted, then he went back inside, bolting the door behind him. He didn't want any more unexpected visitors.

Somehow when he returned to the sight of the dead man, the scene looked even more horrible. Seeing the position the body had been forced into, Murdoch felt a rush of anger that was also tinged with fear. Was he truly dealing with a lunatic? First a brutal whipping that had brought about the death of Daniel Cooke, now this. He could only assume the two deaths were connected.

He made the sign of the cross over the body.

"May the Lord have mercy on your soul."

CHAPTER TWENTY-NINE

urdoch took out his notebook and his tape measure and began to walk slowly around the body, trying to understand what had taken place. There was no sign of any struggle. Talbert's armchair was where it had been when Murdoch visited him. Murdoch picked up the briar pipe that was perched on the brass standing ashtray beside the chair. There was still unburned tobacco in the bowl and a spent Lucifer next to it. He had lit his pipe once only. Murdoch was a pipe smoker, he knew how ornery they could be sometimes, refusing to draw on first light. So Talbert was just getting settled in and then he heard something, perhaps something as innocuous as the door knocker. He couldn't call on his housekeeper to answer, so he put his precious pipe on the rim of the ashtray, placed the newspaper down on the floor, picked up the lamp that Mrs. Stokely had thoughtfully filled with oil for the night, and went to see who was visiting him at this hour.

And who was it, indeed?

Murdoch walked back into the hall and looked around, but his first impression had been correct. Nothing had been disturbed. The clay pot of ferns just inside the door was intact. If it had been knocked over, it would have smashed to pieces. There was a rather worn dhurrie rug covering some of the plank floor and it did not seem to have been moved. All of the framed pictures on the walls were straight. Murdoch glanced at them briefly. Talbert had favoured nature paintings. He had two of the noble stag, one standing at bay with the hounds, the other overlooking his harem of does on the hillside. Murdoch could not imagine anybody overpowering the old man in this narrow hall, however strong they were, without knocking something off the wall. Talbert had not been threatened by his visitor. He had led the person into the parlour.

Murdoch returned to the corpse. First he measured the distance of Talbert's head from the fireplace fender: eight inches. The location of the bullet hole below the jawline was strange. If he had been shot while he was in this crouched position, the entry wound would surely have been much higher. That would be easier to determine after the post-mortem when he could see where the bullet had exited and the trajectory it had followed.

Next he went to measure the length of the blood spatters. The longest had actually hit the edge of the couch, but the streaks grew shorter like the struts of a fan closer to the fireplace. There were two breaks in the lines: one fairly close to the right edge and the other where Talbert was lying. It made sense then that Talbert had been standing, facing the opposite armchair, when he was shot. His killer had been a few feet away to his left. As he was shot, he spun to his left and collapsed, likely on the hearth, but Murdoch could not definitely determine that until he could move the body and check for a contusion on Talbert's head. The brass fender around the hearth seemed untouched.

He bent down and removed the bank notes that were scattered on top of the body and placed them carefully to one side. There was one Imperial Bank ten-dollar note, two Bank of Montreal five-dollar bills, and eight two-dollar and five one-dollar bills from the Dominion Bank. Forty-one dollars in total. The blood-stained bills were in varying states of newness and some had stuck together.

Talbert's wrists had been tied with a striped green and gold necktie. Before he undid the binding, Murdoch made a careful sketch of the way the body had been positioned. Then he examined the hands. The fingers were caked with dried blood, as were both palms. Talbert had probably clutched his neck in an instinctive but vain attempt to stem the bleeding. The necktie, however, showed few blood stains and the knot had been fairly loose. It would seem that his hands had been bound after he had been shot and he must have then been pulled into the ball position. It was grotesque. Obviously, binding his hands would serve no purpose when the man was already dead, so why do it?

There was a thunderous knocking on the front door and he went to answer it.

Four rather breathless constables were on the doorstep. He let them in.

"Thomas Talbert has been shot, sometime last night by the look of the body. He's in the parlour. You might as well have a look at him but don't go too close. I haven't had a chance to examine the carpet yet."

The men crowded into the hall.

"Sergeant Gardiner was able to reach Dr. Ogden," said Crabtree. "She'll be here as soon as she can."

"Good. I was afraid we'd have to take Johnson."

Burley, who was a young rather sensitive constable second class, let out an involuntary gasp when he saw the carnage.

"Who'd do that to an old man like Talbert?" asked Crabtree.

"Was it a robbery, sir?" Fyfer asked.

"I'd say not. The assailant actually left money on the body in the amount of forty-one dollars. I'll give you more of a briefing later. Right now we need to get the proceedings moving. George, you stay with me. Fyfer, I want you to round up a jury, fast as you can. Dewhurst and you, Burley, start going through the house. Don't rush, use your wits, and just try to determine if anything at all is out of order or if you see anything that might be related to the murder."

"What sort of thing, sir?"

"I don't know, Dewhurst," Murdoch answered impatiently. "A threatening letter, a bloody handprint. Use your noddle."

Murdoch beckoned to Crabtree. "George, he's stiff as a board, but I want to get him up so I can see the exit wound and the blood pattern underneath him."

Together they hauled up the body, which moved in one grotesque piece. There was a large hole just below the right temple where the bullet had exited.

"That must have blown out some pieces of bone. Hold him there for a minute and I'll find them."

Murdoch moved away from the body, creeping close to the floor. There they were. Several small fragments of the skull were on the floor where the body had covered them.

"I was right," said Murdoch. "He was shot while he was standing and facing that chair. The bullet travelled on an angle upward, so either his killer was sitting or crouching or he was much shorter than Talbert, who was tall, about six feet at least. We can get an exact measurement later. Rigor is complete so he has been dead at least twelve hours, which gives us time of death anywhere between eight and eleven o'clock last night. Dr. Ogden might be a little more precise."

There was another knock on the door. "Speaking of Dr. Ogden, that's probably her now. Let her in, will you, George?"

Murdoch smoothed out a sheet of the newspaper and placed the bloodied bone fragments on top of it.

"Goodness gracious, Mr. Murdoch, what have we here now?"

Dr. Ogden, looking slightly dishevelled, as if she had dressed in a hurry, came into the room. Murdoch was not surprised to see Professor Broske at her heels.

"Detective, we meet under the worse of circumstances, don't we?"

Getting rather drunk on grappa last night wasn't a particularly bad circumstance, but Murdoch knew what he was referring to.

"What have you ascertained so far, William?" Dr. Ogden asked.

Murdoch related the conclusions he had come to about how the murder had happened.

"So he was tied up post-mortem?"

"I'd say so."

"And why would somebody do that?"

Before Murdoch could reply, Broske said, "It has to be a statement, does it not? A message of some kind. There's a secret society that exists in my country. They call themselves the Cosa Nostra. Apparently they will sometimes mutilate the body of their victims as a warning to others, to intimidate them."

"What others?" Murdoch exclaimed, exasperated. "If I hadn't come here early, his housekeeper would have discovered him. I cannot imagine she is a target of this intimidation, she's a middle-aged woman."

"Is she of the same race?" Broske asked.

"No, she's a white woman."

"And the dead man was a negro," continued the professor. "Perhaps there are those who objected to him employing a white woman as his housekeeper."

Dr. Ogden looked shocked. "Surely not here, professor? The situation is unconventional to be sure, but I cannot imagine anybody in this city being so incensed they would shoot an old man and commit such an indignity to his body."

Broske shrugged. "Alas, one cannot underestimate the depth of depravity human beings can sink to, and in my experience the more so when they are filled with righteousness."

It was a sobering thought, and for a moment all of them paused. Then Murdoch said, "I was just about to examine the carpet more closely, doctor. There was so much blood spilled, the murderer would have had to walk through it, especially when he was tying Talbert up."

"It is perhaps best if we stand aside then?"

"Thank you, ma'am."

Crabtree, Broske, and Dr. Ogden watched while Murdoch got to his knees and studied the blood stains. A partial print was clearly visible.

"This is from a man's boot, blunt-toed, average size. Ah." He bent closer. "There's another print here. Just the toe, and it's not that distinct, but it's a rounder shape than the other."

"So, there were two people here," said Broske.

"I believe so."

"Poor fellow didn't stand much of a chance, did he?"

CHAPTER THIRTY

"I don't know where to put you, sir." The Pollards' butler was a stooped, grey-haired man who looked as if he should have been pensioned off a long time ago. He was highly flustered.

"Where is Mrs. Stokely?" Murdoch asked.

"She is in the servants' hall, but Cook has to prepare luncheon and there really is no room there for you to interview her."

"That's all right, the drawing room will suit me." Murdoch was being rather cruel and he knew it. This old man was only obeying the rules he'd lived with all his life. Unfortunately, Murdoch found himself more and more irritated by those rules.

The butler dithered. He had a runny nose and a drop of mucus was hanging from his right nostril. "I'm afraid that won't be possible, sir. Mrs. Pollard is entertaining her discussion group this afternoon."

"What time?"

"Two o'clock."

"I'm sure I'll be finished by then. And I would like to speak to your mistress as well."

"She isn't downstairs yet." The droplet fell onto his lapel.

"Would you be so good as to call her? You do know what has happened?"

"Oh yes, sir. It was I who telephoned your station when poor Mrs. Stokely arrived on our doorstep. A terrible tragedy, indeed."

"I wonder if I might ask you a question, Mr. . . . ?"

"Neely. My name is Neely. I will try to answer."

The butler was looking so alarmed that Murdoch almost didn't proceed, but he knew any information could be useful.

"You have worked for Dr. Pollard for some time, I gather?"

"Yes, sir. For thirty years. He had just started his practice."

"And Mr. Talbert has been your neighbour for all that time, I understand?"

"That's right. And he hasn't been a moment's trouble. His house is as neat and clean as a pin. He paints it regularly, keeps his garden immaculate, removes the leaves when they fall."

"Have you ever noticed him receive visitors who you might regard as sort of, well, sort of shady?"

Neely took a spotless handkerchief from his pocket and wiped his recalcitrant nose. "Never. He lives, that is, oh dear how dreadful to speak of him in the past tense, but I suppose I must. He *lived* a very quiet life. It was on rare occasions that I even saw him."

"How long has Mrs. Stokely been his housekeeper?"

"At least six years. She took up the position shortly after she was out of mourning." He glanced over his shoulder and lowered his voice. "My wife, Mrs. Neely, who is the housekeeper here, was quite inclined to make a friend of Mrs. Stokely, but the mistress put a stop to it."

"Really? Why was that?"

Neely shifted uncomfortably. "Mrs. Pollard is most diligent

about maintaining the dignity of the doctor's household as is appropriate to his position. She was not in favour of her cook, my wife that is, bringing a woman into the house who was, er, who was cohabiting with a coloured man."

That explained Mrs. Stokely's comment about not going bare-headed into the Pollard house, thought Murdoch.

"It's my understanding Mrs. Stokely was employed by Mr. Talbert in the position of housekeeper," said Murdoch.

"So she was, but you know how it is . . . no other live-in servants." His voice trailed off. "Do you have any idea who killed him, sir? We had gypsies through about a month ago. Dreadful vagabonds, they were. Perhaps they returned. They might have determined Mr. Talbert was a man on his own."

"I shall keep that in mind, Mr. Neely, but, no, I don't know yet who his assailant was. And I should therefore speak to Mrs. Stokely without more delay."

Neely moved back. "I'll have to get permission from Mrs. Pollard first, sir. She is most particular, as I said." He paused. "My goodness, I almost forgot. We have two maids here, Molly and Betty. They are young girls from the country, good, sensible girls but when Mrs. Stokely came and told her story, Molly almost went into hysterics. She said that, last night, as she was drawing the curtains in Mrs. Pollard's retiring room, which is on the second floor, she happened to look out of the window and saw two people knocking on Mr. Talbert's door. When she realized she was probably looking at the murderers, she almost fainted. Cook had to fetch her smelling salts. She's still not quite right and has refused to move from her chair all morning, even though Mrs. Neely is sorely busy."

"I must speak to her as well then. Now be so good as to tell your mistress that I have temporarily commandeered the drawing room. But fetch Mrs. Stokely first, will you?"

"Oh dear, yes sir. Come this way, if you please."

Murdoch followed him down the wide hall. Carpeted stairs swept in a graceful curve up to the second floor where the walls were covered with ornately framed paintings. Murdoch wondered how the Pollards' taste in art compared with Thomas Talbert's. Landscapes, rather similar from what he could see, except that the doctor's pictures were larger.

Neely opened the door to the drawing room.

"Mrs. Pollard hasn't requested a fire to be lit as yet. I hope you will be warm enough. May I bring you some tea, sir?"

"Better not, thank you. Mrs. Pollard might not take too kindly to me occupying the drawing room and taking tea."

He'd hoped to get a smile from the old man, but Neely just looked even more apprehensive. He backed out.

Murdoch made his way to a Turkish couch adjacent to the fireplace, an impressive piece in white marble. A large brass fan was in front of the hearth, and the mantel was laden with figurines and gilt-framed photographs. Murdoch had been in several drawing rooms since he had become a detective, and he had come to the conclusion that a fixed principle of society was that the more money you had to spend on objects, the more you were impelled to display them. The Pollards' drawing room was crammed with furniture, more drapery than you would find in Mr. T. Eaton's department store, and enough paintings on the walls to start a gallery.

There was a timid tap on the door and Mrs. Stokely came in. "Mr. Neely said you were here and wanted to speak to me, Mr. Murdoch."

Murdoch got to his feet. "Please sit down, ma'am. How are you feeling?"

He didn't need to ask. Her round face was blotchy with crying and in spite of her stout figure, she seemed frail. She sat down and wiped at her eyes.

"Not too well, sir. It has been the most dreadful shock."

"I know it has, Mrs. Stokely, and I do thank you for your help in the circumstances. I need to ask you a few questions, but I won't keep you long."

In spite of her upset, he noticed that her gaze had been wandering around the room. This was probably the first time she had been in the Pollards' drawing room. He waited until her attention returned to him.

"You told me earlier that Mr. Talbert had no visitors last night, nor seemed to be expecting any."

"That's right."

"How did he seem to you when you left? Was he his usual self? Was he preoccupied at all? Did he appear to be afraid of anything?"

She shook her head vigorously. "Not at all afraid. Thom was not a timid man. He wasn't preoccupied either. Of course, he was upset about what had happened to Mr. Cooke. They didn't get along too well, but he had known him for a long time."

Murdoch had taken out his notebook and was making discrete notes. He looked up at her. "Why do you say Mr. Talbert and Mr. Cooke didn't get along?"

She dabbed at her eyes again. "He didn't speak about it really, but they had a falling out some years ago now. Thom, Mr. Talbert, that is, used to own those stables, you see, but he fell on hard times. There were two fires that destroyed all his carriages and killed most of his horses. Mr. Cooke offered to buy the stables. I don't think it was a very good offer, but Mr. Talbert was forced to accept or starve. He didn't want to because he was very proud of what he'd built up over the years. He was always talking about those old times and the position he'd made for himself in society." She sighed. "I'm only telling you what Thom said to me, you understand, but he once let it slip that he wondered if Mr. Cooke had set the fires himself. I was shocked to hear that, of course, and asked him why he thought so. 'Because my run of bad luck was all too convenient for him,' was his answer. Apparently, Mr. Cooke did offer him a job at the stable afterwards, but Thom absolutely refused. He only went back recently to help out young Elijah."

"Are you saying, Mrs. Stokely, that the animosity was all on Mr. Talbert's part?"

"I suppose I am, aren't I? Thom was a very kind man and most generous, but he could hold a grudge like a limpet. You hadn't better get on his bad side."

"Were you yourself acquainted with Mr. and Mrs. Cooke at all?"

Mrs. Stokely paused and glanced away from Murdoch. "No, we didn't mix much in society . . . but I have heard that his marriage was not a happy one. Mrs. Cooke is not what I'd call a warm-hearted woman."

"I've been hearing stories that Mr. Cooke was a gambler. Did you know that?"

She shifted in her chair. "Well, it did come out one day. In the last little while, he'd been late paying Elijah's wages. When he heard about it, Thom said Mr. Cooke was wasting money on cards and betting rings."

At that moment, the door was flung open and a large, pear-shaped woman burst in. Her hair had obviously been hastily pinned and she was still in her housegown, but her anger was palpable. Murdoch stood up politely.

"I must ask you, sir, how you have the temerity to enter my house and make use of my own drawing room? The affair is sordid enough without it coming right to my very hearth."

Mrs. Stokely shrank back. There was sufficient ambiguity in the other woman's remarks to pierce her soul. Murdoch stepped closer to the irate Mrs. Pollard.

"Madam, I am conducting an inquiry into the death of your closest neighbour. It was at my request that his housekeeper, Mrs. Stokely, came to your house so that I could summon help. She has had an appalling shock, as you can see. There was nowhere else where I could have the privacy I needed to speak to her. I apologize for not getting your specific permission, but I assumed that like most ladies in your position you would be gracious enough to accommodate us." .

The bite in his tone was apparent to Mrs. Pollard and she flushed.

"You assumed incorrectly, sir. I will not have my drawing room turned into a common police hall. I understand you wish to interview my entire household, including myself."

"That is correct, madam. I am told that your maid may have seen visitors at Mr. Talbert's house last night. Her description will be helpful to me."

"Nonsense. She is an empty-headed country girl who would say she sees elves and fairies if you were to ask her."

"The people who visited Mr. Talbert last night were neither elves nor fairies, Mrs. Pollard. They were likely murderers capable of shooting an old man . . ." He had been about to tell her about Talbert being tied up after death so that he could shock her into some humanity, but unfortunately the person who would most suffer from that information would be Mrs. Stokely. He held his tongue.

However, Mrs. Pollard either read something in his face or his words got through to her. Whatever it was, her puffery subsided like a collapsed balloon and her tone became more conciliatory.

"I see. Well, you must do your duty, obviously. I would appreciate it if you would move to the dining room for your interviews, however. I am entertaining my ladies discussion group here this afternoon."

"I would be glad to move to the dining room, Mrs. Pollard. It will be more convenient. But I must tell you that there will be no discussion group, ladies or otherwise, here this afternoon. Until my search of the Talbert house is complete, I will be using your dining room as a base of operations. You and your staff are confined to the house until further notice. I also will require to look at the boots and shoes of every occupant."

This puffed her up again.

"Surely not Dr. Pollard's?"

"Yes, ma'am. Including Dr. Pollard's. I am sending for one of my constables, who will be here on duty as long as I find it necessary."

The thought of what Inspector Brackenreid's reaction might have been if he was at the station ran fleetingly through Murdoch's mind. The inspector would have been apoplectic about Murdoch's behaviour. Commandeering the house of one of the city's doctors was unheard of.

Murdoch indicated the door. "Now, if you don't mind, Mrs. Pollard, I haven't quite finished my interview."

CHAPTER **THIRTY-ONE**

Although he would have liked to find a justification for leaving Constable Dewhurst on duty at the Pollard house, Murdoch knew he was stepping on the edge of the law if he were to do that, so after about two hours, he returned to Talbert's house and sent the constable to start questioning the nearby residents. He assigned Burley the task of informing Elijah Green about what had happened.

"Note carefully how he reacts. If he has any information at all that might be helpful, bring him over to the station right away."

Burley went off, sober at his first serious task. Crabtree was assigned Mrs. Cooke and Fyfer the cabbies.

The Pollards' maid, Molly, had turned out to be so nervous, constantly on the verge of hysteria, that Murdoch had hesitated to push her. The problem was her testimony seemed to change from minute to minute. Yes, she had seen two people being admitted to Talbert's house just before eight o'clock the previous evening, and she thought one of them was a man, rather short and dressed in a long, dark mackintosh. On the other hand, it was raining and the person was holding an umbrella so she didn't get a good look. The other person could have been a woman, but she had gone into the house so quickly it was hard to tell. She supposed it might have been a man in a cloak, but she wouldn't swear an oath to it. About half an hour later, Molly had heard a loud noise, a sort of bang, but thought it was Cook dropping a pot. She hadn't realized it was a gunshot until she heard about the murder. Murdoch had hastily ended the interview at this point and sent the girl off with Mrs. Neely.

Mrs. Stokely had confirmed that the necktie used to bind Talbert's hands did not belong to him. She also remembered noticing that his good worsted coat, a navy blue one, was missing from the hall stand. Given that at least one of the murderers would have been splashed with blood, Murdoch assumed the coat had been stolen so the stains would be hidden.

He told her about the money scattered on Talbert's body, but she had no explanation for it. He didn't keep much money in the house, just enough to pay for monthly housekeeping expenses, rarely more than fifteen dollars or so. She told him where to look in the upstairs bedroom dresser, and indeed Fyfer had found about fourteen dollars in a cash box.

"Did Mr. Talbert have a will?" Murdoch asked.

"Yes," she said. "He had no children so he left what little he had to . . . me." She averted her eyes. "You might be surprised to know, Mr. Murdoch, that I was Thomas Talbert's legal wife. We married five years ago."

"Why did you keep it a secret?"

"Thom insisted. He thought it would be better if I was known as his housekeeper. He said people would no doubt gossip about me behind my back, but at least they would talk *to* me. If I were known as Mrs. Thomas Talbert, there were many who would not do even that. Perhaps he was right. My granddaughter has married a man who aspires to city office, and she had made it clear she doesn't approve of my living arrangements. To know that Thom and I were married would probably turn her away from me forever." She twisted her thin gold wedding band. "Do you think I shall be able to keep it secret, that we were husband and wife?"

"I don't see why not. As far as I know at this point, it has no relevance to our inquiry."

"Thank you, Mr. Murdoch."

Then he recalled what Broske had said about the ever-present prejudice against miscegenation. "Who else knew about your marriage?"

"Hardly anybody. Only the preacher at our church and his wife." She wept again. "Thom was such a good companion. He deserved to die peacefully in his bed."

She had unconsciously echoed Professor Broske's words about Daniel Cooke.

Murdoch bicycled back to the station. He had just entered when Gardiner beckoned him over. He had a conspiratorial expression on his face and his eyes were lively with curiosity.

"We received an urgent telephone call for you. The speaker had a strange accent, possibly Irish, and he sort of whispered. Callahan could hardly make out what he was saying, but he wrote it down as best he could."

He handed Murdoch a slip of paper.

Murdoch. I am in dire need of that book you promised me. I hope you have it and will bring it over this evening. Same time and place as before. Never mind the fire inspection.

"He wouldn't leave his name. He said you would know who it was," added Gardiner. He touched his forefinger to the side of his nose. "Big reader, is he?"

Murdoch nodded. "You might say that."

"I didn't know you were doing a fire inspection. Isn't that Inspector Brackenreid's job?"

"Yes, it is. Strange comment, I must say."

"Callahan thought the voice was oddly familiar but couldn't identify it."

Murdoch shrugged. "There are lots of Irishmen in the city." He headed for the stairs. "I'll be in the inspector's office."

"Enjoying that, are you, Will?"

"Probably a little too much."

Murdoch sat behind the desk and pushed on the button that opened the cigar dispenser. He selected a cigar and lit it. The inspector's message had come at an awkward moment, but he didn't feel he could ignore it. He was hoping to convene all the constables working on the Talbert case at about five o'clock, and Dr. Ogden said she would be ready to do the post-mortem examination at six. He decided he'd better go to the Ollapod Club now and see if he could get to talk to Brackenreid earlier than planned. He wondered why there was such urgency.

Keeping in mind Brackenreid's warning that he would not be allowed admittance to the institute under any circumstances, Murdoch parked his bicycle at the corner of the street and walked casually back to the main gates. Here he bent down and pretended to tie his shoelace so he had a chance to look into the grounds through the railings. Several men were strolling in the direction of the main building, and he remembered that this was close to the time when the residents received their injection. At first sight, he couldn't see Brackenreid. He fussed a bit more with his shoe but noticed that one of the attendants was glancing over his shoulder in his direction, so he stood up and moved on. Frankly, he had no idea how he was going to get inside. Then he had a stroke of luck. A tall, spindly man came trotting across the road, heading for the gates. Murdoch hurried back and got to him just in time.

"Hold on, good sir, I'd like a word with you. Do you work here?"

The fellow shook his head. "I do, but I can't talk to you right now, I'm already late."

Murdoch grabbed hold of the gate so he couldn't open it. "That's too bad, but you'll have to be even later. I'm a police officer and I am here on a serious matter."

That stopped him for the moment. "What sort of serious matter?"

"We've had complaints that the institute is being run in ways that break the law."

The man stared at him in disbelief. "Such as?"

"I'm not at liberty to say at the moment, but I need to gain entry to the building and in such a way that nobody will know who I am."

"You can't. No visitors allowed."

"I wouldn't call myself a visitor exactly. I'm an investigating officer. What is your name, by the way?"

Murdoch took out his notebook to make it all the more official-looking.

"Robert Tennyson. But see here, I've got nothing to do with anything illegal. I just do my job best I can and do what the doctor tells me."

"I believe you, Mr. Tennyson, but that doesn't mean to say the magistrate will. I might have to take you to the court right now and testify."

Murdoch could see that all the residents were inside now. Tennyson also saw that and he looked very nervous.

"Lord help us, they've gone in. They lock the door and I'll get the bird if I don't get in there. I have to assist with the injections."

"Do you, indeed?" Murdoch took out his wallet, hoping he had some money in it. He had a five-dollar bill, his last until next week. "I am authorized to recompense citizens at special times for their inconvenience. Here's five dollars and I promise that, if I have to, I will put in a good word with the magistrate on your behalf."

Tennyson stared at him, then back through the gates into the now-empty lawn. Murdoch waved the bank note under the man's nose. The scent of free money could be very persuasive. The attendant took it.

"All right. I think I can manage something. Go around to the back. I'll meet you at the gate in about ten minutes."

"Done."

Murdoch stepped back and Tennyson shoved open the gate and ran to the door, just getting in before it slammed shut.

CHAPTER THIRTY-TWO

Tennyson stashed Murdoch's clothes in a locker in the attendant's common room. He had outfitted Murdoch in a black short jacket and beige linen trousers. They were intended for a shorter man, but Murdoch hoped nobody would notice.

"Tell them you're replacing Davis for the day," said Tennyson. "They won't question it. We get temporary help quite often. You can do the check in. I'll put the list in front of you. Tick off the residents' names when they call them out and when the attendant gives you the signal, send them for their injection."

"That sounds easy enough."

"Come on, then."

Murdoch followed him down the hall and into the lounge. There were about twenty or so men standing in a curving line that was aimed at a cloth screen at the back of the room. They were chatting with one another and nobody paid him any attention. Murdoch took a quick look around and saw Inspector Brackenreid near the front of the queue. Their eyes met and Brackenreid, cool as an old pro, turned his surprise into a fit of coughing that elicited a concerned few pats on the back from one of his fellow residents. The inspector obviously hadn't yet been able to comply with the rules and he was still in his dressing gown and night shirt. His watchdog, Cherry, was nowhere to be seen, and Murdoch hoped he was off the leash for the time being.

"Here's your list," said Tennyson. "Sit at that table next to the screen. I'll be at the back serving the tea and coffee, but I'd rather you didn't know me."

Murdoch took the chair and put his list confidently on the table. There was another attendant standing near the screen. He was a plump fellow, clean-shaven except for a wide, bristling moustache.

"Who are you?" he asked.

"Davis's replacement."

"Get sharp then. We should have started already."

He disappeared behind the screen and Murdoch looked at the first resident who was standing in front of him in the queue.

"Leiter, Frank," said the man.

Murdoch found his name on the list and checked it off. Leiter knew what to do and he walked behind the screen, out of sight. Meanwhile, Murdoch checked in the next resident and after a few minutes the first fellow reappeared.

"It's all yours, Hennessey," he said. The second man went in and the procedure was repeated, although Hennessey seemed to take a little longer. Nobody questioned Murdoch's presence at the table. He could see Tennyson at the far end of the lounge walking among the residents with a tray of refreshments. One or two of the men were in night clothes like Brackenreid, but most were dressed in suits, none of them shabby, which was to be expected. As far as Murdoch could tell, they all seemed healthy and happy and the hubbub of talk was animated.

Brackenreid was at the table and he said his name.

"Who's doing the dirty?" he asked with a jerk of his head in the direction of the screen.

"Er, I'm not sure. He's got . . ." Murdoch made a gesture indicating the attendant's startling moustache.

"That has to be Raymond and I won't have him," said Brackenreid loudly. "No. I absolutely refuse. The man should have been a veterinarian, not a doctor's assistant."

Raymond popped his head from behind the screen. "I heard what you said, Mr. Brackenreid, and I must say, I take offence to your remark."

"Do you, indeed, then the arrow must have hit the target," said Brackenreid in his best bully voice that Murdoch was so familiar with. "I'm still hurting from your attack yesterday."

Murdoch could hardly believe this performance. The inspector had missed his calling.

He pointed at Murdoch. "I'd rather have this man here give me the medicine."

"That's not possible," said Raymond. "He's only a temporary help."

"I don't give a damn about that." Brackenreid glared at Murdoch. "You know what to do, don't you?"

Murdoch nodded vigorously. "Of course."

"Come on, then." Brackenreid headed toward the screen. There was no stopping him and Raymond stepped aside.

"Why don't you do the check in? I'll just deal with this one." Murdoch winked at the attendant and whispered, "Don't worry, I'll fix him."

Brackenreid led the way behind the screen and Murdoch pulled it closed around him.

"Quickly, Murdoch," he hissed. "We don't have much time. If I don't get out of this place today, I'm stuck here indefinitely.

My wife and my doctor are coming tonight to sign commitment papers. In my best interest, of course."

"How is the program working, sir?"

"It's a heap of horse plop, if you ask me. For which people pay a hell of a lot of money. Did you get that medicine analyzed?"

"Yes, I did. It contains quite a sizable amount of cocaine."

Brackenreid guffawed jubilantly. "I thought it was something like that. Cavanaugh is getting men off drink by getting them addicted to cocaine. No wonder his patients are so loyal. Who did the analysis of the medicine?"

"Dr. Julia Ogden."

"Excellent, she's an acquaintance of my wife's. She'll believe her."

"Is everything all right in there?" Raymond called.

"Yes, we're almost done," Murdoch replied.

Brackenreid indicated a dresser on which were lined rows of vials filled with golden liquid. There was a hypodermic syringe on a cloth on top of the dresser.

Then to Murdoch's horror, Brackenreid turned his back, bent over, and lifted up his night shirt, presenting a rather plump and somewhat hairy bottom.

"Do it, man."

"I beg your pardon, sir?"

"The syringe. You've got to give me the needle."

"Good Lord, is it absolutely necessary?"

"Yes. The vials are counted. And if you breathe a word of this to anybody at the station, I'll have your liver for breakfast. Understood?"

"Yes, sir. But I do want to warn you, I am not familiar with syringes."

"You've played darts, haven't you?"

"I have but –"

"Same thing. Come on, hurry up."

Murdoch picked up the syringe, balanced it between his forefinger and thumb, and aimed it into the inspector's right buttock.

Brackenreid let out a banshee scream and he wasn't acting. The syringe was left dangling. He took a step backward, tumbled onto his rear, and crashed into the screen, bringing it down. "You fool, you incompetent ape. You're even worse than Raymond."

The fall had driven the point of the needle deeper into his flesh and he was roaring in earnest. Raymond and some of the residents came rushing to help. Brackenreid struggled to his feet, shaking them off. With a grunt, he extracted the syringe.

"I'm going to report this," he shouted. "You!" he pointed a dramatically accusing finger at Murdoch. "You come with me. We're going straight to see Mr. Cavanaugh."

"I'll send for somebody," said Raymond.

"Never mind. I want the man himself to give an explanation to the superintendent himself or I'll see he never works here again."

The attendant smirked. "I warned you he was only a temporary staff."

Murdoch lowered his head, looking suitably chastened. Tennyson had come hurrying over and he was righting the screen. "Let them go, Raymond, we've got to finish."

The attendant looked as if he would protest, but Brackenreid shoved Murdoch ahead of him toward the door. "Come on, you."

They got out into the hall, leaving a ripple of excitement behind them in their wake. The residents hadn't had such a lively afternoon since the most recent inmate had an attack of the delirium tremors.

Once in the hall, the inspector halted and rubbed his buttock with a moan.

"Sorry, sir," said Murdoch, "but you did say to think of darts."

"It felt more like you were throwing a bloody javelin."

"Where to now, sir?"

"I've got to get home to my wife and convince her, this is absolutely the wrong place for me." He looked at Murdoch. "Where are your own clothes?"

"There's a room just down here that the attendants use. I bribed one of them to get me in here."

Murdoch thought it wouldn't hurt to let Brackenreid know that he'd paid out his own money.

"Good thinking."

Luck was still with them and the hall was deserted. Murdoch opened the door to the room and they went inside. He handed Brackenreid his clothes and the inspector changed into them immediately. He had lost weight during his stay at the institute. Murdoch's trousers and jacket were tight but not as bad as they would have been a while ago.

"There's a rear door that the attendants use," said Murdoch.

He checked the hall first to see if they were safe, then led the way to the door. They practically ran down the path, through the gate, and didn't stop until they were at the end of the street where Murdoch had left his bicycle. Brackenreid was gasping for breath, but he thrust out his hand.

"Murdoch, I am forever in your debt. I shall have your clothes sent round to you tonight. And all being well, I will return to the station tomorrow morning."

"Yes, sir."

They shook hands and Brackenreid scurried off, Murdoch's hat pulled well down over his face.

Murdoch waited until he was out of sight, then let go of the laughter he'd been choking back. It would take him a while to get the image of Brackenreid's buttock as dartboard out of his head.

CHAPTER THIRTY-THREE

Three constables and Murdoch were seated around the table in the duty room. All of them were enjoying meat pies courtesy of the station petty cash, which Murdoch had seen fit to filch. He knew they had all worked a long day, and in his opinion, hungry men were easily distracted from the task at hand by thoughts of supper. He'd also ordered Fyfer to make a pot of tea, fresh leaves, if you please. Inspector Brackenreid was a miser when it came to doling out the small allowance the officers were permitted for tea, milk, and sugar. He actually checked to make sure they were reusing the tea leaves in the big pot.

Murdoch was drawing a map of local streets on the brown wall of the duty room. "I'll wipe it off later," he said.

"Might be a good thing to have permanently," said Fyfer. "It's certainly helpful."

"Inspector Brackenreid wouldn't like that," said Dewhurst, who always took a perverse pleasure from being the voice of doom.

Murdoch wondered how much he was going to be able to draw from the bank account of Brackenreid's gratitude before it ran out. "You never know, he may come back a new man and totally approve."

He couldn't help but notice how much at ease the constables were without the inspector's unpredictable presence. Murdoch had invited them to undo the top buttons of their uniforms in the warm room. Their helmets were on the hooks by the door.

He checked his watch. "I don't know what's keeping Crabtree, but we should start. Let's hear what you've got."

Burley, the youngest, spoke up first.

"Elijah Green appeared to be genuinely shocked by the news of Thomas Talbert's death. He said he couldn't understand why somebody would want to kill a man of Talbert's age. He asked if the motive was robbery, and I said we didn't think so. He had no suggestions or opinions as to who or why."

"Fyfer? What about Mrs. Cooke?"

"She was in the company of Paul Musgrave so they received the news together. Both expressed great surprise. Neither had any idea, they said, who had done the murder, but Mrs. Cooke is convinced there are gypsies in the area. She took it for granted that robbery was the motive, although she said she didn't expect that Mr. Talbert would have had much to steal. She became quite tearful and she said the news brought up the tragedy of her own husband. All this time, Mr. Musgrave was a great comfort to her."

He let the inference hang in the air.

"Constable Dewhurst, anything from the cabbies?"

"I'd say nothing different from what you've just heard. Shock, surprise, no ideas as to who did it. Like you told me, Mr. Murdoch, I didn't let on about the way Talbert was tied up, but the cabbie, Wallace, did remark that we'd probably find it was, as he put it, 'a tribal matter.'"

"What the hell did he mean by that?"

"He thought the murderer must have been another negro man, sir."

Burley gave a little cough. "I think I have something promising, Detective Murdoch. After I had spoken to Green, I returned to the scene of the offence and I began to interview the residents of the area. I questioned Mr. Magnus Shewan, who lives at 205 Shuter Street near Jarvis. Last night, he was returning from his place of work, which is on Yonge Street. He is adamant he walked by a peculiar-looking couple. So I asks him why he thought they were peculiar and he said the woman was walking a few paces behind the man, as if she were a coulee or some such. The man was definitely shorter than the woman, and he swears they were both dark-skinned. He didn't notice if they turned into any of the houses on the street. He says it was about half past seven when he saw them."

Murdoch drew a dotted line on the wall map, along Shuter from Yonge Street to Jarvis and wrote *MS (7:30)*. He noticed that Dewhurst was smirking.

"Yes?"

"I can top that, sir. I spoke to a Mr. and Mrs. Mario Marino, who live at 243 Church Street, which is a few houses north of Shuter. They are of Italian extraction and I would say you'd call them swarthy, especially Mrs. Marino, who has quite a moustache. Mister is quite short, but Missus is taller and stout. They were going to St. Michael's Cathedral for a special prayer meeting. An Italian man would never hold his wife's arm, as they consider it beneath them and the wives usually walk a few paces behind. They saw Mr. Shewan coming home. They know him slightly as their habits occasionally coincide, but they don't exchange greetings. They find him a very ill-mannered man and said they have tried to be sociable but have been rebuffed."

Burley interjected. "I myself found Mr. Shewan a little taciturn, sir, but I realized he is rather deaf and fairly short-sighted into the bargain, so his lack of manners toward Mr. and Mrs. Marino might not be altogether in his awareness."

Dewhurst's expression made it clear what he thought of that, but Murdoch added the Marino couple to his map.

"Did you confirm there was indeed a church meeting at the cathedral?"

"Yes, sir. There was, and it went from eight o'clock to eleven."

"That's us Catholics for you. We have a lot to pray about, and for," said Murdoch, and the constables dutifully smiled at his little joke. "Sorry, Dick, but I think we can eliminate the swarthy, strange-looking couple from our list of suspects. Anything else?"

"The people I spoke to were generally complimentary in what they said about Mr. Talbert, although he kept to himself by all accounts. Some of them were acquainted with the livery and had met Mr. Cooke. The words used to describe *him* were *moody, irascible, unpredictable*, although one lady on Queen Street who said she used his cabs regularly described him as a most charming and thoughtful man. To tell you the truth, sir, she is elderly and I think she was getting him mixed up with one of the cabbies who generally takes care of her. Her description of him fits Paul Musgrave."

"Anybody else glean anything as to the general opinion in the neighbourhood about either of the two men?"

Fyfer nodded. "I heard much the same really, although a couple of ladies who live on Shuter Street expressed some disapproval about Mr. Talbert living with a white widow lady."

"They must be members of Mrs. Pollard's discussion group," said Murdoch. "She's of the same opinion."

At that moment, the door opened and George Crabtree came in.

"Sorry, I'm late, sir. I had some business at home to attend to."

"Have a seat, George. There's a pie for you and some fresh-brewed tea. I hope you've got something for me. So far we haven't got much to go on."

Crabtree took out his notebook. "I do, sir. I talked to a Miss Laura Brown. She lives on Shuter Street near Sherbourne, 292. She has a little pug dog called Tiger and come rain or shine, every evening, she walks him from her house along Shuter Street as far as Church Street and back. And it's always about the same time. She leaves her house between eight and nine o'clock, except on Sunday when she goes at six so she can go to Evensong at St. Peter's. She says that last night, on her return trip, she saw two people walking west on Shuter. She estimates this would be about a quarter to nine. She was able to give me a good description because Tiger was doing his job just then and she had to stand and wait for him. Her impression is that they were American. There was something about the woman's hat apparently that was different from what you can buy in Toronto. The man was most definitely a negro, and he was wearing a long coat and a fedora hat. She couldn't say if the woman was coloured or not, as she was veiled. They were walking quite fast, but the woman seemed to move stiffly. Just as they approached her, they crossed to the other side of the road and she noticed the man helped the woman to step off the curb. She wasn't sure where that was exactly, but she thought she had just gone past Church Street. She continued on her way after that."

Murdoch put in another line on the map and wrote *(Miss Brown, 8:45) negro and woman* on Shuter Street, near Church.

"What side of the street was Miss Brown on?"

Crabtree looked discomfited. "I'm sorry, sir. I didn't think to ask her."

"I want you to find out. I want to know exactly which tree Tiger was pissing on. Take her back there if you have to. Talbert lived on the south side of Shuter Street. It might mean something or it might not if the two people, possibly American strangers, one a negro, were walking on that side from that direction. The time certainly fits. Talbert was shot somewhere between eight and nine o'clock."

Murdoch was irritated that George hadn't thought to ask the woman such an obvious question. He leaned over and chalked in a square on the northwest corner of Shuter Street and Church. The Elliott Hotel. An American lady with a coloured servant, even though she was female and Miss Brown had seen a male, was too much of a coincidence to be ignored. He'd better go and have another chat with the redoubtable Mrs. Dittman. And soon.

There was a tap at the door and Sergeant Hales entered. "Dr. Ogden telephoned to say she is sending over her post-mortem report on Mr. Talbert, sir. She says she was able to start sooner than expected and preferred not to wait for you as she has a social engagement for this evening." He glanced over his shoulder. "Hold on. I think I hear something right now. Might be the report. Shall I bring it in?"

"Please do. Maybe there'll be surprises."

There weren't. Dr. Ogden wrote that Thomas Talbert was "well nourished and in excellent health for his age." When he read that, Murdoch thought of Mr. Stokely's sad words: *He should have died peacefully in his bed.* As they had pretty much determined when he examined the body, death was caused by a bullet severing the carotid artery and was probably instantaneous. "The bullet was still lodged in the skull. I have extracted it and will keep it for your perusal. Professor Broske says he has experience in these matters from his time in the last Italian war, and he will be happy to share with you a simple but effective method by which you can determine if the bullet matches the revolver."

"He will, will he? First I have to find a revolver."

He'd been reading the report out loud to the constables.

"Dr. Broske is a friend and colleague of Dr. Ogden's. A man of considerable knowledge, which he is always happy to share."

They didn't miss the irony in his voice, and they grinned at him except for Dewhurst, who probably thought he was serious.

He continued. "The trajectory of the bullet was as we discussed. At an angle of forty-five degrees from entry to exit. The revolver was therefore about two feet lower than Talbert's neck. He is five feet, eleven inches tall.

"There was some slight scarring on Talbert's right kidney and some fatty tissue on the liver, which indicated to me that the subject might have been a heavy drinker at some time in his earlier life. Certainly not now, I would say, from the condition of his other organs. The only other thing unusual was that he had a condition known as hexadactyly or, in layman's language, he was born with six fingers on each hand. He had the more common form known as ulnar hexadactyly, that is to say, an extra little finger. Both of these fingers had been surgically removed in adult life. The most common practice is to suture the small fleshy finger as soon as the child is born and then it simply falls off. However, this did not occur with Mr. Talbert and part of the bone had developed. He had mastoids at some time in his life, which left some scarring in his ears. He also had an undescended right testicle, which would have occurred at birth.

"Yours sincerely,

"Julia Ogden. M.D.

"P.S. There is no doubt he was already dead when he was tied up."

The letter ended abruptly and the writing was hurried. Off to a social engagement with you know who, thought Murdoch. He looked over the constables.

"Any questions? The most relevant part of this for us is the angle of the bullet, of course."

"Can we assume that the assailant was indeed shorter than Mr. Talbert?" asked Fyfer.

"Let's say that's a strong possibility, but be careful about putting on blinkers. He could have been sitting down and been seven feet tall."

"So if what the maid said is true, it could have been the woman, the taller one, who shot him."

"That is true, Fyfer." Murdoch rubbed his forehead hard, realizing he was very tired. "All right, I'm dismissing you for tonight. You can get right back at it tomorrow. George, stay for a moment, will you?"

The three young constables collected their helmets and with various buttonings of collars and tightening of belts, they filed out. Crabtree remained at the table. As soon as the door had closed, he said, "I'm so sorry, Mr. Murdoch, I don't know what I was thinking of, or not thinking of, more likely."

"It's not at all like you, George. Is something the matter? Something that's distracting you? Is it what you were telling me about the other day?"

Crabtree put his hand to his eyes and bent his head. Murdoch realized with a shock the man was trying to push back tears.

"Yes, sir. Forgive me, sir, but I can't help myself. I know I was whinging about another babe on the way, but I never thought . . . I never . . . She's done away with it, sir. Ellen has got rid of the baby."

CHAPTER THIRTY-FOUR

Murdoch had comforted Crabtree as best he could, feeling all the while hopelessly inadequate. Apparently, Ellen had acquired some herbs and brought about a miscarriage. "It would have been difficult to have another babe," cried Crabtree, "but we could have managed. I never would have expected her to do this." What she had done was, of course, illegal, but there was no fear that Murdoch would pursue that.

Finally, he sent the constable home and headed down to the Elliott Hotel to speak to Mrs. Dittman and her maid.

He found them seated on one of the benches in the hotel grounds, and he observed them for a moment, unseen. Mrs. Dittman was leaning against the back of the bench, Faith was sitting upright, staring into space. He thought he saw tension in her body, as if she were bracing herself. Then she reached over and caressed her mistress's arm in a way that was too intimate for a maid. Mrs. Dittman didn't respond and Faith made the gesture again, then she noticed Murdoch and must have said something because Mrs. Dittman looked up immediately. The bench was deeply shadowed, and they were sitting away from the lamp, but even so, he saw that since their last meeting she had slipped further into illness.

"Good evening, ma'am, Miss Faith. I wonder if I might have a few words with you?"

Mrs. Dittman sighed wearily. "More words, Mr., er, forgive me, but I have once again forgotten your name."

"It's Murdoch, ma'am. Detective William Murdoch."

"What is it you wish to have more words about, Mr. Murdoch?"

The evening breeze rustled through the branches behind her and she shivered.

"Faith, will you bring me a shawl?"

The maid frowned. "Won't he want me to be here too?"

"If he does, he can speak to you when you return. Please hurry. I'm quite cold. It should be in the wardrobe."

"We can go inside if you prefer, Mrs. Dittman," said Murdoch.

"No, it's really quite pleasant out here. Besides, what will the manager think if you are seen questioning me for a second time? We will be asked to pack our bags, won't we, Faith?"

"Yes, madam."

The maid darted a quick glance at Murdoch, which was full of malice and fear, then she got up and stalked off before he could offer any objection. He studied her briefly. She was a short woman, perhaps about five feet tall, verging on being stout. Nothing about her was particularly mannish, but he supposed any woman in trousers and a fedora hat could pass herself off as a man. He turned back to Mrs. Dittman and realized she, too, had been watching, but it was he she was studying. Her expression was cold. Then when their eyes met, she gave him a rather charming smile.

"Well, sir?"

"Mrs. Dittman, since I spoke to you last I'm afraid there has been another murder. A Mr. Thomas Talbert was found shot to death in his house early this morning."

"I had no idea Toronto was such a wicked city, Mr. Murdoch."

"This is not at all typical, I assure you. Mr. Talbert lived not too far from here. We have a statement from a witness who was on Shuter last night. She said she saw a couple walking along the street, a man and a woman. The man was a negro of small stature and the woman she described as taller and fashionably dressed. She couldn't tell if this woman was a white woman or a negress, but she was sure both man and woman were of middle age and the witness believes they were American. She claims to have seen them shortly after the time Mr. Talbert was killed. They were walking in a westerly direction, that is they would have been coming toward the Elliott Hotel."

"What is this to me? I did not stir from my room last night. I cannot believe I am the only American in the city or that my maid is the only coloured person here. Besides, you say the woman saw a man and a woman. Faith is female, I assure you, and I have no male servant with me, as I already told you."

"It is not that difficult for a woman to disguise herself as a man."

She laughed. "I suppose not and just as easy for a man to disguise himself as a woman. Perhaps it was really two men your witness saw."

"Point taken, ma'am, but there was another coincidence, the witness described the woman as moving with some difficulty, as do you."

She turned her head away with a wry smile. "As do many women of my age. Growing older can be a curse. You are too young to know it, but you will."

In the gloom, seeing her in profile like that, Murdoch had a sudden teasing sense of familiarity, as if they had met before. Not at the interview he had conducted yesterday but before that. He couldn't place it.

He continued. "When our witness reached her own house, she said she turned to look down the street, but the couple had disappeared. There is no cross street close so we can only assume that they went into a house . . . or a hotel. The Elliott is the nearest place."

"Really, sir. I'm afraid I do not care for the insinuation. I have nothing to do with this man's death. He is a stranger to me. I do not possess a revolver. I am a visitor here and, as you see, in poor health. I was not expecting to be harassed by the local police about an affair that belongs to this city, not to visitors, however American they may be. Must I be forced to speak to the chief constable? You are all too happy to accept our money, but it would seem we are convenient scapegoats when you are confronted with a difficult case that has you running in circles."

In spite of her obvious ill health, she was formidable, and Murdoch for a moment doubted himself. But only for a moment. Bluster all she liked, there was something going on with Mrs. Dittman and he was sure she was hiding something. It might not be the worst thing, the murder of Talbert, but there was something there.

Faith came hurrying down the path from the hotel, carrying a shawl over her arm. She immediately wrapped it around Mrs. Dittman's shoulders.

"Thank you, Faith. You did not have any trouble finding it, I hope?"

"Not at all, madam."

Murdoch felt a flash of anger. They were talking in code, damn it. What maid wouldn't know where her mistress's shawl was? Faith had remained standing beside the bench. He turned to her.

"Mrs. Dittman said she never left her room last night after the evening meal. Am I to take it that you kept her company?"

He didn't expect a denial of Mrs. Dittman's statement, but he wanted to see how convincing Faith would be.

"Of course I did. She was not at all well and needed me to look after her."

She spoke in a monotone voice rather carefully, as if she was choosing her words. Her face was expressionless.

"I am investigating the murder of a negro gentleman by the name of Talbert. Did you know him, by any chance?"

Mrs. Dittman interrupted. "Really, Mr. Murdoch. If you visited New York I would hardly expect you to know every white man in the city. Why should Faith know Mr. Talbert simply because he was a coloured man?"

"I didn't mean that, ma'am. It was meant to identify only."

"I've never heard of him," said Faith quickly.

Mrs. Dittman pulled her shawl closer about her. "There, you see. Now, if you don't mind, I will go indoors. I don't want to contract pneumonia on top of all my other troubles, as we intend to leave on Monday morning."

Murdoch decided to take a chance. "There is one other thing, ma'am. As I said, Mr. Talbert was shot and the coroner believes he must have died instantly. However, very soon afterwards, he was bound in a most peculiar position." He reached in his pocket and took out his sketch. "It looked like this. He was tied by the wrists and pulled up into a sort of crouch position with a poker under his knees and over his arms at the elbow."

Mrs. Dittman was a woman of great control, but she couldn't quite hide the shock his words gave her. She glanced at the drawing.

"It is, as you say, a peculiar position. One would hardly tie an animal that way."

"Lucky for the man, he was already dead," said Faith.

"Yes, indeed," said Mrs. Dittman.

"And the position is of no significance to you? To either of you?"

Faith shook her head. "None," said Mrs. Dittman. "Was there no robbery, then? Isn't theft usually at the bottom of these crimes?"

"The only thing missing was his coat. I believe that the assailant took the coat to cover the bloodstains that must have been on his apparel."

She shuddered. "This becomes more gruesome as you tell it, Mr. Murdoch. If you will excuse me, I think I have heard all I can handle for tonight."

She held out her hand to Faith, who helped her to her feet. But Murdoch wasn't done yet.

"Mrs. Dittman, I would like to have a look around your room. I do not have a warrant on me, but I can soon get one."

She stared at him. "If I refuse, you will take it as an indication that I have something to hide and presumably I am connected in some way with these two dead men."

Murdoch hadn't mentioned Cooke's name or his relationship to Talbert.

"Oh, let him come, madam," said Faith. "He's the sort won't take no for an answer. He'll keeps coming around like a fly on offal. You need your rest. The sooner he gets his look around, the better."

Murdoch knew then that whatever there might have been to hide in that room, Faith had disposed of it.

CHAPTER THIRTY-FIVE

Murdoch heard the clock in the hall strike midnight. He was still awake and sleep seemed to have no intention of visiting him. He couldn't calm down his thoughts.

The house is quiet. I wonder if Amy is asleep. I'm sure she is, she's never troubled with insomnia the way I am. Thoughts are chasing their tails through my brain. "Count sheep, Will," Mama used to say. "Imagine them jumping over a fence one by one. One, two, three." But that rarely worked. Sleep came eventually when I knew Harry was asleep and I could hear his drunken snore. But even then I'd lie there, sometimes until dawn, tense and agitated, going over the latest ugly scene in my mind, rehearsing responses I never had the chance to act upon until I started to grow taller and Harry knew I would fight him if I had to. Oh God, why am I thinking of that again? Is it the whipping that was laid on Cooke? I've seen corpses before and violent death is always disturbing, but these two are among the worst. The pain inflicted upon Cooke was lingering and he wasn't a young man. Neither was Thomas Talbert, he must have been well into his seventies. At least he died immediately. But why? Had he known he was going to die? Had he been afraid? He seemed like a man of courage but faced with death, don't we all quail? Wouldn't I? George is determined the culprits are Elijah Green and his brother, but I can see no motivation. Robbery in the case of Cooke makes sense, but the whipping changes that completely. What was the connection between Cooke and Talbert except that long-ago purchase? Did Talbert and an accomplice whip Cooke? And then that accomplice turn around and shoot Talbert? Thieves falling out? But why leave forty-one dollars? – Wait a minute! How could I miss that? Two of the notes were stuck together. Perhaps it was meant to be only forty dollars. The price of betrayal, Judas money. So Talbert's murderer considered he had been betrayed. That makes sense except that . . . there were two people present at the shooting. Thieves then falling out. On the other hand, it could be nothing to do with money. A deliberate ruse to mislead. Did somebody truly consider Talbert a traitor to his own race? Or an impudent coloured man cohabiting with a white woman? Mrs. Stokely and Talbert seemed to have kept their marriage a close secret, but perhaps it had leaked out. The murderer or murderers were familiar with Talbert's routine or they were lucky. He was always by himself on Friday nights. Would they have killed Mrs. Stokely as well if she had been at home? But why was Talbert tied into that cruel position after death? Is Mrs. Cooke involved? She stands to gain much by her husband's death. I can easily see her shooting somebody, yes, but not the whipping or the desecration of Talbert's body. But then again, as Amy reminds me, I tend to be sentimental where women are concerned. Was the intention to whip Cooke to death or whip him so many times and then shoot him? Thirty-seven to thirty-nine stripes. Why does that sound familiar? Where have I heard that before? Prisoners here are usually given ten or fifteen lashes. Thirty-seven is a lot. Oh, thoughts switch off. Think of sheep, fluffy happy sheep jumping over a fence. One, two, three, four . . . Charlie is so happy I almost envy him. Would I feel like that if Amy agreed to marry me? Yes, I would, but she says she loves me now and asks *why I feel the need for some fossilized ritual? Because I do. Because I'm not a New Man, I suppose. I want to stand in front of the altar and say, "I take you, Amy Henrietta Slade, to be my lawful wedded wife, in sickness and in health . . . till death us do part." That's it, isn't it? As if making a holy vow out loud before God makes it certain that death will not separate us. As if we are then protected against typhoid, consumption, and all the other ills the flesh is heir to. That's why I want to have and hold her the way I never got the chance to with Liza. I am as superstitious as a Protestant peasant, as my mother would say. Life is so transient. I see Mrs. Stokely weeping for a husband she is not able to tell the world about. Jump, little sheep. Why did my mother ever tell me to count sheep? We lived in the country and I saw sheep all the time and if they did jump a fence it was because they were afraid of something and fleeing for their lives. I cannot fall asleep if I see frightened sheep. I want them to be secure, ignorant of the fate that awaits them, just enjoying lush grass and sun. I'd better think of something else to count. Count how many times I can strike another human being with a whip for no reason except to hurt him. I know we still punish some of our prisoners like that. I had to witness Pryor being whipped, tied on the triangle, sentenced to be punished with fifteen lashes for raping a child of ten. A heinous crime, but I couldn't bear to stand and watch his back as the welts raised until they were oozing blood. To hear his screams of pain. Only fifteen lashes for him and that was enough. And now we're back to crime and punishment, are we? What punishment fits the crime and what doesn't? I accept imprisonment, but lashing or hanging even doesn't undo the crime or reverse time, and whipping Pryor gave no solace to the raped child, although perhaps it did to her parents. Revenge is Mine, sayeth the Lord. Mrs. Dittman's maid isn't that far removed from slavery in terms of her age. I wonder if she once was one. She could have been. Is that it? Are these two women the ones I seek? Is it a vendetta that I don't know the details of? If so, why these two particular victims, one white, one coloured?*

He sat up in bed and leaned over to light his candle. Maybe a pipe would calm him down. He took out his tobacco pouch from his drawer, tamped his best Badger into the bowl of his Powhattan, lit up, and took in a deep, satisfying draw.

After his request to Mrs. Dittman to search her room, he'd felt he had to follow through although he suspected it would be a waste of time. And it had been. He'd looked in the wardrobe for Talbert's missing coat, but it wasn't there. He'd asked both her and Faith to empty out their suitcases; nothing there either. Nothing unusual except a bottle of laudanum in Mrs. Dittman's valise and a bottle of liquor, unlabelled, in Faith's. If they were implicated in the murder of Talbert, they could have disposed of the revolver anywhere. He finally left them, both still and silent, Mrs. Dittman looking haggard. What was the secret they were afraid he'd discover? Were they lovers? Things like that happened and he had witnessed that peculiarly intimate gesture in the garden. Was Mrs. Dittman afraid of the scandal if it came out that she, a white woman, had a liaison with her coloured maid? That was possible, he supposed, although he sensed there was something about their relationship that could not be explained that way. Faith reminded him of a dog whose entire life was focused on its mistress. A fierce dog, he thought, one that wouldn't hesitate to bite. And Mrs. Dittman? She gave orders the way one would to a servant but . . . but what? Was she too solicitous? Too careful not to be autocratic, or was that just an American trait? He wondered again why she had been so shocked when he told her what had happened to Talbert. No doubt most women would be appalled, but she had reacted to the post-mortem violation, not to the murder itself. Faith had not been shocked.

He was feeling sleepy at last, and he was just about to extinguish his pipe when he heard a light tapping at the front door, the knock of somebody trying to gain access without waking the entire household. There it was again. He got out of bed, pulled on his trousers, picked up his candleholder, and hurried downstairs. No other lights were lit, so the knocking evidently hadn't yet disturbed anybody else.

Paul Musgrave was standing on the steps, and Murdoch could see a carriage at the curb behind him.

"Sorry to disturb you, Mr. Murdoch. I saw your light so I knew you was still up."

"What is it?"

"I thought you might like to take a little ride with me, sir."

"At this time of night?"

"Yes, sir. It has to be at this time of night because this is the only time it happens."

Musgrave was clearly enjoying being mysterious, and Murdoch felt like shaking him. He heard the wail of one of the twins from the back room. He stepped across the threshold and held the door closed behind him.

"You'd better have a good explanation, Musgrave. We have two babes living here and it sounds as if you've woken one of them up. What do you want to say, man?"

"Just this, sir. You know Mrs. Cooke complained that somebody was taking out the carriages and horses without permission or payment. Well, it's true and if you come with me, I'll show you who it is and where they go."

"Tell me now."

Musgrave touched the peak of his cap with his forefinger. "Allow me my bit of fun, Mr. Murdoch. I'd rather you see for yourself. I promise you it will be worth your while."

"Damn it, Musgrave. If you're leading me by the nose, I warn you I have sharp teeth."

"I don't doubt it, sir."

Murdoch stared at him. The man was full of his own importance and clearly was not going to yield up any information until the last minute.

"I'll get my clothes on."

"I'll be at the carriage, sir."

Both twins were howling and the light was showing underneath Katie's door. He hesitated for a moment but decided not to disturb things even more. He dressed quickly and went outside.

Musgrave gave him another irritatingly conspiratorial wink. "We have a companion." He opened the carriage door and Murdoch got in. The blinds were down on the windows, but an oil sconce was burning on a low wick and he could make out a woman's figure in the corner. It was Mrs. Cooke. She had abandoned her widow's bonnet and veil and was wearing a plain felt hat.

She flicked her hand at the cabbie. "Get going, Mr. Musgrave. We don't want to get too far behind. Good evening, Mr. Murdoch."

"Good evening, ma'am."

Musgrave called to his horse and the carriage started to move at a good clip.

"Where are we going?" Murdoch asked. He lifted the blind sufficiently to determine they were heading west along Queen Street.

"I don't know. I have put myself entirely in Mr. Musgrave's hands. He is the one who is determined to get to the bottom of this pernicious thieving. I'm thankful that somebody cares." Her tone was aggrieved, as if Murdoch had been negligent in not pursuing the matter with the ardour it deserved. Their eyes met, and for a moment he saw something soften in her expression. "I am aware, Mr. Murdoch, that you consider me an unfeeling woman who has not shed a tear for her husband. I will not stoop to divulging my private affairs to you, but suffice it to say that my marriage had been unhappy for some time, and we were husband and wife in name only. My affections for Daniel were destroyed many years ago."

She leaned back against the seat and closed her eyes, giving Murdoch no chance to pursue the topic.

"Paul warned me the journey might be a long one," she said. "So, I will take the opportunity to rest a little. This has been a most wearing time."

Murdoch had felt a twinge of sympathy for her when she had spoken so honestly, but the moment had passed and all he could see on her face were the marks of entrenched discontent. He took the opportunity to check out her boots. They were of good leather, old-fashioned and round-toed. She hadn't said a word about Thomas Talbert's death, but he didn't have the impression that she was trying to hide something. She seemed to be completely preoccupied with her own affairs. After a few minutes, he, too, leaned back.

He was awakened by the carriage door opening. Musgrave pulled down the step.

"Here we are. Mr. Murdoch, I suggest you come with me and Mrs. Cooke should remain in the carriage."

"I will most certainly not," she said and followed right behind Murdoch as he climbed out.

"Are you sure, Adelaide? They're a rough crowd."

"I haven't come all this way to sit in a carriage."

So, it is Adelaide now, thought Murdoch. Musgrave handed him a grubby woollen scarf that smelled of tobacco.

"Wrap this around your chin and pull your hat low. You don't want anybody to recognize you. It could make things most awkward. Follow me. Adelaide, give me your arm. We should hurry."

They had stopped on the edge of an open field that sloped away from them and disappeared into a thick stand of trees. The air was pungent with the smell of crushed grass and horse droppings. Oil lamps were hanging from posts around the perimeter and he could see several other carriages. Musgrave had unhooked the rear lantern and he led the way down a path of trampled grass. In a few minutes, Murdoch could hear voices that grew louder as they finally emerged from the trees. About fifty feet in front of them was a dense crowd of men, buzzing with excitement and all facing a brightly lit, roped-off ring.

"It's a prize fight," said Murdoch.

"Quite right about that, sir. They happen here regularly, but don't let on I told you."

CHAPTER THIRTY-SIX

Prize fighting with bare knuckles was illegal, but Murdoch was in no position to enforce the law at the moment. Musgrave had taken him for a ride in more ways than one.

The ring was cordoned off by four posts with ropes strung between them. Four taller posts were also strung with ropes that crossed and from the centre hung an iron chandelier, incongruous in this setting but which threw a good light onto the ring. About six feet away from the first ring was a second rope barricade behind which were pressed the noisy spectators.

"Can we move closer?" asked Mrs. Cooke. "There's space around the ring where nobody is sitting."

"I'm afraid not, Adelaide. That area is reserved for the high-paying Fancy and the officials."

"Who are those men with whips?"

Six men, two of them negroes, were stalking around the inner space.

"They look most ferocious," she added.

"They *are* ferocious," said Musgrave. "All of them are former bruisers. Their job is to keep the riff-raff behind that second rope. You'd be amazed how excited men can become once the fight has got underway."

"Goodness gracious, isn't that Alderman Jolliffe down there, just to the right of the post?"

It was indeed Alderman Jolliffe, an ardent and self-righteous Orangeman who was vocal about his anti-Catholic sentiments. Murdoch thought that he just might let it slip to the newspapers that the councillor was attending an illegal prize fight.

They had been speaking in low voices, but one of the men in front of them turned around. He had a notebook in his hand.

"It's not common to see ladies at these fights, ma'am. I hope you can stand it."

"She's a nurse," said Musgrave, smooth as cream.

The man tipped his hat. "Indeed. Well, I do hope, ma'am, for the sake of the sport that you won't intervene. I've got a wager that says the match will go to twenty-two rounds and I'd hate to lose that money."

"Get on with your own business, Charlesworth. Nobody's going to spoil your story." Musgrave winked at Murdoch. "Mr. Charlesworth here writes up these little donnybrooks for the Fancy to peruse at their leisure."

The chatter of the crowd suddenly subsided, the spectators responding to some signal that Murdoch hadn't noticed. On the other side of the ring, a few feet up the slope, was a stone fence and beyond that a barn. At that moment, the barn doors were flung open and a cheer went up from the crowd. Out stepped a posse of men. The two in front were carrying lanterns burning at full wick and behind them was a tall man dressed in white knee-length knickers and a blue singlet. A flowered silk belt was around his waist. He strutted down the path to the fence gate, which was quickly opened for him by two bystanders. Here he paused, removed his old-fashioned tall hat, and tossed it into the ring to the yells of the crowd.

"Who is that?" asked Mrs. Cooke.

"He's the challenger. He goes by the name of the Chopper. He's from up north somewhere. The story is he's a full-blooded buck."

"Who's he fighting?" asked Murdoch.

"Ah, sir. That's the question, isn't it. There he is, look."

The barn door opened again. There were shouts from the crowd but considerably less enthusiasm. A single man held the lamp ahead and behind him, wearing a singlet and black knickers, was Lincoln Green. His belt was red and yellow. Elijah was directly behind him, carrying a towel over his arm.

"Well, I don't know about you, Mr. Musgrave, but I'm not surprised. Green is the one stealing my horses," said Mrs. Cooke. "I never trusted that man and I was right."

Murdoch thought the cabbie would prove himself a first-rate liar if he admitted to surprise at the presence of the Green brothers, as it was obvious he was quite familiar with the whole goings-on.

Lincoln tossed his hat, a brown tweed crusher, into the ring and another roar went up.

The two entourages, each making a circle around their champion, climbed through the first set of ropes. A little terrier of a man in a black cap and fisherman's jersey hopped into the ring.

"He's the referee, name of Christopher," said Musgrave. "A good man, by all accounts. He won't allow any funny business."

Christopher made beckoning motions, and Elijah Green and a man with the battered face of a pugilist who was standing next to the Chopper both ducked under the ropes and walked to the centre of the ring. Here Elijah marked out a line on the grass with the heel of his boot.

"That's called his scratch line," said Musgrave, who seemed to be enjoying his role as teacher. "Each fighter has to be able to come up to scratch for the next round or else he forfeits the match."

Mrs. Cooke nodded. She was completely engrossed in what was happening. The reporter, Charlesworth, was scribbling in his notebook.

Now Christopher beckoned the two fighters into the ring. Under the brilliant light, Murdoch had a better opportunity to assess each man. The Chopper was a good head taller than Lincoln and looked a lot heavier. He had wide, well-muscled shoulders and long arms. His legs, however, were spindly, and Murdoch wondered if he'd been a lumberjack. When he'd worked at the camp in Huntsville, he'd seen lots of men with similar physiques, all of the heavy work being done by the arms and shoulders. Lincoln was better proportioned, his leg muscles were well developed and his arms looked powerful. The skin of both men gleamed with oil, and both of them were clenching and unclenching their massive fists.

The referee pointed at Lincoln. "First call to the African," he said and tossed a coin in the air. Lincoln called out, "The Queen" in a loud voice. Christopher checked. "Her Majesty it is." There was a mixture of cheers and boos from the crowd.

"He'll take the north corner, or he's a fool," said the reporter in front of them. "The field slopes upward and when they tire it'll give him a bit of an advantage." He glanced over his shoulder. "And he needs all the advantages he can get. The Chopper outweighs him and outreaches him. In my opinion, the African doesn't stand a chance, even though, of the two of them, I'd say he has the most bottom."

Mrs. Cooke frowned and Musgrave interjected quickly. "That's a term the Fancy use for courage."

Lincoln looked at his brother, got the nod, and pointed to the north corner. This elicited another wave of jeers mingled with a few cheers from the crowd. He was not a favourite.

The fighters touched knuckles briefly and then went to their respective corners. Here each man's second was ready in position on one knee. Murdoch could see Elijah talking in his brother's ear. Then he stood in front of him and held up his hands while Lincoln did a few warm-up punches into his palms. The Chopper seemed content to sit on his second's knee and have one of his entourage massage his shoulders.

"Gentlemen, your attention, please," called out the referee. "We are about to begin. Now, I shall remind you in case there are virgins here that this match will be run under the old rules." He shouted out the last two words and a roar of pleasure came from most of the spectators. Murdoch thought they were already acting as a mob, cheering or booing all together. Christopher held up his hands for silence. "I haven't finished yet. There will be thirty seconds between rounds; a drop will end the round and the fighter must go, or be taken, to his own corner. At the sound of the bell he must come up to the scratch line immediately or he will forfeit the fight. The winner will be determined by a knockout or by one of the boxers being unable to continue. In which case, his second must so indicate by throwing in his towel. Are we clear?"

"Yes! Get on with it! Stop blathering!" yelled a number of voices.

"There is one more thing before we let these men at each other, and they will be at each other, I promise you. This is a grudge match of unprecedented ferocity. The Chopper has defeated the African once and the African has in turn defeated the Chopper –"

"We know all that," shouted one man.

The referee scowled. "I should remind you that this boxing match is under my authority just as much as a courtroom is under the authority of the judge. I will not tolerate any brawling or any interfering with the fighters. That is why we have my capable constables."

He indicated the men who were patrolling the space in front of the spectators, and they all slapped their whips into their hands.

"I should also remind you I do not want to see any wagering going on. As we all know, Her Majesty's government has declared prize fighting and wagering to be illegal. And far be it for us to break the law. Right, gentlemen?"

A chorus of "Rights!" came from the crowd.

"Besides, you never know if there are narks among us. It wouldn't be the first time."

Murdoch felt his heart jump a beat. Had Musgrave laid a trap for him? The cabbie must have noticed.

"Don't be alarmed, Mr. Murdoch, nobody knows you're here, but there might be more than one of your previous nabs among this lot so you should keep muffled up."

Christopher continued. "So, we're all understood then? I don't want to see no money changing hands." He paused, "Mind you, I am unfortunately blind in one eye like the Great Admiral himself." He pointed to his right eye. "I don't always see what is going on."

There was a roar of laughter from the crowd. He turned to the Chopper. "Ready?"

The fighter nodded.

Then to Green. "You?"

Lincoln waved his fist in the air in assent.

"Seconds, ready? Timekeeper ready." The referee's voice was as strong and hoarse as a carnival barker's. "Gentlemen, let us begin. Come to the scratch line, if you please."

The flat-nosed timekeeper clanged the bell. The Chopper threw off the blanket that his handler had put around his shoulders and walked to the centre of the ring to take up his position, standing slightly sideways, his right leg foremost, left arm extended, right arm across his chest.

On the other side of the scratch line, Lincoln took the same stance. The two men began to circle each other. Green attacked first, throwing three jabs in rapid succession, then a hard swing to the side of the Chopper's head. He caught him high on his nose and a spurt of blood flew out. The Chopper fell to the ground.

"First blood to the African," called Charlesworth. The timekeeper rang his bell.

"A fall," cried Elijah. He was echoed by some of Lincoln's supporters, but a rumble of disapproval came from the crowd.

Charlesworth scowled. "That wasn't a fall, he backed off and slipped on the grass."

"I don't know about that," said Musgrave. "He's looks a bit wobbly to me."

The Chopper's two handlers were out in a flash and hauled him up and took him to the corner. He sat down while the second flapped a towel in front of his face.

The timekeeper rang his bell and both men jumped up. The next blooding went to the Chopper, who gave Lincoln a stinging blow to his eye.

"One on the peeper," called out Charlesworth.

Musgrave brought his head closer to Murdoch and started to whisper in his ear, "You know that quarrel I told you about? The one between Mr. Cooke and Elijah? I didn't tell you everything . . . didn't seem up to me. But I did hear more than I let on. Cooke wanted Green to make his brother take a drop and Elijah wouldn't hear of it. He's been grooming Linc for months now to be a champion."

"I see."

The cabbie's hot breath was on Murdoch's ear. "He was a fighter himself not so long ago. I saw him fight. He's got the killer instinct, if ever I saw it. They both do."

As if on cue, Lincoln stepped toward his opponent, forcing him into the ropes, and with a powerful swing caught him on the side of the neck. The Chopper staggered away and Lincoln followed, aiming jab after jab at the other man's torso, which was already showing ugly blotches. It was impossible to tell how much bruising Lincoln was receiving, but his left eyebrow was trickling with blood. The flurry had got the crowd excited, but the Chopper was strong and he suddenly retaliated, throwing vicious punches, landing most of them. Lincoln's face began to puff up on one side, distorting it.

Murdoch scanned the crowd. The spectators were in deep shadow, but he could see there were five or six negroes standing silently together near the barn on the north side of the field. There was something in their stillness that spoke more than if they had been shouting like the rest of the crowd. From where he stood, he thought they were young. None was particularly small of stature.

"He's down!" the spectators gave vent as one voice.

The Chopper had managed to grab Lincoln by the throat with one hand while landing two hard jabs to the side of his head with the other. Finally, the Chopper released a huge swing and Lincoln fell to the ground, where he lay writhing.

A loud "Get up" burst from Mrs. Cooke. Elijah and the other second were in the ring helping Lincoln to his feet. They half-dragged him to the corner, sat him on the second's knee, and Elijah dumped a bucket of water over him, then sponged away the blood that was pouring down his face.

The bell clanged and the crowd quieted down. Both men came out slowly, but Lincoln pounced first.

"One to the snorter, the ruby flows," said Charlesworth as he scribbled frantically in his notebook. "Oh, the African has got this round easy. The Chopper is staggering."

Staggering he might be, but the round continued for almost thirty minutes, neither man giving quarter until the Chopper took a fall and the two men walked wearily to their corners.

The next two rounds were shorter, the Chopper taking both falls. It was now obvious that both men had taken dreadful punishment. Their hands were swollen and Lincoln's right arm seemed almost useless.

"He could have broken it on that last parry," said Charlesworth.

Round five had hardly begun when the Chopper threw out a swing, all the weight of his body behind it. He caught Lincoln high on the temple and he dropped like a felled ox and lay unmoving. The crowd was shrieking and calling at him, but Elijah and both seconds had to pull him by his feet to the corner.

"He's done," said the reporter, and Murdoch had to agree. Lincoln could hardly sit on his second's knee. His brother was holding him upright. One of his eyes was completely closed, the other almost so. The bell rang to mark the end of the round, and the Chopper advanced to the scratch line and took up his stance. Lincoln struggled to his feet, took one step forward, waving his arms in front of him as if trying to find his opponent. He staggered backward and leaned against the ropes, panting and spitting blood.

"Mr. Green," called the referee, "is your man up to scratch or not?"

Elijah spoke urgently to his brother, who shook his head and feebly pushed him away. He tried again to get to the line, but he was swaying too much. The Chopper walked toward him, his clenched fist at the ready, but before he could go any farther,

Elijah grabbed the towel from the ropes and threw it down. They had forfeited the fight. The spectators began to shout, a mixture of cheers and catcalls. Murdoch could hear cries of "coward, cheaters." They wanted the fight to continue. The mood was ugly, and Murdoch felt alarm for the Green brothers and their entourage. All together, the fight had lasted about an hour and ten minutes. Not long enough, obviously.

"Damnation," said Charlesworth. "There goes my five dollars."

An ill-kempt, odorous man standing next to him said angrily, "That bloody darkie's a Miss Molly if you ask me. He didn't hardly put up a fight at all."

"I don't know about that," answered Murdoch. "He caught a good one from the Chopper. You could stop a train with a blow like that."

Another man beside him chimed in. "That's all right by me. I had a wager on the Chopper to win. Mind you, a scrap that don't last ain't worth a candle if you ask me."

"I thought you weren't supposed to bet. Didn't the referee say it's against the law?" said Murdoch.

The man released a spurt of tobacco on the grass. "I don't give a fart about that. I just hope my tout is going to pay up promptly. Everybody was betting against the African so he'll have to shell out a lot of dosh."

Musgrave tapped Murdoch on the arm. "I've got to have a quick chin with a pal of mine, I'll be right back. Excuse me, Mrs. Cooke, I'll escort you back to the carriage first. You have been a complete soldier, if I may put it that way, a complete soldier, but the situation might not be safe."

"Not at all."

To her credit, Mrs. Cooke didn't even pretend to be of a delicate sensibility. She had enjoyed herself.

Murdoch could see two men shoving at each other on the far side of the ring. Around them, angry men were waving their fists. It wouldn't take much to turn the whole event into a full-scale riot, he thought. Charlesworth had vanished into the fray. The Green brothers had left the ring, and Murdoch could see them forcing their way through the crowd toward the barn. Lincoln was still unsteady on his feet and the cloth he was holding to his eye was soaked with blood. The knot of negro men Murdoch had noticed earlier also shoved through and he saw them all disappear into the barn. The Chopper was submerged in a sea of well-wishers but he, too, looked groggy.

"Mr. Murdoch, I've changed my mind," said Mrs. Cooke. "I need time to consider what to do about Green. We can't throw out an unjustified accusation. I would prefer you didn't charge him at the moment."

"I'm not officially on duty, ma'am, and I'd be insane to try to make an arrest for illicit gambling in this crowd, and as for stealing one of your horses and a carriage, I don't have any evidence at the moment. I will go and have a word with Green, however. Please don't wait for me, ma'am. I'll find my own way back."

"Very well. Come and see me tomorrow and we can discuss how to proceed. No sense in being hasty, is there? We must forgive those who trespass against us, after all."

She was singing a different tune now. Whatever had caused her to change her mind and had given her such a lively air, Murdoch suspected had little to do with Christian charity.

CHAPTER THIRTY-SEVEN

A s he pushed through the crowd, Murdoch had to sidestep a man who had lifted a boy, presumably his son, onto his shoulders. The lad could have been no more than seven or eight and his face was alive with excitement as he swung his fists in mock battle, his father urging him on. Murdoch had a sudden memory of his own father taking him to see a prize fight when he was about eleven. It was a paltry affair compared with this one and took place in a local farmer's field. Even to a young boy's eyes, the two fighters seemed ridiculously mismatched, one of them a strapping blacksmith's apprentice, the other a flabby, older man who had once been a champion. Harry had got them a place close to the ring, no beaters needed at this match. The ex-champion was canny and seasoned and at first that stood him in good stead, but after less than half an hour, the younger man's better conditioning began to show. He landed blow after blow on his opponent's face, closing both his eyes and causing his lips to puff out to twice their size. One blow landed square on the older man's nose and as his head jerked backward, the blood spattered over young Will's shoulders. Harry had laughed. "Got baptized, did you, son?" Murdoch couldn't bear to let his father see how close he was to retching and he wiped off the blood as stoically as he could. The old champion's seconds didn't throw in the towel for another four or five rounds until the brawler's face was no longer recognizably human. Later, Murdoch asked his father if the man had died. "No, but the poor bastard won't be able to recognize his wife again," was the reply.

The bruiser who had served as Lincoln's other second blocked Murdoch's entrance to the barn.

"No visitors. Sorry, mister."

"I'm an acquaintance of Mr. Elijah Green. Tell him William Murdoch would like a word with him. He knows me."

The man eyed him suspiciously, but he backed off.

"Wait here."

In a few minutes, Green himself came to the entrance and stopped abruptly when he saw Murdoch. A few paces behind him was one of the young coloured men who had been standing aloof from the match, watching.

"Don't worry, Green. I'm not going to arrest you, I wouldn't be so foolish. I'm here unofficially."

Green grimaced. "I didn't think coppers were ever off duty if it suited them."

"Well, this one is. Is there somewhere we can talk in private?"

"I suppose so."

Green jerked his head in the direction of the man in his wake. "Jim, you stay on the gate. I'll be back in a minute. Follow me, Mr. Murdoch."

He led the way down the path. Fortunately, the crowd was drifting across the fields toward the carriages calmed by the fact that most of them had bet against Lincoln and had won their wager. A couple of men were taking down the chandelier and others were dismantling the ring.

They'd only gone a few feet when a man, thick-set, drunk and dirty, got in their path.

"Why'd you throw in the towel, Green? He could have gone on."

"Not in my opinion," said Green calmly. "He didn't hardly know his name."

"Lost me a lot of money."

"That ain't my fault, O'Rourke. It was a fair fight."

The fellow didn't budge. "So you say."

He was shorter than Green but much heavier and there was a menace to him that Murdoch didn't like. He'd met the man before. He stepped forward.

"You heard him. I saw it too. The Chopper landed a good one."

Murdoch still had his muffler around his face so maybe his voice didn't come out as strongly as it might have. The Irishman glared at him.

"I'm talking to this nigra, not you, whoever you are. Keep your nose out of it."

Murdoch pulled away the scarf. "As a matter of fact, I have a very long nose. And I'm sticking it into your business. As I recall, Judge Robinson said the next time you were booked for taking wagers he'd make sure you were given the opportunity to visit Kingston."

O'Rourke stared at him, the light was dim, only one lamp was left hanging on the nearby post.

"You're a copper, ain't you?"

"That's right. Murdoch's the name. Now like I just said to Mr. Green, I'm here unofficially so I can't take you into custody for uttering threats or for taking wagers illegally, much as I would like to. But if you don't bugger off I might suddenly find my badge."

The Irishman muttered under his breath, looked as if he was considering defiance, then retreated.

"I thank you, Mr. Murdoch," said Green. "I'm not in any mood to deal with the likes of him."

They continued on the path that led to the rear of the barn. Here was another lantern and Murdoch could see a tethered horse and a carriage with the familiar yellow C painted on the side.

Green opened the door. "Come into my office."

He climbed in and took a seat. Murdoch followed and sat across from him.

"What do you want to talk about, Mr. Murdoch? I can't stay long. I've got to get Linc home."

"I understand you're managing prize fighters."

Green looked weary. "I wonder who told you that? At a guess, I'd say it was Musgrave."

"Is that what you do in the barn when nobody's there? With the skipping rope? Very good exercise, that. And the Indian clubs."

"You've got to keep yourself fit in my line of work. Training's not illegal."

"But taking a horse and carriage without permission is. It's called theft."

Green smiled. "I had permission. Daniel Cooke gave that to me a couple of years ago. 'Take the carriage whenever you need, Elijah,' were his very words. Let's say it was a barter. He paid me next to nothing and in return I could have use of the horses as I needed. I have to travel around to find good venues and to see other fighters. I saw no reason not to pass on my opinions as to who might win to Mr. Cooke."

"Do you have that agreement in writing?"

"No. It was a gentleman's agreement."

"Did he come to the fights with you?"

Green sat back so that Murdoch could hardly make out his face. "Sometimes."

"Musgrave says he heard you quarrelling about one of the fights. Cooke wanted you to fix it so that your brother lost. Is that true?"

"If I say yes, I can be charged with running an illegal game. You might put your badge on. As it is, I'm claiming what you've seen is just one of many sports that gentlemen come to for pleasure. Nobody can say one way or the other, now can they?"

"Cooke's death could be convenient for you."

"The opposite, Mr. Murdoch," Green answered sharply. "First of all, who will believe he had given me permission about the carriages? Not his wife, I'm sure. If she knew I was here, she'd probably have me arrested."

"She does know. Musgrave brought her."

Green's shoulders sagged. "Is she charging me with theft?"

"Frankly, I don't know what she's going to do. She said she wanted to consider the matter."

Green stared at Murdoch. "Did she now? I wonder what that means? From what I know about the lady, it won't be good." He peered out of the window at the now-empty field.

"You can always leave," said Murdoch.

"Not now. She'll make sure I never work anywhere else. She's got me fast."

"It's my impression she won't stop you from the fights. Perhaps the opposite."

Green digested that. Neither possibility was a good one.

Murdoch didn't know if there was anything he could do about it. On the other hand, he might have a little leverage over Mrs. Cooke himself.

"Is that everything? I should see to Lincoln."

"In a minute. I'm curious about that paper Crabtree found in your box. The words have a different look to them now I've seen this fight. Were they really copy for your son?"

"Just that. I took some words from Mendoza's papers. He was a celebrated man of the ring, an excellent fighter. Lincoln and I have been studying him. My Donnie is interested in the old sport, so I thought I'd give him the words to learn. Believe me, it had nothing to do with plotting Mr. Cooke's death, as your constable suspected."

"And the bloody sacking?"

"Just what I said. I had to bleed Bendigo's abscess. Why waste good sacking?"

Gingerly, he touched the bump on his forehead. "Now this I was fabricating just a bit. The beam I said I walked into was Lincoln's fist when we were sparring." He shifted. "I must go now."

"Sorry, I'm not quite done. First, I wanted to let you know I was sorry about what happened to Thomas Talbert."

Green rubbed his hand over his face. "I'd almost put that out of mind with the fight happening, but I must say I was mighty shocked when I heard. Thom was nobody's enemy."

"At least one person's, I'm afraid."

"But he didn't have much money, I'm sure."

"It wasn't a robbery. There were banknotes dropped on his body, obviously deliberately. All small denominations amounting to forty dollars."

Murdoch was watching Green, but the man seemed genuinely bewildered. "What was the point of that? Oh no, don't tell me you're connecting it with some kind of wager?"

"Judas betrayed our Lord for forty pieces of silver. I was wondering if there was a message in that money. An indication of betrayal."

"You've lost me, detective. What sort of betrayal?"

"I don't know." Murdoch took his sketch out of his pocket and held it in front of the lantern. "After death, Mr. Talbert was tied into this position."

Green studied the drawing and Murdoch saw that tears had sprung to his eyes. "Was he, indeed? Such desecration to an innocent old man, I don't understand."

Murdoch replaced the sketch in his pocket. "Nor do I, at the moment. Was Mr. Talbert ever mixed up in placing bets on the fights?"

"No. He came to one about a year ago and said it made no sense to him to see two sane, healthy men who had no grudge with each other try to batter the other into raw meat."

Murdoch was of much the same opinion, but he didn't comment.

"I know Constable Burley already asked you this, but since you talked to him, has anything come to you? Any suspicions? Anything at all?"

Green shrugged. "If Cooke hadn't been done in first, I might have pointed the finger at him. There was some enmity between them. They didn't hardly see each other, mind, but sometimes Thom would drop a comment about Mr. Cooke that would have set light to straw and Mr. Cooke never seemed comfortable around him. I couldn't understand it. Another owner would have got rid of Thom, I suppose, but Mr. Cooke kept him on. He wasn't even that good a worker any more. I often had to do his job over again."

They heard somebody calling. "Murdoch, where the hell are you?"

Murdoch looked out of the window. Musgrave, swinging a lamp, was walking around the field.

"You'd better see to your brother," he said to Green. "If he's not back to his normal self tomorrow, I want you to take him to a physician I know, a Dr. Ogden on Gerrard Street. I'll speak to her. She won't ask difficult questions."

"Thanks, but he'll be all right. He's tough as shoe leather. It's all part of the game. Next time, he'll learn to be more careful. The Chopper just got in a lucky blow." He hesitated. "What are you going to do? Are you going to arrest me?"

"That's the second time you've asked me that. I'm starting to think you're hankering after the good cooking in the Don Jail."

Green managed a grin. "Not likely."

"No, I'm not going to arrest you. I'm not here officially, as I said. It all looked like good clean fun for gentlemen to enjoy to me. I didn't see any money changing hands."

Green offered his hand. "Thank you. If I can return the favour sometime I will."

"You can help me get back to the city. I don't fancy an hour in the carriage with Mrs. Cooke."

CHAPTER THIRTY-EIGHT

The small church was filled to capacity, but there were only two white people in the congregation, Mrs. Stokely and Murdoch. For the first time in his life, Murdoch was conscious of being physically different from everybody around him. Growing up as a Catholic in a Nova Scotian village that was overwhelmingly Methodist had introduced him early on to prejudice and discrimination, but until somebody knew about his faith, he at least appeared to be like everybody else he met and was treated accordingly.

He had decided to go to the Sunday service at the Baptist Church on Queen Street, and on the way he had met Mrs. Stokely. She was touchingly glad to see him, but she looked wretched, wrung out by grief.

"We can't have a funeral until after the inquest, but Pastor Laing will say some words of tribute today," she said. "I'm sure Thom would have appreciated you coming, Mr. Murdoch."

Murdoch felt uncomfortable. He hadn't come from any fondness for Talbert, although he'd liked him. He came because he wanted to know more about the coloured residents of the city and he knew this was where most of them came to worship. He offered Mrs. Stokely his arm and they entered the church together. They were met at the door by Elijah Green, who was acting as an usher. He greeted Mrs. Stokely warmly and nodded at Murdoch in a cool, polite way. What had happened last night was in another life.

"Good morning, Mr. Murdoch."

"How's Lincoln?" Murdoch asked him quietly.

"He's recovering just fine but having a bit of rest today. Will you come this way, please?"

He led them down the aisle to a pew near the centre.

Murdoch had been about to make his habitual genuflection to the altar as he entered the pew but stopped himself just in time. He had no idea how the Baptists would feel about such outlandish Papist practices, but he felt peculiar not doing it and not crossing himself, as if he were being disrespectful to God. He cringed at how well he'd been indoctrinated. Mrs. Stokely had slid in next to a plump, matronly woman who was exquisitely dressed in a bright blue taffeta walking suit with a matching flower-bedecked hat.

"My dear, please accept my condolences. I'm sure Thomas Talbert was the best of employers."

She was being kind, of course, but Mrs. Stokely was being given the status of housekeeper, not wife as she deserved.

"Yes, he was," murmured Mrs. Stokely. She was dressed in mourning clothes, but she'd been careful not to overdo it. Her plain black hat was unveiled and her suit a navy wool. Murdoch wondered if she would ever reveal the true nature of her relationship with Talbert.

"Such a terrible tragedy," the matron continued. "He will be sorely missed by this church. I know Pastor Laing is awful upset by it." She shook her head. "The Lord sometimes sees fit to take those he loves before their time. It is not for us to question His mysterious ways, is it?"

She leaned forward and included Murdoch in her words. He nodded noncommittally but felt like a hypocrite. There had been many times when he questioned why a supposedly loving God would inflict such misery on the human race for no good reason that he could fathom. When Liza died, Murdoch's faith had been seriously shaken, and so far no priest nor his own prayers had completely restored it.

A woman in front of them turned and also offered condolences to Mrs. Stokely, and they entered into a soft conversation that had to do with the woman's recollections of Talbert's piety.

Unlike the sombre, supposedly reverent silence of Catholic worshippers, this congregation were happily chatting among themselves. A pleasant smell of violets wafted over to him. Everybody was in their Sunday best, gaily decorated hats for the women and well-brushed, sombre suits for the men. On any Sunday morning that was true, of course, of all worshippers across the city, no matter what the church. Murdoch himself was wearing his good houndstooth jacket and fairly new worsted trousers, and he'd spent ten minutes polishing his boots. He should have been attending mass himself but had used the investigation to ease his conscience about skipping. Not that he'd gone last week either or the week before, but he'd deal with that later when he met Father Fair.

Murdoch glanced around. It wasn't the only Protestant church he'd ever been inside, but it was the first Baptist one. The straight-backed pews were oaken and the windows filtered light through pastel-hued stained glass. There were no gilded columns, no statues, no ornate carvings on the ceiling, as there were in his own church of St. Paul's. At the front of the church was a raised platform and a vibrant painting of Jesus at prayer. Below the painting, two curtains framed an alcove, rather like a stage, which displayed another picture, this one of a river. To Murdoch's left was a pulpit with a cross in front of it, the kind he'd once heard a child call a "naked cross," because there was no figure of the suffering Jesus nailed to it.

He was curious about the Baptist service. Not too long ago, he'd been smitten with Mrs. Enid Jones, a young widow who had been sharing his lodgings. She was a Baptist, and every Sunday she went off to her church and he to his. He had come close to proposing marriage but had not done so, for complicated reasons he himself didn't completely understand. Perhaps he just wasn't ready to let go once and for all of his attachment to Liza. If that was so, it wasn't the case any longer now that he had fallen in love with Amy Slade.

He felt a timid touch on his arm.

"Are you all right, Mr. Murdoch?"

"Yes, yes, quite all right, thank you, Mrs. Stokely."

"I just wondered. You seem cast down."

He was saved from a reply by a newcomer entering the pew. Murdoch slid over to give the woman room, then realized with a jolt of surprise it was none other than Faith. She of the no surname.

He tipped his hat to her.

"Good morning, ma'am."

She nodded a greeting and sat down.

"Are you here for the memorial to Thomas Talbert?" he asked.

Her eyes flickered at him. "Is there one? As you've been told already, we didn't know the gentleman. I'm here because I never miss church meeting if I can help it, even when I'm in a strange city."

"How is Mrs. Dittman?"

"Not too well this morning. She had a bad night."

"I'm sorry to hear it."

She turned and looked at him straight in the eyes. "'Twas your visit what contributed to her going down."

Her anger was palpable, but before he could respond, a door at the back of the church opened and the pastor entered. He was tall and thin, younger than Murdoch had expected, dressed in a black suit but no vestments. The organist, who was tucked away out of sight to the side, hit some chords and right behind the pastor came a choir singing loudly and vigorously. Murdoch looked around quickly to see what the ritual was and stood up with the rest of the congregation while the singers filed into place on each side of the altar. All around him, people were clapping their hands in harmony with the hymn that was unfamiliar to him but so lively in tempo he almost started clapping too. After two or three verses, the hymn ended and everybody sat down. The pastor held up his hands. "Hallelujah. The Lord is our Saviour."

"Amen, amen," chorused various members of the congregation. Faith spoke particularly loudly.

"My dear friends in Christ," said the pastor. "Welcome to you all. We have many prayers to request this morning. Mrs. Mabel Forester is not well, suffering bad in her legs and she asks for your prayers."

"Praise the Lord, Jesus saves."

"Our good friend Charles Compton is in sore need of employment and asks for your prayers that he might find work that will help him support his family in the knowledge and love of our Saviour Jesus Christ."

"Amen, Lord."

"But, particularly, this glorious morning, I must ask for your prayers for our dear brother, Thomas Talbert, who has been so cruelly snatched from the world."

Somebody in the congregation sobbed.

Reverend Laing raised his voice. "The Lord shall smite down our enemies yea even as they hurt and revile us. We are in Jesus' hands and he loves us, every child, every man, every woman, no matter how black with sins our souls have become, the blood of Jesus will wash us clean and on the Day of Judgment we will stand before him and if we have taken him into our hearts, our souls will be as clean as the driven snow."

His speech was punctuated by startlingly loud, sporadic cries of "Amen," "Yes, Lord," and "That's right!" from the congregation.

The pastor retired to a chair beside the pulpit and the organist began to play. One woman stood up in the midst of the choir and began to sing. This time it was a hymn Murdoch had heard before. Her voice was so beautiful, it made the hairs on the back of his neck prickle.

Nearer my God to thee . . .

Tho' like a wanderer,
The sun goes down,
Darkness be over me,
My rest a stone.

When she had finished, there was a moment of appreciative silence among the congregation, then the pastor launched into an impassioned prayer that went on for a long time and was often overwhelmed by exhortations from his flock.

Finally, he concluded and faced the congregation, stretching out his arms.

"Welcome, dear sisters and brethren in Jesus. I see that we have some visitors here today. Will you be so good as to stand, tell us your name and where you're from."

Almost as one, the congregation turned to look at Murdoch and Faith. She actually smiled and stood up.

"Thank you, pastor. I am Faith and I usually reside in New York City."

There was a muttering of "Welcome, Sister Faith," "Good news," and she sat down again. Murdoch felt a gentle prod in his side from Mrs. Stokely and he had no choice but to stand.

"My name is William Murdoch and I live here in Toronto."

As with Faith, there was a chorus of "welcomes" and he could see friendly smiles all around him. He spotted Elijah Green sitting in the front pew, his wife and children beside him. None of them was smiling.

The pastor spoke again. "Welcome to you both. Now brothers and sisters, let us show our visitors what sort of welcome our church puts out for any of those who come to our doors. Remember our Lord, who said, 'I was a stranger and you took me in.'"

"That's right! Amen. Yes, Lord."

Murdoch sat back down, but all around him people were standing up and shaking hands with one another. On each side, his neighbours, including Mrs. Stokely, reached out their hands to him and Faith. In the melee, however, she avoided shaking hands with him. Finally, the hubbub subsided, although Murdoch would have sworn almost everybody in the congregation had come over and greeted him.

The pastor raised his arms again. "The deacons will come among you with plates. Do not hesitate to offer whatever you are able to. Remember the widow's mite, which was acceptable to our Lord."

Murdoch was glad he had a dollar left in his wallet and he placed it on the silver plate that was passed along the row. Faith put on a five-dollar bill. That done, the pastor stood again at the podium. "Thanks to our brother, Councillor Hubbard, we have sufficient hymn books now to go around. Whether you can use them or not, let us raise up our voices and sing out joyfully, 'What a Wonderful Saviour Is Jesus my Lord.'"

Mrs. Stokely leaned to Murdoch. "That's hymn number fifty-three."

The woman in front turned, holding out her hymnal. "Here, take mine."

Murdoch accepted the offer. There was more prayer, more singing, another offering to which he could only contribute fifty cents, and it was time for the pastor to give his sermon. A rustling of taffeta skirts, little clearings of throat, and soft "Amen, Lords" as he went to the podium. The congregation settled in.

Pastor Laing's message was simple: Turn the other cheek to those that hurt and abuse you. Murdoch had heard many a variation of this and had long ago dismissed it as an impossible text, noble in theory, but impossible in a real world permeated with injustice and violence. Nevertheless, as he sat in the midst of people whose lives he knew were not so long ago racked with terrible hurt and abuse, he was moved in a way he had not been in a long time. There seemed to be no rage or indignation in the pastor's voice but no servility either. This was what the Lord Jesus taught, and he was going to live by it. Murdoch watched Elijah, head bent, apparently intent on what was being said.

The pastor concluded his sermon and Murdoch heard a particularly loud "Praise the Lord's word" from Faith. Mrs. Stokely was quiet, and Murdoch wasn't sure how much she was actually listening.

"Let us leave today by singing together a hymn that I know was a particular favourite of Thomas's. His voice ringing out for the Lord is forever in my heart."

"Amen. Amen. That's right."

The choir stood up and launched into a song that quickly had everybody on their feet, clapping and swaying together.

"Oh! Oh! Oh! What He's done for me."

This was repeated three times and followed by "I never shall forget what He's done for me."

In spite of an initial self-consciousness, Murdoch was soon moving to the rhythm with everybody else. Faith was singing and swaying enthusiastically beside him. She had a lovely, vibrant voice and he would have complimented her afterwards if he hadn't thought she would spit in his face.

The song ended.

"Go in peace," said the pastor, hands uplifted. Released, the congregation burst into chatter. Mrs. Stokely shook hands with the woman beside her, and the woman in the front pew who had lent her hymn book turned to Murdoch with her hand outstretched.

"The Lord bless you," she said.

He wasn't quite sure what the correct response was, but he mumbled, "And the Lord bless you too."

Faith left immediately without acknowledging him or anyone else. Murdoch escorted Mrs. Stokely outside. The pastor was on the steps, greeting his congregation. When it came to Murdoch's turn, he gave him a warm smile.

"Welcome in Jesus' name, sir."

"Thank you," said Murdoch awkwardly. "I apologize for intruding on a place of worship, but I am actually a police officer. I am investigating the death of Thomas Talbert, and I wonder if I might have a word with you?"

The pastor showed no surprise and Murdoch suspected that the entire congregation knew from the moment he walked into the church who he was.

"Will you come back at a later time, Mr. Murdoch? I must finish my duties, but I will be happy to speak to you if it will in any way facilitate your inquiries. Thomas was a most valued member of our church."

His words were cordial enough, but once again Murdoch could sense his wariness. He was getting accustomed to it. The police asking for a word about a murder case usually didn't bode well for a coloured man, even a man of God.

CHAPTER THIRTY-NINE

Murdoch spent the rest of the afternoon alone. Charlie was on duty and Katie had taken the twins to the Toronto Islands for the day. Amy was visiting one of her students who was ill, she feared with the consumption. In the late afternoon, feeling restless, he decided to drop in at the station to see if any of the constables had come up with new information. Then, on impulse, he turned along Queen Street to St. Paul's Church. He had been in another church this morning, an apostate one, and even though it was a visit conducted in the line of duty, as it were, he knew Father Fair would assign him a penance if he heard about it. Not that he was looking for absolution, but something drew him to St. Paul's, some need he could hardly articulate.

As he was arriving, a flock of birds swooped around the bell tower, twittering frantically, and landed in the big maple tree that grew in the front yard. The din continued as Murdoch walked up the steps. The light was growing softer as the day began to wane and he was finding it hard to shake off his mood. He'd dealt with other cases before that were soaked with tears, cases where people of blameless lives had been murdered, but this latest death had affected him. Talbert was an old man and had surely not deserved to be killed violently and certainly not to have his body treated with such indignity.

Murdoch pushed open the heavy oaken doors and entered into the vestibule where the smell of incense from morning mass hung in the air. A bank of votive candles flickered, and a woman was kneeling at the prayer rail. Whatever she was saying a novena for absorbed her completely, and she didn't glance up when Murdoch took up a taper and lit a candle. He, too, dropped to his knees. *Dear Lord, I ask your prayers for the soul of Thomas Talbert. May he be with you in eternity. I ask this in Jesus Christ's name. Amen.*

There were so many candles burning they were giving off heat. He regarded them for a moment, each tiny flame representing a plea to Almighty God to intercede or perhaps to give thanks for a prayer heard. He crossed himself and got to his feet. The woman didn't stir. Her rosary was threaded through her fingers and he could see her lips moving silently. Her face was careworn and her clothes shabby. There was something about her that reminded him of his mother, perhaps the desperation with which she told her beads. He'd seen his mother do that many a time, trying to find solace in her faith, and he remembered how intense his own feelings were, a mix of anger and helplessness. Anger at the source of her unhappiness, his father, and helplessness because he was too young to do anything about it. As he found himself doing so often, Murdoch wondered where Harry was.

He reached for a taper, dropped a nickel in the box, and lit another candle. He didn't kneel this time but said quietly, "Help me to find forgiveness in my heart, Lord, for those I perceive as having wronged me and those I loved."

The candle flame danced in its red dish, as if it were mocking him.

As soon as he walked into the station hall, Murdoch knew something had happened. Charlie Seymour and a young constable third class, the stenographer, Bobbie McCarthy, were the two officers on duty. Charlie greeted him. His face was alive with humour as if he'd just been exchanging a joke with McCarthy.

"You look like the cat that got the canary," Murdoch said to him.

"I feel as if I ate a pigeon, not the canary," Charlie replied. "You will too when you see who's here." He grinned. "Go down to your office. He's waiting for you. Oh just a minute, there's also a letter come for you. Don't ask me who from because I don't know, some urchin brought it in then took off like a rabbit seeing a fox. It must have been the sight of McCarthy here."

The stenographer laughed, not minding the teasing that was often directed at him. He was a country boy, apple-cheeked, hardly a frightening figure even to the half-wild boys of the city poor, who were ever wary of the frogs.

"Who's waiting for me?" Murdoch asked Charlie.

"It's a surprise. Go on. He's been here at least half an hour."

Murdoch put the envelope in his pocket and went through the rear door to his cubicle. He pushed aside the reed curtain. At his desk, leaning back comfortably in his chair, arms behind his head, was Inspector Brackenreid.

"Murdoch! Come in."

"Well, I, er . . ."

Brackenreid stood up. He was not in uniform but was wearing a fawn suit that anticipated summer. He had put a stylish bowler on the desk.

"Do you want your chair?"

"No, that's all right, sir. I'll sit here."

He took the sagging chair that served for visitors.

"I couldn't wait to get back to the station, Murdoch. I think I surprised our duty sergeant out of a year's growth." He frowned in the old, familiar way that was something of a relief. "A bit much, if you ask me, I'm not exactly Lazarus returned from the dead."

"No, sir, I suppose he wasn't used to seeing you out of uniform." *Or in such a jovial mood.* "How are you feeling, sir?"

"Good. Better than I've felt in years." He patted his pocket. "Don't happen to have a cigar, do you, Murdoch? I could do with a smoke."

"No, sir. I'm sorry, I don't."

Brackenreid pulled open the desk drawer. "Yes, you do, you rascal. Here's a box of the best Cuban." He placed the box on the top of the desk and chuckled. "I thought the least I could do was treat you to a cigar, Murdoch, considering I owe you my life."

Murdoch thought the inspector must still be in the grip of the lingering effects of inebriation. "Not exactly that, sir."

"As good as." He took one of the cigars, took a pair of cigar cutters from his pocket, and snipped off the end.

"The matches are in the other drawer," said Murdoch.

Brackenreid lit up and enjoyed a luxurious draw of smoke. "Good Lord, Murdoch, I almost forgot to offer you one. They are for you, after all."

"I won't at the moment, thank you, sir, but please help yourself."

The inspector waved his cigar tip. "You could do with a new office, Murdoch. This isn't fit for a broom closet."

Murdoch winced. Small and unlovely as his cubicle was, it had served him well for a long time.

"What I've been thinking is that the room next to mine just down the hall would be a more suitable space for one of my most promising officers. At the moment, there's nothing in it but an old filing cabinet, a couple of broken chairs, and a table with three legs. What do you say if we moved all that stuff out and fitted the room up as your office?"

"Well, sir . . . I don't know what to say."

"Good, it's done then. You might as well keep this desk, but we'll get you a couple of better chairs and a decent cabinet." He grinned at Murdoch. "The room could do with a coat of paint to liven it up. I'll order work to start right away. But you'll have to promise me you won't draw your damn maps on the wall."

Bob Cratchett must have had similar mixed feelings when Scrooge went through his metamorphosis, thought Murdoch. Brackenreid was positively beaming at him.

"Thank you, sir. That is very generous, but really I'm so used to this space by now, it serves me very well." *And it's far away from your office.*

The inspector was not to be denied, however. "Nonsense. I'll order everything tomorrow." Suddenly the rather ridiculous air of conviviality dropped away. "I am trusting to your discretion, Murdoch, about what happened at the spa. My wife was most upset that I had left, but she is willing to see how I do, as she put it. I have to stay sober or I won't have a place to hang my hat any more. So I'm counting on you, William. If you see any signs whatsoever that I am backsliding, I want you to pull me up short. No matter what I say or however much I fight you, you must tell me the truth."

Murdoch groaned inwardly. It was not a responsibility he relished, but all he could do was to agree.

"Would you put that in writing, sir?"

"What? Oh you're poking fun at me. But I will, if you insist."

"No, sir. I was joking. Perhaps we could shake hands on it as gentlemen though. No matter what you say, if I deem it necessary, I will speak out what's on my mind."

"Only if you see me backsliding, Murdoch. Not about everything."

"Quite, sir. Another joke."

Brackenreid knocked the ash off his cigar. "I must be going. If I'm a minute later than I said I'd be, Mary will be in hysterics. I'll be in tomorrow, Murdoch, and then I'd like to be briefed on what's been happening here. You look as if you are in the middle of a case."

"Yes, sir."

"Tell me tomorrow then. You will have my full attention."

As that was an experience Murdoch had not had professionally for a long time, he merely nodded. This new inspector was going to take some getting used to.

After Brackenreid left, the reed curtain snapping and cracking behind him, Murdoch went around the desk and sat in his usual chair. He pulled open both drawers in case the inspector had left other gifts, but the cigars were it. Then he remembered the letter that Seymour had handed to him and he took it out of his pocket.

Dear Mr. Murdoch. I am in dire need of your help. Will you please meet me in the stables this evening at six o'clock sharp. This must be in strict confidentiality. I have in return some information to impart concerning the death of Thomas Talbert, which you will find very helpful. Please do not fail me.

Yours, Adelaide Cooke.

Murdoch pulled out his pocket watch. Damn. It was almost six. He had five minutes to get to the appointment. He wondered what it was she needed. His sense of Mrs. Cooke was that, whatever it was, she wanted it immediately and it didn't matter whether it was convenient for anybody else.

CHAPTER FORTY

J ust as he was about to jump on his wheel, Murdoch discovered he had a flat tire. He didn't have time to repair it, so he left the bicycle and jogged as fast as he could over to Mutual Street. It was ten minutes past six when he got there and the stables were in darkness. Damn. Had she left?

He tried the side gate, which yielded to his push. It was unlocked. He crossed the courtyard. Dusk was falling rapidly, but there was just sufficient light remaining that he could make his way to the barn. As he approached, he could see the door was slightly open and could hear a soft nicker from one of the horses. He wished he had his bicycle lamp with him and he cursed himself that he hadn't brought a truncheon or even a revolver. He'd rushed out of the station, completely accepting that the note was from Adelaide Cooke, but what if it wasn't? Now as he tried to look into the darkness of the barn, he could almost hear Amy's voice chastising him. *It doesn't take manly muscle to fire a gun, you know.*

"Hello," he called. "Mrs. Cooke? It's Detective Murdoch here."

There was no answer except the stamp of a horse's hoof and the chink of a bridle.

He pushed open the door all the way, standing to one side so he could not be a target if anybody inside had that intention. Nothing happened. He stepped across the threshold and again quickly moved away to the side. Again nothing.

"Hello, anybody here?"

"Over here," said a hoarse, barely audible voice. He couldn't tell if the speaker was a man or a woman, and he could see nobody.

The voice had seemed to come from one of the stalls at the end of the row. He took a couple of steps forward, straining to see.

"Are you alone?" the voice asked.

"Yes, I am. I was expecting to meet Mrs. Cooke."

"You won't be. I was the one who sent you the note. I took the liberty of using her name."

"And who are you?"

"Never mind. You don't need to know. You're late, I thought you weren't coming."

Murdoch was about to apologize as if he had committed a social indiscretion, but he stopped himself. The situation was absurd. His neck was prickling at the back and he could feel the tension in his gut. He shifted his weight slightly forward. The unseen speaker had an advantage over Murdoch as his eyes had not yet adjusted to the darkness.

"The letter asked for my help and in return I would receive information about the death of Thomas Talbert. Is that true?"

"More or less."

Murdoch peered into the dark, trying to make out if there was more than one person hiding there. "Will you come out into the open? It is difficult to talk to somebody that I can't see."

"Don't be so impatient. We have all evening."

Murdoch had pinpointed the location of the voice by now. The speaker was in the far stall, but the mare didn't seem perturbed and was placidly munching on the hay in her manger. Whoever it was had no fear of horses and must be crouched down and peering through a slit in the stall wall.

The voice came again, more conciliatory. "Mr. Murdoch, I do thank you for coming, but I need assurance that you are to be trusted. I would like you to come farther into the barn. There is a stool in the alley. Please sit down, facing the door."

The voice was still hoarse and low and the words were pronounced with almost an English accent and a peculiar preciseness that sounded artificial. He hesitated. He supposed he could run out of the barn and go for help, but he would probably lose the chance to question his shy informant if he did that. Besides, he was more and more convinced he was talking to a woman.

"How do I know *I* can trust *you*?" he asked.

"Regrettably, you don't know. You'll have to take that chance. As I said in my letter, perhaps we can help each other. Do you want to or not? If not, please leave. If you do, please take the stool."

Murdoch walked cautiously forward and almost banged into the stool. He sat on it as instructed, facing the open door.

He was attacked so suddenly and violently he was taken completely off guard.

A heavy cloth bag was dropped over his head from behind and pulled so tight he was almost choked. At the same time, something hard hit him on the back of his head and he fell face down on the stones. He must have lost consciousness for precious seconds because when he came to, his wrists were tied tightly together in front of him with some thin cord that bit into his flesh.

Something was jammed hard against his neck just beneath his ear.

"This is a gun. I did not come here with the intention of shooting you, but if I have to I will. Don't struggle. Now sit up and bring your knees to your chest."

The string at the neck of the bag was pulled tight, jerking him up. He had no choice but to obey, and in a moment his assailant had bound his ankles. The pressure of the gun at his jaw didn't relax.

"Come into a crouch position."

He was slow to move and there was a sharp blow to the back of his head that made him want to retch. He forced himself not to.

"Don't try to be brave, Mr. Murdoch, it really isn't worth it."

Then the gun was removed and a stick of some kind was thrust underneath his knees and over his elbows, forcing him into a painfully tight ball. It was the same position in which he'd found Talbert. This time he couldn't stop himself from gagging, and there was a fumble at his neck and he felt the cords of the bag loosen slightly.

"What do you want?" Murdoch managed to say, although the bag was still so tight against his nose, he could hardly breath. He realized it was a horse's nose bag. He could see nothing but blackness. "You said you don't intend to shoot me, why are you tying me up then?"

"What did you say, Mr. Murdoch, I can hardly hear you?"

The mockery in the voice filled Murdoch with a rush of rage that overrode his initial fear, but he also knew his best chance to survive was to keep a cool head.

"I asked why you have tied me up in this way."

"A lesson, shall we say?"

Murdoch tried to free his mouth so he could speak with more force. "I don't know who you are. Surely I'd learn a better lesson if I knew what I had done wrong."

"It is not only the guilty who have to suffer, Mr. Murdoch. How much easier life would be if that were only the case."

"You said you needed my help. Is that true?"

"Alas, no. Not in the least. I thought an appeal to your chivalry would get you here quickly and, you see, I was correct about that."

Murdoch coughed violently as some of the dust from the bag went down his throat. Again there was a fiddling at his neck and the heavy bag was pulled away so he could breathe more easily. He would have given his soul for some water, and it was his voice now that was raspy.

"Are you the one responsible for the deaths of Cooke and Talbert?"

"In the strict meaning of the word, I suppose I am, but in truth, they were responsible for their own end."

"You were getting revenge, then?"

He felt another slap to the side of his head, not quite as hard as previously but still jolting.

"I've answered enough questions." The appalling voice came close to his ear. "I have punished two, I have one more to find." There was an odd, chilling chuckle. "What God joined should not have been. First, the father, then the son, and last the holy one and we are done. Somebody will discover you eventually, Mr. Murdoch, police officer. Every minute will be an increasing agony to you, but you won't know just how long you will have to stay like this. It will seem like eternity. However, you, sir, unlike many other unfortunates, can assume that when you are rescued you will be safe from further harm. Those who release you will not hurt you and you will be set free. That should be a comforting thought."

There was another tap to his head, then Murdoch sensed that his attacker had moved away. He heard the door close.

He twisted in the bag so he could relieve the pressure from his nose and was able to gain some space. His head had started to throb from the blows he'd received and he had to fight back waves of nausea.

"Help! Somebody help me!"

He knew how muffled his cries would be and stopped. Perhaps he could wriggle himself somehow over to the door. But which direction was the door? He could see nothing. Nevertheless, action was better than inaction and he rolled onto his side and started an agonizing sideways slither. It was excruciatingly slow and he didn't get far when his head banged into a stall partition. He heard the horse snuffle and stamp its foot. He lay still. All he needed was to end up close to a horse's hooves and he'd risk a good chance of being kicked to death. He tried to reverse directions but had no sense whatever of where he had come from. The pull on his legs and the pressure of the stick was becoming more and more painful.

Every minute will be an increasing agony to you, but you won't know just how long you will have to lie like this. It will seem like eternity.

"Help!" He shouted again. "Help!"

What time was it? He must have arrived in the barn less than half an hour ago. He knew no cabbies would come until tomorrow morning, but when did Elijah Green arrive to tend to the horses? Surely he'd be here before too long?

Unless he had a good reason for not doing his chores tonight.

Once again Murdoch tried to move, but the more he did, the more everything hurt. Finally, panting, he lay still and waited.

However, you, sir, unlike many other unfortunates, can assume that when you are rescued you will be safe from further harm. Those who release you will not hurt you and you will be set free. That should be a comforting thought.

CHAPTER FORTY-ONE

He had lost all sense of time, but he thought he'd been lying like this for more than two hours. The cord had been tied very tightly around his wrists and ankles and they were throbbing, but the worst agony was from the pressure of the stick against the back of his knees and his elbows. He found that by rocking forward onto his toes he was able to alleviate some of the strain on the back of his legs, but he couldn't sustain that for long periods. To make matters worse, he was finding it increasingly hard to get enough air inside the bag. The material was a heavy linen and was barely porous enough for him to breathe. Flies crawled across his exposed hands and he was power-less to shoo them away. He was also aware of an increasingly urgent need to void his bladder. Unbidden, Professor Broske's words came back to him, insinuating themselves into this brain.

Let us remember that fear is a disease to be cured. The brave man may fail sometimes, but the coward always fails.

At first, he had forced himself to concentrate, trying to work out who had attacked him – somebody who knew him, knew where to find him, who had even winkled out a truth about his character. A man or a woman? He still wasn't sure. These thoughts went round and round in his brain for a while, but before too long the agony took over everything. He began to despair that no one would discover him before morning.

Suddenly, he heard the door open.

He shouted as loud as he could. "Help! Over here!"

He hoped to God it wasn't his attacker returned to torment him some more.

There were footsteps, the sound of boots on the flagstones. Suddenly there were hands at the back of his neck and the bag was jerked off his head. The stick was pulled away.

Murdoch gasped and gulped. Oh, blessed sweet air.

His eyes were dazzled by the light of a hurricane lamp that was on the ground beside him, but he could just make out the worried face of Elijah Green.

"Who did this to you, Mr. Murdoch?"

"I didn't see." He could hardly speak. "Whoever it was came from behind and took me by surprise."

"Let me get that rope off. Sorry, this will hurt a little. The cord is tight."

He removed a knife from a sheath at his belt and forced it in between Murdoch's swollen wrists, nicking the skin as he did so. The rope fell off and he did the same with the cord at the ankles. Murdoch licked his dry lips.

"I'll get you some water."

"No, wait. I've got to piss first."

Green grabbed a pail from a nearby bench.

"Use this. Can you stand?"

Murdoch tried to straighten up, but there was no circulation in his legs and he was weak as a babe.

"I'll hold you," said Green.

"No! I can do it myself. Just give me something to lean against."

Green dragged a bail of hay in closer, but Murdoch couldn't stand and his hands had gone numb. He had no choice but to accept the offer of help.

When he was done, Elijah lowered him gently to the ground, then he lit the big hurricane lamp that was hanging from a hook on the beam. "I'll be back in a tick."

As sensation returned to his limbs, Murdoch's entire body felt on fire. Cautiously he tried to straighten his legs, but they felt as if they no longer belonged to him. Elijah was back at his side almost immediately. In one hand he had a tin mug, in the other a brown bottle.

"This first." He handed the mug to Murdoch, who gulped the cool water. "Now drink this, but slower." He poured some liquid from the bottle into the mug.

Murdoch took a sip and some burning fluid slid down his throat, causing him to cough. Tears came to his eyes.

Green guided the mug to Murdoch's lips as if he were an invalid. "It's not the best brandy money can buy, but it should do the trick. Take another sip."

Murdoch did so and the second and third swallows were easier. The warmth from the liquor spread quickly through his body.

"Good, you're starting to look alive again. I wasn't sure for a minute there."

Murdoch grabbed hold of Elijah's wrist.

"You're late, aren't you? Don't you do your chores earlier than this?"

Green stared at him. "We were celebrating with my son. It was his birthday."

Holding the man this tightly was shooting pain up Murdoch's arm, but he didn't let go.

"How do I know you weren't the one who attacked me? It's an old trick. You pretend to leave, then wait a while and come back as if you're just coming in to work."

In the shadowy light of the lamp, Green's face was almost hidden so that Murdoch couldn't see his expression, but he didn't struggle or try to get away. Murdoch tightened his grip and felt the other man wince.

"Whisper at me. Say, 'Somebody will discover you eventually, Mr. Murdoch.' Go on say it! 'Somebody will discover you eventually.'"

Green started to repeat the words, "Somebody will discover –"

"No! I said *whisper*. Like this." Murdoch imitated his assailant's hoarse voice. Green tried again. There was no resemblance to the voice Murdoch had heard and he released Green's arm. Besides, his sense was that his attacker wasn't the same size as Green. Whoever had attacked him was very strong but smaller. The voice had consistently hovered just above Murdoch's head level.

"All right, I believe you."

Green let out his breath. "I'm glad to hear it, Mr. Murdoch, because I had nothing to do with tying you up."

Murdoch struggled to get to his feet, but his legs still couldn't hold him and he staggered. Green caught him.

"I think you should sit a bit longer."

"No. I've got to move. Whoever it was attacked me said he still had one more person to get."

"Did he tell you who?"

"No."

"Then better to hold off for a while. Frankly, sir, you're not fit to help anybody at the moment." He was right. Murdoch sat down on the bale of hay.

Green peered into his face. "You've got quite a goose egg over your eye. Did he hit you?"

"Not there. I fell forward and met with the flagstones."

Green stood up and took a round tin from the nearby shelf. Murdoch noticed it had a picture of a horse on it and there was a whiff of a strong-smelling ointment when he opened it.

"This'll sting for a second or two," said Green, and he daubed some of the sticky substance on the lump. Murdoch jerked away from him.

"I almost forgot you've had a lot of experience dealing with bruises, haven't you?"

Green answered calmly but stopped what he was doing. "That's right."

Murdoch felt himself flush with anger. "Is that what this is all about, Green? Are you trying to warn me off? Are you? Or did you send somebody else to do the dirty work?"

But even as he said it, he knew the circumstances didn't really fit. Why would his attacker have whispered those chilling words in his ear. *I have punished two. I have one more to find.* Of course, that could be a ruse to throw him off track, but somehow he knew it wasn't. He – she – had meant every word.

"Have you got any more of that brandy?" he asked.

Green handed him the mug. Murdoch gulped the raw brandy to the dregs.

"I want you to work on me."

"Beg pardon, sir?"

"Work on me the way you would with one of your fighters. I've got to be up and moving now. Be quick."

Green took up the lantern and disappeared into the gloom of the barn. Murdoch was glad his back was protected and reached for the stick, but Elijah soon returned carrying a battered doctor's valise, which he put on the ground.

"Let's get you out of your jacket first."

The slightest lifting of his arms sent white-hot stabs of pain racing through Murdoch's muscles, but he managed to struggle out of his coat.

Green removed the cufflinks from Murdoch's shirt, shoved up the sleeves, then took out a bottle from his bag, uncorked it, and splashed some of the liquid into his cupped hand. There was a pungent smell of wintergreen. He started to rub the liniment into Murdoch's forearm. His grip was firm and sure, and in spite of himself, Murdoch began to relax as the pain abated.

"Why were you here in the barn?" Green asked as he turned to work on the other arm.

"I received a letter that was supposedly from Mrs. Adelaide Cooke, asking me to come here and I'd be given some information about Talbert's death."

Green shook his head. "Mrs. Cooke isn't in town. I got a message that she's gone to visit her sister in Georgetown and she left Musgrave in charge."

"No, I know it wasn't her."

"Did you get any information?"

"No. Nothing."

"I wonder why they wanted you here in the barn."

"According to my attacker, so I could be taught a lesson. I was tied up in the same way that Talbert was tied, although in his case, they used a poker not a broom."

Green stopped what he was doing. "It'd be easier to work on your legs if you removed your trousers."

"Never mind about that. Do the best you can." Murdoch felt he had experienced enough humiliation for one day. Green didn't insist and returned the liniment bottle in the valise and wiped his hands on a piece of sacking. Then he started to knead deep into

Murdoch's thigh muscles. Murdoch yelped and tried to keep talking through his groans.

Finally, Green leaned back on his haunches. "That'll do you for now, but you're going to be stiff for a few days."

"Thank you." Murdoch eased himself back into his jacket. "My attacker said something very strange. He, or for that matter, she, said, 'What God joined together should not have been. First the father, then the son, and last the holy one and we are done.' Does that mean anything to you?"

Elijah looked puzzled. "Sounds sort of Papist. Don't they say prayers like that?"

"The blessing is in the name of the Father, the Son, and the Holy Ghost."

"Somebody pretending to be Papist then?"

"Maybe, but it didn't sound like that to me. They used the word *punishment*. Two had been already punished and there was one more to find. I assume the two are Cooke and Talbert, but I'd better find out soon who is meant by the holy one."

"You said, man or woman. You think it might have been a woman who attacked you? She'd have to be real strong."

"I was taken by surprise and the person had a revolver and threatened to shoot me. As I couldn't see if it was an idle threat or not, I complied."

Green closed up his valise. "Sounds like sensible thinking to me." There was something in his voice, sympathy perhaps, and Murdoch realized he must have been conveying the sense of shame that was gripping his gut. How could he have been so foolish and so inept as to let himself be tricked like that? Rationally, he knew there hadn't been much he could do to defend himself, but he felt he'd behaved like a coward. His embarrassment made his voice sharp.

"Help me up, will you?"

Green tucked his arm under Murdoch's and got him to his feet. Murdoch felt wobbly but managed to take a couple of steps forward. His knees were shaking. He perched for a moment on the stool from which he had been so ignominiously thrown. He leaned his hands on his knees and paused, taking in a deep breath.

"Because somebody got the better of you doesn't mean you're not a man of bottom, as we say in the fight business," said Green. "In my books, you've got considerable bottom. If I'd been tied up like that for two hours I'd have been screaming for my mammy. You can have the courage of a lion in your heart, but if you've got no power, courage won't do you any good and it will eat at your innards instead."

Murdoch felt a rush of gratitude to the man, but it was himself he had to forgive. "Well? Do you have any ideas you'd consider sharing about what I just said?"

Green hesitated, then pursed his lips. "The reference to the holy one could be significant to us. In the old days, in the Baptist Church we often called our preachers Holy, especially if they weren't lettered but had God in them. You know like, Jeremiah Holy, or Mariah Holy. You don't hear it as much these days because the preachers go to school and are educated. I suppose you'd say holy was an honorary title."

"Do you know anybody, anybody at all, who might have been referred to that way?"

Elijah nodded. "Come to think of it, I do. He used to be the pastor of our church before Pastor Laing came. I think he was lettered as well, but he was such a good man, people often called him, Preacher Archer, Holy."

"Is he still alive?"

"Yes, he is. He's elderly now, and his mind isn't always clear, but he might be worth talking to. He would certainly have known

Thom Talbert from the early days. He lives in the manse next to the church with his wife."

Murdoch heard the raspy voice in his ear. *We have one more to find.* He hoped to God he would get there first.

He tried out his legs again. Better this time. His muscles were tingling and burning, but he thought he'd suffered no lasting damage except to his pride. Green had got him up to scratch. He almost grinned. He'd forever have sympathy with fighters after this.

Green caught hold of his arm. "Is the preacher in danger?"

"I don't know, but he's the only possibility at the moment. I've got to get over there."

"I'll come with you. He's one of us. And forgive me for saying so, Mr. Murdoch, but you'd have trouble apprehending a three-legged dog at the moment."

Murdoch could see it would be a waste of time to argue and he also needed him. "Come on, then."

CHAPTER FORTY-TWO

t was Green's suggestion that they borrow one of the carriages and drive to the church. Murdoch accepted the offer gratefully, and while Elijah was hitching up the horse, he limped into the office and telephoned the station. He was relieved to hear Charlie Seymour's voice. Briefly he filled him in as to what had happened and reassured him that he was all right.

"Send a constable to 183 Mutual Street. Mrs. Cooke is supposed to be away, make sure she is. If she isn't, bring her into the station. I don't care if you have to drag her there in cuffs. Also, I want to talk to one of the cabbies, his name is Paul Musgrave. Bring him in too. I'll be there as soon as I can . . . No, I don't know if they are our culprits, but somebody was able to get into the barn here and I'm taking no chances. I don't have time to tell you everything at the moment, Charlie, but there's one more person I hope to God can fill in the missing pieces for us. Have Fyfer get over to the Baptist Church on Queen Street. Tell him to go to the manse. I should be there before him, but tell him to expect to stay all night."

There was still a light burning in the front window of the manse and when Green knocked, the door was answered promptly. An elderly woman whom Murdoch recognized from the church stood on the threshold.

"Good gracious, Elijah. What is it?"

Murdoch stepped forward and introduced himself quickly. "I do apologize for the hour, ma'am, but I'm afraid it is a matter of some urgency. I wonder if I might speak to Reverend Archer?"

He assumed this woman was the pastor's wife. She wasn't budging.

"It is very late and he's already had one visitor this evening." Mrs. Archer might be tiny, but she was as daunting as a mother doe defending her young. Her feet were braced, her eyes fixed on Murdoch. "Can your business wait until tomorrow?"

Murdoch forced himself to speak calmly. "I would prefer to deal with the matter tonight, ma'am."

Green interjected. "I can vouch for the detective, Mrs. Archer. The matter is most urgent. It has to do with Thomas's death."

She stepped back. "Come this way, then."

They followed her down the hall, through a large kitchen that smelled of baked bread, then through another door into a short hall. Pastor Archer's apartment was an addition to the house.

Mrs. Archer glanced over her shoulder. "I told my husband that Thomas was dead, but I don't know if he quite understood. I do ask you to be careful what you say to him."

She rapped on the door.

"Stanley? Stanley? Elijah Green is here and somebody from the police who wishes to speak to you."

There was no answer, and Green and Murdoch exchanged worried glances. Then they heard the sound of an old man's rheumy cough and a muffled "Enter." Mrs. Archer ushered them past her into the room.

An elderly negro, small and stooped with a fringe of beard and close-cropped white hair, was standing by the fire, warming his hands. He was wearing an old-fashioned brown velvet smoking jacket and matching cap. He looked as dry and brittle as a grasshopper.

"Come in, both of you, come in." He waved his hand politely. "I do apologize for the untidy state of my home, but I was just going through my papers."

The living room was fairly spacious although it was untidy, papers scattered all over the floor. The walls were lined with high bookcases, all of them stuffed with stacks of bound papers. The air was thick and smoky from tobacco.

"I've been asked to write down my life story, you know," the pastor continued. He glanced over at his wife. "Isn't that so, Leah?"

"Indeed it is, Stanley. How are you progressing?"

The old man sank into an armchair that was drawn up close to the hearth. "Slowly, I must admit, it is going slowly."

"How long did your visitor stay?" she asked him. "She must have let herself out while I was upstairs."

"Who are you referring to?"

"The American lady who was here to see you. Did you have a good chat?"

The pastor sighed. "That was a long time ago, Leah. You can hardly expect me to remember that. I see so many people."

Mrs. Archer's eyes flickered over to Murdoch and he understood.

"Stanley, you remember Elijah, don't you?"

The preacher's eyes were vague. "I'm afraid I don't. Have we met before?"

"Not for some time, Pastor."

"And this is Mr. Murdoch. He is a police officer and he wants to talk to you on matters of great urgency that can't wait until morning."

Archer eyed Murdoch calmly. "Is that so, sir?"

"Yes, it is."

"Then you had best have a seat. Leah, would you be so good as to bring us some of your splendid coffee. The detective looks as if he could do with some. And I'm sure the young man would like some as well."

"Not for me, thank you, sir," said Murdoch. Green shook his head.

"Make some for me then, Leah. I'll have it afterwards."

Mrs. Archer headed for the door. "Don't tax him, Mr. Murdoch. He's just getting over a cold. I'll be back directly."

Murdoch turned to Green. "Perhaps you could help Mrs. Archer while I talk to the reverend."

Green hesitated.

"Don't worry," said Murdoch. "I'll be careful."

Mrs. Archer looked surprised. She was too well mannered to give into her anxiety and curiosity both, but Murdoch knew she wouldn't be away long.

"Don't mind my wife," said the preacher after the door had closed behind them. He smiled. "She's as fussy as an old hen. Praise the Lord." He waved his hand. "You'll have to take me as you see me. I'm writing my life story, which is what all those papers are about. I have almost finished. I'd never have thought when I was a young man that there'd be anybody in the white world interested in reading about the misery of the coloured folk. They seemed like they didn't want to hear, see, or speak about what was happening to us. But now it's different. I've got a publisher who can't wait to print my memoirs, as he calls them. 'The more misery you put in, Stanley, the better it will sell,' was what he said. Amen to that, says I. Not that I've got to make any of it up, you understand. I surely don't. My mammy and pappy were both slaves, hallelujah, and my relations likewise, so I've got plenty of misery enough to fill ten books."

The pastor appeared quite lucid, and he reminded Murdoch of Thomas Talbert, although he was probably a few years older.

"Have a seat, sir. You can just move those papers to the floor. That's it. I'll stir up the fire a bit. I don't have that much flesh on my bones any more and I feel the cold."

The fire was already blazing, but the pastor added a couple more pieces of coal from the shuttle.

Murdoch did as he said, his muscles complaining. His head was pounding.

The old man fussed with the fire, then returned to his armchair. His expression changed and he looked at Murdoch, his face full of worry.

"Leah said you were a police officer. Have you found her then?"

"Found who, sir?"

"Thomas's daughter. There's no word yet?"

Murdoch had no idea what he was referring to. "Word about what, Reverend?"

The question disturbed the preacher, who picked up his pipe from the table. "I'll think better if I have my trusty friend in my hand."

"Do you mind if I join you?" asked Murdoch, and he took his clay from his pocket. He was about to share his packet of tobacco when Archer handed him a tin.

"Try this. You won't find this in the stores here. I get it sent up from North Carolina."

When they'd both settled the business of tamping and lighting and drawing, Murdoch tried again. He thought he had better tread carefully.

"I understand you have known Thomas Talbert for a long time, sir."

"I have indeed. Poor Thom, he's had a mighty trying time of it lately. Did he tell you if he was going to accept Mr. Cooke's offer? I advised him to." The old man was speaking as if Talbert were alive.

"Er, yes, I believe he has."

The pastor drew on his pipe and was temporarily lost in a haze of smoke. Suddenly he looked at Murdoch in alarm. "Are you from America?"

"No, sir. I'm not. I live here in Toronto."

"Amen to that. I feared you were tracking them down. If you are, don't expect me to help you because I won't."

"No, sir," said Murdoch gently. "I'm not tracking them down at all."

Archer seemed not to hear him and he went on, speaking quickly. "They have nothing, most of them, when they arrive. But we do the best we can, hallelujah. My wife lives the gospel, and she is wondrous capable at getting them clothes and places to stay." He shook his head and tears welled up in his eyes. "Such terrible stories I hear from them."

Archer puffed on his pipe and abruptly his focus changed. "Thomas took the offer, did he? I'm surprised he hasn't told me after all the to-do he was making. But I'm glad to hear that because I've been afeared for some weeks that he would do Mr. Cooke harm."

"How so, sir?"

Murdoch looked at the preacher, waiting. The man looked back, searching for something in Murdoch's face that presumably he found because finally he let out a sigh and said, "I don't know if you are familiar with the practices of the Roman Catholic Church, but in their faith, the priest listens to confessions of sins, misdeeds, and so on that he then absolves –"

"I do know of it," said Murdoch.

"Then you must also know that these confessions are considered to be of the utmost confidentiality. A priest is not allowed to reveal what is said, even if threatened by law . . . in that faith I believe the priest is considered to have a direct connection to God. I don't accept that myself." He smiled sheepishly. "Sorry, I am wandering from the point. You see, as a pastor, I am frequently called upon by my parishioners for counsel from anything of the most trivial, what should I plant in the garden this year, to matters of great moment, how can I settle my affairs when I die so that my children don't quarrel with each other? I do not repeat what my people tell me." He struggled for words. "On the other hand, I am not a Romish priest and sworn to a vow of secrecy."

Murdoch didn't think the priests actually took such a vow, it was more a matter of canon law, but he wasn't about to correct the pastor. "Please go on, Reverend. I do respect your position, but what you have to say might be very helpful to me. Thomas Talbert confided in you?"

"Yes. We have been friends since boyhood. We went to Sackville School together. Thom was always determined to become a man of means, which he is now, of course, and I have been called by our Lord to spread the Good News."

Murdoch nodded, but Archer didn't pay attention, lost in his thoughts. Whatever they were, it was clearly disturbing to him.

"Poor fellow. He doesn't want to part with the stable, I know that, but God's ways are mysterious to us and He has visited Thomas with severe misfortune. He must consider himself lucky to be able to get any of his money out of it at all."

He fell silent again and Murdoch began to wonder if that was the extent of the confidence that Talbert had shared with him. However, the old man continued.

"Thom is a hothead, he always has been." He looked over at Murdoch. "He is convinced that Cooke is responsible for the fires, although it seems quite unlikely. Worse, he insists that Daniel has poisoned his horses. I know that was a most mysterious affair, but these things happen to animals, don't they? He had to admit his veterinarian couldn't find any poison, but he is unshakeable. What troubles me, though, sir, is that he is so intent on revenge. I have reminded him, Revenge is Mine, sayeth the Lord, but he will have none of it." Archer drew deeply on his pipe. "His desire is like a poison itself. He will wait, I know he will. He said so himself. I cannot talk him out of it."

Suddenly, the old man stared at Murdoch. "We've got off the topic again. I know that Thomas darsn't go to America himself. Has he hired you?"

"Er, no, sir. I'm a police officer."

Archer stared at him in surprise. "Are you, indeed? I'm glad to hear it. I thought that the matter was of no concern to the city."

"It is, sir. A matter of great concern."

"Good, good. Would it help if you saw a picture of the girl yourself?"

Before Murdoch could find an answer, Archer got to his feet and shuffled over to his desk. He rummaged in the back for a few minutes, muttering to himself, then returned carrying a flat, oblong leather case. He took out a small *card de visite* case. It was pretty with a gilt finish.

"Such a dreadful tragedy. Praise the Lord, who moves in mysterious ways. But we are all praying for a happy outcome." He handed Murdoch the case. "This was taken recently. She herself gave this to me shortly before her marriage." Murdoch took the case and opened it. The place where the picture would have been was empty.

"What has happened to her, Reverend?"

The old man looked bewildered. "Why do you ask me? I thought that was why you were here?"

"No, sir. I'm afraid I don't know what has happened to Miss Talbert."

"Nobody can find her. Her husband has been searching for weeks to no avail."

"Why is she missing?"

"I'm astonished you don't know. It happened right after she was married. They were in Niagara on their wedding tour. The unfortunate man blames himself, of course."

"And what has happened to her?"

"She has been kidnapped and sold into slavery."

"My God!"

"We must not take the Lord's name in vain, sir, but we are praying constantly for her safe return."

"Who is her husband, Reverend? Who did she marry?"

"Don't you know? He is one of Thom's cabbies."

The pastor's eyes drifted away.

"Who? Which cabbie do you mean, Reverend?" Murdoch asked, trying desperately to contain his impatience.

"His name is Daniel Cooke."

CHAPTER FORTY-THREE

Murdoch was still reeling from this information when the pastor said, "Are you of the Baptist faith, Mr. Murdoch?"

"No sir. I am a Roman Catholic."

"Indeed? Well I don't suppose Christian prayer is so much different, is it?"

Although he had the feeling Father Fair's hair would stand on end at this blasphemy, Murdoch nodded. "I don't think it is either, Reverend."

The pastor picked agitatedly at the crocheted armrest cover. "Emeline needs our prayers. She must be found before it is too late. Her mother came to see me this very night and I know she is distraught. I could hardly comfort her. Forgive me, sir, my memory is not as good as it was, things slip away like papers off my desk. But as I recall she was asking me about a child. She said his name was Isaiah, but I don't know a boy by that name." He shrugged. "I don't know why she was inquiring about him, she never said." He sighed. "The poor woman was in such pain and although I say it I shouldn't, I don't believe she is long for this earth. The Lord is ready to receive her . . . but we were about to do something, weren't we?"

"You wanted to pray, Reverend."

Somewhat stiffly, the pastor got off his chair and went down on his knees. He clasped his hands and raised his eyes to the ceiling.

"Oh Lord Jesus, who we know loves his children as a shepherd loves his sheep, I pray to you this night for guidance."

Murdoch didn't dare trust his legs to kneel, but he, too, clasped his hands and bowed his head. The pastor's voice grew louder.

"Help me, Lord, to know Your Will in this matter. You who gave your only begotten son that we might have eternal life, you who know what it is to suffer, show us the way, Lord. Show me the way that I might do what is right for those of your children who have particularly suffered from the wickedness of the world and those sinners who do not know the glory of thy Love. Show me, Lord, I pray. This child is in need of a good family. May that family be presented to me by your grace."

He was swaying back and forth and seemed almost to have gone into a trance. Murdoch waited uncomfortably. Finally, the pastor came to a halt and unclasped his hands. He remained on his knees.

Then the door opened and Green came in carrying a tea tray. Behind him was Mrs. Archer. She went over to her husband. "Look at you, you should be in bed. Enough praying for now."

Green helped her to get her husband to his feet and back in his chair. He looked exhausted.

"Emeline needs our prayers, Leah. We cannot fail her. I have let her down once, I cannot do it a second time."

"Never mind that for now. We will get the entire congregation to pray for her." She tucked a blanket around the pastor's legs. "I want you to drink your posset and then it's off to bed with you."

He took the mug she handed him and drank the hot milk greedily. When he looked up, he had a white moustache on his upper lip. Gently, his wife leaned over and wiped it off with a napkin.

He replaced the mug on the table and closed his eyes. "So much sorrow, Leah. So much sorrow." In a moment, he seemed to have fallen asleep.

Mrs. Archer stood back and addressed Murdoch. "There is a constable at the door, sir. I didn't let him in because I thought it would upset Stanley too much."

"Thank you, ma'am. I'll speak to him."

Green followed him into the hall.

"I should get back to the stable and tend to the horses, Mr. Murdoch. Is the pastor in any danger?"

"I'm still not sure. Things are falling into place, but I don't intend to take any risks. I'm going to have a watch put on the house until we find our culprit."

"Good. And I'll put out the word too." He gave a grim smile. "I am acquainted with some good bruisers. We will make sure he is quite safe."

Murdoch put out his hand. "Thank you for your help. I apologize that I was not particularly gracious before."

Green shook hands heartily. "I wouldn't have been either. How are you feeling?"

"Maybe not as bad as the Chopper and Lincoln, but close."

Fyfer was standing at the bottom of the steps and he watched Green as he left.

Murdoch beckoned to him. "Frank, I want you to patrol this street. Don't allow anybody to approach the house. In particular, be on the lookout for a stocky, middle-aged coloured man. He may be wearing a fedora and long mackintosh. Be careful. He is dangerous."

Fyfer saluted. He liked this kind of assignment.

Murdoch returned to the apartment. The pastor was still asleep. Mrs. Archer looked up at him anxiously.

"What is happening, Mr. Murdoch? Elijah told me you had been attacked and probably by the same person who shot Thomas. And now you have a constable at the door. Surely we are not under suspicion?"

"Good gracious no, Mrs. Archer. But I am afraid your husband might be in some danger."

"Why?"

"I believe it has to do with something that happened a long time ago, and that the deaths of Daniel Cooke and Thomas Talbert are connected. My attacker spoke of teaching them a lesson and that there was one more to do. He used the words *the holy one*. Elijah tells me your husband was once referred to in that way."

"That's right. It sounds strange to hear now." She sank back into the chair. "Will we ever be free from the past? That terrible tragedy haunts us yet."

Like her husband, she seemed tired, her sprightliness evaporating, and she suddenly looked old and frail, like him.

"Did he talk to you about Thomas Talbert's daughter?" she asked.

"Yes, he did. He seemed to think I was here because she has disappeared. Abducted, I gather."

"Thirty-eight years ago."

"The pastor said she married Daniel Cooke."

"Very few people knew of it. The marriage was kept secret."

She sat down next to her husband and just as he had picked up his pipe for comfort, she picked up an embroidery sampler that was on one of the chairs and took out the needle. She was picking out the words *The Lord is our saviour*, and the linen cloth was thick with flowers. While she spoke, she concentrated on her sewing and hardly looked at Murdoch.

"Did he tell you that he's been asked to write his life story?"

"Yes, he did."

"Did Stanley say what the publishing man said to him?"

"About including the misery?"

"That's it. If that man had said it in front of me, I would have turned him out of doors. We have too many tales to pick from. Girls barely out of childhood raped by the men who owned them; women treated like brood mares, only not as well; young men mutilated because they glanced the wrong way at the white missus. My own father was whipped into unconsciousness because he himself refused to beat another slave. Which story do you want, sir?"

Murdoch had no easy words of comfort. He could only wait until she was ready to continue. She bit off the end of her silk thread and examined her work.

"Emeline Talbert was sold into slavery immediately following her marriage to Daniel Cooke. They were on their wedding tour in Niagara Falls, and an American slave trader kidnapped her. She was never seen again. Amen. Poor Thomas lost most of his hardearned money trying to find her, but about four years after she disappeared, Daniel Cooke received a letter from a doctor who said he had been at her deathbed. So that was that. Very soon afterwards, Daniel married Adelaide Peckwith, who, I might say without implying anything, had a substantial dowry. But you said your attacker spoke of teaching somebody a lesson?"

"Yes, and I was one of them apparently. And I now believe Daniel Cooke and Thomas Talbert were also recipients."

"And my husband might be another?"

"Yes. But please don't worry. My constable is outside and Elijah is bringing over some men who I'm sure will have very strong arms."

She rethreaded her needle and began to sew, fast and deft. "Thank you, Mr. Murdoch, but we are no strangers to danger." She smiled at him, a sweet, wry smile. "On the other hand, neither my husband nor I could be said to have the strength of our youth, so I will make no protest about accepting your help."

"I will make sure our villain is soon behind bars."

She didn't speak for a few moments, preoccupied with her own thoughts. A primrose began to take shape on the sampler. "Marriages between a white man and a coloured woman were rare at that time. Emeline Talbert was beautiful, she could have passed for white easily, but she wasn't white, and I always wondered why Daniel Cooke wanted to marry her. He wasn't that intelligent a man in my opinion, but smooth as butter around the ladies. There were many eligible white women who would have jumped at the opportunity to marry him. But he swept Emeline off her feet. Alas, even then I suspected his motives." She sighed. "Even if I had voiced them to Emeline, she would not have listened. Thomas wasn't rich, but he had worked hard to make money and his stable was thriving, but Daniel acted as if he were bestowing an honour on the family. A white man marrying a coloured girl." She jabbed her needle into the cloth. "She would have made a good match without him, I'm sure. And one among her own people."

The preacher let out a soft snore and she glanced over at him.

"Stanley has not really forgiven himself even for officiating at the marriage. He had the same misgivings I did, but he allowed himself to be talked out of them. He feared that if he refused to marry them, they would have eloped, and that would have been worse. She was a headstrong, motherless girl."

Murdoch needed to probe further. Carefully. "The pastor thought the woman who came to see him earlier today was Mr. Talbert's wife."

"Did he? Well she's long gone too, poor soul. She died before Emeline was wed and sometimes I tell you frankly, I praise the Lord, that she never knew about that wedding and what happened to her daughter."

"I interviewed Mr. Talbert before he died and he never mentioned that Daniel Cooke had been his son-in-law."

"No, he wouldn't have. He was ashamed of ever giving his permission, and I know he always blamed himself. He had no reason to except that the long illness of her mother had made Emeline grow up without a guiding hand. Thomas at that time was far too concerned with becoming rich and he drank too much, so the child was left to servants to manage. I'm not saying she wasn't a good girl at heart, I believe she was, but when Cooke came a calling, she was only seventeen and she was determined to have this man. Thomas knew nothing would stop her." She glanced over at Murdoch, her face drawn with sadness. "He married a white woman a few years back, a widow she was. She's a good woman, and they suited each other in my opinion, but there are those in the white world who believe fervently that the races should never mix . . . except illicitly when a white man has his way with a negro girl. I presume that is acceptable."

She studied her husband for a moment.

"I should get him into his proper bed. He often falls asleep in his chair and he always gets a stiff neck from it."

He hesitated. "Are you suggesting that somebody is punishing Cooke and Mr. Talbert for marrying outside of their race? Mr. Cooke's marriage was many years ago."

She gave a little shrug. "Sometimes a wound festers for a long time before it kills."

Murdoch's thoughts were starting to go in a different direction. "I have no wish to upset you, ma'am, but there are one or two things I need to ask you. Mr. Cooke was whipped at least thirty-seven to thirty-nine times, although he died from a heart attack midway through the beating." He took out the drawing he had made and held it out to her. "Mr. Talbert was tied after death into this position. Are those two things significant?"

She looked at the sketch and flinched, turning her head away. "I would say they are very significant. They were both common forms of punishments for slaves. Thirty-nine lashes meted out for the most trivial of transgressions: a strange look, being too slow to come when called, singing God's hymn when you shouldn't." She indicated the paper. "That method of tying was what was known as the Spanish Stoop. Slaves would be left in that position for hours. It was a way to break their spirit."

Murdoch was still suffering from that punishment.

Mrs. Archer wiped at her eyes. "My husband and I were very active in what we called the Underground Railroad. We helped many fugitive slaves who came up from America that way. Some of them were children, infants even, sent by desperate mothers to safety." Once again she studied her sampler, as if it comforted her. "For so many of us, Canada was the Promised Land, where the wounds would all be healed. But the Lord in his wisdom has seen fit to keep us in this valley of the shadow and I know not when we will see our green pastures. I fear it will not be in my lifetime."

She fell silent, full of memories, and when she spoke, she did so with her head lowered. "By law, you see, we are free and equal in Canada, but true equality does not necessarily rest in law only, as I'm sure you know, Mr. Murdoch. True equality has to exist in the heart. And there are always those who do not have open hearts and think we should be in our place. Not slaves, oh my goodness no, that is an American abomination but not equal, God forbid, never equal. Perhaps you read in the newspapers only last week, Mr. Murdoch, a coloured man was lynched by a mob in the city of Newark. He was attempting to save his two daughters who were being accosted. You could no doubt sit here for an hour or more and I could tell you similar tales and not repeat myself."

Murdoch had read in the *Globe* about the incident but hadn't paid much attention.

"The hope lies with the children, does it not?" she continued. "Children who are born free." Her face was soft in the firelight. "The youngest child we rescued was barely three months old. He came to us so sickly we were afraid he might not live but, hallelujah, he did and has thrived. He was born with six fingers, you see, and somebody had tried to remove the extra finger by binding it with twine. One hand became infected and it was a miracle, the Lord be thanked, that he didn't lose either his hand or his life. But he thrived in the love of our Saviour and he's a grown man now with a family of his own."

Murdoch stared at her. "I beg your pardon, ma'am, but did you say the child was born with six fingers?"

"That's right." She regarded him, wary now at his reaction. "It is not uncommon, sir. It means nothing. It is not a sign of the devil."

"I apologize, ma'am. That was not what I was thinking. But this boy, do you know where he is now?"

"He was placed with a good Christian family who were themselves fugitives. Why are you asking?"

"Did you keep a record of this placement?"

He could see her fingers clenching the hoop of her sampler. "We did, but I should tell you, Mr. Murdoch, my husband holds strong views about the necessity for keeping those records confidential. He saved many a child from shame by quietly and privately arranging for them to go to a good Christian family. Frankly, sir, many of these children were the result of rape, usually a white man on a coloured girl. Stanley believes that if it's God's will for those children to know their parentage He will ensure it happens, otherwise we will not interfere."

Murdoch leaned forward, trying to temper his urgency. "Mrs. Archer, I will respect your views, but I do need some information. This child, did you yourselves know his parentage?"

She shook her head. "No we did not. A Quaker family brought him to us. They were from Ohio and all they could tell us was that his mother was a fugitive, a very young girl who had barely escaped with her life. She had been able to hand the baby over to a minister of God who in turn got him to Mr. and Mrs. Scott. The pastor, alas, died in a fire that was deliberately set when he returned to his church."

"Will you tell me this child's name? I wouldn't ask if I didn't consider it most important."

Mrs. Archer hesitated, and he was afraid she would refuse to answer. He knew he could get a warrant to see the records, but he didn't want to do that. Finally, she slumped a little as if she could read his thoughts.

"I must stress that he himself does not know his parentage. He believes that Mr. and Mrs. Gr –" She stopped and her hand flew to her mouth.

Murdoch finished the sentence for her. "Mr. and Mrs. Green. Elijah was that boy."

"Yes."

Now that she'd said it, Murdoch realized what had been nagging at him. Green didn't look anything like his brother, Lincoln. He was taller, lighter-skinned, with sharper features. And at the same time, Murdoch recognized who he did, in fact, resemble, he who also had six fingers, hexadactylis: Thomas Talbert.

Both Murdoch and Mrs. Archer heard the sound of footsteps outside in the hall, then the door burst open. A woman stood for a moment on the threshold, then she lifted the revolver she held in her hand and fired straight at Stanley Archer.

CHAPTER FORTY-FOUR

"There you are, Fiddie. Come and sit down, I have something for you." Lena handed the sepia-coloured daguerreotype to Faith. "I thought you might like this." The other woman viewed it suspiciously. "Where'd you get it and why are you giving it to me now?"

"I stole it from the poor old preacher. He's quite senile, so it wasn't hard." She stretched out her hand again. "Please, take the picture."

Faith slapped her hand away so that the daguerreotype fell to the floor. "I don't want it. You're a planning to stay here, ain't ya? Well, don't think for one blue second I'm going anywhere without you."

Lena's voice was sharp. "Yes, you are, Fiddie. And you're going tonight. It's only a matter of time before we're caught."

"You didn't do nothing. It was me. I thought he was goin' to punch you, father or no father, when I shot him. And I'm sorry, I've said I'm sorry."

Lena stood up, took her cane, and began to walk up and down. They were in the hotel room, the lights burning low. Bursts of laughter came from outside on the lawn where there was some kind of birthday celebration in progress.

"It doesn't matter any more, Fiddie. You did what you thought was right for me. In fact, I'd say my father died to me a long time ago."

"He was lying, you know. He was in on the sale just as deep as the other one."

Lena winced as she made a turn. "Was he, Fiddie? I was starting to believe him."

Faith was almost yelling. "Well, don't. He was lying. Do you think he's going to come right out and say he sold his own daughter? No, he ain't."

"There was an expression on his face when he saw me . . . it was joy."

"No, it weren't. It were pure shit fear."

"Calm yourself, Fiddie. We don't want the manager knocking at the door. I've told you it doesn't matter to me any more and it doesn't."

"Why'd you go to see the preacher man? You crept out as cagey as a white massa coming down to the quarters. You was up to no good. Why're you speaking so sweet and honeyed about him? 'Poor old preacher.' I thought he was the last one for us to do? Did you change your mind?"

"Yes, I have, Fiddie. I've had my fill. Believe me, things look different when you're moving toward death. What seemed of consummate importance once, no longer is that way. Besides, Pastor Archer was kind to me when I was a girl."

"That's not what you were saying afore."

"Wasn't it? I hardly remember any more."

Faith glared in exasperation. "That's mighty convenient. Well, I'se remember. I remember everything you'se said over all these years. 'First the son, then the father, then the holy one who should a knowed better.' All those years, we talks about it and we plans and we saves our money till we could come here and eat that sweet meat of revenge. And now you'se waving it away like it were no more special than a mosquito landing on your arm. You says it was nothing when you knows it was everything."

"Fiddie, please. We mustn't quarrel now of all times."

Faith was not placated. "Did you tell this good old preacher man who you were?"

"I didn't have to. He's confused in himself. He thought I was my own mother." She gazed at Faith. "He said that my father was distraught over my disappearance."

"Any fool can fake that. Ain't hard at all. So that's why you've gone all soft on me. Cos you think your pappy really cared and tried to find you."

"The preacher said Pa had lost almost all of his money searching."

"Well, we didn't hear of it none, did we?"

"No, and I think that's because Daniel took it."

"You're not getting sorry 'bout him too, are you?"

"No. When he saw me and realized I'd come back, it was as sweet a moment as I'd ever imagined it would be."

"And he deserved a whipping. He deserved it a lot more than you and me when we got our thirty-nine."

"I know that, Fiddie, I know that." She moved to the couch by the window. "Come and sit beside me, dearest."

"Not until you tell me why you've got that look on your face. You're going to tell me something bad, and I won't hear it."

She put her hands over her ears. Lena smiled at her.

"You look twelve years old when you do that. Don't be silly. Come and sit close to me, one last time."

"One last time," Faith shrieked. "I told you I ain't goin' nowhere."

"Well I am. You can't pretend any more, Fiddie. I am dying. I want to die in the place I was born."

"That don't make no sense. You ain't been here since you was no more than a child. What about our house? You'll be comfortable there."

"I know that, dearest. But the fact is, it isn't safe for you. No, hear me out. My last days on this earth would be unsupportable if I thought that you had been captured and were in jail. I shall say I killed the two of them, but if you are there they will charge you as an accomplice."

Faith ran over to the wardrobe and dragged out the valise. "We can still get away. We've done it before."

"Fiddie. You're not listening. I don't want to run any more."

"But you'll need me to look after you."

"They won't let you. If we are caught and we surely will be, we will be separated. Come, please, please sit beside me. I cannot go on talking to your back."

Faith reluctantly turned and went over to sit on the couch. Lena put an arm around her shoulder, drew her close, and began to stroke her hair. "Death is going to separate us anyway, so this is only a little earlier than planned."

"I'll die too. I'll die at the same time."

Lena kissed the other woman's forehead. "No, you won't. If you love me, you will grant me this, Fiddie. You've got many years left to live in you. I want to know that you are safe."

"Safe don't mean much if you're in misery. How can I be happy without you? We ain't bin separated since I first knowed you."

"You must try. I'll be with you, just not physically. You've sur-vived so much, Fiddie, you can survive this. Please, for my sake."

Faith stuck out her lower lip. "No, it's too much to ask. I want to stay with you till you pass."

Lena lost patience. "But *I* don't want you to do that. I want you to get your clothes together now and leave. There isn't much time if you want to catch the last train. You've got plenty of money and you can be in New York by tomorrow."

"What will you do?"

"I'll wait here. It's comfortable. I don't think that detective will be too long finding me out."

"He don't suspect anything. He won't come."

"If he doesn't, then I shall send for him. They won't look too hard for you if they think they've already got the killer."

"I don't like it, none of it."

"If you don't do this for me, I shall come back and haunt you."

"You can't haunt somebody who's already a ghost. What do you think I am, the little pickaninny from the garden still? Well, I ain't."

"I know that, my dearest. I know what you feel, but I'm asking you to do this for my sake. I want you to promise to live out your natural life, and you'll know I'll be waiting for you on the other side."

"Mebbe there ain't another side. Mebbe this is all we got."

"Of course it isn't. I'll be there and I won't have any pain any more and I'll open my arms and take you in them just as before."

"You and your pretty words."

Lena straightened up. "You must go, Fiddie. Travel as a man, it's safer and less conspicuous. Go, my little nigger gal, before I start crying myself. We can't have two of us blubbering at the same time."

"Why not, we've done it before many a time?"

"Come on, there's a good girl. Get your things."

Suddenly, Faith seized Lena's face between her hands and gazed into her eyes.

"I just told you, I knows you better than my own soul. You still ain't telling the entire and whole truth. You wants to send me away because you can't find it in your heart to forgive me for what I done. I shot your pappy just when you were thinking he cared for you. Ain't that the case, tell me true from your heart."

"I know you were trying to defend me, Fiddie."

"But you're mad 'cos I tied him up in the Stoop when you had run out of there to look at the garden or whatever it was you was doing."

Lena shrugged. "He was dead. He would not feel it."

"If it's not that, what is it, then? There's something come between us for all your pretty words. I shall go mad if you don't tell me."

Gently, Lena removed Faith's hands. "Nothing is important now except that we part this last time with love for each other. You have been my right hand for so many years. It is not only you who will find it hard to be separated, Fiddie, I will find it agonizing."

"No, I won't go anywhere. You ain't telling me all the truth that's to tell. You went to that preacher man because you wanted to make sure about Isaiah, didn't you?"

Lena grew stiff and she looked away. "Why would I do that? I know he died. You told me so."

"But I always knows you didn't believe me. Never did. Even after all these years, you thought I was lying to you."

"No, Fiddie, not lying. Never that. It's just that I sometimes thought, or hoped, you were mistaken. You never saw his body, after all."

"I didn't need to. I sees the church on fire. And I hears later that the preacher was burned to death. I'd given him the babe so I knows he must be dead. I've told you this a dozen times."

"You're acting jealous and you don't have to. I was curious, is all. I just wanted to make sure before it was too late that my son had not made it to Toronto as I requested, as you swore to me you told the minister. 'Take him to Toronto, Canada, and hand him over to Reverend Archer.'"

"I did say that. That's exactly what I tells the pastor before I runs for my life. If he could have got the child out, he would have. And I ain't being jealous. Why should I be jealous over somebody who ain't alive? So, what did the old man tell you?"

"He couldn't tell me anything. He lives in the past."

"You're a liar. He told you s-something and it-it has come between us." Faith was sobbing so hard she could hardly speak. Finally, Lena reached under the cushion that was on the couch and pulled out a little blue linen jacket.

"He showed me the boxes where he kept his records and mementoes of the children he had saved. There was one labelled *Unknown*, but the date seemed right so I opened it. The jacket I sewed for Ise was in there." She pointed at the collar. "The place where I'd sewed the paper with his name and my name and the date of his birth, remember?"

Faith nodded sullenly.

"The paper was still there unread and untouched," Lena continued, "but I knew for certain he had survived." Tenderly, she picked up the jacket and pressed it against her cheek.

Faith stared at her in horror. "I swear to you – I didn't . . . I didn't know. I thought he died in that fire."

"When I asked you if you had seen the body, you said you had."

"No, you are remembering wrong. I said I hears from some-body who told me the minister had been found all burned up and there was a baby's body there too."

"But that wasn't the truth, was it, Fiddie? You preferred it if I believed my child was dead."

Faith was rocking back and forth and moaning. "I didn't want you to fret. You – you would've wore yourself right out trying to get to him if you thought he was still alive. I thought it better to let him go." She caught Lena's hand and kissed it passionately. "Tell me you don't hate me, darling Lena. I did what I thought was best."

"Fiddie, I will never hate you. How could I?"

"But when you die, it won't be me you'll be thinking of, it'll be him and how you never knew him. And whether he's alive now. Won't it? Tell me the truth, it'll be him, won't it?"

"It's all in the past. It's too late for regrets."

"You didn't answer my question. It'll be him you thinks about on your deathbed, ain't it?"

Lena's eyes were filled with tears. "Yes, Fiddie. In all likeli-hood, it will be him."

"So what you're saying is you ain't ever going to forgive me."

Lena sighed. "Yes, I suppose that is what I'm saying."

CHAPTER FORTY-FIVE

ater, Mrs. Archer swore that the good Lord himself had deflected the bullet. Murdoch thought that God had been assisted by the surprise that the assailant had experienced on seeing Murdoch leaping toward him. Unfortunately, he was detoured by Mrs. Archer's cry and the necessity of determining the condition of the pastor who had blood pouring from the side of his face. Murdoch just had time to register that the shooter had fled. He ran over to tend to the old man. The bullet had shattered the lamp beside him and shards of glass had cut his scalp and cheek, but otherwise he was unhurt. Minutes later, Fyfer ran into the room and Murdoch was about to berate him for neglecting his duty when he saw that he, too, was bleeding. He had an ugly bruise on his temple.

"She knocked me down, sir. I'm sorry."

"Never mind that now. We should get a doctor for Mr. Archer."

"I can look after him," said Mrs. Archer. She used her sampler to staunch the blood.

"You're a tough old rooster, aren't you, Stanley? You've survived far worse than this." She nodded at Murdoch. "Go and do your duty, detective, we'll be all right."

Murdoch left them in Fyfer's care.

It took him almost half an hour to get to the Elliott Hotel as, in spite of his willpower, his muscles refused to move quickly. His back had gone into a painful spasm and at one point he doubted whether his legs would ever support him again.

The hotel was in darkness and he went around to the rear where Mrs. Dittman's room was, afraid she might have already fled.

He need not have worried. The curtains were not drawn and there was a low light shining. He could see her seated in a chair by the window and he knew she was waiting for him.

She saw him coming and stood up to let him in by the French doors.

"Good evening, Mr. Murdoch. I was expecting you. Please come in." She indicated the tea trolley. "I can offer you tea if you would like, but I cannot answer as to how warm it still is."

"No thank you, ma'am."

Normally, Murdoch would have been angered by this hypocritical facade of good manners, but there was something about the woman that softened his response.

"I shall have to take my medicine, if you don't mind, Mr. Murdoch. I can speak with a clearer mind then."

"By all means, ma'am."

She limped to the dresser and poured something from a brown vial into a cup on the side table. She took a deep swallow and shuddered slightly. "Not the best taste in the world. It quite ruins the tea, but it does its job."

Murdoch had taken the chair in front of the fireplace and she sat down opposite him.

"I suppose you are expecting me to go through a song and dance of denial, Mr. Murdoch, but frankly I don't have the energy. I know why you have come and I am willing to be quite truthful with you." She paused and smiled a wry smile. "On the other hand, perhaps I should hear from your own mouth why you are here. I should not be too premature."

She thinks it might be better to stall a little longer, thought Murdoch.

"I have come because I believe you are implicated in the deaths of Daniel Cooke and Thomas Talbert and in the attempted murder of Reverend Stanley Archer."

That startled her. "What do you mean, the attempted murder?"

"Somebody shot at him tonight in his home. Fortunately, they missed, but the intent was to kill him, there is no doubt about that. I was present. The assailant was a woman. It was your maid, Faith."

She stared at him in horror but made no protest.

"Where is she? I'd like to speak to her."

"I'm afraid that won't be possible. I have sent her back to New York."

"How long ago did she leave?"

"Some time ago."

Murdoch pointed to the telephone set on the desk. "I would like to make a call, ma'am."

"By all means."

Murdoch could see how much his news had upset her. She hadn't known anything about the shooting.

Fortunately, the unctuous clerk, Oatley, hadn't yet left, and Murdoch was able to get him to connect him with the police station. He gave the order to send two constables to Union Station and gave a description of the maid. "She is armed and dangerous."

Mrs. Dittman had hardly seemed interested in his call, and when he returned to his seat, she said, "A few moments ago, you said I was implicated in the deaths of a Mr. Cooke and a Mr. Talbert. What do you mean by *implicated*?"

"You were complicit in the whipping of Daniel Cooke. You were present and a witness to the shooting of Thomas Talbert."

"I see." She had laced her fingers in her lap and had been studying her hands and now she looked up at him. "I said I would be honest with you, sir, and I will be. I am totally responsible for the deaths of those two men. Daniel Cooke died more by God's hand than by mine, but in the case of Thomas Talbert, I was the one who shot him."

"You realize that I will have to arrest you?"

"Yes, I do realize that and I am prepared for it."

"Mrs. Dittman –"

"That is not my real name. I borrowed it."

"Should I call you Mrs. Cooke then?"

"No!" she spat out the word. "But I see you have discovered me, Mr. Murdoch."

"I paid a visit to Reverend Archer. You were there shortly before me, I believe?"

"Yes. He was an old friend. I was sorry to see his state. I am relieved that he was unhurt. That had nothing to do with me."

"I know you did not pull the trigger, if that's what you mean."

"I repeat, the attempt on his life had nothing to do with me. I swear to you I am not implicated in that, as I am with the other two deaths."

"Forgive me saying so, ma'am, but I don't believe you alone would have had the strength to haul up Mr. Cooke to the rafters, or to whip him in that way."

"You would be surprised what strength passion can bestow on a person, Mr. Murdoch. I have had many cruel years to contemplate what sort of revenge I would visit on Daniel Cooke. Thirty-nine stripes seemed fitting. I had to endure them more than once."

Murdoch spoke gently. "Mrs. Archer has told me your story."

Again she returned to studying her fingers. "I expect she told you I was sold as a slave many years ago."

"Yes."

"What she probably didn't tell you, Mr. Murdoch, because nobody here knew, was that my husband of one week was the one who sold me."

Murdoch had suspected as much.

"He received three hundred dollars. The slave trader resold me for four hundred. I should say that it seemed like a sign from God that Daniel had that precise amount of money in his safe."

"Which you stole?"

"*Stole* is a harsh word, Mr. Murdoch. It suggests I participated in a robbery. In fact, I was merely recovering my dowry, you might say. I took what was mine."

"And you whipped him until he had an apoplectic attack and continued to whip him after that?"

"Yes."

She was watching him defiantly. He changed tack.

"He must have been shocked to receive your message."

"He was, indeed. His crime returned from the grave. He was still quite pale when he arrived at the stable. I suppose he thought I was dead."

"Yes. He did. He had received a letter from a doctor saying he'd been there at your deathbed."

"He must have bribed him. It would have given him an

excuse to stop searching. I had no encounter with a physician, even perhaps when I needed to, until recently." For a moment her thoughts turned inward, and Murdoch didn't have to guess what she meant by that.

He brought her back to the present. "I understand your motive concerning Cooke, but why did you shoot your own father?"

She frowned as if he were rather a dull student and she the teacher. "Because he was complicitous. I saw his signature on the bill of sale."

"According to Mrs. Archer, your father had nothing at all to do with the kidnapping. He almost went bankrupt trying to find you. Signatures are easy to forge."

She stiffened. "I don't know if that is the case."

"Is that why you threw money onto his body?"

"Yes. Judas wages."

"And then you placed him into the Spanish Stoop?"

"Yes, that is correct."

Murdoch leaned toward her.

"Miss Talbert, you promised to tell the truth, but you are not doing so. I think you have sent your maid away so she cannot speak for herself. A witness says that a man and a woman visited Thomas Talbert the evening he was killed. Perhaps you went there with Elijah Green."

"Who is that?"

"The man from the stables? The man that Faith spoke to when she was getting the lie of the land."

"Why do you say that? I don't know him."

"Miss Talbert, when you were talking to the Reverend Archer, he was confused. He thought you were your own mother. But you were inquiring about a boy named Isaiah. I assume that you were asking about your own son."

She moved away from him. "I have no son."

"I think you do, ma'am. He was rescued as an infant and brought to Toronto by way of the Underground Railroad. He was adopted and he is a grown man. His name is now Elijah Green."

Murdoch waited, and he felt as if the entire world was balanced on the edge of a razor.

"Was Green your accomplice, Miss Talbert? Was he helping you to get your revenge? He didn't know Thomas was his grandfather or that his mother had been married to Daniel Cooke and been cruelly betrayed. Did you tell him and ask for his help?"

"No! Absolutely not. I have never met the man you speak of. Faith was the one who spoke to him when she went to the barn to inquire about a carriage. No, you must believe me, I have had nothing to do with him."

She could contain herself no longer and she burst into deep, gulping sobs, all the more painful to watch because they were almost soundless. Murdoch stood up and went over to her, putting his hand on her shoulder.

"Your maid was your accomplice, wasn't she?"

She could not speak at first, then she looked at him through her tears. "Yes, she was."

"Did she whip Daniel Cooke?"

She nodded. "I also took part at first, but when we saw that he had died, she continued."

"She was the one who shot your father?"

"Yes. I was accusing him of betraying me and he went to come over to me, perhaps to convince me he was innocent. She thought he was going to attack me and shot him."

"Then she tied him into the Spanish Stoop?"

"Yes. I was not present when she did that."

"You didn't know she had made an attempt on the life of the Reverend Archer, did you?"

"No, I did not."

"Were you aware that she also attacked me? She put me in the Spanish Stoop. She said she was teaching me a lesson."

Emeline drew in her breath sharply. "I did not know that either. I am sorry. I was distressed after you left here. I suppose she was referring to that. She was ever my bulldog." She caught his hand and held on to it as if she were drowning. "Mr. Murdoch, please believe me. I did not know about Elijah Green until this moment. He does not know of my existence, and I swear I have not involved him in any of my affairs." She looked at him beseechingly.

"I believe you, ma'am."

Her body almost collapsed as she sank back with relief into the couch.

"Thank you."

"Forgive me for bringing such grief upon you, ma'am. Reverend Archer did not know Elijah was your child, and Elijah has grown up not knowing that Thomas Talbert was his grandfather. I don't believe he even knows he was adopted."

She shifted slightly on the couch, and he saw pain shoot across her face. "As I am sure you have guessed, Mr. Murdoch, my life's thread is about to be shorn in two. I assume you will arrest me now?"

"Yes, ma'am."

"For being an accessory?"

"That's right."

She gave him a wry smile. "Mr. Murdoch, I must have you know that Faith, or Fidelia, as is her real name, is not in any way my servant. We took those roles because we could move freely about the country. She is my dearest friend, truly my soul sister."

"I see."

"I have told *you* the truth about what happened, but I will not repeat that to a judge. No, it will be useless for you to try to make me. I will deny I ever said what I have said to you. But I have seen the sin of my ways, and I intend to confess to the murder of both Daniel Cooke and Thomas Talbert. I worked alone and unaided."

"I cannot go along with that, ma'am. I will have to report what you have said."

"Of course. But I tell you now that I was saying all those things only to avoid being charged. I am totally responsible. I do have a plausible motive, after all. A jury will believe me."

"I intend to find your ma – your friend."

She gave him a wan smile. "Fiddie and I long ago learned to get out of tight corners, Mr. Murdoch. She won't be at the train station. You will never find her."

She reached out as if to touch his hand, but she stopped herself.

"Mr. Murdoch, you took me by surprise a little while ago. I consider myself a shrewd judge of character, and I must now throw myself on your mercy. It will serve no good purpose for, er, for Elijah Green to know that I am his natural mother. He has a family. He appears to have lived a good life to this point. Why should I shatter that with the news that his mother is a murderess who killed his own grandfather? You seem a man of conscience, Mr. Murdoch. I beg you to give me your promise that you will not reveal this to him. As you can see, I am ill. I have a tumour that is eating my stomach. There is nothing to be done. Please, keep my secret, Mr. Murdoch. It is the last wish of a dying woman."

Murdoch hesitated. He couldn't see much would be served by bringing Green into the picture. The selling into slavery was enough reason for the revenge that Emeline had long sought. The newspapers would rejoice in that.

"Please, Mr. Murdoch," she said again.

"Very well. I promise I won't tell him or anybody else unless I deem it absolutely necessary to the case in question."

She placed her hand on his. "Thank you again, sir. I'm sorry that I will put you in a rather difficult position, but I know it is for the best. You simply first heard the panicky ramblings of a distraught woman. I repeat, I am totally responsible and that is what I will say from now on."

She got to her feet and paused while a wave of pain rippled through her body.

"Perhaps you would be so good as to bring my valise."

EPILOGUE

Murdoch was lying close beside Amy. It was almost midnight, and she had been waiting for him to return from the jail. The doctor who had examined her immediately placed Emeline Talbert in the infirmary. She was not going to live long enough to go to trial, so Judge Rose was content to accept her supposed confession and leave things as they stood. The wondrous thing was that when the story had been reported in the newspapers in all its lurid details, Mrs. Archer had gone to visit her. "God in His infinite Wisdom has given her punishment enough," she said. "It is not for me to judge her." Soon afterwards, a few members of the Queen Street Baptist Church had also begun to visit, and Murdoch thought Emeline was comforted by their company. He himself went every two or three days. At first, Emeline was aloof, but he never pressed her to retract her story about the crimes and she gradually relaxed in his presence.

"How is she tonight?" Amy whispered.

"Weaker. She may last one or two more days, if that."

Amy stroked his thigh. "You have been kind to her, Will."

"She has been dreadfully mistreated. After she escaped from captivity, she and Faith, or Fidelia as she sometimes calls her, settled in New York. She managed to build a decent-enough life for herself, at first by writing letters for those who couldn't, then by owning property. She is quite a wealthy woman, I understand. When she found out she was dying, the poison of her hatred overwhelmed her, and she decided to return to Toronto to avenge herself on her betrayers."

And the half-acknowledged longing to find out if her son had lived or not. He hadn't told Amy that part of Emeline's story.

"Is there any chance you will find her maid or, should I say, her lover?"

"No, not her lover, but a beloved one certainly. And no, I don't think we will find her."

They were quiet for a moment, then Murdoch rolled over onto his side and gazed into Amy's face. In the candlelight, she looked soft and young, her hair loose about her shoulders.

"What's the matter? You have something on your mind. Do you not want me any more? Are you beginning to see what being involved with a policeman means? Long hours, strange habits?"

She gave him a quick smile. "It's none of those things, Will."

"What then? There's something going on."

"There is something I have to tell you."

He experienced a twinge of anxiety, never quite sure of her even though tonight she seemed especially fond and loving.

"What? For God's sake, Amy, don't keep me in suspense."

She took a deep breath. "Tomorrow, I want you to go to Father Fair and have him put up the banns."

He sat straight up in bed in astonishment. "You'll marry me, after all?"

She nodded. "Give me your hand."

He did so and she guided it to her belly. "I don't care a nickel about marriage, but this one deserves a proper start in life."

Murdoch yelped. "This one? What do you mean, this one?"

"What do you think I mean? I am with child and you, I assure you, are the father."

Murdoch's eyes filled with sudden tears.

"Amy, my dearest, dearest girl."

He pulled her to him so tightly she exclaimed in pain.

"You had better not squeeze me quite so hard, Will, or you might remove the reason I am taking such a step beyond my principles."

He loosened his grip sufficiently so that he could look at her, and he saw and finally accepted that she loved him and he wept. Laughing, Amy wiped away his tears with the sleeve of her nightgown.

"And I thought all this time you were a tough-hearted policeman."

"I am, I will be, it's just that you took me by surprise. To have you and a family of our own is more than I can encompass." He was forced to stop.

Amy sat up and stared into his face.

"William Murdoch, will you stop it? I'll have to send Charlie for Dr. Ogden."

His tears turned into laughter. "Oh no, please don't. She'll bring the professor and he'll attach me to one of his machines and study me the way you told me he did with poor Mary Blong."

"And so he should. But she was a fake and is cured, whereas I believe you are quite genuine, a hardened case and an odd one to boot."

He touched her. "I know a good way to convince you of my normality."

She smiled, and they lay together for a while not saying

much, Murdoch absorbing her news. Then he said, "Amy, I want your opinion about something. When is it permissible to break a promise?"

She propped herself on her elbow. "Oh, Will, I'm not your confessor. What do you mean? I hope this hasn't anything to do with what I've just told you. You're changing your mind?"

"Of course not. But what if you had given somebody your solemn promise, but circumstances now seem different and you think a greater good would be served by breaking that promise?"

She reached up and kissed him on the lips. "You are such a dear, good man, William Murdoch, few people would torment themselves with this question. Have you made a promise you wish to break?"

"Yes."

"Then I am sure you will not do it lightly and the greater good will be served."

He sighed. "In that case, I have to get out of bed right away."

"No!"

"I'm afraid so."

"At this time of night?"

"Time is what we don't have. I must bring two people together, one of whom does not know of the other's existence and God help me, I think he should." He turned to her. "Will you promise me you'll be here when I get back?"

"Of course. Isn't that what wives do, wait for their husbands to get home?"

"Amy Slade, was that an old-fashioned viewpoint I just heard coming out of your mouth?"

"It was. Sometimes tradition embodies wisdom."

"Do you promise me then?"

"I do. Until death us do part."

AUTHOR'S NOTE

The germ of the idea for this book came from a true story, that of James Mink and his daughter, which is a significant part of black history in Toronto. However, like most writers, I have gone on from there, and the plot and events of this book are entirely fiction.

The ideas, some of the actions, and many of the words I attribute to Professor Broske I took from an astonishing book, *Fear*, written by Angelo Mosso in 1893.

The Ollapod Club is an amalgam of the many such rehabilitation centres that flourished in the 1890s. Many of the principles we use in our attempts to deal with alcoholism were also used then. I have not included anything that was not done at the time, I've just attributed them to one club.

By 1896, bare-knuckle or prize fighting, as it was sometimes called, was illegal. I don't know whether a fight took place in Mimico, but other than that I have been as true as possible to the rituals and language of these events.

ACKNOWLEDGEMENTS

I want to thank the people who shared their expertise with me while I was writing this book, especially Cindy Boht, who knows horses as well as she knows dogs, and Anthony, Jayne, and Jim, who allowed themselves to be twisted out of shape for a few painful moments to demonstrate the positions I needed to see.

Al Greene took time out of a busy schedule to talk about his life growing up in North Carolina; Stanley Grizzle kindly shared his house and his time so I could talk to him about the life of a black man in early Toronto.

As always, thanks must be given to my astute editor, Dinah Forbes, and my agent, Jane Chelius.

Any errors of fact are mine.